An Unexpected Match

GAYLE ROPER

HARVEST HOUSE PUBLISHERS
EUGENE, OREGON

Cover photos © Chris Garborg; Wollwerth Imagery / Bigstock

Cover by Garborg Design Works, Savage, Minnesota

Published in association with the Books & Such Literary Agency, 52 Mission Circle, Suite 122, PMB 170, Santa Rosa, CA 95409-5370, www.booksandsuch.com.

This is a work of fiction. Names, characters, places, and incidents are products of the author's imagination or are used fictitiously. Any resemblance to actual persons, living or dead, is entirely coincidental.

AN UNEXPECTED MATCH
Copyright © 2014 by Gayle Roper
Published by Harvest House Publishers
Eugene, Oregon 97402
www.harvesthousepublishers.com

Library of Congress Cataloging-in-Publication Data

Roper, Gayle G.
An unexpected match / Gayle Roper.
  pages cm — (Between two worlds ; book 1)
ISBN 978-0-7369-5618-5 (pbk.)
ISBN 978-0-7369-5619-2 (eBook)
1. Women teachers—Fiction. 2. Amish women—Fiction. 3. Afghan War, 2001—Veterans—Fiction. 4. Man-woman relationships—Fiction. I. Title.
PS3568.O68U55 2014
813'.54—dc23

                                                                2013044764

Printed in the United States of America

        14 15 16 17 18 19 20 21 22 / LB-CD / 10 9 8 7 6 5 4 3 2 1

In memory of Chuck, my hero.

Acknowledgments

MANY THANKS AND MUCH APPRECIATION TO THE FOLLOWING:

Irma Swartz for your insights and experience with Amish life.

Maggie Mills for sharing your Amish neighbors and stories.

Georgia Shaffer, Pat Johnson, Deb Strubel, and Nancy Meyer for years of listening to my stories. Critique groups don't get any better.

Vicki Junkins for being my first reader. I'm so glad you enjoyed the book!

Nick Harrison and all the fine folks at Harvest House Publishers. You are all wonderful!

Janet Kobobel Grant of Books & Such Literary Agency for taking such good care of me.

Chapter 1

Rachel Beiler unpinned her organdy *kapp* and laid it on the bureau in Maxine's spare bedroom. With a shaking hand she released the bun at the base of her head and brushed out her thick hair. The bristles bit into her scalp and scored their way through the rich brown mass.

So many Amish women had thin hair, a combination of genetics and the tight pulling of the hair to confine it. Rachel's was so heavy that sometimes it gave her a headache, all that weight pulling at the back of her head. Unbound, it fell well past her shoulders, the ends curling with a life of their own in spite of her ardent and lifelong wish for straight hair like her sisters.

The thought of leaving that curl falling free made her slightly dizzy.

Aaron had always found her curls disconcerting, un-Amish somehow. He made believe he didn't see the wildness in her hair because he feared it reflected a wildness in her. Not that he ever said so, but she knew.

It's falling free, Aaron. Unbound.

Of course if he had his way, she wouldn't be acting so forward. She'd be fighting to be the good wife he deserved for he was a good man, a kind man, an Amish man through and through. It was his cross to bear that he loved her.

I love him! True, but not as much as he loved her.

She put the brush on the bureau and took a deep breath. Loose hair didn't have to be a symbol of a loose life regardless of what Aaron had thought or any of the rest of them. It didn't. But she couldn't rid herself of the fear that she was doing something terribly wrong, something sinful.

If people found out what she planned…

She ran her hands through her hair, pulling it tight above her face as a good Amish woman would wear it, as she'd always worn it. She dropped her hands, and the thick mane with the sun streaks burned in over the summer months fell free, a sign that she wasn't a good Amish woman after all.

She'd tried. *Gott* knew she'd tried! For all her twenty-six years she'd tried.

She sighed. She was different. That's all there was to it.

She gathered her hair at her nape and clasped it with the large black barrette Maxine had bought for her. Somehow that bit of confinement made her feel a bit more herself, a bit less a rebel.

Taking a deep breath, she unpinned her apron, then her dress, laying them neatly on the bed. It wouldn't do for them to be a mass of wrinkles when she put them back on. She stared at the denim skirt and white blouse that waited for her.

The blouse had a collar.

"Hurry, Rachel," Maxine called from the living room. "You don't want to be late for your first class."

No, she didn't. An education was the reason she was taking such terrifying risks.

She reached for the blouse and slipped it on. She fumbled with the buttons, her first buttons ever, and thought how much easier the straight pins were to manage. She slipped into the skirt, which fell to her knees. Her mother would find the length deplorable, but Rachel had worn her skirts even shorter during her *rumspringa*.

Aaron had liked her legs. She knew because she'd caught him looking.

She smoothed the skirt over her hips with sweaty palms, afraid to look in the mirror and see the reprobate she'd become without her husband's guiding hand.

But she couldn't stop herself from taking this frightening step. She had to find out what a college classroom was like. She had to be part of discussions and write papers and listen to lectures live, not on the computer. Since all these things were forbidden, it was as if she were going through her rumspringa all over again, only this time she was old enough to recognize her rebellion for what it was.

She stared at herself in the bedroom mirror. Did she check how she looked in *Englisch* clothes merely because she was curious about how she looked in them or because she wanted to be certain she looked good? She had to admit to both, and suddenly she felt vain. Worldly.

Her blouse might be buttoned to the neck, tucked carefully in the skirt, modest enough even by Amish standards, but her hair felt wild around her as curls peered over her shoulders. The humid late-August air made the tresses flowing down her back more untamed than when newly washed and she'd have to sit and dry her hair before the heat of the wood stove. The little wisps that always curled at her hairline looked extra messy, extra unruly.

Her stomach kicked and rolled. What did she think she was doing? She was risking everything. Everything! But the pull toward education and the excitement of learning drew her on as surely as her love for her family and the teachings of the *Gmay* pulled her back.

She froze for a moment, unable to draw a breath, knowing she was caught on the edge of a steep slide into—what? A fall from grace? A life of rebellion? A hidden shadow life? A freedom to choose what her life would be?

Maxine appeared in the doorway, all practical encouragement. "You look lovely, Rachel."

Rachel blinked and managed a faint smile in return. Being told she was lovely wasn't something she was used to. Compliments, like Englisch clothing with its buttons, multiple styles, and varying patterns, made you proud. But there was no denying; compliments were nice—and reveling in them sinful, just like rebellion and pride. And education and knowledge.

"I'm terrified, Max."

Maxine smiled. "Of course you are, dear. Everyone's afraid her first day in a new school. Now let's get going." She turned and walked briskly to the door leading to the garage.

Max's straightforward, unemotional attitude put the starch back in Rachel's spine. She could do this. She wanted to do this. The risk was worth taking.

She picked up her backpack and slung it over her shoulder. At least the strap and the weight felt normal. She'd been carrying her teaching materials back and forth in this bag for the past three years as she taught at her district's Amish school. She grabbed her black sweater, the only garment that was familiar, because air conditioning often made her chilly since she was rarely in it.

Rachel closed her eyes. Would Gott punish her for her evil? She pressed her hand over her churning stomach and followed Max to the garage.

"Feel like you're going to throw up?" Max paused before climbing into the passenger seat.

With her short dark hair and her kind hazel eyes, Max was Rachel's anchor in this adventure. Rachel managed another tight smile for her. "Feel like it, yes. Do it, no."

She took her place behind the wheel of the black Honda. She turned the key in the ignition, amazed as always that she was driving an automobile. She, the Amish woman who had a history of keeping all the rules because that was what you did no matter how you felt. Now she was only a week from getting her license. At least she was driving a black car. Somehow it didn't feel as wrong as a white car or a red car would have. Like color minimized the sin.

Wouldn't Johnny fall down laughing if he knew what she was doing? Her brother had made such a big thing out of learning to drive when he began his running around. When he bought his first broken-down car at sixteen, he drove it proudly to the farm and made believe he didn't see the disapproval in *Datt's* eyes. The little boys had climbed in and out, laughing the whole time, and Jonah, who just turned twenty and recently made his vows, had tried not to look intrigued.

If Rachel was counting correctly, Johnny was on his third junker now, and Jonah was twenty-eight and married with three kids.

Concentrating intensely, she backed the black car out of the garage into the rainy evening. She didn't want to look left toward the family farm. What if Mom was there? What if she had come up the road to see what Rachel was doing at Max's house? The fact that she'd never done such a thing before didn't matter. Nor did the fact that there was no way she knew where Rachel was. Rachel hadn't lived in their house since she and Aaron married. Still tonight would be the night she'd catch Rachel for sure.

But Mom wasn't walking up the road in the rain, and Rachel pushed on the accelerator, setting herself on this new, exciting, and forbidden path.

The wipers flicked back and forth, back and forth, their rhythm setting off a line: I'm going (wipers left) to college (wipers right). I'm going…to college. I'm going…to college.

What am I doing? I'm going to college!

Aaron, don't be mad!

"Do you have your lights on?" Max asked.

"What? Oh, no." Rachel reached out and twisted the lights on.

Max made a humming noise. "I know it's not dark out yet, but the law says that when the wipers are on, the lights should be on too."

"I know. I forgot. What if it's raining next week when I take my test and I forget my lights? I'll fail."

"You won't fail." Max's voice held an assurance that Rachel did not share.

"This playing at being Englisch is hard, Max! There's so much to remember!"

"Like your turn signal as you approach the turn?"

Rachel flipped the signal on. "I'll never manage it all."

"You will if this is what you want." Again that calm, practical voice. "How many years have you wanted to do just what you're doing tonight?"

"Always." In fact, Rachel couldn't remember a time when she didn't want to learn more. There was a world out there full of people and places, thoughts and ideas. When her schooling stopped with eighth grade and she was expected to be satisfied helping her mother around the house and with her younger brothers and sisters, she came as close to being depressed as someone with her personality could.

At the corner she turned left, away from Honey Brook and all she knew, toward Lyndale and Wexford College. "My heart's pounding so fast I can barely breathe."

"We can still turn back," Max said. "In fact, you can turn back any time you want."

Rachel gave a jerky nod, her knuckles white as she gripped the wheel. "I don't want to leave, you know, but they're going to make me if they find out. They're going to make me choose. Why can't they understand that all I want is the chance to learn? To study? I want to stay Plain. I like being Amish. It's what I know. It's where I'm comfortable. I just want to learn things too."

Max didn't comment, and Rachel wasn't surprised. There was nothing to say that could counter centuries of tradition and the *Ordnung*. The rules were firm, as immutable as the Ten Commandments, and they said education made you proud and was therefore wrong.

Rachel drove on and the two women settled into an understanding silence. A half hour later, the exit sign for her turnoff appeared and Rachel put on her turn signal. Moments later, she drove onto the campus, past the daunting sign that read Wexford College: A Christian Institution of Higher Education. The fall semester began this week, and young men and women in jeans and shorts, tees and sleeveless blouses, walked in groups, laughing and talking. Belonging.

She was here whether she belonged or not. Her stomach felt hollow and her mind alive with possibilities.

When she drove up to the classroom building, there were already several cars parked in the lot, commuting students like her. She pulled into a slot, put the gearshift in park, and turned to Max. "Do I look as frightened as I feel?"

"You can do this." Max smiled her encouragement.

Rachel made an uncertain sound as she watched a girl in jeans and a T-shirt climb out of a car and hurry to the building, her flip-flops splashing in the puddles as she ran. She looked so—Englisch! So at ease.

"You can do this," Max repeated. "But just in case, I'll wait right here for fifteen minutes. If you feel you need to leave, you just come out."

Somehow that eased the coil of tension knotting her chest.

A little red Smart car zipped past them and into a parking spot. A girl who looked about sixteen—she had to be at least that old to be driving, didn't she?—climbed out and opened an umbrella printed with red roses. Huddling under its cover, she hurried to the building, backpack bumping her as she ran.

"They're all so young!"

"Trust me," Max said. "There will be some gray heads in there."

"If you say." Taking a deep breath, Rachel grabbed her backpack and opened the door. Damp air rushed in.

"If class ends early, just call," Max said. "I'll come right away."

Again, Max's calm voice steadied Rachel, who nodded and stepped into the rain. It splashed on her black shoes and beat on the open black umbrella she clutched. She began walking, her skin prickling and her mouth dry.

Daniel couldn't have felt any more afraid when he faced the lions.

Her step hitched when she saw a parallel between herself and that great man of God. He'd broken the law by choice because he wanted to worship God, and King Darius punished him by sending him to the lions' den. She was breaking the Ordnung, and she was doing it by choice, so she was breaking the law just as Daniel had.

But—and it was a big but—she wasn't doing it for faith. She wanted an education. No lions would tear her apart for her choice, but if she were discovered, her life would be torn apart just as painfully. And she couldn't expect God to send an angel to protect her when her motivation was so selfish.

She squared her shoulders, reached out, and pulled the door to the building open.

Chapter 2

As he watched the federal prison recede in his rearview mirror, Rob Lanier thought how much he despised the place and all it stood for. *Despised* it.

Not that Allenwood was ugly. It was just the opposite. The minimum security facility was attractive and clean and as nice as such a place could be, but it was still a prison. He had to be cleared to enter the facility, then scanned with a security wand, and cleared again to enter the visitors' room. He had to be cleared to leave. He shuddered.

Of course, some of the revulsion he felt was due to the fact that it was his father he had just visited. You'd think after twelve years he'd be used to it, but the resentment flared every time he sat at a table in the visitors' room and studied the once-elegant man who had worn only hand-tailored suits and was now reduced to khaki prisoner garb. Rob had been in uniform the first time he visited after boot camp, and they almost hadn't let him in since he was wearing the same color as the prisoners.

Like he'd willingly switch places.

Today was the first time he'd come since he got out of the Army. He'd put it off as long as he could, but his conscience finally got to him.

Lord, I could do without such a tender spirit, You know? Then he could feel free to ignore his father. He could become just like his mother and brother.

"So you're finally going to do something worthwhile with your life,"

Dad had said when Rob, searching for conversation material, mentioned that tonight was to be his first night of class.

Something worthwhile. He'd stared at his father, amazed as always at the man's gall. Here he was, sitting behind the walls of a prison, but he still had the nerve to demean his son and his accomplishments over the last twelve years. It was but one more indication of the scope of the man's self-delusion. Even in his present, highly circumscribed circumstances Eugene Lanier saw himself as the exception to the rule, the brilliant one with the right to look down on all lesser beings including his son.

Oh, Lord, please don't let me take after my father! How many times through the years had he prayed that prayer?

"It's one of the last three classes I need for my degree," he told his father.

"Big deal. Second-rate Christian college." The scorn scalded the air. "You should have gone to Williams as we planned."

And whose fault was it he hadn't? Not that Dad would ever acknowledge his responsibility for the family finances going south, one of the many ramifications of his actions. Rob took deep breaths to tamp down his anger.

"Whatever you think, serving my country was an honorable way of life, and I'm proud to have done so." He looked around the lounge. "It's certainly a better choice than those you made." He let his contempt seep into his words and immediately felt petty. He was a better man than that.

Though his father's face flushed, he expressed no regret. Rob wasn't surprised. Even before his arrest, the man made no apologies to anyone, not to his wife, his sons, his business associates, and since his arrest certainly not to the many people he'd bilked. That was the worst part for Rob, the least honorable part.

Rob glanced in the rearview mirror again. Just looking at the prison through the rain-streaked back window gave him a creepy feeling. It irked him that his conscience drove him to visit a man who wasn't the least bit pleased to see him.

Slough it off, Lanier. The man's not worth it.

He shook himself much like Charlie, the big brown oaf of a dog he'd rescued from the shelter two weeks ago. Somehow the thought of Charlie cheered him.

He glanced at his watch and depressed the accelerator. If he didn't hurry, he wouldn't have time to eat before class. He needed some good Mennonite cooking to replace the bitter aftertaste of the visit with Dad. Pork and sauerkraut, real mashed potatoes, creamed dried corn, shoofly pie, sweet tea. Rob smiled in anticipation.

Of all the things he'd missed in the Army, home cooking was at the top of his list, especially on his deployments. While the other guys dreamed of hamburgers and steak, he yearned for ham loaf and whoopie pies.

His phone rang, and he pushed the button on the steering wheel that activated it.

"A very cool feature," the salesman had said of the hands-free device.

Very cool indeed. "Hello."

"Rob. Where are you?"

Rob took a deep breath. His headache wound itself tighter, and he felt ashamed of his reaction to his mother's voice. He tried to sound upbeat. "Mom. How are you?"

"Fine." But the abrupt tone said differently.

"What can I do for you?" he asked, aware that was the time-bomb question.

"I am furious! Livid! Do you know no one will give me a loan so I can buy a car like yours?"

No surprise there, either at her desire for a new car like his or at the lack of a loan. She was an if-you've-got-it-so-should-I person of the first magnitude whose credit rating was in the cellar. Loans didn't magically appear, no matter how much your selfish nature knew you deserved your latest craving.

"Two things, Mom." Rob forced himself to talk in a mild tone. "One, you have a very nice car. You don't need another one." He knew this because he'd bought her the silver Cruze three years ago. He'd just finished paying it off.

She made a sniffing sound. "It's tiny."

"It's more than adequate for one person."

"Then why did you buy yourself a big SUV?"

It wasn't that big, but she'd never grasp that fact in her current mood. She was distressed because it wasn't the size of a Cruze. "I've got Charlie."

"You bought a car for a dog." He heard the disbelief.

"My money, my choice, Mom—which reminds me of reason number two you're getting a no on the loan. You don't have the money to pay for a new car."

"And whose fault is that?" she snapped.

Rob rolled his eyes. He knew the answer as well as she did.

"Your father—" she began.

He cut her off. "I'm not going to talk about him with you, Mom. We've covered the topic like sweet on sugar. Enough."

"But you don't understand me and my pain."

She was right; he didn't. He'd tried, but he couldn't understand remaining a victim for twelve years. If she'd get a job, it would pull her out of her self-pity and dependence, not that she wanted to hear that again any more than he wanted to hear a rant against his father. "Talking about Dad upsets both of us and doesn't fix a thing."

He heard her sniff of disapproval. After a couple of beats of silence during which he suspected she was analyzing why he wasn't going along with her wishes, she said in a wheedling voice, "Well, you could—"

"No, I couldn't. I have to pay for my own."

Her anger at his comment hummed down the line, but he didn't apologize. Sometimes he almost missed the snapped commands and uncompromising orders from his superior officers the past twelve years. At least they hadn't been loaded with attempted manipulation and hidden meanings.

When she finally spoke again, her voice was ice. "I suppose you spent the afternoon laughing with the reason I don't have any money."

He couldn't remember the last time he laughed with his father. It certainly hadn't been this afternoon.

"Mom," he warned, refusing to be drawn into a bash Eugene Aldrich Lanier conversation. Not that he blamed her for her anger. One morning she'd been rich and pampered, her every wish granted. The next her husband was in jail and everything she thought was hers was whisked away. Still, twelve years was more than enough time to move on.

He looked at the green Pennsylvania countryside rushing by, so lush and lovely after the arid brown of Afghanistan and the debilitating heat of Iraq. *Home.* And he was in one piece. He smiled in spite of everything.

"Rob? Rob, are you still there?"

He rubbed at the tension behind his left eye. She represented home too. "I'm here, Mom. Just thinking."

"You shouldn't think during a phone call. Dead air. You need to clear your mind of your bad thoughts."

He looked at the wonderful tall trees, deciduous and conifer, flashing light and shadows over him like a strobe. "Who said they're bad thoughts?"

"Of course they're bad thoughts. You saw your father."

"I did. First time in a long time."

"I told you not to go. I told you he isn't worth your time. I told you to forget him like he forgot us."

"Goodbye, Mom. Gotta go." He reached for the off button.

The car came out of nowhere.

One minute he was driving along with no one in sight; the next a gray bullet disguised as a late model Jeep Wrangler rounded the curve in his lane, aimed right at him. Even as his heart went wild with the awareness of the coming crash, he saw the driver look up from fiddling with something—his CD player? his phone?—and watched the man's eyes go wide. The driver wrenched his wheel, trying to swerve back onto his side of the road. The car's skidding action threw up a great gout of muddy water that covered Rob's windshield and robbed him of his vision.

Rob pulled his wheel to the right reflexively to get out of the car's path even as he hit the brakes. The cinder and mud shoulder was narrow, edged with a metal guardrail that was supposed to keep cars out of the deep gully beside the road. As he crunched on the cinders, he tried to see through the muddy window.

Help, Lord! The arrow prayer was as ardent as any uttered in the field.

As he waited helplessly for the arc of the wipers to clear the windshield, he clutched the wheel with all the intensity he'd gripped his rifle as he walked through remote Afghan villages just waiting for a Taliban sniper or an IED to get him.

Instead of a terrorist round in a rocky mountain stronghold, it was going to be a gray bullet on a Pennsylvania road in a rain storm.

Come on, Lord! Not fair!

In the excruciating seconds of blindness, Rob heard the scrape of metal as the car slid along the guardrail and the skid of his tires on cinders as his wheels sought for traction. He struggled to keep control of the bucking wheel. How long was the strip of guardrail? Was there time to stop before it ran out and he went over the side?

The wipers cleared the window at the same time the brakes grabbed. He slowed and then stopped, still plastered against the guardrail. The silence was intense as he sat, head dropped back against the rest, heart thundering. He felt limp even as he felt he'd pop out of his skin.

"Rob! Rob! What's going on? Rob!"

It was Mom. He'd never had time to push the off button.

"Hey, Mom," he managed.

"What happened? Are you all right? I heard terrible noises."

"Car in the wrong lane, but I'm okay. Can't say the same for my car, but I'm fine."

"Thank heavens! I don't know what I'd do without you!"

He smiled to himself. Maybe she cared after all.

"Who'd take care of me if you got hurt? Or killed! How would I manage? How would I get along?"

He gave a mental shrug because he was too weary to give a real one.

"The whole time you were in the Army, I just knew you were going to get killed. I knew I'd be left on my own with no one to care. Certainly your brother would be no help. He never is. I knew—"

He cut in. "I've got to check the car, Mom. See you soon." And this time he definitely depressed the off button.

He sat, watching a red-tailed hawk alight in the dead top of a nearby tree and stare down at him. He sketched a wave at the bird. "I'm fine. Really. Fine."

The hawk flew away.

When he felt his legs would hold him, he pushed his door open and climbed out.

The Jeep Wrangler was nowhere in sight. Surprise, surprise.

Muttering under his breath, he climbed out into the rain. He walked around the back of the car to examine the damage to the passenger side. The whole length of the car was scraped and dented, the paint scoured off down to the metal. The guardrail wasn't looking too good either, but it had done its job and kept him from going into the gully. He peeked over the side. Long way down.

He sighed. "Okay, Lord. It's not that I'm unappreciative, but the car's only three weeks old! I haven't even had to wash it yet."

Chapter 3

All the people seemed to be funneling down one hall. Rachel followed, looking for the stairs, her closed umbrella dripping down her leg. She needed to find room 203. She would be going there for an hour and a half every Friday and Monday night at 6:30 for the next three months.

She trailed three girls in shorts up a flight of stairs, her shoes squeaking on the tile floor. All those long legs ahead of her made her swallow. And the scoop necks of their tops. The one girl's bra straps showed, but she didn't seem to care. The three giggled as they walked down the hall and entered room 203. Her classmates.

She was used to seeing and talking to Englisch people, especially at her parents' produce stand where she worked all summer. Still, seeing the girls here, so confident, so blatantly immodest by her standards made her feel terribly out of place.

She looked down at her denim skirt and white blouse. They'd felt so Englisch in Max's bedroom, but now they looked so conservative compared to the shorts and tops of the others. She'd gotten it wrong in spite of her care.

But her Amish clothing would have been wrong too. It would have attracted attention, something she did not want. In some strange way she would be a symbol if she was the lone Amish person present, and she didn't want that. It didn't seem right to expose herself and, by extension, her people to the searching eyes and prying questions an Amish woman in a college class would cause.

So she'd just have to feel awkward in her Englisch clothes. She wasn't here to impress anyone. Impressing people was so Englisch. Humility and blending with the community were the Amish way, her way. There was a lot to be said for everyone dressing alike. You always felt right. You always were right. You never worried about being wrong.

She paused in the doorway, telling her heart to slow down and her skin to stop prickling. She wanted to feel brave but knew she was failing miserably.

A lady she assumed was the teacher stood at the front of the class studying something on the lectern. The woman wore slacks and a silky red oversized shirt over a scoop-necked top, but the scoop wasn't as low as the girls'. She wore trendy red glasses that made her look like she controlled her world. Lucky woman.

"Excuse me." A man had come up behind her, his tousled hair and wrinkled shirt showing clearly he'd gotten caught in the downpour. He didn't look happy, but at least he wasn't sixteen like most of the class. Not that they were really sixteen. More like eighteen. It was a basic comp class required of everyone.

Rachel moved into the room to let the man pass. Without another glance at her, he took a seat in the back row. There was an empty chair in the row ahead of him next to the girl who'd driven that red Smart car. Rachel took a deep breath and forced herself to take one step, then another.

She'd be okay. She would. She had to be okay. This was her dream come true. And Max was still waiting outside. She could still leave if her tiny dab of courage failed. She could go back to being who she'd been all her life. She knew her place there, knew what was expected of her. In this room she had no idea.

She blinked. She had a choice. She could give up her dream. She could go back to feeling intellectually stifled. Half alive. Forced into a mold that didn't fit.

If only she wasn't loved in that mold. If no one cared what she did, this would be so much easier. If no one cared, no one would be hurt if she was discovered. But they did care. They'd always cared, and when Aaron died, they'd been so wonderful to her. If they knew she was here, they would be so distressed.

She took a seat by the Smart car girl. She pulled her AlphaSmart out of her backpack and put it on the desk. When she'd discovered the battery-operated little word processor, she'd almost cried. She didn't have to feel sinful when she wrote on it. Granted it didn't do anything but allow her to write, so she still had to go to Max's to print her material or to access the Internet, but she loved the little machine for the clear conscience it allowed her.

The Smart car girl looked at her and smiled. Perky was the word that came to Rachel's mind. It was probably the short pixie hair, the button nose, and the small body.

"Hi. I'm Amy Steiner."

Rachel's return smile felt stiff. "I'm Rachel Beiler."

"My first college class." Amy looked around the room. "I'm nervous. I don't know anyone."

Somehow knowing someone else was unsure of herself made Rachel relax. "Me too. Nervous and first class. I don't know anyone either."

"But now you do. You know me." Amy beamed. "BFFs before you know it."

Uncertain what a BFF was, Rachel's stomach turned. "Sounds good." What else could she say?

"It does, doesn't it? I always wanted a best friend, but I wasn't allowed one."

Okay, the BF was for best friend. The other F would become obvious eventually. At least she hadn't committed herself to anything obscene or immoral. But Amy had no close friends? Rachel couldn't fathom it.

"I'm sorry," she said. "That must have been hard. Lonely."

Amy made a face. "Long story. Too long and depressing for just meeting someone."

"Okay." Rachel became busy with her knapsack.

"That sounded very impolite." Amy frowned as she berated herself.

"Not impolite at all," Rachel assured her. "Sometimes you just don't want to talk about things, especially with a stranger."

"Too true." Amy flipped open her laptop and turned it on. "But we're not strangers. We're BFFs. What's that thing?" She gestured at the AlphaSmart.

Apparently being BFFs allowed you to ask anything you wanted. "It's a word processor."

"Like a computer?"

"A limited one. It works on three double A batteries."

"How long do the batteries last?"

"Hundreds of hours."

"No kidding! How cool is that."

"Cool indeed."

Amy spun in her seat to face the row behind. "Hi. Did you ever see anything so cute in your life?"

"What?" It was the unhappy wet guy.

"Show him, Rachel." She pointed to the AlphaSmart.

Rachel turned and held up the machine.

"Double A battery-operated computer," Amy announced. "Lasts forever. Genius."

He grunted what could have been agreement or "leave me alone." Amy apparently heard agreement.

"It's our first class," she confided to him. "I'm Amy and this is my friend Rachel. We're nervous, Rachel and me. What about you?"

Wet Guy gave a half smile that quirked one side of his mouth. "I'm Rob and it's my first class too. At least first class live. I've done some work online."

Rachel wanted to say, "Me too," but she was too shy. Englisch men always scared her—which she knew was ridiculous—and this one was big and strong, overwhelming. And handsome.

"I'm jealous." Amy grinned, looking anything but jealous. "I always wanted to study online, but I couldn't."

"I couldn't do anything else," Rob said. "No other options."

Why no options? Rachel knew why for her, but why for him?

"So where are you from that you had no options?" Amy asked him, her manner friendly and slightly flirtatious.

"I'm local," he said. "You?"

"I lived in the northwestern part of the state, an hour from Erie."

He nodded like he knew exactly where she was referring to. "It gets cold up that way."

"In my little town, winter freezes were the least of it." Amy's voice became as chill as the winters. Then she beamed, the sun after the blizzard. "But I'm not there. I'm here!" As she turned to face front, she looked at Rachel. "And I'm *never* going back."

As Rachel tried to think of a response, the professor cleared her throat.

"Welcome, everyone. I'm Dr. Selma Dyson." She didn't speak loudly but everyone immediately quieted. "I don't have many require-ments of you as a class, but I have two absolutes. No cell phones for any purpose. This is *my* class and I expect you to give *me* your atten-tion, not some friend or, worse yet, some game. Turn them all off. Now."

After the general gasp of dismay, everyone pulled out phones and began turning them off. Rachel watched Amy punch commands into her pink flowered phone. Rachel didn't pull hers out. It only had Max's number in it, and she wouldn't call.

"And my second requirement—" Dr. Dyson continued, "—a paper every Monday. At least a thousand words." She rolled her eyes at the mutters. "This is a comp class."

"How many pages is that?" asked a boy in the front row.

"Four."

"Four!"

"Four. And I take off for grammar and spelling. This is not your comfy high school anymore, people. I have one goal for this class, and that's to make you think for yourselves. I want to read what *you* think, what *you* feel, what *you* believe, not what someone taught you or, worse yet, what someone else wrote on the internet. This class is all about you learning to be a thinker."

Yes! Excitement bubbled through Rachel. That was exactly what she wanted. To think and to be challenged to think.

"Now," Dr. Dyson said, "let's talk about what makes good writing."

Rachel typed away on her AlphaSmart, completely engaged.

The time fled by. In what seemed like only minutes, Dr. Dyson was wrapping up the evening with, "The oldest maxim of all is to write what you know. Write what you feel passionate about. So your first assignment is to write about something you find interesting. Could be yourselves. Why are you here? Sure, you want an education—or your parents want one for you—but why Wexford? Or maybe you'd rather write about a topic that excites you. Or a subject you've been thinking about. This paper is your choice."

"What if you don't like my choice?" muttered someone. Rachel didn't see who.

Dr. Dyson heard. "I'll like it as long as you write about what you think, not just the facts. The *why*. Why do you love sports? Why do you hate politics? This paper is all about you. No research needed." She grinned. "At least this week. I'm making it easy for you, people. Write an autobiography if you want. Just no 'I was born on—' beginnings, please. Be a little creative." She closed her notes and then looked up. "Oh, and no fancy fonts to take up lots of space. Calibri or Times New Roman, size twelve. No exceptions."

Half-formed thoughts raced through Rachel's mind. Could she put into words why she was here? She couldn't wait to try, and she had the whole weekend to do so.

Chapter 4

Maxine Englerth sat in her favorite recliner in the living room and checked the clock. Almost time to go get Rachel. The evening had passed without a come-get-me phone call, and Max felt a zing of satisfaction.

Earlier in the evening when she'd watched Rachel walk into the building at Wexford and disappear behind the tinted glass, all her doubts about her complicity in Rachel's actions gnawed at her.

She'd sighed and waited the allotted minutes to see if Rachel would come back out. She wouldn't blame the girl if she changed her mind. The potential consequences of what the two of them were doing were immense, more so for Rachel than for her. All she'd lose would be the respect of the Amish community. Rachel would lose everything.

Max had put her hand over her suddenly pounding heart as she stared through the rain streaked windshield. Was she wrecking Rachel's life? If she were caught, there was nothing but shunning in her future.

Am I doing the right thing, Buddy?

As always when she talked to her late husband, she heard no answer.

Throughout her marriage, Max asked Buddy what he thought about all kinds of situations. She didn't always follow his advice or agree with his thoughts, but he was her sounding board, the one who helped her reach a decision. She ached for him now.

He was one year gone, the victim of a rampant cancer that took him much too young. Most of the time she felt like half a person, especially when she wanted to talk with him. He had been so practical, so principled that she always trusted what he said.

Buddy, tell me I'm not making a terrible mistake. That she's not making a terrible mistake.

Instead of an answer she had rain pounding on the car's roof on a gloomy Friday evening. She blinked back tears of uncertainty and loneliness.

Why'd you leave me, Bud? Some days she got so mad at him for going. She was only fifty-four. He could have at least waited until she was eighty-four. Or better yet ninety-four.

She wanted to tell God she was mad at Him too, but she didn't have the courage. Not that He didn't know exactly what she was thinking even if she didn't say it.

A man with the side of his car seriously messed up pulled up beside her. He climbed out, clothes wrinkled as only rain can wrinkle, expression as dark as the stormy sky. Another member of the Bad Day Club, poor guy.

Max stared at his retreating back as he jogged through the rain. Once upon a time Buddy had jogged like that, easily, without thought. She wanted to remember that Buddy, not the one who could barely walk, not the one who was stooped with pain.

The anniversary of his death had been last week. People said the second year was worse than the first. Did that mean the hollowness inside would get hollower? How could it?

With a sigh she started the car. Rachel had been inside longer than the fifteen minutes they'd agreed on. She turned toward home.

Do you mind me letting Rachel drive your car, Bud? She made a sad smile. Of course he didn't. He had no use for it anymore. She frowned as a stray and totally frivolous thought flashed across her mind. How did people get around in heaven? Did they sort of float? Or did they walk like down here?

I'm going to give the Honda to her, you know. Why have two cars in the garage when there's only one driver?

Of course there would still be two cars in the garage. Rachel couldn't take hers home with her. But the papers would read it belonged to Rachel Miller Beiler, not Bernard Thomas Englerth.

The family's involvement with Rachel had started so simply about twenty years ago. Her brother Jonah, two years older than Rachel, had come first, a little towhead with a Dutch boy haircut and straw hat almost as big as he was.

"I heard a boy laugh," he said as he stood at the edge of the stand of trees that separated Max and Buddy's new house from the Millers' farm.

"You did." Max had been enchanted by the little boy. She called over her shoulder to her son, "Ryan, come meet your new friend."

Ryan had come rushing around the corner of the house in his T-shirt and shorts to meet the Amish boy in his broadcloth shirt and broadfall trousers. They became fast friends and appreciated each other even today, though their paths had diverged as their cultures intervened.

Now Jonah was married and a father several times over with his own business, a nursery and garden center. Ryan was in graduate school finishing up his PhD in Materials Science at Lehigh University in Bethlehem. At least he lived in state even if he was rarely able to come home. Jonah lived down the street.

Rachel had eventually trailed Jonah to the house, a little sweetheart in her apron and dress with hair knotted at the nape of her neck. Though Ashley was a year older than Rachel, the two girls enjoyed each other as much as Ryan and Jonah. The girls grew apart when Ashley discovered boys and makeup.

For several years Max didn't see much of Rachel. Then one night she appeared on their doorstep, a beautiful girl of seventeen or eighteen, wearing her heart-shaped kapp and dark dress, her feet in flip-flops in spite of the cool March air.

"I have a question, Mrs. Englerth." Rachel swallowed, obviously nervous.

"Rachel! How wonderful to see you! Come on in. Buddy, look who's here."

Buddy glanced up from the Final Four long enough to smile at Rachel. "We've missed you."

Rachel flushed and Max couldn't tell if it was from pleasure at the comment or embarrassment that he noticed her.

Max smiled at her husband as she said to Rachel, "We won't hear from him again this evening. Come on. Let's you and me go into the kitchen and you can tell me all that's happening over at the farm."

Max loved having a young person to talk with. The house had become so quiet, too quiet, with both kids off at college. She bustled around the kitchen getting glasses of sweet tea and slices of apple crumb pie.

She set Rachel's pie and tea before her as the girl sat at the table. "I know it's not as good as your mom's, but I hope you enjoy it."

"Where's mine?" Buddy called from the living room.

"How does he do that?" Max asked Rachel. "He's deaf to everything but the game and still hears me cut pie?"

"Maybe he smells it?" Rachel suggested.

"Bingo! That's it." Max took a piece and a glass of tea to her husband and then returned to the kitchen to sit with Rachel.

The girl had waited for Max before she ate and now took a bite. She was still nervous and her smile was tight when she said, "Um, good."

Max smiled back. "That's a compliment since I've had your mom's. Tell me how each of your brothers and sisters are doing."

Rachel talked and Max listened. The pie disappeared and so did Rachel's tension as she spoke about her four brothers and two sisters.

When Max heard about Levi, six, offering up three of the family's chickens as sacrifices because of a sermon on Sunday, she decided it was time to get to the point.

"So, Rachel, what can I do for you? What's this question you want to ask? I'll do my best to answer it."

Rachel studied the flowers on her pie plate with great interest. Then she straightened her shoulders as if grasping courage. "May I come and use your computer sometimes?"

Max blinked her surprise. She had been expecting to be asked to drive someone in the family somewhere—shopping perhaps, or to the doctor or chiropractor. "Oh, my dear, of course!"

Rachel glowed with pleasure.

Max studied her visitor. Was using the computer Rachel's running-around rebellion? She was of the age for her rumspringa. "I remember Ashley taught you to play some computer games when you were young. We have some fun new games she and Ryan loaded for Buddy and me before they went back to school."

Rachel nodded. "That's nice. Is there a time that's best for me to come over?"

Max thought. "It'll have to be at night because Buddy works and I'm in and out with various projects and meetings. I'm home most nights, just never Thursday. It's our small group from church."

"Evenings are good. I have to work too."

Max thought of the PC that was so old both kids refused to take it to college. It was in the extra bedroom and would be perfect for Rachel. "You can start tonight if you'd like."

Rachel's eyes sparkled. "Could I?"

"Come on. I'll get you set up."

It took Max a couple of months to realize Rachel wasn't playing games or looking for funny movies on YouTube. She was reading. Frequently she'd leave the house with a thoughtful look or faraway expression as if she was thinking about something. When Max checked the history of Rachel's web investigations, she found blogs and e-zines that covered a variety of topics from women's issues to history to writing to science. The only things missing were fashion and celebrity gossip. And games.

The girl wanted to learn, which shouldn't have surprised Max. It had always been clear that Rachel was smart as a whip. Apparently she was chaffing under the limited education her people espoused. As Max pondered that realization, an idea took root in her imagination.

"I think Rachel is a very intelligent girl," she told Buddy.

"You're just realizing that?"

She waved that comment aside. "She ponders things."

"She does. I've always felt sorry for an Amish man or woman with a questing mind."

Max was delighted Buddy agreed with her perception of things. She determined to take what she saw as the logical next step.

One evening as Rachel prepared to leave after spending almost four hours on the computer, Max said "Have you ever thought about having a real purpose to all your reading and learning?"

Rachel looked at her in question.

"How about going for your high school diploma? You could get your GED by studying online."

Rachel looked out across the woods toward her family farm. "I've thought about doing that."

Max was encouraged by the comment. "I think you should do it. You're a very smart girl."

"Two problems," she said. "One, I have to wait until I'm eighteen, but that's only a couple more months."

"Why eighteen?"

"Younger you need a letter from a school authority saying you left school but need the diploma equivalent because of work or higher education or the Army or something." She gave a rueful smile. "Who would I ask? I don't think anyone on our school board will write me such a letter."

Max thought of the little one-room schoolhouse a mile down the road and the Amish men who formed its board. Fine men all, but there was that cultural divide.

"The other problem," Rachel continued, "is that I'd have to go to a testing center."

"You can't take it online?" Obviously Rachel had looked up the information.

"No. You have to go to an official GED testing center. The closest is Reading."

Max had been thinking Philadelphia with the fifty-mile drive through dense traffic and then the chaos of the city, but Reading was only about twenty miles. Not bad at all. She looked at Rachel. Unless you drove a buggy.

"What if I drove you?" Max said.

Rachel's face lit up. She took a deep breath as if she were about to admit to something that had been a deep and closely guarded secret previously. "I've got the money saved from work to pay for it."

Max hugged the girl. "Then you go for it."

Rachel didn't say yes, but she didn't say no, something Max considered encouraging. Three months later, just past her eighteenth birthday, Rachel told Max she'd signed up to do the deed.

When Max told Buddy what Rachel was doing and her part in it, he raised an eyebrow. "You sure you're not interfering where you shouldn't?"

Max frowned. "I thought you agreed with me."

"I did?" Buddy scratched his head. "When?"

"You said you felt sorry for an Amish man or woman with a questing mind."

"And you translated that into my saying it was a good idea she get her GED?"

"Well, yes."

"Maxie, don't you think that's stretching my comment a bit?"

"It's only high school, Buddy."

He shook his head. "It's way more than their culture would encourage."

"But she's so smart! And she's working cleaning houses." Not that there was anything wrong with cleaning houses, but the thought of this superintelligent girl settling for less than she could be, saddened

Max terribly. "God doesn't give brilliance to many. It shouldn't be squandered."

"Babe, she's not your daughter." Buddy's voice was gentle as he pointed out the obvious.

"I know." She felt her confidence that she was doing an all right thing momentarily slip, but then she pictured Rachel's radiant face as she talked about something she had learned on the computer or in a book she got from the library.

"I used to think we'd never get our Ashley through school. Remember, Buddy? For her, life meant fun. But Rachel—" She grabbed her husband's hand as if touching him would transfer her confidence to him. "She yearns to learn, Bud. She's an intellectual in a community that sees education as a seat of pride. How does someone like her survive when she can't learn? When she can't explore new ideas?"

"Maybe you're opening a door to nothing but grief for her, Maxie. I know you want to help. I know you've always had a soft spot for Rachel. But are you doing her any favors?"

Now as she sat in her lonely living room and waited for it to be time to go get Rachel, Max still didn't have a definitive answer to Buddy's question. All she knew was that Rachel kept taking one step, then another, then another, and she couldn't do anything but help.

I hope you're not too upset with me, Buddy. Please don't be upset. But what else can I do?

Chapter 5

By the time class was over, Rachel's hands might have been tired from all the typing, but her heart was soaring. Professor Dyson was going to be very demanding, and she loved it.

As she began collecting her things, Amy peered at her. "Rachel, you want to go for coffee?"

Rachel's hand stalled in the middle of sliding her AlphaSmart into her backpack. Talk about unexpected. She took a breath as she turned to say no thanks. The air leaked out of her slowly when she looked at Amy's face, a mix of longing and uncertainty, all perk gone.

Amy glanced away quickly when Rachel didn't immediately answer and spotted Rob gathering his things. "You too, if you want, Rob."

He looked up in surprise. "Me too what?"

"Go get a coffee. Rachel and I are going. Come with us."

He paused for a moment, shot a quick look at Rachel, and then shrugged. "Why not? Charlie will keep for a few more minutes."

If Amy's delighted smile was an indication, Rachel thought the girl was as surprised as she was by his acceptance.

"Great!" Amy did a little dance step in place. "Who's Charlie? Does he want to come too?"

"Probably, but I don't think it'd be a good idea. He's my dog. A big brown thing I rescued a couple of weeks ago."

"Yeah?" Amy's smile settled into normal. "I have a dog back home. A beagle named Bagel. I miss her. A lot." She looked at Rachel. "You got a dog?"

"We've got two at the farm, a mom and her son. Pepper and Corny." Named after crops by her little brothers.

"Cool. What kind?"

"Collies." Rachel threw her book bag over her shoulder. "Look, I'd love to go, but I've got someone picking me up."

"Call her and tell her not to come," Amy said without hesitation. "I'll take you home. Where do you live?"

"Honey Brook."

"Where's that?"

"About a half hour that way." Rachel pointed.

"Not a problem. I'm going that way."

There was something about Amy's obvious longing for friends that tugged at Rachel. She pulled out the phone Max had insisted she buy and tapped the one number she had in it.

Max answered on the first ring. "You okay?"

"Fine. In fact, better than fine. Class was great! I've got a ride home. Is that okay? We're going to go out for coffee."

Max laughed in her ear. "And here I've spent the night worrying! Go. Have fun. Is he handsome?"

"Max!" Rachel tried not to look at Rob who was indeed handsome with his brown hair and very blue eyes. "Her name's Amy."

"Rats." Max sounded disappointed, making Rachel smile.

They walked into the fading light of a now rainless dusk. The campus coffee house was one building over, and it was uncomfortably crowded.

"And they're all too young anyway," Amy said. "Way too young."

Both Rachel and Rob looked at her, startled.

She held up a hand. "I know, I know. I look sixteen." She shrugged. "What can I say? I'm really twenty-five."

"Huh," Rob sounded unconvinced.

"Really. I can prove it. Didn't you say you're local? Do you know a coffee place around here?"

"Sure. Well, not a coffee house as such but a place that has great coffee as well as other stuff. The Star Diner is a couple of miles down the road. Want to follow me? I'm the SUV with the caved-in side."

"Ouch." Amy said when they stopped to examine the side of Rob's car. "How'd it happen?"

"Forced off the road this afternoon. Saved by a guardrail."

No wonder he'd looked upset when he came to class. Ouch was right.

"Could have been a lot ouchier." He flicked his key fob and one brake light flashed. He sighed. "At least that's what I'm trying to convince myself."

"You need this coffee," Amy declared. "We'll follow you."

Rachel shoehorned herself into the passenger seat of Amy's little red Smart car. Amy swung behind Rob, a bright red David following a hulking black Goliath.

"Don't you love this little thing?" she gushed. "I do. It's such fun to drive. And I can zip all over the place. I drove this old junker when I left home and barely managed to keep going until I got here. Thought it would die several times on the trip. What a relief to have a car I don't have to pray over, you know?"

Rachel had never thought about praying over a car, but she'd known some horses she'd talked to the Lord about, and not very kindly.

Without taking a breath, Amy switched topics. "Isn't he gorgeous? Don't you just melt when he smiles?" She gestured with animation as she drove. At times Rachel wasn't certain either hand was on the wheel. "I saw the way he checked you out before he said he'd come. He likes you. I can tell. I can always tell about stuff like that. Not that I've had lots of experience calling romances, but when I have, I'm always right. I'd give anything to have a guy look at me like that. Well, not *anything*, but you know what I mean. I mean, he's gorgeous! Those blue eyes! Just like Bradley Cooper."

Rachel had no idea who Bradley Cooper was, and her head was spinning by the time she climbed out of the car. Certainly Amy was imagining things about Rob checking her out. No big, handsome Englisch man would look on her with interest. Plain old Rachel Beiler? Forget it.

Amy's comments made Rachel even more self-conscious than she'd been and that was saying something. As a result she couldn't make herself look at Rob as she and Amy followed him across the parking lot. It didn't help that he was the first man besides her brothers she'd been around socially except in large gatherings like district dinners since Aaron's death.

A couple of men in her district had made it known they would be happy to call on her, but she'd always said no. At gatherings she made sure she was busy in the kitchen with the women. Marriage had been fine, but she wasn't anxious to be married again, at least not yet. Maybe someday. After all, she'd like to have children.

"It's been three years," her mother would say. "Time to move on. Milton Fisher is nice. Or Benjie Zook. Or Davy Yoder."

"Mom! No! They're your age. They just want wives to raise their children. I want to love my husband, not merely respect him."

"You need a man, Rachel," her father told her. "You need a family. Find another man your age. Find another Aaron."

But deep in her secret heart she didn't want another Aaron, and that made her feel guilty. He had been such a fine man, and she had been happy with him. She would have been satisfied married to him for fifty years. But when he died, she found she liked living alone. She could be herself in her own home. She could read and think and stare into space, and no one thought she was wasting her time. No one lectured her about idle hands or useless thinking. And she could slip over to Max's unseen.

Rob cleared his throat, making her jump and look up. He smiled and held the door for her and Amy. Amy practically danced through while Rachel lowered her head and studied the scuffed floor. She didn't try to stifle her shy smile.

"Wow! A gentleman," Amy hissed to Rachel. "Looks *and* manners! It doesn't get any better."

Rachel couldn't help glancing at Rob to see if he'd heard and caught him shaking his head in bemusement. She smiled and he smiled back, flustering her completely.

A hostess wearing a weary face turned to them, menus in hand. She saw Rob and her face lit up. "Well, Rob Lanier. I heard you were back in town."

"Patsy Turner," he said, giving her a hug. "How are you?"

She held up her left hand, wiggling her ring finger. "Patsy Witmer these days, and I'm fine."

"Pete Witmer the lucky guy?"

Patsy grinned. "His brother Phil."

"Whoa. You nabbed an older man."

Patsy smiled as she led them to a booth. "The better man in my opinion. You?" She glanced at Amy and Rachel.

He shook his head. "Still single. These are my friends Amy and Rachel."

With a smile, Patsy left to greet two couples who'd just come in.

Rachel and Amy sat on one side of their booth and Rob across from them. Rachel studied her menu without seeing it. What was she doing, having coffee with two Englischers? She wasn't worried about someone seeing her. It was too late in the day and they were too far from home. Except for running-around kids, everyone would be home getting ready for bed.

Their waitress appeared. "Hey, Rob." She grinned. "Patsy said it was you."

"Betts." He stood and repeated the easygoing hug. "Good to see you. How are Bill and the kids?"

"We're all in one piece, which I consider the sign of a successful day. What can I get you all? We've got great peach crumb and shoofly pies."

When she left with an order for two peach crumbs and a shoofly, all à la mode, along with three coffees, Amy studied Rob.

"You know everybody in town?"

"Not really."

"Sure seems like it."

"The Star's been owned by Patsy's family for years, and a lot of the guys who went to high school with Pats and me worked and still work here, like Betts. We used to hang out here all the time."

"I couldn't imagine staying in my home town." Amy shuddered. "It took me a while, but I got out and I'm never going back." She spoke the last words slowly and with emphasis.

Rachel studied her new friend as Betts served their coffee. This was the second time Amy had mentioned leaving home; both times her voice had been edged with sharp anger and deep pain. Maybe when they knew each other better, Amy would tell her story. *If* they knew each other better. *If.* Not *when.* She had to be careful not to mix too much with Englisch people. She'd be polite, kind, but not overly intimate. Not BFFs.

"I felt I'd never come back either," Rob stirred two creams into his coffee. "Yet here I am."

Betts brought their pies and Rob surprised Rachel by asking if the girls minded if he thanked God for the food.

"It's something I've gotten in the habit of doing." And he prayed a prayer made up on the spot. Rachel knew because it thanked God for peaches and molasses. She'd never in her life heard such a prayer.

When her people had a meal, they bowed for silent prayer before and after they ate. She had no idea what the others prayed, but she usually repeated the Lord's Prayer in her mind. How could you do better than Jesus's prayer?

"Do you always make up your own prayers?" she asked before she thought.

"Sure," he said with an easy grin. "I do it all the time."

"Me too," Amy said. "I figure if David could make up his prayers, so can I."

Rachel had never considered the Psalms in that light before. The great Amish/Englisch divide yawned wide in the strangest places.

Amy pointed her fork at Rob. "How long were you gone?"

"Twelve years, give or take. I left right after I graduated from high school."

"Long time. I repeat: I'm never going back."

Rob saluted her with his coffee cup. "I'll check on you in twelve years."

"Why'd you come back?" Rachel asked, her curiosity overcoming her shyness.

He frowned at his pie. "I'm not sure. When I figure it out, I'll tell you." He looked right at her and smiled that warm smile that quirked one corner of his mouth higher than the other.

Rachel couldn't not smile back. "A pair of wanderers." She included Amy in her smile. "What does it say about me that I live down the street from my family, see them almost every day, and like it that way?"

"That you have a nice family?" Amy said immediately.

Rachel laughed. "Good guess and very true."

Amy sipped her coffee after adding two creams and a packet of Splenda. "How about you, handsome? Now that you're back in your hometown, do you live at home? Or down the street?"

"Not a chance." Rob cut off a piece of his peach crumb and stabbed a bit of his ice cream. "Charlie and I have our own place on the other side of town. It's not very large, but it's working for us for the time being."

"What do you have? A house? An apartment? A condo?"

"We're renting an apartment, but I've got to get something bigger for poor Charlie sooner rather than later. He needs a yard."

Rachel thought of Pepper and Corny who had the cows to herd and the farm to enjoy. Charlie would love their lives.

"What are you doing for money?" Amy asked him. "Where are you working?"

"I'm interning at Ingram and Harper for now."

Rachel looked at him blankly as did Amy.

"Financial planners. I love economics. I love watching the markets and analyzing what's happening. This comp class—which I've put off until the last possible moment—is one of three classes that stand between me and my degree. Then graduate school. Then financial planning for my own clients."

Rachel watched him as he talked. How fascinating that he found money as interesting as she found teaching. To her, money was for buying what you needed; nothing more, nothing less. To make a career of it seemed boring. People were what made life interesting, not numbers.

But he was far from boring.

He forked up the last piece of his pie. "I've managed to put off this comp class for years, but it's to the point that I won't graduate unless I take it."

"You're at the end and I'm at the beginning," Amy said.

"The end." He smiled. "Sounds great. What are you two doing for work?"

"I'm waitressing," Amy said. "I sort of like it, and it lets me pay my rent. What about you, Rachel?"

"I'm a teacher. Children. I love it."

"That's what I want to be some day!" Amy bounced in her chair.

Rachel felt all her dreams rise as she caught Amy's enthusiasm and found herself saying, "I want to be Dr. Dyson." She blinked in surprise and dismay but knew she'd just articulated her heart's desire. A college professor. She'd never been that specific before, and she'd certainly never told anyone, not even Aaron. Especially not Aaron. And she knew it could never be.

"Good for you," Rob said. "You'll have to get glasses for that professorial look."

"Red ones like hers." Amy grinned. "You'll look good in red."

Rachel, who'd never worn red in her life, suddenly wanted red glasses even though her vision was 20/20.

She smiled at the surge of pleasure their encouragement brought. She was so used to either being silent about her dreams and yearnings or being misunderstood.

"And if your eyes don't need them," Amy said, "you can get cool frames with plain glass."

For a moment she almost considered it.

She scraped the last of the peach crumb and ice cream from her plate and to her surprise regretted that it was time to go home. Maybe she needed to be more social after all, but it was hard when everything in her culture was built around either family or couples. She was not a couple anymore, and was not interested in finding a husband. She had too many secrets.

Just another sign of how different she was.

Rachel swallowed a self-pitying sigh as she and Amy told Rob goodbye, and he and his damaged SUV turned one way out of the parking lot as she and Amy turned another.

Amy talked the entire trip to Max's, asking question after question and sometimes waiting long enough for Rachel to answer. Rachel kept her answers as truthful as she could without mentioning her Amishness. That part of her life was private.

They turned off Route 322 onto the winding roads of Chester County at the very edge of Lancaster County. It always amazed Rachel how quickly a major highway was replaced by rolling farmland and a way of life at odds with the speed and frenetic pace of the Englisch.

Blinking red lights flashed on the road ahead.

"Slow down, Amy." Rachel's voice was urgent. "That's a buggy."

Amy slowed. "Cool. I wish I could see inside, but it's too dark."

They came up behind the buggy quickly and slowed to a crawl.

"What do I do now?" Amy asked. "There's a double yellow line and a hill I can't see over. I can't pass. Someone might be coming."

"Just wait till the top of the hill, and then pass. Forget the yellow line. Everyone does."

Rachel could feel Amy's impatience as all the horses under her hood were reduced to the one horsepower of the slow-moving buggy. What felt like a good clip in a buggy was agonizingly slow in a car. They finally crested the hill and with a burst of power, Amy passed the buggy.

"They are so dangerous! But so cool!" Amy grinned, her face illuminated by the dashboard's lights. "I've only ever seen pictures before. I need to come back in the daylight so I can really see."

Rachel looked over the dark countryside. "All the farms have their fields full of corn this time of year. And cows, since many of them are dairy farmers. Or sheep. Or goats. Or chickens. Or all the above."

"You are so lucky to live here."

"I am. And I love it. Turn left here. The brick rancher with the light post lit is where I'm going."

"You live right in the middle of Amish farms?"

"I do." If Amy only knew.

"Lucky you. Let's plan to get something to eat next class, okay?"

"Thanks, Amy. For everything."

"Thank you. I was scared to death I wouldn't have a friend."

"Me too."

"I'll wait till you get inside."

Max threw the door open as Rachel crossed the porch. They both waved as the little red car sped off.

"So tell me all," Max demanded as she shut the door.

Rachel laughed. "Let me change first."

In the bedroom she struggled with the unwieldy buttons on her blouse and relaxed when she slid the pins into her dress. Now she felt like herself. She pulled her hair back and secured it at her nape. She covered the bun with her kapp. Rachel Beiler was back.

"Max," she called. "What shall I do with the clothes?"

"Hang them in the closet."

Rachel slid open the louvered door and found hangers, even one with clips to hold the skirt. She studied the blouse and skirt, which would be waiting for her when she needed them for her next class.

She thought of people she'd read about in the paper and in books who led multiple lives. Some were spies living a secret life not even their wives knew about. She stopped for a moment as she considered the ethics of spying but put it off for another time. Too complex by far. Besides she wasn't a spy.

Other people with double lives had two families, each secret from the other. When she read their stories, she was fascinated at how they kept their lives separate—until something gave them away and everything blew up.

Well, she was living two lives. Amish widow/school teacher and Englisch college student. As she slid the closet door shut, she wondered how long she would be able to keep her two lives as neatly separated as her clothes. Or would it all blow up?

She shivered.

Chapter 6

Rachel walked into Max's living room. "I hope my going out with Amy didn't make problems for you."

"Not at all. It just saved me a trip back to the college. I've been sitting here dying to know everything that happened. Now tell me."

Rachel gave a quick recap, talking about Professor Dyson, Amy, and even Rob.

"It was better than I hoped, Max, though I think that's because of Dr. Dyson." Rachel could feel her cheeks stretched in a broad smile. "It's going to be wonderful. Challenging. I'm not quite certain how I'm going to write a piece about why I'm there without giving away that I'm Amish, but that'll be part of the fun."

Rachel rose and Max walked her to the front door. "I'm just so pleased your evening went well. I worried about you."

"Why?"

"I was afraid you'd be disappointed."

"Just the opposite! Thanks for all your encouragement and help."

Max held out a set of car keys.

"What's this?"

"Buddy's car. I want you to have it."

Rachel felt the blood drain from her face. "Max, I can't—"

Max waved her comment away before she finished. "I'll sell it to you for one dollar, cash." She wagged her finger. "I expect you to pay promptly."

She smiled and Rachel knew an excitement almost equaling going to class.

Max patted her hand. "We'll take care of the transfer when you pass your driver's test."

Rachel felt her eyes fill with tears as Max pressed the keys into her hand. "Don't your kids want their father's car?"

Max shook her head. "They each already have their own just as nice or nicer. I told them my plans, and they know what I'm doing. They approve."

Rachel's throat tightened with emotion. She hugged Max, who returned the embrace.

"I insist on paying you a fair price, Max. I got all that money from the insurance settlement when Aaron died, and I want to pay you. After all, you're a widow too, and I know you've still got terrible medical bills from Buddy's illness. I won't miss a few thousand and you can use it."

It still surprised Rachel every time she remembered she was financially well off. She'd never have pursued any kind of compensation or reparations. Things happened and Gott knew. She had been willing to accept that. It was Aaron's boss who had sought the money on her behalf.

"Aaron shouldn't have fallen from that roof," Mr. Nathan told her. "It was a faulty safety harness. Someone should be held accountable."

"If it had been willful, I'd agree," she told him. "But no one planned what happened."

"Please let me do this for you, Rachel. I feel so bad that a wonderful guy like your husband died on my watch."

"Don't feel responsible, Mr. Nathan. Gott knew. I must accept His will."

Mr. Nathan just looked at her, and she recognized what she'd just said as Amish-think. Didn't Englisch people acknowledge God's will?

"Okay, if you say it's God's will, maybe it is, but that doesn't mean you shouldn't be compensated for Aaron's lost wages. Perhaps you can see that as God's will too. Under better circumstances, Aaron would be supporting you for years to come. And I've been paying on this insurance for years. I want you to benefit from it. I need you to be cared for."

She could see that he did need this. Somehow he felt guilty, and helping her would help him. Mr. Nathan pursued a suit on her behalf and won her a hefty sum that she didn't know what to do with. It sat in the hands of a financial advisor he'd recommended, and every time she got a report, she had more.

Rachel slipped her backpack over her shoulder. "I'll look up the car's value and write you a check."

Max blinked against tears. "You're a good girl, Rachel."

Rachel swallowed. Maybe once upon a time, but not now.

Her conflicted feelings must have shown because Max looked concerned. "I hope things don't explode in your face."

"Mmmm." She handed the car keys back to Max. "I'll have to leave these here. I can't risk anyone finding them in my house or my purse."

Max nodded. "I'll leave them in the bowl by the garage door with my keys, just like Buddy kept them. There's a garage door opener clipped to the visor. I'll get a house key made so you can come and go as you need."

The women hugged good night, and Rachel walked slowly down the short stretch of road to her house. Pepper appeared and walked beside her, the soft click of her paws on the pavement somehow comforting. She thought about her two lives. If she could just keep them both, she'd be happy. Satisfied. No, more than satisfied. Fulfilled somehow. She'd have her people and she'd be learning. She knew she could never be Dr. Dyson, not really, but if she could gather knowledge...

She spread her arms wide to the warm night air, listening to the crickets and watching the stars shining overhead, pulsing balls of heat and energy throwing their light over millions of miles. The pictures taken in space fascinated her with the beauty and complexity they revealed. Surely Gott was amazing to create such variety and wonder, and it had all existed for century upon century without human eyes being aware until recently.

The words of one of her favorite hymns flowed through her mind. "*O Gott Vater, wir loben dich.*" O God the Father, we praise you.

With her heart happy, she crossed the street to her house. She climbed her front steps to the wide porch, Pepper padding beside her. She pulled a key from her pocket and unlocked the door. She hated having to lock her house away, but times had changed. She was a woman living alone.

"Thanks for the escort, Pep."

The dog turned, went down the steps, and disappeared into the night.

She walked into the large room that ran the width of the house, struck by the silence after her people-filled night. She shrugged the lonely feeling away. That's how it was when you lived by yourself. Quiet. Silent.

Her home was a wonderful two-story house, part stone, part clapboard though it was really vinyl, not boards. Aaron, his father, and his four brothers had built it as a wedding present for Rachel. Their three acres were a gift from Rachel's father, located at the far edge of the Miller farm.

A wood fireplace made of stones filled one side wall. Building it had taken the brothers hours, gathering the stones and fitting them together. It was Rachel's favorite feature of the house and she had placed comfortable furniture around it. She loved sitting in front of the fire on cold winter nights, thinking, wondering, and watching the flames leap and fall.

"Don't you sew or quilt on the long dark nights? Knit?" her sister Sally asked. Sally was a person who never sat still. Contemplating ideas and concepts with one's hands at rest was outside her experience or imagination.

"I don't sew and knit like you," Rachel always answered though she could do both. Mom would never have allowed her daughters to reach adulthood without those and other homemaking abilities. "You will have to keep me in scarves so my neck doesn't freeze."

And with a shake of her head at such incompetence, Sally did.

The stove in the kitchen was efficient and provided heat on those cold winter nights. The first floor bathroom was convenient. The basement had room for Aaron's workshop and shelves for her to store the vegetables and fruit she put up. These days the workshop was quiet and the shelves empty. Datt fixed anything that needed fixing and Mom kept her in preserves.

The second floor held two baths and five bedrooms, rooms she and Aaron had meant to fill with *kinder*.

"You and Aaron have your own bathroom?" Mom had been amazed when she first saw it beside their bedroom. "I heard the Englisch did this, but my daughter?"

"Aaron's two brothers work for a construction company, Mom. They're using the plans from a house they built at work."

Mom shook her head. "At least you don't have to de-electrify a house like if you bought a regular one."

"And we have a big open room in the front instead of a separate living room and dining room and an entry hall. We can take our turn hosting worship."

They had done so once near the end of the first year they were married. They'd been so excited when the closed wagon holding the meeting benches and hymnals was driven into the yard. Her brother Jonah, who was Aaron's best friend, had come to help them move their regular furniture to the storage shed out back and bring in the benches.

Rachel had cleaned and re-cleaned the kitchen, and all three of the bathrooms sparkled. No one used the one by Rachel and Aaron's bedroom, but the other upstairs and the one downstairs were very popular.

After the meeting and after the tables were erected for the meal, Aaron took great delight in showing the men his pride and joy, the latest thing in generators powered by a combination of solar power and battery. Rachel was glad the sun shone that day or maybe the power to make the wonderful bathrooms do their job might have run out. She thought briefly about having an outhouse dug behind the shed just in case they hosted on a cloudy day.

Then Aaron died and it no longer mattered.

Chapter 7

Rob walked around the common area behind the apartments with Charlie as the dog rushed from shrub to shrub as if he was afraid he'd miss some interesting scent. He tore off after a rabbit that disappeared under someone's shed and came rushing back with a great grin, happy for the exercise and for Rob's company.

"Just don't take off after a skunk like that, my man. Believe me when I tell you that you won't like it."

Charlie woofed his understanding and took off again, big feet covering an amazing amount of territory very quickly.

When Rob went to the shelter and looked at dogs, he hadn't expected to fall in love. But there was something about Charlie with his too big feet and expressive face that was just what he needed. Charlie was a companion who didn't intrude, company who was happy to let him alone for a good nap, and a warm body who demanded little in exchange for giving his whole heart.

For the past twelve years Rob hadn't been alone. In the Army he was surrounded by men and women, many of them great people he'd have given his life for. But now that he was home, he realized how much he was enjoying his solitude. Charlie kept him from being lonely in that solitude.

Not that Rob wanted to be alone forever. He imagined he'd get married someday, but he hoped he'd choose better than his parents had. He was going to pick someone uncomplicated, undemanding, and utterly honorable. A committed Christian.

Rachel flashed through his mind, her guileless face open and lovely. And that wonderful curly hair. He spent half of class studying it, thinking how he wanted to run his fingers through its silkiness to see if it felt as wonderful as it looked. She was the reason he said yes to Amy's invitation to get some coffee.

Before the world blew up with his father's arrest, the kid he'd been back then always assumed that someday in the far distant future he'd marry some nice rich girl. Of course he'd get his education first, get a job that paid lots of money like Dad's, and have some serious fun. Then, when he was old, like thirty, marriage.

These days he wondered where he'd ever find a woman, rich or poor, who'd willingly accept the wonky people he was related to. An unrepentant jailbird father. A narcissistic, demanding mother. A mommy-dependent, charming but useless brother. The Laniers were quite the brood. What he himself would be like if he hadn't met Chaplain Roussey and through him met Jesus he shuddered to think.

Pre-Dad's fall, life at the Lanier home had been unremarkable for moneyed families. Dad made money hand over fist in his investment business, and Mom happily spent it. Rob had a new car for his sixteenth birthday and money for whatever he wanted to do, wherever he wanted to go. His brother, Win, four years younger, smiled his way through life, charming everyone and letting life spin golden about him.

While Win drifted in happy times like their mother, Rob excelled like their father, and he did so academically and athletically. He was not only the football captain but the class valedictorian. He had been accepted at Williams College in Massachusetts, a feat he was justly proud of as it was one of the top small colleges in the country. Life was good and could only get better.

Then came the lightning bolt of the arrest. Thunderous accusations were followed by the stormy trial and the end of the world as he knew it. Their money disappeared overnight and with it their house and his car. Williams became an unrealized dream, way beyond the reach of a boy with no financial backing and a father whose crimes made the mainstream news and a Talking Point by Bill O'Reilly.

The worst part was the shame. He hadn't committed any crime. He hadn't built an elaborate Ponzi scheme that cost hundreds of clients their life savings. He hadn't siphoned off exorbitant fees and hidden them offshore. He hadn't stared down everyone without a word of apology or remorse.

But he'd been ashamed even if his father wasn't. He developed severe stomach pains and ended up on medication for ulcers. Guys he thought were his friends didn't know what to do with him now that he couldn't provide a weekend at the family shore house or pay for tickets to the latest rock star's concert. He didn't know what to do with himself any more than they did. The main reason he joined the Army was to get away, to go where no one knew or cared that he was Eugene Lanier's son.

And now he was back. It made no sense. All he knew was that he felt God wanted him here, and he was trying to be obedient even though the up close and personal with his family often cost him his equanimity.

"They're so much easier to deal with from a distance," he told the Lord. Here at home frustration was his daily companion.

His whole body twitched whenever he thought of his mother's positive reaction when he told her he planned to become a financial planner. "Like your father? Oh, good. Then we'll be able to get the house back. Or maybe a bigger one."

"Not like my father!" he wanted to shout at her but forced himself to speak respectfully. "I want to be honorable."

"Just so you're rich." And she laughed.

No wonder it had taken him more than ten years to admit he had his father's feel for money. During that time he'd day-traded his Army salary into a considerable nest egg and done the same for a few close buddies.

"You have the golden touch," one said.

"No!" He'd practically yelled it. He didn't want that ability. He didn't want to be his father.

His friend shrugged. "You can deny it all you want, but you're amazing with money and the markets and economics—all that stuff. God has gifted you."

It felt like a curse.

One day Chaplain Roussey sat him down. "Say there was a professional athlete who made a lot of money throwing games. Eventually he was caught and disgraced. He's got a son who has inherited his father's athletic gifts. You're saying the son should never play?"

Rob wanted to say, "No, never," but that was obviously the wrong answer. It wasn't the gifted kid's fault the gifted father threw games.

"I get what you're saying," he told the chaplain.

"So you're not going to tell God He made a mistake when you inherited your father's Midas touch?"

"Midas was given the gift that everything he touched turned to gold including his food and water and even his daughter whom he loved very much. The Midas touch is a gift that brings no good." Rob rolled his shoulders to relieve the tension. "I know whereof I speak."

"The *love* of money is the root of evil," the chaplain agreed. "But what if you don't love it? What if it doesn't control you, but you control it?"

"Is that even possible?"

"Are all money managers in jail?"

Bazinga! Even now, years later, Rob had to smile. He whistled to Charlie, who came running with great loping strides.

"You're a good man, Charlie Brown." Rob stroked the dog's ears. "Let's go in."

Tongue lolling happily, Charlie led the way into the apartment.

The red light on the answering machine was blinking. What did Mom want this time? He made himself push the button.

"Hey, Rob." The deep voice was a surprise. Win instead of Mom. "Guess what? I lost my job today. Can you believe it?"

Actually, Rob could.

"Just because I was late. So not fair. Anyway, can I borrow a couple hundred? I'll pay you back as soon as I get another job. Promise."

If Mom had trouble accepting that she was responsible for taking care of herself, Win was worse. Somehow he felt entitled. The world—and any employers unfortunate enough to hire him—owed him. He shouldn't be expected to be on time, and when he wasn't, he should be forgiven. After all, he was Win Lanier.

Trouble was, no one cared.

Rob collapsed in his lounge chair. Charlie lumbered over and sat at his feet, his great head resting on Rob's knee. Rob absently rubbed the dog's ears and thought over the day. The remembered screech of his car against the guardrail made his teeth ache. His mother's narcissistic griping and his brother's assumption that Rob was there to support him both annoyed and appalled him.

If it weren't for the few blessed minutes after class when he'd been able to laugh with Amy and soak up Rachel's beauty, the day would have been a total loss—no offense meant, Dr. Dyson.

He leaned his head back and heard Charlie collapse at his feet. When he realized he was falling asleep, he pushed himself to his feet.

"Come on, Charlie. Time for bed."

As he lay gazing at the ceiling, he became aware of Charlie staring at him from his spot beside the bed. Ah, why not? The dog was the only one in his family who was normal. Might as well reward him for that fact.

He patted the mattress, and Charlie jumped up, turned in circles, and with a heartfelt groan, settled, taking up most of the lower half of the bed.

With a smile, Rob let himself drift off, Rachel's face his last thought.

Chapter 8

*J*ohnny Miller walked into Corner Bob's and slid onto a stool at the bar. Just because Merle and Bennett had called it a night didn't mean he had to. No sir. He checked his watch. It wasn't even midnight yet. Last call wasn't for a couple of hours.

"Hey, Harry." He nodded at the morose man slumped on his regular stool at the bar. "Have a good day?"

Harry gave his usual grunt and kept his concentration focused on his beer.

Whatever made Harry so miserable, the man wasn't sharing. Johnny shook his head and raised a finger. "Beer, please."

From his place behind the bar the Bob of Corner Bob's looked at Johnny with sympathy but no beer.

Johnny felt his stomach cramp. That look meant only one thing. He'd seen it before and laughed at the poor guy it was directed at.

"Beer," he said again, but this time it was more a plea.

Bob shook his head. "I don't recommend it until you talk to Mr. Sherman."

All the swear words Johnny'd learned in his years since leaving the farm raced through his mind but he didn't say any aloud. He didn't want his fear to show. "Why would I want to talk with Mr. Sherman?"

"I have no idea." Bob pulled a glass from the soapy water of his little sink behind the bar and began drying it with a Joseph's coat striped towel that had seen better days. "But he's looking for you."

"What if I don't want to see him?"

Bob laughed. "Like that matters."

Johnny hoped he wouldn't hyperventilate. "Come on, Bob. A beer."

"After your talk. I don't want you puking in my establishment like the last guy Mr. Sherman talked to."

Johnny closed his eyes as if he could close out Corner Bob's and everything—everyone—in it. "Is he at his table?" It was barely a whisper.

Bob nodded toward the back of the dark room. "Sitting like an itsy bitsy spider waiting to pounce, only he's blubby tubby, not itsy bitsy. And here comes Mick to escort you back."

Johnny spun slowly to see Mick Morrison, big, powerful, and as handsome as a GQ model, coming toward him. Maybe it was the combination of too many muscles and too hot a temper, but Mick was scary nuts. He made Mr. Sherman—who scared any sane man—look like your favorite uncle.

"Hello, Johnny." Mick clamped a heavy hand on Johnny's shoulder and squeezed. Johnny paled at the pain. "Mr. Sherman wants to say hello."

"Soon as I get my beer." Though if Bob caved and gave him one, his hand would probably be shaking too much to hold it.

Mick gripped the muscle beside Johnny's neck and squeezed harder. He smiled as Johnny flinched at the pain. Slowly he released the pressure so Johnny could stand and follow.

Tail between his legs, Johnny did just that.

Jules Sherman, a jowly chubby man in his fifties, sat at a table in the room's darkest corner, his back to the wall as if he expected bad guys with tommy guns to come in and strafe the place. Not that the wall would help if that happened.

As Johnny trailed Mick past the side room with its pool tables and players, he tried to walk confidently, but his fear made him stumble. He had to force himself to look Mr. Sherman in the eye. He made believe Thomas, Mr. Sherman's other bodyguard/goon, didn't exist.

Thomas with his curly hair and crooked nose never seemed to do anything but stand at parade rest behind Mr. Sherman anyway.

"Well, Johnny." Mr. Sherman smiled, the oh-so-polite business professional meeting with a favored client. "How are you this evening?"

Johnny swallowed bile. Why had he ever let himself get involved with this man? Bennett and Merle had warned him.

"Don't do it, Johnny," Bennett had said.

"You'd be stupid." Merle was always blunt. "The man's slime."

"Don't worry," he told them with confidence. "It's a sure thing. I'll pay him back the next day."

He should have listened to his friends, not some guy who didn't know what he was talking about.

When he lost his money, Bennett shook his head. "Too good to be true is always too good to be true, Johnny."

"We warned you." Merle slapped him on the back. "Gotta tell you, I got no money to help you out with." Merle had then turned to Bob that night a week ago. "Give Johnny a beer. He needs it."

He needed one now. "Hello, Mr. Sherman. I'm fine, thanks."

"Johnny, I think we need to talk." He didn't offer Johnny the chair that faced him. That was for those who came to ask for something or for those who came to repay his favors, not for those who owed him. Not for Johnny.

"Five thousand, Johnny." Again the friendly smile. "I lent you five thousand in good faith. You had a sure thing, you said. Double your money, you said. You promised."

Johnny smelled his own flop sweat. "I'll get it. I will." Though how and when were questions Johnny couldn't answer.

"Just so you know, the figure is $6000 starting tomorrow. Next week it'll be $7000. A thousand a week for every week you don't keep your agreement with me." He brought his hand down sharply on the table with a crack that made everyone in the bar except Mick and Thomas jump. Johnny turned faint. "Got it?"

Johnny nodded, throat too dry to speak.

"Got it?" Mr. Sherman repeated.

"Got it," Johnny managed after he swiped his tongue around the inside of his mouth to make some saliva. He turned away.

"Oh, Johnny." Mr. Sherman called as in afterthought. "After next week, it's no more Mr. Nice Guy. After next week, I get serious. Right, Mick?"

Mick's crazy nuts smile made Johnny wonder which countries had no extradition agreements with the U.S. It was a useless question even if he knew the answer. He didn't have the money to go there any more than he had the money to pay back Mr. Sherman.

He managed to make it to his bar stool without his legs giving out or his bladder emptying. Bob shook his head sadly as he shoved a beer into Johnny's hands.

By the time he was on his third, Johnny felt somewhat in control. A group of about ten people had wandered in and the bar was now full of conversation and laughter. Harry still sat on his stool, lost in his private despair. In the corner opposite Mr. Sherman a darts tournament was winding down.

Johnny glanced over his shoulder at Mr. Sherman. He continued busy with others, some sitting in the chair, some standing as Johnny had.

"Where'd he come from?" Johnny asked Bob under cover of the noise. "How'd he get the power?"

Bob shook his head. "Don't know." He raised a finger in the wait-a-minute sign and moved down the bar to fill another order. Johnny sipped and waited.

When he returned, Bob rubbed at a water ring on the bar with the towel he dried his glasses with. "He just showed up one night about five years ago and let me know that table was his."

"Just like that?"

Bob didn't even bother to take offense at the implied call of cowardice. He just rolled his shoulders and gave a slight shudder. "There was more."

Johnny nodded wisely. "With guys like him there's always more."

"Always more," Harry muttered, making both Johnny and Bob jump in surprise. "Always more." He slid off his stool and was gone.

Johnny watched him stumble out the door. "I never heard him speak before."

"Mr. Sherman's got his claws in him somehow. Poor guy."

Last month Johnny would have thought Harry an idiot to have anything to do with Mr. Sherman. Now he was one of the idiots, just like Harry and Bob. He studied Bob. "What's he got on you?"

Bob rubbed harder at the long dried water mark. "If I interfered with anything he did or if I went to the cops, he said, that cute little daughter of mine would be in trouble."

"He threatened Trixie?" Johnny couldn't believe it. "Aren't kids off limits?"

"Not with him. He showed me pictures of her taken on the school playground, at the store with the wife, even playing on the swings in our backyard. It got the desired result."

Johnny looked over his shoulder at Mr. Sherman again. What kind of a man went after a kid? His eyes met Mick's, and the crazy man smiled like the crocodile eyeing his helpless victim.

Bob pulled a dry towel from a cabinet. "I haven't said a word to anyone about anything, and I never will."

Johnny nodded slowly. He didn't have cute daughters to worry about, but he had sisters.

Chapter 9

As Rachel walked slowly up the farm lane to Mom and Datt's house Sunday afternoon, Pepper wandered over to join her. "Hey, girl, how are you?" Rachel scratched the dog's head.

Pepper made no answer except to lean against her for a moment before she wandered off.

The produce stand by the road was shuttered for today, the No Sunday Sales sign prominently displayed. Tomorrow Datt would have the last of the freshly pulled corn. The end of sweet corn was the sign that the beginning of her new year at the one-room school down the road was almost here.

But it wasn't her students or her lesson plans that filled her mind. It was the class in which she was a student, and the people there.

Dr. Dyson spoke with such precision as she discussed writing. Sometimes all Rachel wanted to do was write, but she had so many things she wanted to say, so many stories she wanted to tell that she was overwhelmed. Professors had to publish, didn't they? It would be fascinating to see what Dr. Dyson wrote. She'd go on Amazon and look the professor up.

She never went to Max's on Sunday to use the computer. Sunday was the Lord's Day. It was bad enough that she was disobeying on other days. She refused to do so on the Sabbath. It was to be kept holy.

Tomorrow night she had class, so it would be Tuesday evening before she could look up Dr. Dyson online. She would buy at least one book the woman wrote. She knew she wouldn't be able to resist.

The one good thing that had come from the settlement Mr. Nathan had gotten her was the freedom to buy as many books as she wanted. Her mailbox was always filled with brown boxes from Amazon.com or cbd.com.

She scratched her right palm. It itched every time she thought of Amazon and a Kindle. The idea of having scores of books in her hand at one time fascinated her. If only it didn't need to be plugged in.

Think about something else, she ordered herself.

Amy popped into her mind and Rachel smiled. That woman had never met a question she didn't ask or an answer she didn't find interesting. But in spite of all her enthusiasm for everyone, she talked very little about herself and when she did, there was an edge to her comments.

"I'm never going back."

Her memories must be very bad, but Rachel wasn't sure what that meant.

Did she want to find out?

She suspected that if she pushed, Amy would tell all. She couldn't resist. But did Rachel want to get involved in Amy's life like that? After all, she had her own secrets to keep. And Amy was Englisch, another complication in Rachel's already complicated life. And it wasn't like she could fix the problems Amy was dealing with.

When she'd pictured herself going to college, Rachel always pictured sitting in class learning new things. The people in the class with her were vague shadow people except for their contributions to stimulating classroom discussions. Having peach pie with them had never crossed her mind. Being driven about in a Smart car by a young woman who finally showed Rob her driver's license to convince him of her age was more than Rachel's exceedingly fertile imagination could have conceived. Getting to know that woman, really know her, was a world fraught with both exciting possibilities and unspeakable dangers.

And there was Rob. She smiled as she approached the farmhouse.

Anyone watching would think she was glad to be coming home. And she was. Of course she was. She pushed Rob away.

She studied the white clapboard house with the black trim. She'd had a wonderful childhood here, loved by Mom and Datt. Her parents were not just Amish by culture but by belief. Their family and their faith were the centers of their lives. Here she'd been taught to work hard and to love well.

Still she was glad she didn't live here now. Her marriage might have been short and certainly Aaron had died too young, but she'd liked the freedom being married had given her. She and Aaron had set their own schedule, one dictated by his work with the roofing company, not by the rhythms of farming. Unless there was a bad storm and roofs were damaged, he worked regular hours, and she liked knowing when dinner should be ready.

Over the one summer they were married, they grew their own garden, and Rachel, who did not enjoy homemaking, much to Mom's distress, put up the vegetables and fruit. She had actually enjoyed the task with Mom and Sally working with her. But the truth was she hadn't canned a single fruit or vegetable since. Nor did she miss the chore.

Aaron had enjoyed the garden and its care, but he was adamant that he didn't want to be a farmer. "Too hard. Dawn to dusk. I like having free time to relax. I like having time to spend with you."

Perhaps it was the fact that they were both untraditional Amish that drew them to each other. She with her dislike of homemaking was much more out of step than Aaron with his disinterest in farming. Many of their male friends didn't farm either. Lack of land in the area was one reason. The dependability of working regular hours for a known salary was another.

When Aaron was killed, Datt wanted her to move back to the family home.

"It will be too lonely to live by yourself," he said.

And it was lonely. But in another contrary quirk, she found she enjoyed solitude. Living alone suited her. And Mom and Datt were only around the bend in the road. Jonah and his family lived a half mile in the other direction. Both Jonah and Miriam and her parents had her for dinner at least once a week. She was often invited to the homes of her students too.

When she was first approached by the school board about teaching at the local school, Rachel was surprised and overjoyed. They had had a seventeen-year-old teacher the previous year, a very nice girl who didn't like teaching and wasn't interested in finding ways to make the children learn. Rachel was older, twenty-two, almost twenty-three when she was asked. She was so thankful for something to do with the long hours of the day that she cried herself to sleep that first night.

She might not be able to make a dinner that made people's mouths water like Mom and Sally, even Ruthie, but she could teach.

As she walked past Mom's garden with its border of pink petunias to keep the rabbits out, she saw Mom sitting on the front porch reading another of the Amish novels she loved to criticize.

When she saw Rachel, Mom smiled and stuck her bookmark, a lovely strip of needlework Aunt Sarah had made for her last birthday, between her pages. "How nice you came to visit," she greeted Rachel. "I was hoping you would."

Rachel took the rocker beside her mother. "I'm surprised you don't have company."

"We were at Sarah and David's for the noon meal. Datt wanted to come home to read the paper. There is so little time with harvest on us."

"The corn has been good."

Mom stood. "Very. Would you like some lemonade?"

"I'd love some if you'll share it with me." Rachel followed her mother into the house. Datt sat in his favorite chair reading *Die Botschaft*. Rachel always loved the gossipy news in the paper, even when she was reading about people she'd never met and would never meet. The masthead read, A Weekly Newspaper Serving Old Order

Amish Communities Everywhere. She'd thought all newspapers were as folksy and personal until she'd started reading the *New York Times* and the *Philadelphia Inquirer* online.

Datt looked up. "Did you know Anna Esh was making cheese and ice cream to sell from her house?"

"I think I heard," Mom said as she opened the propane refrigerator. "Say hello to Rachel."

"Hello, Rachel. Why didn't I know? And Old Abe Mast had a stroke."

"I didn't know that." Mom paused with the lemonade pitcher in her hand. "Does it say how he is?"

"He's staying with his daughter and her husband and writes what he needs on a piece of paper."

"Is this Old Abe who always had an opinion?" Rachel asked. "Or Old Abe who had the farm on Cambridge Road?"

Datt shook his head. "Opinion Abe. God's will can sometimes be very hard."

Rachel watched her mother pour three glasses. She made her lemonade these days with a powdered mix but always made sure real lemon slices floated for authenticity.

Rachel carried a glass to her father and took a sip from her own. "Where are Levi and David?" The house was quiet without her younger brothers rushing around.

"The Weavers are having the youth for volleyball and a sing," Datt answered. "Are there any cookies to go with the lemonade, Ida?"

Mom got down an earthen crock and lifted its lid. She arranged molasses cookies on a plate Rachel brought her. "Give these to your father and help yourself."

Datt took a bite. "Good, wife, but I miss Sally's molasses cookies. She has the touch."

"She does," Mom agreed. "But now Eben gets to eat them."

"I noticed last time we visited he didn't share. He is going to get fat with her cooking."

Rachel grinned. "Maybe Jake will share when he and Ruthie get married."

"Sure he will," Datt said. "She isn't as good a cook."

"Now stop that, Ammon. She's a fine cook."

Datt looked at Rachel and his eyes twinkled. "Especially compared to our Rachel."

"Ammon!" Mom made believe she was appalled at his comment.

Rachel took one of his cookies. "For being mean on the Sabbath."

Datt winked at her and rattled his newspaper back into place. "Did you know that Joe Borntreger down Tennessee way is eighty-three?"

"No, I didn't," Mom said. "I don't believe I know him."

Mom and Rachel went back to the porch. "I have to leave the room when Datt reads the paper," Mom said. "Otherwise he tells me all the things he reads. I want to read them myself, not hear them secondhand."

Rachel smiled. Most of the time Datt didn't say much, but when he read, he seemed to feel obliged to repeat all he was reading. It was a family joke how they all fled when he picked up *Die Botschaft*.

As she and Mom sipped their lemonade in companionable silence, Rachel wondered what Mom would think if she knew what Rachel had done Friday evening. Would she swallow and make believe she didn't know as some parents did when they learned of their children's activities? Or would she feel bound to tell the bishop?

If he found out, he'd be forced to take action against her. The thought made her stomach cramp.

She loved her People with all her heart. She was in danger of losing them and all she held dear and for what? Learning stuff? Stuff she may or may not ever use?

But the thought of not learning new things, of not stretching her mental muscles made her insides shrivel.

Mom looked her way. "So what have you been up to, Rachel?"

Rachel gave a slight smile to cover the constriction in her throat and took a drink of the sweet-tart lemonade. "Yesterday a car from New York stopped at the produce stand. 'Are you Amish?' the lady kept asking, making the A in Amish have a long sound like in apron." Rachel laughed. "It was so strange!"

"Tourists," Mom said, as close to scornful as she ever got. "I don't mind the Englisch like Maxine because they're respectful. But tourists like that one? I'm glad you run the produce stand, not me."

"It's fun, and I have to do something while school's not in session."

Mom grinned. "You will have Little Jonah in September."

She smiled at the thought of her nephew. "I know. He'll keep me busy all by himself."

"Miriam has been teaching him some English so he'll be ready for school."

"That's *gut*. I feel sad for the little ones who come and have never even heard English before."

"Jonah takes Little Jonah to the nursery sometimes, so he at least hears it spoken even if they don't speak it at home." Mom smiled.

They rocked in companionable silence for a few minutes.

"How is Max doing?" Mom asked. "It's been hard on her since Buddy died."

"She misses him a lot. And her kids are busy with their own lives. They're good to her, but she has a lot of time alone."

"You are good to her too."

Rachel brushed away the compliment. "We're good for each other. We understand each other."

"I think she should get a job," Mom said.

"Mom!" Rachel tried not to laugh. The ultimate homebody wanting someone to work?

"It would give her purpose. I see how your job gives you purpose. You have to have purpose in life."

Rachel looked at her mother, plump, work-worn, and content. "And yours is caring for all of us."

"Of course."

Of course. It was a given that women took care of their families. But when you didn't have a family or your family was busy?

Mom smiled at Rachel. "I think you had an extra purpose this past year helping her get over Buddy."

The comment was so far from the truth it was like a punch to Rachel's heart. While she was glad to spend time with Max, she was usually in the bedroom at the computer. Her purpose in going to Max's was selfish and far from the godly gesture Mom was imagining.

Rachel stared at the barn and the horses standing nose to tail in the field beyond, flicking flies away for each other. "She isn't finding getting over Buddy to be very easy."

"Well, they were very close, and she's only had one year. You on the other hand have had three."

Uh-oh. Here it came.

Mom gave her version of a stern look, something she had never mastered because of her positive outlook on life. "Now, tell me why you wouldn't talk with Jem Weaver last Sunday. He was just trying to be nice."

"Jem Weaver? Mom, he's old!"

Mom sniffed. "He's two years younger than I am. I know from school days. That is not old."

Rachel laughed. "Not to you maybe, but to me it's old. He just wants someone to take care of his house."

"Of course he does."

"I don't do houses well, Mom; you know that. And I want to care for a husband, Mom, not a house. And I want him to care for me. I want someone to look at me like Jonah looks at Miriam."

"You had Aaron." As if she couldn't expect another man to love her.

"And he was a wonderful man. Why should I settle for less?"

"Jem is not less."

Rachel didn't respond, but her silence made her opinion clear.

"I worry about you," Mom said. "I don't want you to spend your life lonely and alone."

"For now I'm fine, Mom. I'm alone, yes, but I'm fine that way."

"You need babies."

Rachel's heart caught. She did. But not enough to marry Jem Weaver. "You just want more grandchildren."

"*Ja*, I do. And I want you to have children while you're still young. Raising Abner at this age is a challenge. He was upset because he couldn't go with Levi and David to the volleyball game. Crying babies never used to upset me."

Rachel looked at her mother. She had to be fifty-two. That was old to have a four-year-old underfoot, even one as adorable as Abner.

Rachel laid her hand over her mother's on the arm of the rocker. "When I find a man I love and who loves me back, then I will make you happy."

The face of Rob Lanier flashed across her mind. She blinked him away as totally inappropriate. An Englisch man would not make Mom happy.

Chapter 10

When she heard the knock on her front door late Monday afternoon, Rachel looked up from the peanut butter sandwich she was eating.

"Rachel." Her oldest brother pushed open the door and peered into the room. "You have a moment?"

"Jonah! Come in. Come in." She rose and smiled. She rarely saw him these days. Between his work, his family, and his duties as deacon, he was a very busy man. "Come in. Have a seat. Let me get you something to drink."

"Something cold would be wonderful." He hung his straw hat on the peg by the door and slid into the second chair at the kitchen table.

Rachel glanced at her battery operated kitchen clock that looked like a teapot. Having Jonah visit was wonderful, but Monday evening at 5:15? She soon had to be at Max's to change clothes. She took the glass of cold sweet tea to him and sat, feeling guilty for hoping he wouldn't stay long.

"That's your dinner?" He pointed to the sandwich.

"I didn't want to cook. And look. I'm having an apple too."

"Like that's supposed to make me think you're eating well? I don't know about you, Rachel." His smile took away any sting to his words.

Jonah was such a fine man, and she was blessed to have him as her brother, but what would he think if he knew she hoped to eat at the Star later this evening?

It was only last spring when Red Jake died that Jonah had become a deacon. She had been surprised when his name was called as one who had at least three nominations from the men and women of their Gmay. She had whispered another name to the leaders as she passed by the room where they were assembled. She hadn't even thought of her brother.

Her surprise wasn't because of his character but his age. She knew every male who joined the congregation understood that he might be chosen as bishop or preacher or deacon. Refusing the responsibility wasn't an option. It was a great responsibility to stand as those who oversaw the obedience and spiritual lives of the group. Often those nominated were older. Datt had been nominated several times, but the lot had never fallen to him. She suspected he was relieved, though he'd never say so.

She'd watched Jonah walk forward with the six other men who had at least three nominations. It was a solemn moment because the life of one of the seven men would never be the same. She glanced at Miriam sitting down the bench from her. Her head was bowed in prayer as she sought God's leading in the man about to be chosen. How did she feel about the possibility that for the rest of his life, the health of the Gmay might be her husband's responsibility?

The tension in the room grew as the seven took seats at the front. Seven books lay on the table, one for each man, but only one had the slip of paper in it that read, "The lot is cast into the lap; but the whole disposing thereof is of the Lord." That man would be the new deacon.

One by one the seven stood and took a book from the table. Rachel held her breath as the bishop moved from man to man, opening the book, looking for that slip of paper. Jonah was the fourth man. When the bishop opened his book and found the paper with the Bible verse, he asked Jonah to stand.

"The lot has fallen on Jonah Miller," he said solemnly. He laid his hand on Jonah's shoulder and ordained him then and there to his new position, one for which he had no training beyond being part of the Gmay all his life.

Now she smiled at Jonah. "What are you doing here when you should be home awaiting dinner? Or should you be at the nursery still?"

"I have stopped to talk with you for a few minutes."

With her or at her? The thought jumped unbidden, and she tried to send it away. She forced herself to smile pleasantly. "How are Miriam and the children?"

"Miriam is doing well." He got that look of one besotted, the look she had noticed before, the look she wanted from whoever she married if she married again. "We will have another child in March."

"Oh, Jonah, how wonderful!"

"We think so. Don't mention it to Mom. We haven't told her and Datt yet. Miriam just told me this morning."

"Number four." Rachel thought of the empty bedrooms upstairs, and she swallowed around the yearning squeezing her heart.

"Little Jonah is so excited about going to school," he continued. "Hannah and James can't wait their turns. They want their own red and white lunchboxes just like Little Jonah has." He smiled as he thought of his children. "He thinks having Aunt Rachel for a teacher is a wonderful thing."

"It'll be fun to have him in school. He's so sweet. Quick and smart. But then you know that."

"Smarter than me," Jonah agreed. "Just like you are."

It wasn't a compliment like the Englisch might make. It was merely a statement. A true statement. Rachel didn't respond.

"But I'm not a *dumkopf*," he said, his voice a bit sharp.

Rachel blinked. "Of course you're not. You did well in school, and you were smart enough to pick Miriam. You've got your own business." She felt a sudden concern. "It's going well, isn't it?"

"It's going well, but that's not why I'm here. I'm here to talk with you."

Rachel's stomach knotted. "Is something wrong with Mom and Datt that I don't know about?"

"Nothing is wrong that I know of."

She looked at him, hoping her guilt didn't glow like a firefly at dusk. "Then what concerns you, Jonah?"

His expression turned somber. He leaned forward, his arms resting on his knees, his face serious. He carried an authority that increased her nervousness.

"Do you think we don't notice, Rachel?"

Rachel fought the panic rising and clasped her hands to keep them from shaking. "Notice what?" She held her breath.

"All the time you spend at Max's house."

Rachel blinked. This was about the time she spent with Max? That was all?

"I like Max, Jonah. She's been good company for me, another single woman I can talk with."

"I know." He fingered his beard, a habit when he was uncomfortable. "I like Max too. I always have. And I liked Buddy. He was a fine man for an Englischer."

"She misses him so much, like I missed Aaron. She and I are two widows who understand each other's feelings and lives."

Jonah nodded. "I know but—"

Rachel interrupted, something she rarely did. "In case you haven't noticed, everyone else my age is married and has a busy life taking care of their husbands, children, and homes. Talking about giving birth and the best way to get out stains is not interesting to me, Jonah. Max talks about other things, things that interest me and make me think. We have good conversations about things that concern us as women alone."

He studied her. "But is talk what you really do?"

Rachel frowned. "What do you mean?"

He squared his shoulders. "I'm not here as a deacon, Rachel. I'm here as your brother. I have to know. What do you do at Max's house?"

She couldn't lie, but she couldn't tell him about the computer and expect him to understand. "What do you think I do?" She held her breath.

He pressed his lips together as if he couldn't bear to say whatever was coming. "You watch television."

"Watch television?" That was it?

"You watch television and fill your mind with the world."

"No, Jonah."

"People are talking, Rachel."

She didn't doubt it. They always talked about her because she was different. She didn't follow the expected pattern. She thought. She asked questions. She didn't like housekeeping when everyone knew women were to be keepers at home. She still wondered why they trusted her with teaching their children.

With great relief she looked at her brother. "Jonah, I can tell you in all honesty that I have not been watching TV at Max's house."

He studied her, his brows drawn together in a fierce frown, but his eyes brimmed with concern. "You worry me, Rachel."

She felt her heart crack. Here was Jonah, giving up time with Miriam and the kids to come talk with her. To warn her. He and the rest of the family were why she didn't just get up and go. Who would she love if they weren't in her life?

"You mustn't worry about me, Jonah. I'm fine."

She wasn't. She was torn in two, but he didn't need to know that. If he sensed where she was going, what she was doing, he'd be forced by his position as deacon to confront her, maybe start proceedings against her.

"Ask yourself what would Gott want from you," Jonah said. "Obey Him, Rachel. Don't let the world corrupt you, even through a woman as nice as Max. The price is too great."

With that he stood, grabbed his hat, and left. Just before he closed the door, he looked back at her. "Take care, Rachel."

What he meant was be careful. There were lines not to be crossed, and she and her actions were under scrutiny. She heard the jingle of the horse's bridle and the creak of the buggy as he drove away.

The price is too great. Jonah's words cut at her heart.

She bent forward, laying her head on her knees. The price was too great no matter which way she went.

Chapter 11

Max sat in the passenger seat per Pennsylvania law while Rachel drove what would soon be her car to class.

"When you go to school on Friday," Max said with a smile, "you'll be a licensed driver able to drive your very own car."

"I hope so."

"Uh-uh," Max was adamant. "No negativity. You're going to do fine. You remembered to use your turn signal at every turn this evening."

Rachel perked up a bit. "I did, didn't I? As long as I remember the headlights if it's raining during the test."

"The weather's supposed to be great on Wednesday, but if it isn't, I'm sure you won't forget."

Rachel glanced at Max. "At least you won't have to go everywhere with me anymore."

"I have not minded in the least." She moved her shoulders, trying to make herself more comfortable. The seatbelt in this car always rubbed her neck. "It's not nearly as nerve-racking riding with you as it was with Ryan and Ashley. I thought we'd never survive until they got their licenses. Then I worried they'd never survive to reach their majority. So you're a delight, Rachel. A delight. Besides what else would I be doing?"

Max heard her own sadness, lostness in that last question and flinched.

Rachel glanced over at her. Apparently she decided to take what was meant to be a rhetorical question seriously. "Maybe you should take a class, Max. We could find something we'd both enjoy, and we could drive in together next semester."

Max made a face. "I don't think so. I have no desire to put myself back under some demanding professor." The very thought made her feel old and tired. "I've forgotten how to study."

"You could—"

"I could but I don't want to." She hoped Rachel heard her end-of-discussion tone.

Evidently not.

"Maybe a night-school class where you learn a new craft or skill. You could try quilting. Or knitting."

"Are you serious?" If she didn't know better, she'd think Rachel was trying to convert her to Amish, not that they welcomed converts. "I'm no good with a needle of any kind."

Rachel laughed, which made Max feel a little less lectured. "Me either. How about learning how to fix a motor?"

Now Max laughed. "That's why there are mechanics."

"Cooking?"

"No." Her heart clutched as she thought of the constant reminder that cooking for one was.

"Computers?"

"Double no. I feel about them the way I feel about cars. I want them to work but I have no desire to learn how or why."

"Or you could get a job."

Max blinked. That was unexpected, the shiv to the heart when you were looking for a handshake you could ignore. She studied Rachel. "What's brought on the sudden need to give me advice?"

"Well." Rachel hesitated as if she feared she'd pushed too far. "We all need a purpose. That's what my mom says. With the kids and Buddy gone, I guess I'm worried you've lost your purpose."

Max felt only slightly miffed, not really angry, which surprised her. Usually when people tried to tell her what to do, she got mad.

The only times she'd ever gotten angry at Buddy were the times he pushed too hard.

She looked at Rachel, face intent as she concentrated on her driving. She was only saying these things because she cared. Max knew that. And she was only saying things Max had already been wrestling with.

"Maybe you're my purpose," Max said. "Maybe I get a lot of satisfaction from helping you." Which was very true.

Rachel nodded. "But you won't be helping me forever."

True. She was pretty much launched and soon wouldn't need Max anymore. Another death of a sort. Max took a deep breath and tried to keep her voice steady. "I'll figure it out."

"I know."

The uncertainty in Rachel's voice made Max wonder what she saw. A poor, flailing, drowning woman trying to reach a lifesaving ring to pull her from this sea of pain? How pathetic. She was a strong woman. Or she had been. How strange to realize her independence had been dependent on Buddy's strong arms to catch her if she fell.

They pulled up in front of the classroom building. Rachel climbed out and grabbed her backpack. At the last moment she leaned back in the car. "I love you, Max."

Max nodded as tears stung her eyes. "I know. I love you too."

"And you don't have to wait to see if I'll be okay like you did Friday." Rachel smiled and a cluster of her curls fell forward over her shoulder. She was so beautiful!

Max sat in the passenger seat long after Rachel disappeared into the building, staring out the windshield. She wasn't waiting to see if Rachel came running out. She was waiting to see if she could identify a purpose, any purpose, in her life. Rachel's questions had upset her, not in a bad way like hurting her feelings. They'd upset her because she had no answers to them. She suspected she could wait here all night and still not know what her purpose was these days.

For years people always said Buddy and Max or Max and Buddy.

Who was she now that she was only Max? She'd been trying to figure it out for a year now, and she still didn't know the answer.

All she knew was that Rachel's mother was right. A person needed a purpose and she'd lost hers.

Last Sunday in church Mrs. Nelson, an elderly woman whose husband of almost sixty years trailed her everywhere, had approached from Max's blind side. She appeared like a genie in the church aisle, her orange jacket clashing with the maroon carpeting and pew cushions.

"How are you doing, Max dear?" She peered at Max from rheumy eyes full of curiosity as opposed to concern.

"Okay, I guess." She forced a smile. "It depends on the day."

Mrs. Nelson patted her hand. "You just keep on keeping on. After all, all things work together for good, you know." Then she and Mr. Nelson hobbled off to cheer up some other poor victim.

Recalling the incident, Max shook her head. Surely the old lady didn't mean it was good that Buddy was gone, even if that's the way it sounded.

Oh, Lord, it's so not good!

All year Max had told the Lord exactly how she felt. He was God. He could take it. Besides while she was mad at Him on one hand, she also knew she wasn't the only woman whose husband had died prematurely. It wasn't like God singled her out and said, "Max, I have chosen you to go through the pain and agony of loss." Well, He had, but not only her.

And would it have been any easier if Buddy died when he was Mr. Nelson's age, and she had to face his loss in the middle of the many other losses that came with old age? At least she had her health, her mind, her home, her, well, her everything but Buddy. And a purpose.

With a great sigh she climbed out of the passenger seat, walked around to the other side of the car, and climbed behind the wheel. Time to go get her dinner. She planned to try the diner Rachel had told her about.

A flutter of panic chilled her. Had she remembered her Kindle? She checked her purse and felt a great flood of relief wash away the alarm. She had it. Somehow eating out alone was easier when she had something to read. She could fill her mind with a story rather than regret or discomfort at dining by herself in a public place.

Now if she could only figure out a purpose.

Chapter 12

The first thing Rachel saw when she walked in the classroom was Amy saving a seat for her, the same one as last week.

"You know," Amy began before Rachel even sat, "I forgot to get your phone number last week. We could have done something over the weekend if I knew how to get ahold of you. I looked in the phone book, but there are lots of Beilers. And Bylers. I thought about calling them one by one, but then I decided that was pathetic. I could survive one weekend without my BFF. But I need your number, like, right now."

Rachel blinked and got out her phone. Her number was probably in there somewhere, but she didn't know where. It wasn't as if she planned to call herself, and the people she knew wouldn't be calling her either.

She stared at the phone with all its little apps staring back. It felt alien in her hand. She knew lots of her People used cell phones for business, but she didn't. It wasn't like she had to call her students.

"I know," Amy said. "Who knows their own number, right? Here, I'll figure it out. I'm good that way."

Rachel felt great relief when Amy took her phone. She pushed a few buttons and then hit some numbers on her own phone. Then she pushed some numbers on Rachel's phone.

"I just entered my number for you."

She pushed some more buttons on Rachel's phone and held it up facing herself. She pushed again, and a flash went off. More fiddling and she handed it back.

"My picture's by my number. Now when I call, you'll see my picture pop up and know it's me."

Her phone could show pictures of the person who called? It was a sad thing when your phone was smarter than you were.

"You only have one other person's name in there." There was genuine concern on Amy's voice.

Obviously having only one name was suspect. "New," she managed.

"Ah." Amy seemed satisfied. She looked past Rachel's shoulder. "Hey, Rob."

He was every bit as tall and handsome as Rachel remembered. And Englisch in his jeans and T-shirt with a logo over the heart. When he took the empty seat next to Rachel, she was able to read Wounded Warriors.

As he pulled his tablet from its case, Amy leaned to Rachel and pointed at the phone. "Get his number," she whispered. "He likes you. I know it."

But he liked Warriors, and unless they were some team mascot, she didn't. She was Amish. She believed in non-violence. Warriors were the opposite.

Dr. Dyson called out, "Good evening, people. Hope you had a good weekend and a productive one. I look forward to reading your papers."

Again the class sped by. Again Rachel felt herself open up like a thirsty flower to a rain shower. She wished there was some way she could take more than one class, but there wasn't. Amish school started next week, and she wouldn't have the time.

She bit her lower lip. She was getting greedy.

When Dr. Dyson gave them a ten-minute break in the middle of class, Amy searched in her purse until she pulled out a bedraggled and nearly empty roll of mints. She offered one to Rachel. "Do you have someone picking you up after class tonight?"

Rachel nodded as she took one. "But Friday I'll be driving my own car." *My own car.* It was still an unbelievable concept.

"That's nice."

That's nice. That was all Amy had to say? Clearly she didn't understand how momentous having her own car was, but then she had no context.

Amy held the mints out to Rob who took one; then she popped the last one in her mouth. "Why don't you text whoever's supposed to pick you up and tell her I'll take you home again."

Text her? "I'll give her a call."

"Whatever."

As Rachel called Max, she was conscious of Rob watching her. "My neighbor," she said as she waited for Max to answer. "Max."

His eyes narrowed. "Max?"

"It's really Maxine."

"Ah." And he smiled.

Rachel told herself she was smiling back because she was glad Max wouldn't have to drive out again tonight. It had nothing to do with Rob wondering if Max was a man.

As soon as class was finished, Amy stood. "Come on, guys." She fluffed her bangs. "Let's hit the Star. I'm hungry."

"Me too." Rob flipped his pack strap over one shoulder. "If you didn't suggest it, I was going to. I didn't have time for dinner before I came."

As she collected her things, Rachel felt as cozy inside as if she was sitting in front of her fireplace on a winter's night. It was stupid, she knew, but it had been a long time since she had friends who wouldn't talk husbands and babies. Not that there was anything wrong with talking husbands and babies, but she had neither. And there was more to life.

As they walked out of the room and down the stairs, some of the cozy feeling dissipated. She became aware that all around her the others in her class wore clothes in patterns and styles she didn't understand. As far as she could tell, no one wore the same thing they'd worn Friday night.

No one except her. She looked down at her denim skirt and white blouse and knew she had to do something. In not wanting to stand out by wearing her real clothes, she was standing out because she didn't know how to wear Englisch clothes.

All she wanted was to learn things. How did it get so complicated?

On Friday Amy had worn pants that looked too short to be regular pants and too long to be shorts but were apparently in style since a couple of the other girls had them on too. Some of the tourists who came to the produce stand also wore them. Amy's were patterned with flowers, a circus of colors. Friday she wore a pretty pink top with them. Tonight her top was the green of a ripe lime and her pants were dark blue.

Even Rob had on something different than he wore the other night. At least tonight's purple Warrior shirt was dry and wrinkle free, unlike Friday's shirt.

"I'll follow you again, Rob," Amy said as they reached the cars. "I think I know where I'm going, but I'm not sure."

He nodded and they fell into procession like last week.

"You should have gone with him," Amy said as they waited at the first light.

"Why would I go with him? I thought we were BFFs." She had to find out what that second F meant. Tomorrow night at Max's she'd look it up on Google after she bought a book of Dr. Dyson's on Amazon.

"If you need me to tell you why you should ride with a great guy like Rob, then don't bother." She sounded somewhat disgusted.

"Amy, I'm not looking for a guy." Especially an Englisch one who advertises warriors. "I'm a widow. Another guy after my husband seems too strange."

Amy stared at her. "You're a widow? How can that be? You're too young!"

Rachel shrugged. "It happens."

"The war! Afghanistan or Iraq?"

"Neither, and the light's green."

Amy surged ahead to catch up with Rob. "So what happened?"

"He fell from a roof."

"Ouch."

Ouch indeed.

"How long were you married?"

"A year and a half."

"That's all? That bites."

Rachel wasn't familiar with the phrase, but it was obvious what Amy meant. "It does."

"How long ago did he die?"

"Three years."

Rachel braced herself to hear that three years was long enough and she should move on, and Rob would be the perfect guy to move on with.

How should she answer that? Three years was a long time, and she felt guilty when she realized a day—or even several days—passed without her thinking of Aaron. He didn't deserve to be forgotten. But Rob being the perfect replacement? Absolutely not.

"I'm so sorry," Amy finally said. "Is that the right thing to say? The only widows I know are old ladies."

"I'm sorry is the best possible thing you could say." Rachel was impressed. A smart, sensitive lady lived in that perky little person.

"On the cop shows they always say, 'I'm sorry for your loss,' when they go to tell someone about that week's murder."

"That sounds good too."

"What was his name?"

"Aaron."

"Was he good looking? Nice? Did you love him?"

Only Amy. "He was very good looking. Very nice."

"Good looking like Rob?" she asked as they pulled into the Star's lot.

"No. Aaron was slighter and shorter. He had light brown hair, much lighter than Rob's. He was strong though. He and his brothers built our house."

"You have your own house? How cool is that!"

"It's very cool," Rachel agreed. "It meant I didn't have to go home to live with my parents after Aaron died."

"I'm never going home to my parents either." And Amy slammed the car door behind her for emphasis.

After Patsy seated them, Amy looked at Rob. "Did you know Rachel's a widow?"

Rob studied Rachel. "I'm so sorry. The war?"

Why did everyone assume the war? People died for all kinds of reasons. She shook her head. "Accident."

They were all quiet for a minute as they considered Rachel's loss. Then Amy pointed to Rob's shirt logo. "Speaking of the war, do you work with Wounded Warriors?"

"No. It's more I send them money to help the guys who need it and if you send enough, you get a shirt."

Betts came to their table to take their beverage orders, and it was a few minutes before they were alone again. As usual Amy had something she wanted to know.

"Tell me about your families, both of you. You know mine was awful. I need to hear about good ones."

Rob took a deep breath and looked off to the side as if he were uncomfortable. "Not much to tell. Mother, father, brother."

"What's your father do?"

"He was in investments, but he's retired now."

"Huh." Amy looked surprised. "Were you a late-in-life kid or something that you have a father old enough to retire?"

Rob laughed. "Not especially. He was sort of forced to retire."

Betts appeared at the table with a small tray holding their beverages. "Rob's father is notorious." She served the drinks and smiled at Rob. "But we all love this guy anyway. He's as good as they come."

Notorious? That was a strong word with negative connotations. What was Mr. Lanier known for? Rachel waited for Amy to pursue the comment, but she didn't. Maybe she'd somehow missed it. Or maybe, as seemed more likely, she felt the discomfort pouring off Rob in waves and was being as discreet now as she'd been about Aaron.

Rachel looked at the tense Rob. "Tell us about your brother." Hopefully he was a safe topic.

With the subject of his father dropped, he relaxed. "Four years younger than me. Nice guy. Charming. Still trying to find his way."

"That'd make him just about right for me," Amy said. "Age and situation. Would I like him?"

Rob leaned back as Betts set his burger and sweet potato fries in front of him. "Amy, I have no idea. And I don't set up blind dates."

Amy looked at Rachel. "Isn't that just like a guy? No imagination for things of the heart."

"Not true," Rob said. "I just play things of the heart close to the vest." He grinned at Rachel. "Especially at first."

Amy smirked as Rachel felt her face go hot. Again Amy showed discretion and let the topic drop. "It's your turn, Rachel. Tell us about your family."

Her face cooled as Rachel talked with affection about all the Millers. Both Amy and Rob laughed at the story of the chicken sacrifices and smiled at the story of Datt trying to get her to move back home. The biggest challenge was to keep the Amish aspect of her family quiet.

When she stopped long enough to drink the last of her soda, Amy sighed deeply.

"You are so lucky!"

Rachel nodded. "I know."

"Do you think they'd adopt me?"

Rachel laughed as she imagined introducing Amy to her parents. Culture shock on both sides.

As she bit into her grilled cheese, she wondered again what she was doing endangering her life with her family. And how she could do anything else if she wanted to survive.

Chapter 13

Rachel stood just inside Max's living room. "Max, I'm wearing the same thing I wore last week."

Max nodded. "I wondered when you'd notice that. Or if you'd care."

"It's vain to care."

"Not if you want to fit in."

Rachel's closet at home held dresses in varying colors, though the style was the same. For over a year after Aaron's death she'd worn only black and had felt like she was abandoning him the first time she wore another color.

But this situation was different. Englisch styles and patterns were a world she didn't understand, and delving into that confusing world felt strange, another not so tiny step away from the familiar and the correct.

"Time to go shopping?" Max smiled in anticipation.

There it was: that Englisch fascination with shopping. What was so wonderful about walking through malls and stores? All they did was make you greedy. The very idea of shopping for Englisch clothes made Rachel's stomach drop.

Englisch clothes made you want to be pretty or stylish or unique, all things she'd been trained against her whole life. She was used to looking at clothing as one way of yielding herself to the Gmay. Could she make Max understand how looking the same as all the other women was a good thing that fostered humility and unity?

"Do you know *uffgevva?*" she asked Max.

Max shook her head. She was seated as usual in Buddy's recliner. She pointed at a chair for Rachel who sank to the edge of the indicated seat.

"Uffgevva is the concept of giving up your rights, giving up yourself, and yielding to the community. It applies to many things and dress is one of them. The Ordnung tells me what I can wear, and I yield my right to disagree because the community is more important than my wishes. I want to be humble and please God, so I wear the prescribed wardrobe just as I submit myself in other ways to the Gmay."

Max lowered the footrest on Buddy's recliner and sat forward. "I understand the concept of submitting to others. It's a command of Paul's in Ephesians. It's one of the ways the Body of Christ keeps unity, something else the Bible tells us to seek."

Rachel blinked. An Englisch woman who believed in uffgevva? "But it seems to me that you Englisch make a big thing about your rights and being independent. We Amish are working to lose ourselves to God and to the Gmay. We have no rights but rather the duty to love God and serve each other."

"I agree we English love our individuality. But speaking for myself, I recognize my responsibility to yield my rights for the greater good, whether it's for my country or my church or my family. I try to honor others and accept others. I try to remember not to think of myself more highly than I should."

"But—" In many ways that sounded like the Amish way.

"Consider," Max said. "We both believe in dressing modestly since this is what Scripture says. You—your people—define how to be modest differently than I. You don't want to call attention to yourself within your community, so you dress alike. But if I dressed like your community in my community, I'd draw that unwanted attention."

Rachel knew what Max meant because that was why she didn't wear her regular clothes to class. Her mind whirled. She'd always thought of the Amish and the Englisch as totally at odds with each other. The Amish were modest and correct, those who gave up self, and the Englisch were immodest and incorrect, those who cherished self. She hadn't even thought about a third group out there, Englisch who believed in uffgevva. She knew there were lots of Englisch who called themselves Christians, but Englisch Christians who believed in giving up themselves?

Max studied Rachel. "John the Baptist said that Jesus must increase and he must decrease. Is that uffgevva?"

"John the Baptist made following Jesus his whole purpose. Part of following Jesus in that way is uffgevva. It's losing individuality, giving it up."

"But didn't God make us individuals with different personalities and gifts?"

Conversations with Max often made Rachel think beyond herself. She liked this stretching of her faith.

"We certainly recognize people are different and contribute in different ways," she said. "But we should be willing to give up our personal opinions and agendas. We should be humble, serving one another, yielding to each other."

Max nodded. "I believe that. I do. I also believe God gave us different gifts and personalities, that being different is good."

"But self is dangerous." If uffgevva taught anything, it taught that.

Max nodded. "Self can be dangerous. I agree. But are being different and being full of self the same?"

They couldn't be the same. She was different from everyone she knew, but she wasn't full of self. Or was she? Wasn't this whole getting an education thing her being full of self? Or was it just her being different?

"I need to think."

"Okay, you think. In the meantime, do you want to go shopping or not?" Max asked.

Rachel realized that in spite of all her talk about uffgevva, she did. She wanted to fit in. *Gott Vader, am I becoming Englisch?* What a scary thought.

"How will I know what to buy?" she asked Max.

"You buy whatever makes you comfortable."

Max sounded so reasonable, but it was beyond Rachel's experience to buy ready-made clothes. She'd been sewing her own things on her mother's machine as soon as she was old enough to reach the treadle. She could manage that homemaking chore because it was easy when you followed the same pattern every time, and Mom was always there to correct her mistakes.

On Wednesday after she passed her driver's test with no problem, she and Max went shopping.

"I don't want to spend much," she told Max. Buying Englisch clothes did not mean she would forget her Amish frugality.

Wearing her white blouse and denim skirt, Rachel followed Max into a consignment shop. Racks and racks of clothes filled the room. Colors and patterns shimmered on every hanger. It was blinding and bewildering. Overwhelming. How was she ever to select?

"You need a couple of sweaters," Max announced, taking charge.

Rachel obediently followed her to a counter where sweaters of every color lay. She felt panic rise in her chest.

Max looked at her, then at the sweaters. She began pulling out cardigans in several colors.

Rachel reached for a pale blue Max hadn't selected. It wouldn't attract attention and it was a pretty shade.

"No, no." Max took it from her hand and put it back. "With your dark brown hair and eyes, that color would wash you out. You want stronger colors."

She did?

Two hours later, she and Max carried her purchases inside Max's house. The bags filled the large chair in front of the fireplace.

"We bought too much, Max. I need to take some back."

"It's not too much. If you want to see too much, you should see Ashley's wardrobe."

"But I'll only be wearing them twice a week."

"Four outfits that you can mix and match isn't much, Rachel. Believe me. Which outfit will you wear Friday to class?"

Rachel's eye went to the cranberry top. It was the brightest shade of red that she'd ever had, and she loved it.

Max picked up the knit top. "It's a wonderful color for you. Brings out the roses in your cheeks."

Rachel flushed. Did she want roses in her cheeks?

"You should wear it with the long gray skirt we found."

Rachel looked at the skirt. She'd seen girls in class in ones just like it.

"I'm glad that I'm only playing Englisch two nights a week. It's too nerve-racking to do more often. Look. My hand's trembling."

"Go change. You'll feel more like yourself."

So she did. And she did.

Friday evening she dressed for class in her new gray skirt and cranberry top.

"Whoever would have thought I'd be dressed Englisch in a longer skirt than I wear dressed Amish?" she said to Max who was busy in the kitchen microwaving her dinner. "I won't be too late coming home."

Max smiled. "You've got a key, so it's not a problem. Come home whenever you feel like it. I'm a night owl. I'll probably be up. If I'm not, come on in."

Driving without Max in the seat beside her was scary for the first few miles, but by the time she pulled into a parking spot at Wexford, she felt confident. At least she had made it this far without being spotted by someone from the Gmay. Or worse, from her family. She also felt safer in her car than she did in her buggy, especially on the main roads. The suction from the big trucks didn't make the car shudder as much as it did a buggy. She also didn't have to worry about a horse being frightened and acting on that fear. But if she got a flat tire, she was in trouble.

After class, as was becoming their habit, Rachel, Amy, and Rob went to the Star. Patsy showed them to a banquette in the corner instead of a booth. Rachel slid in from one side and Amy from the other. Rob didn't hesitate; he slid in beside Rachel.

Not that he sat close, but it was obvious he deliberately sat by her, not Amy. When Betts came for their order and Rob's attention was on her, Amy not too subtly socked Rachel on the thigh and mouthed, "I told you so."

Rachel flushed. The last thing she wanted or needed was an Englisch guy interested in her. There was no way she could juggle one more thing.

"How'd you two do on your papers?" Amy asked after she ordered a grilled cheese sandwich and Diet Coke.

"Okay," Rachel said noncommittally.

"Sea of red." Rob, looking unhappy, fiddled with the salt and pepper shakers.

"What went wrong?" Rachel asked quickly before Amy asked her how she did and she had to confess she'd gotten an A.

"According to Dr. Dyson, no emotion, no involvement, all facts. 'There's no *you* in here'—you get the idea."

"What did you write about?"

"I wrote about the need for rescuing pets."

"That's a great topic. How'd you personalize it? Did you write about rescuing Charlie?"

"I wrote about the need to rescue animals."

"Okay, but—" Rachel hesitated. She was in danger of falling into teacher mode, and Rob might not appreciate her telling him what she thought was wrong.

"But what?" Rob looked like he really wanted to know. "Come on, Rachel. Help! Otherwise it's going to be a very long and painful semester."

Rachel pulled away a piece of her hair that had somehow gotten stuck in the corner of her mouth and brushed it back over her shoulder. She never had trouble with hair when it was contained in her kapp or a scarf. "Why did you write on that subject?"

"Because it was something I'd just done, I guess."

"So the fact you'd just done it is what makes it personal to you. Personal is the key word for this assignment."

He nodded. "According to the ASPCA, there are thousands of animals put down every day because of the expense of caring for them."

Rachel put up a hand. "No, that's not what she wants. What makes this general topic of rescuing animals personal to *you*?"

Rob frowned as if she'd asked him a trick question. "Charlie, I guess. When I saw him sitting in that cage, his tail wagging and his eyes pleading, I knew I couldn't leave him. In fact I hated leaving any of them." He talked for some time about the poor dogs in cages, all looking so forlorn, and about the little kid who was picking out a dog.

"'I want that big one,' the kid said, pointing to a dog three times his size. And his father said, 'You'll never be able to take him for a walk. He's too big. He'll take you. Pick a small one.'" Rob smiled. "They left with a harlequin Great Dane."

Rachel smiled back. "Did you write any of that?"

He looked gobsmacked. "That's what she wanted?"

"That's what she wanted."

"You mean I spent all that time researching things for nothing?"

"Statistics about animals being abused and in need of rescue, about organizations that do that work, that's not what she's looking for though you could probably slip some of that info in here and there."

Amy agreed. "This isn't a history class or a science class where you spit out facts. It may be a basic comp class, but you have to go deeper. You go into your emotions and thoughts, not just facts. Anyone can find facts. Only you can write your reactions."

Rob ate half his tuna melt before he spoke again. "You mean I have to explain that I wanted companionship? Someone who didn't demand unreasonable things from me? I have to admit I was smitten by a dog's lolling tongue and sad eyes asking for help?"

"Lolling tongue," Rachel said. "She'd like that."

"What'd you write about?" he asked.

"Why I'm taking this class."

Amy pointed a French fry at her. "And I bet you didn't write about the statistics that people who go to college get better jobs and make more money."

"I wrote about my heart's yearning for more education, my consuming passion to learn."

"And I wrote about my need to leave my small narrow home for a larger world," Amy said. "Not about the finances of leaving home or the dangers or the resulting independence. I wrote why I had to get away or die." She grinned. "Got a B."

Rob shook his head. "So she wants us to rip out our guts and write in blood."

"You got it." Amy patted his hand like a mother who was proud of her son.

"I'm going to be a money man. Numbers. Markets. A plus B equals C. I do facts and probabilities, not feelings."

"What are you writing about for next Friday?" Rachel asked. She felt impatient that she had to wait a whole week for the next class because of Labor Day. "We can brainstorm with you."

"I don't know." He grinned that adorable grin of his. "It's not Thursday night yet."

Chapter 14

The banging on his trailer door made Johnny Miller feel his head was inside one of Datt's old milking pails while someone beat on it with the equally old milking stool. Not that anyone had used a pail and stool for years. Sanitation laws and all.

"Open this door, Miller!" Mick Morrison's temper burned in the words, and Johnny wouldn't be surprised to see scorch marks on his front door—if he ever got to see his front door again. "I know you're in there!"

There was an extra loud bang on the door, and Johnny pictured Mick using his baseball bat.

"It's the end of another week, Miller."

As if Johnny didn't know it was Friday evening, and he owed Mr. Sherman another thousand dollars. He hadn't been able to pay the original five thousand. How could he pay an extra thousand? Where was the logic?

But it wasn't about logic. It was about power and fear.

What would happen if Mick broke in and found him cowering here in the shower stall like a spooked mouse? His humiliation would be total, his reputation, such as it was, unredeemable. Johnny wrapped his arms more tightly around his legs and burrowed his head into his knees.

"You should have seen him," Mick would say, laughing as he told everyone where Johnny was. "All that stupid Amish sissy stuff always comes out in the end. Wusses, all of them!" And a whole lot of uglier words. If Mick wasn't beating someone with his fists or his bat, he found whipping them with words almost as satisfying.

Johnny shivered and hugged himself tighter. Being called a coward was better than being beaten or killed. Besides, what else could he do but hide? He didn't have the money to pay. He'd never have the money.

A vivid picture of Mick shooting off the front door lock and storming the place raced through his mind like an action scene from a movie. Or maybe Mick'd just race down the side of the trailer with his automatic, trigger depressed, spitting fire as he laughed maniacally and Johnny jerked in slow motion as the bullets ripped through him.

He whimpered at his imagined demise, then slapped a hand over his mouth to keep any more sound from escaping. *God, help me! Please?*

Not that God was likely to listen to him.

And not that Mick needed a gun. All he had to do was ram the door with that massive shoulder of his and the lock would pop. Johnny shuddered.

The mildew stench of the unwashed and poorly vented shower stall tickled the inside of his nose and made him want to sneeze. He buried his nose in his arm to stifle the urge. He couldn't afford the noise. The flimsy trailer shell was no protection against being heard.

Or being shot.

The banging continued in spite of the lack of lights on inside. Why didn't Mick just bust his way in? Get it over with?

"Miller! Come out here and be a man!"

Johnny cringed at the words. The man terrified him. There was something seriously wrong with the guy, something missing inside, that inner whatever-it-was that kept people from harming others. Mick gloried in hurting those weaker. That would include Johnny.

Usually Mr. Sherman kept him under control, but every so often he let Mick loose.

"You're a dead man, Miller," Mick yelled. "A dead man!"

Johnny felt his stomach heave, and he swallowed mightily. It wasn't the shame of throwing up all over himself that made him fight the nausea and flood of saliva. It was fear of the noise he'd make as he heaved.

Another sound made Johnny go cold all over. His cell phone was playing.

But it wasn't his. It was Mick's. He could hear Mick bellow, "Yeah?"

His voice immediately grew respectful, and Johnny knew it must be Mr. Sherman. What did the fat man have that made the Micks of the world respect him? It was a mystery. If he could figure it out, he'd never cower in a stall again. He'd make others cower.

The murmur of conversation reached him through the flimsy trailer shell, but not words. There was a moment of silence as the call seemed over.

Then Mick slapped the side of the trailer again, making Johnny jump and his bowels turn watery.

"I know you're here, Miller. And I know I could get in there without breaking a sweat. I got my gun." The affection in Mick's voice when he spoke of his weapon sounded obscene.

A loud *crack!* sounded as Mick pulled the trigger. Johnny put out his hands and, fingers splayed, braced himself against the far shower wall to keep from collapsing in a quivering heap.

"I'm just playing with you." Mick laughed. "Think about that, Miller. I'm only playing with you. This time." He laughed again and Johnny felt goosebumps all over his body.

Footsteps crunched. A car door slammed. Then another. Someone was with Mick. Thomas? They were a team of sorts. A motor turned over. Tires spat gravel in the drive, and the sound of the motor diminished to nothing.

Johnny lifted his head and rolled his shoulders, but he didn't stand. Not yet. What if Mick hadn't really driven away? What if he was crouched, bat at the ready, waiting for a sound, any sound, from inside the trailer? Then he'd force the lock and be inside in a flash. Stress sweat made the mildew sweet by comparison.

"You're a dead man, Miller."

But Mr. Sherman didn't send Mick after people to kill them. At least not that he'd ever heard. What good were dead people? They couldn't pay you back. They couldn't be forced to work for you.

People who'd been beaten and tortured and who feared it happening again could be made to do most anything. Johnny felt the shackles binding him to Mr. Sherman snapping on his wrists. Frantically he rubbed them away though he knew the threat remained.

He had to leave the area. California. Mr. Sherman's reach couldn't be that long.

After fifteen minutes he decided Mick was truly gone. The man was too ADHD to be quiet that long no matter his game, too impatient to wait quietly in the dark for a noise. Johnny stood, his legs so cramped that he had to lean against the stall while the blood rushed painfully through them.

When he knew he could move without bumping awkwardly into something and alerting anyone listening that he was here, even though he was pretty sure there was no one out there to hear, he moved to the front window and peered cautiously out. No car, but he already knew that. He'd heard it drive away.

He studied the edges of the cornfields bordering the patch where the trailer sat. An army could have hidden in the green stalk forest.

Not that one was. When you had Mick, you didn't need an army.

Without turning on a light Johnny pulled a bag of chips from the cupboard and a warm beer from the closet. He hated warm beer, but he wasn't risking the fridge light to get a chilled one.

As he chomped and drank, he tried to think logically. He owed Mr. Sherman money he didn't have. Mr. Sherman demanded payment one way or the other. He was afraid of Mr. Sherman and Mick. They wouldn't leave him alone and would have no hesitation about hurting him or those he cared for. He had no fondness of pain or of seeing others in pain. Solution: He had to go into hiding. It was that simple.

So where could he hide? California or someplace far like that. How much would it cost to go that far? Not that it mattered. He could go as far as his money took him, and then work a while until he had enough to go again.

He stood. He needed something sweet to counter all the salt of the chips. He grabbed the bag of Wilbur Buds, the smell of the chocolate telling him he needed a cold drink, not the lukewarm one in his hand. With one final furtive look out front, he opened the fridge and pulled out a cold one.

Trouble with California was he didn't want to leave Honey Brook. He liked Honey Brook. He knew the area; he felt comfortable here. He might hate his job, but it was regular income. And no one at work ever complained when he was hung over. They just told him he was an idiot.

And Becky was here.

Not that she paid him any attention. She wanted a good Amish man, and he sure wasn't that. Still her pretty face filled a lot of his dreams.

He studied the bag of chips and the bag of Wilbur Buds and wondered if anyone had ever come up with a chocolate potato chip. Talk about the perfect combination! He'd have to ask Mom to make some. She could cook anything.

Mom. He narrowed his eyes. Mom and Datt. The farm. No one would look for him there. They all knew how much he hated it. Or said he hated it.

He studied his idea, looking for problems.

Mom and Datt would love for him to come home. Of course he'd have to make believe he wanted to join the church, but he could do that. He knew the rules well enough. He could fake them in his sleep. And Datt could use extra hands around the place. He was getting older every day.

Becky would be so impressed with his choice she'd finally agree to go out with him. Of course he wasn't sure where they'd go. She wouldn't go near Corner Bob's. Of course he couldn't go there any more either, not if he valued his life.

He sat back in the chair and thought as he crunched. Home. Could it really work in throwing Sherman and his goons off his track?

Chapter 15

Amy picked Rachel up at Max's house late the Saturday afternoon of Labor Day weekend.

"I worked six to three today," she explained from behind the wheel of her little red car. "I have to work all day Sunday and Monday, nine to six. This is my time to party!"

Rachel's heart skipped a beat. When Amy phoned and said, "Let's go do something," she'd thought of the Star or a stroll at the mall.

"What do you mean, party?" She was so not a party girl. During her rumspringa her idea of partying was staying out until midnight at a youth gathering.

"Nothing too wild," Amy said. "A quick dinner at Wegman's and a movie."

"A movie?"

Amy jumped in her seat. "Can you believe I've never been to one...ever? My father wouldn't let us. He said movies would corrupt us with the world."

Amy's father wasn't the only one who thought that way.

"There's a great movie all the girls at work are talking about," she continued. "It's PG13, if that's what you're worried about."

Rachel wasn't certain what PG13 meant, but it sounded very suspect, a very slippery slope. She should just admit she'd never been to a movie either, but Amy would want to know why. How could she explain without revealing her secret?

Amy's grin was so wide it split her face. "We are going to have so much fun!"

"I don't know, Amy."

"Oh, come on. Don't let me down on my first wild night." Amy looked over with pleading eyes.

There was that churning stomach again. Whatever she did, it would be wrong. She'd disappoint Amy or she'd break the Ordnung.

"Come on, Rach. I want to find out what everyone else does on a Saturday night. I want to be a real person."

There was no way Rachel wanted to stand before the Gmay and confess going to a movie. She needed to tell Amy no very clearly. Of course she was sinning twice a week with class and more often at Max's with the internet. When she thought about it that way, what difference would a movie make?

She squeezed her eyes tightly shut and said, "Okay. Let's go."

"This is going to be such fun!" Amy backed from Max's drive. Rachel settled down in the passenger seat and told herself she didn't regret her capitulation. But she understood more clearly than ever the influence of friends and the need to keep the community apart. Sin lurked behind every door, waiting to pounce, and it sometimes came in the guise of BFFs.

"What was it like, growing up surrounded by Amish people?" Amy asked as she slowed for a buggy, unable to pass because of oncoming traffic. A pair of little girls with their hair slicked back into buns looked at them out the back window of the buggy, probably as curious about the little Smart car as Amy was about them.

"It was normal." Rachel turned her head so the people in the buggy couldn't see her as Amy took advantage of a break in the traffic and passed the slow moving vehicle. "When you grow up a certain way, you think that's the way it is for everyone."

"True." Amy grinned. "Then you go to school and find out your family's nuts."

"Amy!"

"Well, they are. Nice except for my father, but nuts. I thought only terrible people had TVs until I went to kindergarten and found out I was the only one who didn't have a bunch of them. It was shortly after I went to visit my new friend Amber and came home in love with TV that Dad decided my younger sisters and I should be homeschooled to keep us from being tainted by the world."

Exactly the reason for Amish schools.

"Did you like it, the homeschooling?" Rachel had loved going to school, not only for the learning but also for her friends, the girls whispering their secrets and telling the boys to let them alone. Then there was recess with the baseball games and volleyball games. She'd definitely been a tomboy.

"I guess homeschooling was okay. My mom was a good teacher and made sure we had plenty of extra things to do like helping serve meals at the shelter—where we saw what happened if you let the world in—and knitting caps for cancer patients—where we saw what happened when God had to punish you." Her brow wrinkled at the thought. "Do you think God makes you sick to punish you?"

"I know a lot of fine people who have gotten sick and died," Rachel said. "It's just part of being human, don't you think?"

"It's what I think, but my father and the people at church said differently. I'm trying to figure out who's right and who's wrong." She got an impish look. "I keep wondering what he's going to say when he gets sick. He's got to someday, right?"

Rachel laughed. "Probably. Most of us do. Remember that boy in the Bible who was sick, and the disciples asked what his parents had done wrong that he was sick? Jesus said no one had sinned. He was sick so God could be glorified. Then he healed the boy."

"But what if he doesn't heal you and you stay sick?"

"Then I guess you die like everybody else."

"And go to heaven where you're all better and everything's great! Win/win."

They drove in silence, passing an oncoming buggy holding three teenaged Amish girls in pretty pastel dresses with complimentary aprons, their kapps crisp and white against their dark hair. They were giggling together, their eyes bright.

"Do they mind having to dress alike all the time?"

"It's just part of being in the community. It's just life."

"I always hated having to wear dresses that came almost to the ankles. Always!"

"Amish girls don't wear dresses that long."

"I know, but they're trapped like I was. I look at the Amish kids, and I identify."

Rachel looked at Amy's jeans and sweater. "You've changed."

"You bet! The hardest part was not throwing Jesus out with the long skirts because they were so tied together in what I was taught that I struggle to see them separately."

"How were you different from the Amish?"

"We had computers, Dad drove a car, and we used modern conveniences like phones and microwaves. Dad looked like every other businessman going off to work. It was us girls who looked different." Amy was quiet for a minute. "I resented that. A lot."

Rachel looked down at her flowered navy skirt, reversible so she had another blue pattern that allowed her to appear to have two skirts. Practical. Thrifty. Amish—but so *not*. She sighed. It wasn't resentment that pushed her against the Ordnung. It was curiosity. It was knowing there was more to know and wanting to learn about that more, whatever it was.

"I went to a small school with the neighborhood kids," she finally said. "I always loved school. I still do. I guess that's why I love to teach."

"I fought my parents for years to be able to go back to school."

"Did you win?"

"Nope. And they wouldn't even think about college. 'Foolish for a woman,' my father always said. 'You're just going to get married and be busy caring for your husband and home.'"

Amish-think to a degree. But to the Amish this pattern wasn't to beat women down or keep them in their place. It was to keep the community strong with healthy families where mother and father fulfilled biblical roles. It was to train children in the faith. It was to provide stability where all knew exactly what was expected of them and did it willingly.

"Hey, look!" Amy pointed.

Strutting through Mrs. Meyer's yard were six very large wild turkeys. Rachel had seen them around before.

"Those are some big boys." Amy slowed as the turkeys wandered into the road in front of her. There the birds stopped, pecking at seed someone had spilled. She was forced to stop too.

She blew her horn at the birds. "That'll scare them."

It didn't. It seemed to make them angry because suddenly they were all around the car, cackling and gobbling. They came to the windows and stared in at Amy and Rachel, heads bobbing indignantly. Given the size of Amy's car, the birds loomed large and unexpectedly threatening.

In all the times she'd seen this rafter of turkeys wandering the area, Rachel had never seen them react like this. Usually they looked at you and turned tail, sometimes doing a low level flight for a few yards to get away.

Maybe it was the seed, maybe not, but something had made the birds very territorial.

"They're Amish turkeys," Amy said, giving another delighted-with-life jump in her seat. "They don't like automobiles."

Rachel had to laugh. "I can't imagine what's gotten them riled up."

Amy flinched, her grin scared away, as a bird poked his very sturdy beak against the driver's side window. She fluttered her hands at him. "Go away!" He answered by pecking again.

A second bird began pecking Rachel's window.

"They've got us surrounded." Amy looked slightly panicked. "I can't go forward or I'll run over one or two, and I can't go back because of the one behind me. Given their size, it'd probably disable the car."

Movement drew Rachel's eye. Beyond the turkey looking in the front window and voicing indignation with every bobbing head movement was a horse-drawn cart coming down the road. Abner was holding the reins as he sat in Levi's lap. Mom and Ruthie squeezed in beside the boys.

Rachel turned her head as far to the side as she could, fluffing her hair to help hide her face.

Not like this! Please not like this!

As she watched from the corner of her eye, Levi took the reins from Abner and handed them to Ruthie. He jumped from the cart and began waving his hat at the birds. "Go! Go!"

The turkeys turned their agitation to him and began moving toward him. He stood his ground, brandishing his hat like a weapon. Ruthie had to work hard to keep the horse still as the birds gobbled and griped.

Amy hit the gas as soon as the birds moved out her way, and with a wave of her hand toward Levi, she took off. Rachel wanted to look back to be certain he was all right—the turkeys didn't look like they wanted to cooperate with him any more than they had with Amy and her—but she was afraid to. Levi might see her and recognize her. Or Mom or Ruthie or even Abner.

She glanced in the side mirror and saw Levi staring after the car as he waved his arms halfheartedly. Was it because he liked the cute little car or because he recognized her?

Amy drove out of Honey Brook through Lyndale to Downingtown and the movies. By the time Rachel climbed from the car, her conscience was so divided she could hardly breathe. On one hand Amy danced ahead, pulling her into the unknown as persuasively as the mythical sirens lured sailors to their deaths. On the other were the years of Gmay teaching that an activity like this was *verboten*.

Rachel took her place in one of three lines behind Amy, watching the people ahead of them buying tickets. Behind the cashiers was a big electronic board telling the time and theater of all the movies showing. Somehow she hadn't realized that several movies were showing at once, their starting times staggered. She managed to ask for a ticket for the one Amy had selected.

In the lobby, everything was so bright and busy. People milled about, yet somehow they all seemed to know where to go. She looked right and left and felt a panic attack waiting to pounce. For not having been to a movie before, Amy seemed at ease in the surroundings, even leading Rachel to the refreshment line where she bought a huge tub of popcorn that cost an astronomical amount of money.

"Want a Coke?" Amy asked. "My treat."

"I'd rather have a water." She rarely had any sodas but homemade root beer, and even they tasted too sweet to her.

When they walked into the darkened theater for the movie they were seeing, Rachel carried her water and Amy's soda while Amy hugged her popcorn as if she was carrying a toddler. Seats rose like the lecture hall at Wexford, and they climbed until Amy found two seats together. They climbed over knees and sank into their seats.

"Those turkeys almost made us too late to get seats," Amy whispered. She took a handful of popcorn and held the tub to Rachel. "Want some?"

Rachel looked down at her full hands.

"Oops." Amy set her popcorn in her lap, took her soda, and stuck it in the cup holder attached to her seat. Rachel slid her bottle into the holder beside her, wondering how Amy knew the holders were there in the dark. She took a handful of Amy's popcorn and settled back to become worldly. In a strange and scary way, it was exciting.

She stared at the huge flashing images dancing across the screen. She felt mesmerized as they watched something called previews, bits and pieces of movies to be shown at future dates. There were three she thought looked like interesting storylines.

Then the movie itself started. In no time she was lost in the story, jumping when something unexpected happened, crying at a tender moment, laughing at the visual jokes.

When it was over, she sat, shell-shocked. So this was a movie. No wonder they didn't want her going to theaters. Talk about the world taking over! To her own surprise, as they made their way back to the lobby, Rachel leaned into Amy and said, "I loved it! What a wonderful way to tell a story!"

Chapter 16

*R*achel pinned her kapp into place and ran her hands down her dress to straighten it. She grabbed a sweater though she probably wouldn't need it. Already the day was warm. With her backpack slung over her shoulder, she went to the small barn behind her house. She pulled her buggy from its place, then went to her horse.

"Hey, Rusty. It's the first day of school."

He nickered a greeting and she ran a hand over his sleek neck. She worked the bit and bridle into place, then backed him between the traces and buckled him in.

As she checked to be certain all was as it should be, Rusty shifted. One front hoof came down solidly on the rein that had slipped to the ground as she worked.

"Oh, Rusty, not today." She put her shoulder into his and pushed. He became a rock, a huge immovable mountain. She looked at him and caught the devilry in his eye. He knew what he was doing.

"Rusty! You bad horse. Move!" She pushed again.

He lifted one leg, the one not on the rein, and set it carefully down again.

"Not that leg! This one!" She slapped him lightly. He leaned down and butted her in a gentle movement.

Knowing he'd play the rein game indefinitely, she walked away and put her supplies in the buggy. When she came back, the rein was free and he was twitching his ears, impatient to get going.

Poor Rusty. He didn't get out much over the summer. People were constantly picking her up for events, so he spent his days lazing in the barn. He loved when school started because it meant exercise every day.

At school, Rachel climbed from the buggy and unlocked the padlock on the chain-link fence that circled the property. She pushed the gate wide. She drove behind the building where she unhooked Rusty and tucked him into a stall in the small shed. There was a second stall for her buggy where it was well protected in case of the rain.

She walked around to the front of the white school building and unlocked the door as the first students walked up the lane. She hated that the building had to be locked and circled by a fence, but since the Nickel Mines tragedy, it would be foolish to risk another crazy man. She'd close the gate of the fence and lock it after all the children were present.

Some of her students rode their scooters to school, flags waving high to warn motorists. Several others wore bright green safety vests so they were visible on the narrow winding roads they walked. All carried lunches, most tucked into brightly colored Igloos.

The new little ones looked uncertain as older brothers and sisters or cousins led them into the room.

"Good morning," she said to each one.

"Good morning, Rachel," Little Jonah said when it was his turn, just like all the other students. She grinned at him and he grinned back.

Some of the little ones forgot the English only rule and greeted her with, "*Guten morgen.*"

"Good morning," she said again with a smile.

They all realized their mistake immediately. "Good morning," they said, the D on "good" sounding more like a T.

The day went quickly, and Rachel was smiling as she drove Rusty home. She did love teaching. The entire week sped by, though every morning when she harnessed Rusty, she thought how simple it would be to get in her car, turn the key, and drive.

Finally Friday night came and Rachel drove herself to Wexford.

"I feel like it's been forever." Amy hugged her. "I would have called, but I ended up working extra hours, covering for someone on vacation."

Rachel hadn't expected a call and so never missed it. "Not a problem. School started this week, so I've been busy."

"How come you can teach if you don't have your degree yet?"

Amy was too sharp by half. "My school board has given their approval." Which they'd rescind if they knew she was going for a degree.

She'd read recently about the Colossus of Rhodes standing astride the ancient harbor entrance. She felt like a modern version standing astride two worlds. To teach in one, she'd need a degree. To teach in the other, she'd better not have one.

Rob slid into a seat beside her and gave one of her curls a tug, something no one had ever done before. It felt personal, intimate, and as she smiled shyly at him, she was afraid she liked it too much.

Class sped by as always. They got back their papers on their latest assignment, an essay about what they believed. Rachel was pleased she got another A. She also had a note from Dr. Dyson scribbled across the top: "See me before you leave."

As class drew to a close, Dr. Dyson took a minute to study everyone. "No groans, please, but it's time for that old chestnut, the person who has affected you deeply. I want you to write an analysis of why he or she has influenced you, not a list of this person's accomplishments. I want your personal story with them. What did they do or say that made some change in your life, good or bad. Where were you when you met them, when they said something that touched you? What were you and this person doing? Why were you with this person? Personal. Emotional."

Rachel frowned. Who would she write about? Datt who was so committed to both God and the Gmay and taught his children to be as committed? Max who helped her reach beyond? But could she write about either without giving away her background?

After class she turned to Amy and Rob. "Dr. Dyson wants to see me."

"What's wrong? What did you do?" Amy asked, all concern.

"I have no idea."

"We'll wait down in the lobby," Rob said, then winked. "You might need our sympathy."

"Ha!" Amy snorted. "I doubt it. But we will wait."

Dr. Dyson took a seat in the first row and patted the one next to her for Rachel. With a dry throat Rachel sat. Never in her life had she been reprimanded by a teacher. What had she done wrong that Dr. Dyson needed to speak to her?

"So what's a nice Amish girl like you doing in my class?"

Rachel was speechless for a few seconds while Dr. Dyson waited. Finally she managed, "How did you know?"

"I come from an extremely conservative Mennonite background. I recognize in you and your writing many of the same things that drove me into the broader world."

Rachel stared at Dr. Dyson. Never would she have imagined that this gifted woman grew up wearing Plain clothes and living under rules as binding as the Ordnung.

"Has it been worth it?" she finally blurted. That one question covered all the uncertainties, doubts, and fears that plagued her.

"Leaving, you mean?" Dr. Dyson patted Rachel's clenched hands. "For me, yes. It's been hard. I've hurt people I love, and I deeply regret that. But I don't regret one bit becoming who God made me to be."

"I love my People," Rachel whispered. "And I love learning. I love this class. I don't know how to—" She couldn't finish and gestured with her hands, spreading them wide in a gesture of loss.

"I remember being just where you are, Rachel. I remember how hard it was, being forced to choose."

Rachel felt tears gather. Someone understood. Max sympathized, but she didn't understand. Dr. Dyson understood.

"I know being here is a gigantic risk." Dr. Dyson gestured to the classroom. "If you need someone to talk to any time, I'm here." She stood. "I just wanted to tell you that you don't have to work so hard to write around your heritage. Feel free to write the word *Amish* and all the other words necessary to express yourself." She smiled. "You are a very gifted writer, a true thinker. I suspect you're a closet academic."

Rachel felt herself flush with pleasure and the realization that Dr. Dyson was right. She *was* a closet academic. "Thank you."

Dr. Dyson grew serious. "A double life isn't healthy, Rachel. You will need to choose."

Hearing the obvious stated aloud twisted her insides. "I love the Plain life."

"But you love learning and crave knowledge."

Rachel nodded helplessly.

"Pray for guidance, Rachel. Ask God to give you wisdom. Ask Him to make your paths clear. Ask Him to lead you and instruct you as David asked." She gave Rachel's shoulder a gentle squeeze. "He led me. He'll lead you."

Rachel walked from the room lost in thought. Gott had led Dr. Dyson. He would lead her, Dr. Dyson said. She should ask Him to do so.

That was an interesting thought. In her experience prayers were prescriptive. Certain prayers were read at certain occasions. Silent prayer at meals and other times was, for her, usually the Lord's Prayer.

Dr. Dyson suggested she pray for God's guidance. Maybe she should look up the verses on God's leading and pray them. It wouldn't feel as presumptive as praying spontaneously like Rob, but it would still be personal.

Amy and Rob were waiting in the lobby.

"Everything okay?" Amy asked.

Rachel smiled. "She complimented me on my writing." That was both true and safe to say.

"I knew it." Rob reached for her backpack dangling from her fingers and threw it over his shoulder.

Amy made a face as she followed them to the door. "Whenever the teacher—that would be my mom or dad—wanted to talk to me, it was always because I was in trouble."

The three of them walked out together, went to their separate cars, and caravanned to the Star. Rachel had an egg salad on wheat toast. It was good but not as good as her mother's.

As the evening wore on, Amy became quieter and quieter. She stared at her plate and dipped her last fry in her ketchup several times without eating it.

"What's wrong, Amy?" Rachel asked.

"She must be feeling sick," Rob teased. "She's being quiet."

Amy looked up with a weak smile. "Good one."

"Tell us." Rachel leaned toward her friend. "We'll help if we can." She glanced at Rob, suddenly aware she'd spoken for him. She flushed. "At least I will."

Amy took a big breath. "It's a big favor."

"So ask," Rob said, and Rachel nodded. After all, they were BFFs and that second F meant forever.

"Anything but money," Rob said, then smiled. "That's another joke in case you didn't recognize it. You need money?"

"No money, but thanks." Amy began shredding her napkin.

Rachel and Rob waited.

"Okay, here goes. Will you help me move some of my things tomorrow?"

"Tomorrow?" Rachel ran through her plans for the day. Yes, she would help. There wasn't anything she couldn't do another time.

"I know it's last minute and all, but…" Her voice trailed off.

"That's it?" Rob asked.

Amy nodded. "I know it's asking a lot…"

"No, it's not." He grinned at her. "How much stuff do you have?"

"Bedroom stuff. A chair or two. A desk. Maybe some clothes."

"Piano? I draw the line at pianos."

Amy managed a grin. "No piano."

"Then what's the problem?"

"The stuff is at my family's house near Erie. It's going to be a five to six hour drive each way."

Rob glanced at Rachel and she shrugged. "Okay with me," she said. "I don't have anything planned." Except the produce stand, and Levi could cover that. He'd be happy to since it meant some money in his pocket.

Chapter 17

When Rob pulled into the lot at his apartment complex, a car sat in his parking spot. Granted, no one had painted Lanier between the lines, but it was right in front of his door and clearly his.

Which neighbor had company with bad manners? Mr. Harding, the septuagenarian, to his right? Not likely. The man might stay up half the night watching TV, but neither he nor his friends went out after dark. The Palmiaris on the left? Could be, but—he glanced at his watch. Ten o'clock. Late for a work night, especially since Rocco Palmiari left for work at five in the morning.

He glanced at the visitor parking spots clearly marked with a large sign that proclaimed their purpose. Someone couldn't read. He pulled into visitors' parking.

As he walked toward his unit, the driver's door on the misparked car opened, and a tall man stepped out.

"Took you long enough" the man said. "I thought class ended at eight."

"Win." Rob hoped he didn't sound as unenthusiastic at the sight of his brother as he felt.

"I've been waiting for almost half an hour."

How did a grown man manage to sound as petulant as a teenage girl whose father won't give her more money for clothes?

"Had I known you were here…" Had he known, he probably would still have milked every possible moment with Rachel and Amy. "I've got to walk Charlie. You want to walk with me?"

127

Win shrugged. "Sure. Why not?"

Rob opened the apartment door and a desperate dog charged out, heading for the bushes that edged the parking lot.

"Poor dog," Win said. "How long's he been inside?"

"Too long, poor guy."

The brothers began walking around the complex, Charlie snuffling every stray scent as he accompanied them. For no discernible reason except impulse, the dog would break into a run and dash the length of the lot and back.

"Charlie's working out well?" Win asked.

Charlie took that moment to rush up to them, tongue lolling with joy. Rob rubbed the dog's head. "He's great."

Charlie turned to Win for another rub, and Win complied. "I'd like a dog. They're such great animals."

"So get one."

"Like Mom'd let me. 'They shed, Winston. They smell. They bark. They upset my allergies.'"

"They do all that and more," Rob agreed.

"But they're fun." Win bent down and let Charlie give him a sloppy, slurpy kiss that made Rob want to wipe his dry face in empathy.

The brothers watched Charlie tear off across the open green space behind the complex, long legs stretching as he ran.

Win swiped a hand through his hair which, Rob noted, needed a cut. "Did you ever happen to notice how Mom's allergies only kick in when the issue is something she doesn't like or want to deal with?"

Rob made a noncommittal humming sound. If he wouldn't discuss his father with his mother, he certainly wouldn't discuss his mother with his brother.

After several moments of silence broken only by the brothers' footfalls and Charlie's panting after one of his sprints, Win asked, "So how's class?"

"Good. Very good actually. Great professor."

"Comp class, right? Do you have to write a lot?"

"A lot more than I'd like, but I think I finally figured out what she wants." Rob smiled to himself as he thought of Rachel explaining what Dr. Dyson expected, her lovely face so serious as she talked.

"You doing all right in it? I mean, I always hated having to write something, but I bet you're good at it."

Rob contemplated his brother. This interest in what he was doing and how well was both spooky and out of character. "Let's just say I'm okay."

They continued in silence. Rob knew he should try harder with his brother but every discussion followed the same pattern. Win complained about living with Mom and Rob told him to move out and Win said he didn't have the money and Rob told him to get a job.

"So do you think the Eagles stand a chance this year?" Win asked apropos of nothing.

Rob looked at his brother. "You really want to talk about the Eagles?"

Win shrugged. "They're as good a topic as anything."

"You drove over here and waited till ten o'clock at night for me to come home, and you want to talk football?"

"Why not? Isn't that what brothers do?"

Not these brothers. "Why are you really here, Win? This attempt at pleasant conversation is scaring me."

"Ha ha."

"Win." Rob laid a hand on his brother's arm, and they halted. "Why are you here? Is something wrong with Mom?"

"Can't I visit my brother if I feel like it?"

"Sure, if you ever visited him."

Rob could almost feel Win trying to get up the courage to say what was on his mind.

"Lend me a few thousand?"

Rob blinked. "No." No thought necessary.

"I've got to get out of the house. I've got to get away from her."

Rob stared at his brother. He did sound desperate. "No."

"Then let me live with you. You've got two bedrooms."

"No."

"Come on, Rob."

"Do you have a job, Win? Any kind of a job? An income? Are you even looking?" Rob knew his brother hadn't been looking. Mom delighted in keeping Rob up-to-date during her daily phone calls.

"He lies around all day and sleeps," she'd said today, disbelief in her voice. "Then he watches TV all night. It drives me nuts."

"So get rid of the TV," he told her. He knew he didn't sound sympathetic, but it was the same old, same old.

"How will I watch my shows if I do that?"

"Put the TV in your bedroom."

"We have three TVs."

"Sell two."

"To who?"

"Go on Craig's List."

"And have strangers in my house? No thank you. With my luck they'll rob me blind or maybe murder me."

"Come on, Mom. Don't you think you're getting just a bit carried away? Besides Win is there to protect you."

"Fat lot of good he'd be. He'd probably be asleep."

"Then I could come over when a buyer came."

"You'll be at work or class."

"Set a time when I'm free, Mom. We could make it work."

"Speaking of work, Win isn't and he's not looking."

Feeling as if he was batting his head against a brick wall just for the fun of it, Rob said, "Have you ever thought about not feeding him or doing his laundry or providing him a room rent free?"

"Of course I've thought about it, but he's my baby."

"Mom, he's a grown man, and I've got to go." The headache was a piercing dagger behind his left eye.

"But what am I to do with him?" she asked as he hung up. Hadn't he already given her the answer?

Now he asked, "A job, Win? Income?"

"What's that got to do with anything?"

The thing that frightened Rob was the fear that Win really, truly didn't see a connection between work and life.

"How would you pay your rent if you lived here? Your part of the utilities? Your part of the food?"

"You've got to pay those things anyway. My being here won't make that much of a difference."

Rob ground his teeth. "Of course it will. Aside from the increase in costs, it won't be my home anymore. It'd be ours, and I wouldn't have my privacy. And that privacy is very important to me."

"You'll never know I'm there."

"Win, you're up all night watching TV, and you sleep all day. I work regular hours. I don't want a TV blaring all night and you snoring all day."

"You won't even be there to hear me snore." Win smiled with his look-at-me-aren't-I-clever charm, but what he meant as a joke drew no laugh.

Instead Rob gave him a pained look.

"Okay, okay." Win waved his hand as if he was erasing his comment. "Bad joke."

"But true situation."

"I just live backwards because I'm bored and the best stuff is on at night. If I lived with you, I wouldn't be bored."

"You think I'm going to entertain you?"

"We could go out together. Go clubbing. Fun stuff."

Rob shook his head. "I'm not a clubbing kind of guy, Win. I'm boring."

"Come on, Rob. I'd be a good roommate. We could make it work." He sounded desperate.

"Win, I've been at Mom's. I've seen your messes all over the house. I'd be on your back all the time to clean up and you'd be on mine to lighten up."

"You *can* be a bit of a neat freak." Again the charming smile. "No offense intended."

"None taken. But I like neat. I learned it in the Army. And I would resent big time having you mooching off me."

"I wouldn't mooch." Win seemed offended at the idea.

"So you would pay for food?"

Win looked away.

"Job, Win. Job. Get one and then we'll talk." About how Win could afford his own place.

"You know, for a guy who calls himself a Christian, you're very selfish."

Was he? Maybe, but he wasn't about to enable Win's lack of purpose in life. "The answer is still no."

"But I can't stand living with her any longer."

"Then don't."

Win glared. "You don't understand!"

"You're right there."

"You're so lucky. You got away. You've been all over the world."

"In the Army, Win. Hardly a pleasure trip. And let me point this out to you: you could do the same."

"The Army? Are you kidding?" He looked horrified. "I'd never survive."

"Leaving home doesn't have to mean the Army, you know."

Since he didn't have a ready answer, Win didn't say anything.

By this time they'd circled the complex and were back at Rob's.

"I've got to go in." Rob clapped his hands for Charlie who came running. He knew dinner was coming. "See you, Win."

"You're going to make me go back to her?"

"No. Go get another place if you want. Crash with some friends." Why did tough love end up making a person feel like a jerk?

"Come on." Win smiled his most winsome smile. "You're not going to kick me to the curb."

"Nope. I'm going to tell you to go find a home of your own." Rob grabbed his backpack from the car. "See you later, Win."

"I'm your brother!"

"That you are. I love you, but you can't live here."

"You just want to keep your life to yourself just like you always kept your friends to yourself." Bitterness and anger sounded loud and clear. "You've probably got friends now that you don't want me to meet because you're afraid I'll win them away."

Rob stared in disbelief, not at Win's spiteful tone—he was used to that—but at what his brother had said. Did he really think that? "I'm trying to keep you away from my friends, am I? And I'm worried they'll like you more than me." The idea was absurd. Never mind that he hadn't done anything remotely social since he'd been home except eat out after class.

"Even when we were kids," Win said, his tone pettish, "you never let me play with you and your friends."

As Rob remembered it, Win tagged along everywhere, but this wasn't the time to correct his brother's revisionist memory.

"Two things, Win. First, petulance isn't a good look on you."

Win looked even more petulant.

"Second, you want to meet my friends? I'm more than glad to share. Come with me tomorrow. You'll have to help one of them move, but she's cute and you'll be happy to impress her, I'm sure."

Self-pity became wonder. "Really? I can come?"

Rob looked at his little brother. Didn't the man have a life? Friends of his own? "I'll pick you up at seven. Be ready."

Chapter 18

When Rob turned the corner in the rented pickup, he saw Rachel climbing out of her car. She wore a pair of jeans, and he realized it was the first time he'd seen her in pants. And a pretty sight it was with her long legs. He smiled in appreciation.

Amy was practically dancing down the outside stairs from her second floor apartment, all energy and enthusiasm. She wore jeans too, but somehow on her small frame they were just jeans.

"Which one's yours?" Win asked from his place in the passenger seat. Charlie sat at attention between them.

Rob threw the gear shift into park. "What?"

"Which girl's yours?"

Rob turned to stare at Win and found Charlie regarding him with interest. "Neither."

Charlie looked unconvinced.

Win was unconvinced too. "You think I can't tell you're interested in someone? Even Mom's picked up on it."

Rob felt a chill. "Mom thinks I have a girl?"

"Mom knows you have a girl."

"I haven't said anything. She hasn't said anything."

"Yet." Win laughed. "Be afraid. Be very afraid."

"Believe me, I am. Especially since I don't have a girl."

Win studied Rachel and Amy through the windshield. "It's the little one who can't stay still," Win said.

Wrong. "Why do you pick her?"

"Because you always like them perky."

Rob ran through the small list of women he'd dated in the last few years. Not a perky among them.

"Remember Missy the cheerleader?" Win ticked them off on his fingers. "And Brenda the majorette? Perky."

"That was high school, Win. I don't do perky so much these days." And here was part of the problem with his family. They all saw him as he'd been twelve years ago. He'd been home so little that they had no idea who he was these days.

"You like the quiet one with the pony tail?"

"The curly pony tail and the big brown eyes and the terrific figure and the gentle manner."

"Whoa!" Win looked at Rob. "You've got it bad."

"Maybe." But he was pretty sure Win was right. "But she doesn't know, so keep your mouth shut."

"Do I hear an 'or else' tacked on there?"

"You do."

"Then I've got to ask, 'Or else what?'"

Rob threw the truck in park. "Or else I'll make Mom kick you out."

"I'll move in with you."

"Not a chance. I already told you. You'll be homeless and forced to man up."

"See me quaking with fear." Win laughed. "I dare you to try. I'm her poor traumatized little boy, don't you know."

Rob looked at Win and saw a man he didn't understand. "How can you let her think that of you? Let everyone think that of you? You've let yourself become a cliché for failure to launch."

Win shrugged, unfazed. "Free food, free room, free-dom."

"I thought you hated it. Last night you certainly seemed to."

"It's a new day, and I got out of the house before she was out of bed. No complaints. No rants. Just me doing my own thing." With a self-satisfied smile he climbed from the truck.

Sometimes Rob wondered how he and Win could share the same DNA. They were so different. Back when things went bad with Dad, Rob reacted by proving he could manage on his own in spite of his hurt and bitterness. Win took the opposite tack and fell apart. He clung to their mother and became dependent. Twelve years later neither had changed.

Twelve years ago he decided to prove he wasn't his father. He was still trying to prove it. Twelve years ago as a fourteen year old, Win had fallen apart. The teasing and mocking at school, the seeing their father on trial, the visits to the prison had taken a terrible toll on him. But he was a man now and was choosing to stay stunted and dependent. And he was so charming about it, no one seemed to mind.

As he followed Win to join the girls, Rob worried again about what would become of his brother if he didn't make some changes—like get a full-time job and his own place. An acquaintance with Jesus wouldn't hurt either.

Amy bounced up and down in her excitement, her perkiness on full display. "Two guys! This is so great!"

Rob had to smile at her. When the semester started, he'd been planning to go to class and leave, nothing more. Get the credits and be closer than ever to the degree. Because of the little live wire and her coffee invitation, his life was richer and—he glanced at Rachel—showed a promise he'd never envisioned.

"My brother Win," he introduced.

"I see the resemblance." Amy pointed to their blue eyes and jaw line. "Both handsome."

Rob watched Rachel's slow smile of agreement, and her flush when she realized he was looking at her made him feel the morning was already a success.

Win was clearly taken with Amy. "Will I get arrested for underage stuff if I make a pass at you?"

Amy looked flattered. "Why don't you try and we'll see?"

"You might end up rejected but you won't end up in jail," Rob said. "She's twenty-five."

Win looked as unconvinced as Rob had been the night he and Amy—and Rachel—first met.

"I've seen her driver's license," Rob said.

"I'd have said she was fourteen, tops," Win said, then quickly added with a warm smile, "No offense intended."

Amy grinned back. "None taken. I put up with looking like a kid now because I know I'll look spectacular in thirty or forty years when all my friends are falling apart."

"And we will so resent you," Rachel said.

Amy just grinned and clapped her hands. "Time to get going, everyone."

"So we'll get to meet your family and see if the rest of them are as perky as you?" Win walked beside her to the truck.

"Nope. I picked today because none of them will be home. Better that way."

"Your family must be like mine." Win looked over his shoulder at Rob and grinned.

"Not a chance," Amy said. "I win any contest hands down. Besides your brother's a sweetheart. Right, Rach?"

Rob looked at Rachel for her reaction and saw only a slight, mysterious smile.

Amy pulled open the cab door of the pickup. "Rachel and I'll take the backseat."

"You'll have to," Rob said. "It's too small for Win or me."

Rob was pleased when he found he could see Rachel whenever he looked in the rearview mirror. Even when the two girls were involved in a conversation that excluded him and Win, he could enjoy her expressive face. It made the long trip seem short.

They pulled into Amy's hometown around one, and Rob's stomach was running on empty. "Where can we eat, Amy?"

"There's a café I've always wanted to eat at," she said with a bounce. "Sort of a bucket list thing. This'll be my one chance."

"Are they closing?" Win asked.

"Nope. It's in the next block, Rob." She directed him to a small storefront in the center of the town's block-long business district.

They walked into Maisie's Café and obeyed the sign that said Please Seat Yourself. Amy was practically vibrating with excitement as they slid into a booth. Rob made sure he sat beside Rachel, not a problem since Win homed in on the seat beside Amy.

"You have no idea how many times I passed this place and wanted to come in." She looked around with undisguised appreciation. "Isn't it pretty?"

It was a small town eatery, like hundreds of others Rob had seen. Obviously Amy didn't get around much.

"Looks nice," Rachel said with her gentle smile. "Smells good."

It did that. Rob's stomach growled in anticipation.

"Here you go," said a waitress wearing a shirt reading *Maisie's: nothing but the best.* She slid menus onto the table.

"Thanks, Pam." Amy smiled.

Pam looked at her with a frown. "Do I know—Amy? Amy Schreiber?"

Amy beamed and gave a little bounce. "Yep. It's me."

"Wow! You look…" She paused like she was looking for the best way to say something that could easily come out wrong. "You look great. Like real people, only cuter."

Amy glowed as she patted her cropped cut. "Thanks!"

"I heard you'd left town."

"I did. These are my new friends." She pointed to each in turn as she said, "Rachel, Rob, and Win."

"Isn't this the big weekend for, well, you know."

"Exactly. That's why we're here now."

Pam nodded in understanding. She took their orders and returned in record time with their food and drinks.

"Yum!" Amy all but licked her lips over the vegetable soup. Rob agreed it was good but hardly worth Amy's delighted reaction. It probably could have been tasteless and Amy would have thought it five-star. Eating here was somehow symbolic for her, and symbols of a new life should taste good.

"So does this little town have its own high school?" Win asked her as he watched a quartet of boys eating a mountain of food at the booth across the restaurant.

"The local kids get bused to a consolidated school."

"Long bus ride?"

"I think so."

"You don't know?"

"I was homeschooled."

"There was a time I wished I was homeschooled," Win said, a shadow passing over his face. "Kids can be pretty cruel."

Rob winced. Dad had been arrested in March. June and graduation came well before the trial. Not that the recriminations of those Dad had fleeced weren't painful enough to read or hear, but he'd escaped the worst of the mess by enlisting the day he graduated. Win hadn't been so lucky.

"I guess homeschooling can be good when it's done well," Amy said. "In my case, it was just a prolonged excuse for propagandizing my parents' warped opinions." She took a big bite of her sandwich and let out a long, "Mmm."

Rob studied the perky little blonde. He felt a wave of sympathy for her and the home life she'd been forced to endure. What had her parents been like? Survivalists? Neo-Nazis? Extreme environmentalists? Whatever it was, it had hurt her deeply.

"Does cyber schooling count as homeschooling?" Rachel asked, relieving the emotion of Amy's last comment. "That's how I did high school."

Rob pictured an intense girl staring at a computer screen, listening to a lecture by a person miles away or doing her math problems with fierce concentration. "Didn't you miss group activities—sports, drama, music, stuff like that?"

"I had plenty of interaction with people, believe me. Five brothers and two sisters."

"Eight kids?" Win stared at her. "*Nobody* has eight kids."

"I know lots of people with large families," she said.

"Me too," Amy said. "Our three girls were considered a poor showing."

"Well, there's just the two of us." Win pointed to himself and Rob. "And the way things turned out, it's a good thing."

Pam the waitress appeared with a hamburger wrapped to go.

Rob took it. "Thanks. Charlie will appreciate it."

"Everything was great, Pam." Amy grabbed the check and headed for the door. "Better than I ever thought."

Charlie, who had been waiting patiently tied to an inoperative parking meter, downed his treat in one gulp. Rob squeezed water from his bottle into the dog's mouth, and Charlie happily drank although he got as much down his front as down his throat.

Ten minutes later they pulled into the drive of a large gray farmhouse with white trim. The yard was neat, the walk lined with pretty gold and white flowers.

Rob opened his door and Charlie leaped over him, running full tilt for a cluster of rhododendron at the side of the house. Rob could almost hear the dog's sigh of relief as he assumed the position. A minute later the animal lowered his leg and tore in circles around the lawn.

Charlie ran exuberantly straight at Rachel. Rob pictured her being knocked flat on her back, Charlie standing over her like a conquering hero, drooling his victory and pleasure on her face.

Rachel didn't flinch. "Hey, big boy." She held out her hand and the dog came to a quivering stop. She rubbed his ears. With a great sigh he leaned into her leg for a longer scratch. She was the one who conquered.

Rob watched his dog and the woman he was pretty sure he wanted to refer to as his, and he felt a happiness that was a new sensation to him. Not that he'd been unhappy before Rachel. He'd felt satisfied in the service, useful, and fulfilled. He'd had good friends. This feeling was different. It made him want to smile.

Rob watched Amy climb slowly from the truck and stand on the walk staring at the house. She shuddered and wrapped her arms about her waist. "I shouldn't have eaten all those fries."

Win walked to her side. "Not a happy homecoming." Not a question; a statement and made with more compassion than Rob would have expected of his brother.

"Not a happy homecoming," she agreed. "It's harder than I expected. I thought I'd just run in, grab stuff, and go. No emotion but relief that I had escaped."

He nodded. "Memories. They get you every time."

"Memories." She shuddered again.

He threw his arm around her shoulders. "But we're here with you."

"Thanks." She dropped her head to his shoulder for a minute, then straightened. "Okay. Enough of that. Let's get this over with." She strode purposely up the walk.

Rob studied Win's back as he followed him to the house. Win had said exactly the right things to Amy, offering her the understanding she needed. He frowned. Maybe Win wasn't the only one with preconceived opinions.

Ouch.

Chapter 19

*R*achel watched Amy unlock the door. How brave she was being! Whatever went on here had hurt and hurt badly.

A brown and white beagle raced out as soon as the door opened. He ran to Amy and went crazy, jumping on her, making noises deep in his throat. Amy fell to her knees and hugged the animal who proceeded to lick away her tears.

"Oh, Bagel, I've missed you!" She buried her face in his neck. "I'll never leave you again, I promise. Don't you worry. I'm taking you with me."

"We're taking the dog with us?" Rob asked as Charlie returned from his trip inspecting the backyard.

Rachel looked at Amy and her dog in their frenzied embrace. "Do you really need an answer?"

"I hope her landlord knows."

"Bagel the beagle." Win grinned. "Cute. I wonder who came up with that?"

Amy rose with a final pat on Bagel's head. "It'd be nice if I could say I was, oh, thirteen, and thought it was so cute. I was twenty-two and still thought it cute."

She looked at the dog who sat at her feet with an adoring look on his face. "At least he's cute even if the name's dumb. Aren't you, baby?"

Bagel went into another paroxysm of joy at Amy's attention.

Amy laughed. "I rescued him without telling my father and

brought him home before he got back from work. Everyone was in love with the boy by the time Dad got here. Even Miss Evelyn who happened to be visiting loved him. It was too late to get rid of Bagel without having a bunch of weeping women." She grinned her impish grin, then turned solemn. "Dad never forgave me for outwitting him."

Amy bent, took the dog's face in her hands, and kissed his nose. "But the boy is worth every minute of the anger and abuse the man could dish out, aren't you, baby?"

Bagel kissed her back.

Rachel watched Amy and Bagel and glanced at Rob who was absently scratching Charlie's head. Maybe she should consider a dog. Not an outdoor dog like Pepper or Corny but an indoor one like these two. Maybe it'd help with the loneliness that sometimes plagued her, especially on the long winter evenings.

Amy moved away from Bagel, and he saw Charlie for the first time. Bagel started barking like a mad thing and a ridge of hair rose on Charlie's back.

Then again maybe she was better off petless.

"Stop it, Bagel! No barking," Amy ordered to no result.

Rob dropped to one knee and put his arm around Charlie's back. Charlie looked at him, uncertain. "It's okay, big man. He's a friend." He held out his hand to Bagel.

Amy dropped down beside Bagel and laid a hand on his back. "Shush, baby," she said quietly. "Shush. It's just Charlie." She held her hand out to the big dog.

The animals' original surprise and accompanying animosity defused, Bagel and Charlie began sniffing each other in the time-honored and ill-mannered method of dogs everywhere.

"Catastrophe averted," Amy said happily. "Let's get to work. It shouldn't take long."

Rachel followed Amy into the house. The entry hall held a closet which Amy opened. She sorted through the jackets and coats hanging there and pulled out three, a heavy down jacket, a gray wool pea coat, and a black fleece jacket.

"Cold weather's coming. I'm going to need these soon." She put them on the chair by the front door.

Off to the left Rachel glimpsed a neat living room full of furniture covered in a rather overwhelming brown plaid. A sculpted beige rug covered the floor, and sheer beige curtains hung at the windows. It wasn't as Spartan as an Amish living room, but it was somehow depressing. Or maybe Amy's comments about the place had caused her reaction. Either way she preferred her bare white walls and green shades.

"Come on," Amy said. "Let's go upstairs. That's where we'll find my stuff." She led the way and the others followed.

Pictures of groups of people lined the walls of the stairwell.

Rachel stopped and studied the groups of people crowded together in them. They looked very sober and stiff. "Are you in these?"

"Unfortunately, yes."

Win stopped and studied one picture. "Interesting looking group. A little old-timey with the long dresses and hair."

Amy snorted and kept climbing.

A long hall had several doors opening off it. As they walked past the first two, Rachel saw bedrooms done in basic furniture: a wooden twin bed, a matching dresser, a straight back chair. Plain bedspreads covered the beds, one blue, the other green. A wooden cross hung above each bed.

The rooms looked remarkably like hers at home except for the cross and the bedspreads. Rachel's bed had a lovely quilt done in calicos of soft blues, greens, purples, pinks, and yellows, more a quilt like those made for the tourists than for an Amish home. Rachel loved it because it reminded her of spring even in the middle of winter, and it kept her toasty even in the cold bedroom where her only heat was what her small kerosene space heater provided.

They passed a bathroom, and at the end of the hall Rachel could see the master bedroom with its large bed, again covered with a plain spread, this one gray. A square gray rug covered the floor.

Amy stood in front of a closed door.

"Your room?" Rachel could feel Amy's nervousness.

"My room." Amy reached out a hand that trembled slightly and pushed the door. Its hinges creaked as it slowly opened. Amy gasped.

The room was empty. No bed. No dresser. No rug. Nothing. Only the cross hung where the bed must have stood.

Amy walked in and turned in a circle. Bagel followed her and sat at her side. When she looked at Rachel and the men standing in the doorway, her eyes were tear-filled. "It's like I never lived here. Like I never existed."

"Oh, Amy." Rachel ached for her friend. She walked into the room and reached for her as she would one of her sisters if she were hurting.

Amy took a step back, hand held out to keep Rachel away. "Don't. I'll fall apart and weep all over you."

Rachel nodded. She understood that fragile edge of control.

Amy took a long shaky breath. "I thought Mom would keep my things safe. Or maybe Alice and Annie." She blinked furiously. "I should have known better. He always overpowers them."

Rachel felt her own heart break a bit more for her friend. In the doorway Rob and Win shifted uneasily at such raw pain.

"He thinks he beat me," Amy said, her voice suddenly hard even as tears continued to fall. "He made sure that if I ever come back, it'll be on my knees, begging him to take me in. First I'll have to beg to get in the door and then beg to have a bed to sleep in. He'd have given away the room itself if it weren't attached to the house."

Bagel leaned against her and looked up with sad eyes, like he knew what she was feeling and shared her sorrow.

Rachel couldn't resist. She rested a comforting hand on Amy's back, letting her know she wasn't alone.

"This is embarrassing." Amy drew a deep breath and exhaled slowly. "I bring you all the way up here to get my stuff, and it's not even here."

There was a knock on the front door and a voice called, "Hello?"

"I'll go," Rob said and went down the stairs, Charlie's nails snick-snicking after him on the wooden treads.

Rachel looked out the window and saw a white van with Animal Control painted on its side in black lettering. She looked at Bagel, the only animal she'd seen on the premises.

"Do you think he sold your things?" Win circled the room. "Maybe he just put them in the attic or the basement."

Amy brightened a bit. "Maybe. It's not like him to just give things away. If he put them in the attic, he'd be happy because I'd still have to beg to get them back."

Glancing out the window again Rachel watched a man in a tan uniform walk to the van. In his hand he held a long stick that had a flexible loop at one end, the kind she'd seen vicious dogs led away with. Again she glanced at Bagel who sat loyally at Amy's side.

Rob appeared in the doorway.

"Who was it?" Win asked when Amy didn't seem to notice his return.

"Nothing important. I told him he should talk to Amy's father, and he left."

When the van drove off, Rachel turned from the window and looked at Rob. He gave her a sad smile.

"Let's check the attic." Amy said with a clap of her hands, her usual verve replacing her distress. "This way."

She went to a door at the far end of the hallway, pulling it open and flipping on the light. Bagel raced up the steps, Charlie at his heels, and Amy and Win followed.

Rachel waited until Amy was out of earshot and then turned to Rob. "Animal control?"

Rob nodded. "Here for a vicious dog named Bagel. Its owner asked that the animal be taken while the family was away so the children wouldn't be traumatized."

She thought of Amy's affection for the little dog. Most Amish families saw their animals as working stock, not pets, but they wouldn't send a perfectly healthy dog to the pound where it might be destroyed. They certainly wouldn't lie and call a docile pet vicious. "How sneaky and cruel."

"What is it with fathers?" Rob muttered more to himself than Rachel.

Rachel, who had followed through on googling Rob's "notorious" father, hurt for him. "Too bad you don't know my father. He's the kind of man a father should be."

He looked at her with a light in his eyes that made her warm all over. "Maybe someday. Who knows?"

"Who knows" she whispered. And wouldn't that be a day.

She and Rob climbed to the attic where they found Bagel lying on a dog bed in the corner of the room. His chin rested on a scruffy looking teddy bear that had seen better days.

"He took the dog's bed and toy away because he was angry at me!" Amy knelt beside the dog and stroked his head. His tail slapped the bed. "All Bagel ever did was like me more than him."

And who could blame him? Rachel thought and immediately felt guilty. She didn't even know the man and she was judging him.

"Is this your stuff?" Win called from the far end of the attic which stretched the length of the house.

Amy hurried over and gave a happy bounce. "My bed, my bureau, all my stuff! Yes!"

"Tell us what to take, and let's get it onto the truck before your father comes home." Win rubbed his hand over the headboard. "I don't feel like meeting him today." He paused and then added, "Or any day."

Amy gave a shaky laugh. "That makes two of us, but not to worry. He won't be home until tomorrow evening. This is Meeting Weekend. He's busy listening to Miss Evelyn and Mr. Jerry harangue him, and he's liking it!" Her voice was equal parts disbelief and outrage.

Rob and Win clomped down the stairs with the headboard and footboard of Amy's bed. When they came back, they took the matching bureau. Rachel and Amy manhandled the mattress and box springs.

"Clothes?" Rachel asked as she stood panting by the pickup.

"I don't want most of them. They're embarrassing they're so ugly. Just look at the pictures in the stairwell."

When she went inside and studied the photos, Rachel saw Plain in the women's clothes though there were no head coverings. "Is your family some Plain sect I'm not familiar with?" In every Plain sect she knew of, the women wore head coverings.

Amy came to stand beside her. "I wish. That wouldn't be nearly as weird. They're part of this house church gone off the tracks. When I was a little kid, the group was fine. The people were strict but nice and normal. Jesus was the center of everything. Then Miss Evelyn and Mr. Jerry joined the group, and that was the beginning of going sour. They said God called them to the group to be its leaders and Scripture says you have to obey your leaders. Miss Evelyn said she was a prophetess sent to us by God."

"They just walked in and took over?" Rob asked. "No selection process of those worthy to lead like Scripture says?"

"I wonder about religion." Win stopped on the stairs behind the girls and studied the pictures. "It seems to make people go nuts."

"I guess religion can do that." Rob pointed to the pictures. "That's religion. Rules. Faith is different. Faith is believing, and it should be filled with grace, not rules, though things should be done decently and in order."

"If you say so." But Win's doubt was obvious.

Amy ran a finger over an image of herself in a group of about thirty people, adults and children. She wore a baggy dress and a frown and had her hair pulled back and falling long down her back. "You were supposed to wear your hair long until you married. Then you wore it up. That's Alice and Annie." She pointed to the girls on either side of her, both with hair hanging to their waists. "And that's Mama and that's my father."

Rachel thought Mama looked about as sad as a person could look, and Amy's father looked as stern and unbendable as the strictest bishop. She thought of Mom and Datt and knew she was blessed.

"When I look at these pictures," Amy said, "I have to keep reminding myself not to throw Jesus out with the bathwater."

"I thought that was Moses," Win said, and laughed at his joke. Amy just looked at him.

"You know—the bulrushes and all."

"I know. And you know exactly what I meant."

Win shrugged. "I just didn't expect you and Jesus."

"We're tight." Amy wrapped her fingers together to show how tight.

"Where's the picture taken?" Rob asked. "Looks like tents in the background."

"They take a picture every year at Meeting Weekend. They rent a private campground and have church all weekend. And I mean all weekend. No breaks. No free time. Church." She shuddered. "It was excruciating."

"You wore dresses camping?" Win said.

"Only harlots and whores wear pants." She looked at him. "Didn't you know that?"

"Then this should be a very interesting evening." He wiggled his eyebrows and glanced at her legs in their jeans.

Amy held up her index finger and shook it at him. "Unh-unh, wise guy. Remember, I didn't throw Jesus out."

Rob shot his brother a quelling look. "Easy, Win. I think we'd better get back to work. Personal things, Amy? Jewelry? Photos?"

"I took the photos I wanted when I left and I wasn't allowed to have jewelry. But I had a hope chest. It should be around here somewhere."

"As in I'm-gonna-get-married hope chest?" Win asked.

"It's loaded with the linens and dishes and pots and pans I was supposedly saving for the happy union with someone my father selected for me with the approval of Miss Evelyn and Mr. Jerry."

"He was going to pick your husband?" Rachel thought of Aaron and their courtship and engagement. Certainly they'd sought their parents' approval, but they chose each other first.

"Oh, yeah. Everything was his right as father. Children obey your parents and all that. That's why I had to get out before it was too late. First, I'm not a child anymore. I want to make my own choices. And, second, he'd settled on a guy Mr. Jerry suggested and planned to announce our engagement this weekend at camp. Miss Evelyn was going to bless us so everybody knew this was of God. Who cared what I thought?"

"Do I hear a touch of bitterness there?" Win asked.

"Oh, yeah, and more than a touch. 'He will be strong,' my father used to say, threaten really, because I needed someone who could force me to his will rather than my own sinful selfish desires. In other words, someone who will squash my tendency to think. After all, a man always knows best."

"Sounds good to me," said Win with a smile.

Amy scowled at him, then turned to Rachel. "Come on, there are some boxes of mine in the attic."

An hour later when they climbed back in the truck, Charlie took his seat in the middle of the front seat and Bagel settled in Amy's lap in the back.

"Sweet boy, you are free!" Amy fondled his ears. "Free!"

Rob turned the key and the engine throbbed to life.

Amy gave one final look at the gray house. "He often told us that if we ever defied him, we would never be forgiven. If we left, we could never come back."

"Isn't that what the Amish call shunning?" Win asked.

Rachel couldn't resist explaining. "Shunning is supposed to make the shunned person see his or her wrong and repent. It's a last resort and done with sorrow."

She thought of the people she knew who'd been shunned. Usually it didn't go that far when someone was confronted with a sin. They acknowledged their sin to the Gmay and everything was fine. When it went as far as shunning, the person often was too set in his wrong ways to return.

"With my father, it was strictly punishment," Amy said. "And humiliation."

"Law with no grace." Rob backed out of the drive.

"Exactly." Amy looked at the house with sad eyes. "I miss my mom. She's totally under my father's domination, but she loves us kids. I know I hurt her by leaving, and it makes me feel bad, but I had no choice. I couldn't let them eat me whole. I couldn't let them make me marry some guy I don't even know!"

"You never even met him?" Rachel couldn't imagine such a thing.

Amy shook her head. "He's from another house church that's as weird as ours."

"An arranged marriage." Win smirked. "I thought they only happened in romance novels."

"You read romance novels?" Amy looked scandalized.

"Mom does. And she tells me all about them."

"Another reason to get your own place," Rob said as he drove through town.

Win shrugged. "Small price for home cooked meals."

"I worry about my sisters," Amy said. "Will they be strong enough to leave or will they marry some guy Miss Evelyn and Mr. Jerry pick because they don't think they have a choice?"

"I'm sorry, Amy." Rachel gave her friend a hug. "Maybe someday you can help them escape if they want it."

"Maybe." Amy hugged Rachel back, holding on tightly, Bagel squished between them. "You guys have no idea what your acceptance of me means. That first night of class when I suggested coffee, I was scared to death."

"So was I," Rachel said. "And you seemed so cool and happy. I was glad someone so positive wanted to spend time with me."

Rob nodded. "I'd just visited my father and had an accident on the way home. I was tense and tight and needed that chance to relax and remember life could be normal after all."

"Huh," Win said. "I was probably playing Halo III with some guys from Japan or something, but I'd have come if I'd been invited."

"If I'd have known about you, I'd have invited you," Amy said. "And you're invited from now on."

"I'll happily leave the Japanese guys for time with you." Win turned and grinned at Amy.

Rob looked at Rachel in the rearview mirror and rolled his eyes.

Chapter 20

*S*unday morning was brisk, so Rachel grabbed the black shawl her sister Sally had knitted for her for Christmas. She wrapped it around her shoulders as she left the house. She'd doubtless shed it as the day progressed and the temperature rose, but it'd feel good in the meantime.

She walked to the end of the drive and waited for Abe and Emma Beiler, her brother-in-law and sister-in-law, who stopped for her on church Sundays so she didn't have to get her own horse from his comfy stall and pull the buggy from its shelter at the other end of the small barn. Since Aaron's death, Abe and Emma had taken her under their wing. Since they had no children of their own, Rachel sometimes felt she was their substitute child even if she was only two years younger than Emma.

Emma held a Tupperware container of pickled eggs, their crimson showing through the opaque plastic. On the backseat beside Rachel was another Tupperware container holding two pies. Rachel balanced her offerings for the post-service meal on her knee, the spicy cinnamon scent of the homemade applesauce fighting the acrid smell of fresh tomatoes sliced yesterday evening before she went to bed so there'd be no food preparation on the Sabbath.

As they pulled up to the Zook farm, Abe stopped to let the women out before taking the buggy behind the barn where the Zook boys would serve as hostlers for the day.

"Uh-oh, Rachel," Emma whispered as she watched a round woman

155

with several small children in tow. "Ada has the toys to keep the children quiet during service in a paper bag again. We must be careful not to sit by her or we'll never hear the sermon over the rattle of the bag."

"Emma!" Rachel bit her tongue so she wouldn't laugh.

Emma looked unrepentant. "You know it's true."

They put their food in the kitchen and took seats in the women's section as far from Ada as they could. Emma with the married women, Rachel with the single women.

Rachel loved the Gmay. She watched the benches fill with the one hundred and twenty or so in her district. These were the people she'd known her whole life, the people who knew her.

As the song leader called out the first song and the congregation began to sing slowly and in unison, Rachel sang along as her heart was torn.

What do I do? What should I do?

The first hymn ended and someone began *Loblied,* the traditional second hymn of every service. As the melody of praise slowly rose, Rachel thought on the words, especially the words about being devout and undeceived.

I am not devout. I am not humble. I am not godly. But I love Gott with all my heart and I want to be good.

To make matters worse, she knew Communion was coming soon. What would she do when it was time to affirm her commitment to Amish life, not just belief in Jesus but agreement with the Ordnung? She had fudged when all she was doing was taking classes online. She'd convinced herself such behavior wasn't all that wrong.

She studied her hands folded in her lap. Fudged? She'd lied. She hadn't been keeping the Ordnung then. And what about now?

Now she was going to Englisch college and wearing Englisch clothes, driving a car, and if she were totally honest, becoming attracted to an Englisch man. How could she affirm her commitment to the Gmay?

She looked around the room at these people she'd known all her life. She didn't want to lose them. She didn't want to lose this life. She knew what she should do.

But even as she sang and prayed, she knew she was going to class the very next night and out to the Star with Amy and Rob. She thought of the words Paul had written in the book of Romans centuries ago: *Oh, wretched man that I am.*

After service and the community meal, she staked a spot at the sink and washed everyone's dishes so she didn't have to deal with the attentions of any of the men. Her nails had never been so clean.

Eventually Abe and Emma took her home.

"Do you want me to mow your lawn for you? I could come tomorrow night," Abe said as Rachel and her empty dishes exited the buggy.

"Thank you, Abe, but I can do it. It doesn't take long." Her little push mower clipped the grass neatly as she walked it around the yard.

"But school has started and you must be so busy."

Rachel smiled. Abe was worrying too much about her again. "It has, but I'm fine. I have plenty of time. I thank you for the offer though."

After Abe and Emma disappeared from view and she took her dishes inside, Rachel walked down the road to Mom and Datt's house. The exercise felt good, but if she was honest with herself, she needed her parents. She felt so fragile inside, she needed their secure love.

As she neared the house, Levi came out of the barn riding one of the horses. He trotted down the lane toward her and stopped beside her. His brown hair hung below his black hat and his shirt tail was hanging out on one side. He seemed taller every time she saw him.

"Levi, why are you riding? It's the Sabbath."

He grinned at her. "I'm going to get a saddle with my produce stand money. Did you know the outhouses I've been building are making me a lot of money? The tourists love them. I don't know what they do with them after they buy them, but I don't really care."

"You're getting a saddle? What do you think you are? A cowboy?"

"I want to compete at the rodeo at the Yoders."

Rachel blinked. "The Yoders have a rodeo?"

"Every Thursday. You should go. You can watch Ruthie barrel race."

"Ruthie? Our Ruthie?" She tried to picture her demure little sister astride a horse and had a hard time. Imagining her racing around barrels was even harder. And what about modesty?

"Amish don't do rodeos."

"We may be the only ones who do," he said proudly.

"Pride, Levi."

"Yep." He grinned at her.

"Is this to be your running around?"

"Levi." Mom's voice was loud and clear. "I don't think that's currying the horse."

He grinned at Rachel. "Oops."

She grinned back. "Better get to it before Datt catches you."

"He'll never notice. He's reading the paper."

She laughed as she trailed him up the lane where she found Mom sitting in her rocker on the porch, her shawl wrapped around her shoulders.

Rachel took the chair beside her and they enjoyed the peace of the dying day together.

The silence was broken by the sound of an automobile coming up the lane.

"Who could that be? Tourists on the Sabbath?" Mom scowled.

"Only one car is that bad, Mom." Rachel smiled as Johnny's pathetic excuse for a vehicle pulled to a stop in front of the barn.

Mom got to her feet with a hand over her heart. "Oh, my! Datt, come out. Johnny is here."

Datt wouldn't come. Both Rachel and Mom knew it. He was always glad to see his wayward son on his infrequent visits, but he never rushed to him like Mom did. After all, Johnny had left. It was his responsibility to come to Datt, not the other way around.

Johnny strolled to the porch, his jeans low on his slim hips. He had on a short-sleeved plaid shirt, the kind that always made Rachel think Mennonite farmer. But Johnny was no Mennonite. He wasn't much of anything as far as she knew.

What the shirt indicated was that he'd dressed for the visit. Usually he wore old T-shirts with logos like Harley Davidson and Budweiser, John Deere and International Harvester.

So dressed up why? Johnny was her brother and she loved him, but he always had an angle. And he could be sly.

"Johnny." Mom kept her voice calm though Rachel knew her heart was pounding. Johnny was here. "I'm so glad to see you. Have a seat. Rachel will get you a glass of lemonade."

Johnny grinned as he sat. "I'd love that. I love your lemonade."

As Rachel rose, she thought *flatterer*. She walked inside. Datt quickly raised *Die Botschaft* as if he hadn't been straining to hear what was being said on the porch.

"Johnny's here," she announced as if he didn't know. "I'm getting him some lemonade. Want a glass?"

Datt didn't say anything.

"Come join us on the porch."

"Did you know the Reihls have a new daughter named Anna Mae?"

Rachel looked at Datt in exasperation. "I didn't."

"And Willis Yapp is in bed with sciatica."

Rachel sighed. German stubbornness. She carried Johnny's lemonade to him and settled to hear what he had to say. Whatever it was, she doubted that he'd be open about it. He'd back into it in his own time.

"How's the trailer?" Rachel asked. "Do I need to come and clean it again?"

Johnny shrugged. "It's a roof over my head."

"You should come home, Johnny," Mom said. "You know we'd love to have you."

"I love visiting the farm," he said, and Rachel thought, here we go. He was buttering her up for whatever was on his mind. He hated the farm. At least that's what he'd been saying for years.

"It's so peaceful here." He looked out over the barnyard with an affectionate—and to Rachel, suspicious—expression.

It was peaceful here unless you counted the tensions of weather and crop failure and heavy-duty labor and equipment that always needed repair and livestock that always needed feeding and milking and....

Mom nodded agreement.

He wants to come home. The thought popped into Rachel's mind and almost knocked her off her chair. She'd been expecting a request for money or something like that, but no. He wanted to be back on the farm. But why? She doubted he liked farming now any more than he had when he left all those years ago.

Johnny stood. "I think I'll go in and say hi to Datt. I bet he's reading the paper, right?"

"You know him," Mom said.

Johnny let himself into the house and Rachel heard him greet Datt and Datt's gruff hello.

"It's always so good to see him," Mom said. "I worry about him, and when he comes, then I know he's still all right."

Rachel nodded. *Be careful,* she wanted to say. *Something's up. He's got an ulterior motive.* Mom, who was as aboveboard as could be, wouldn't see hidden agendas. Even Datt, who was more worldly because of his business dealings with the Englisch, would probably not see through Johnny.

What did it say about her that she could? Was she sly too? Or worldly?

It shamed her to admit that yes, she was worldly and becoming more so every day.

"Did you hear his comments about the farm? Do you think he's ready to come home?" To Mom coming home was shorthand for assuming his Amish identity, complete with taking his vows.

"Liking the farm is still a long way from returning to the Gmay," Rachel cautioned.

"I know," Mom said, but Rachel could see the hope rising in her.

To Rachel's amazement, Johnny struggled through a full fifteen minutes with Datt. She couldn't imagine what they talked about given their lack of converging activities and thoughts, but she had to give him credit for persevering. She smiled at him as he came back out, expecting him to leave, but he surprised her and took a seat beside Mom again.

"Datt told me about some man named Reuben Miller in Iowa," he told Mom.

"Maybe a relative?" Mom said.

Johnny shrugged. "Who knows. There are too many Amish Millers to count, and we're probably all related somehow. Anyway he was having trouble with two horses that wouldn't get along. One kept biting and kicking the other, so he tied them together face-to-face. They were too close to bite or kick. Did you ever hear such a thing?"

"I did not," Mom said. "You shouldn't make up stories, especially on the Sabbath."

"I didn't make it up. It was in *Die Botschaft*. If it's a story, then Rueben Miller made it up."

"He would never, not for the paper." Mom looked offended on Rueben Miller's behalf even though she didn't know him, or maybe it was the reputation of the newspaper she felt strongly about. "So how does the story end?"

"After the horses stared at each other, ears back, for a while, Rueben turned them loose in the pasture and chased them. They ran together, then raced each other. He did the same thing a couple of more times, and now they get along. He wondered if people who didn't get along would benefit from the same treatment." Johnny's grin was wide.

Mom slapped gently at his arm. "I must read that story for myself."

"Walk inside and Datt'll tell you all about it."

"That is why I sit out here. I'll read it for myself."

Rachel listened and squirmed. Whatever Johnny was up to, she didn't want him to hurt her parents.

The door flew open and Abner walked out, rubbing the sleep from his eyes. Service was long for him, and he always took a nap on meeting Sundays though he didn't most other days.

"I don't want a nap," he'd usually say. "I'm four." Every day but meeting Sundays.

He spotted Johnny's lemonade glass. "I'm thirsty."

"Hey, guy." Johnny held out his hand down by his knee.

Abner studied it a minute, then walked over and brought his chubby little boy's hand down on Johnny's hard adult one. "High five, Johnny."

"That's a low five, kid, because our hands are down low."

Abner frowned. "High five?"

Johnny raised his hand so Abner had to go on tiptoe to reach it. Abner slapped it again and giggled. "High five."

"High five," Johnny agreed as Abner leaned against his knee. The little boy looked at Mom and Rachel. "Lemonade?"

Chapter 21

Friday Rachel walked to her car in the Star's lot feeling cheerful and happy in spite of the rain. Another week had passed, and it had been good. Both Monday and tonight Dr. Dyson wove a rich tapestry of ideas and thoughts in new patterns and designs; concepts Rachel could think about for hours.

In her real life she enjoyed her school kids more every day, teaching the little ones, trying to challenge the older ones. It could get tricky at times, like when one of the older boys asked, "Where did you get those pictures of galaxies like that? I want to see more." She couldn't answer, "The internet," though that was where she found them. Fortunately she had a library book with similar pictures she could show him.

"See you, Rachel," Amy called as she ran through the weather to her little car. "I'll give you a call about doing something tomorrow night."

Rachel tried to balance her backpack and her umbrella so she'd have a free hand to wave. As she did, she realized her backpack was unzipped and the AlphaSmart Amy had been playing with was back in the Star.

"Rats." She turned and started back to the diner.

"Forget something?" Rob asked, half in, half out of his car.

"I left the AlphaSmart on the table."

She ran through the puddles and stood dripping on the rug just inside the diner's door. Betts was carrying her AlphaSmart to the front desk.

"I figured you'd be back sooner rather than later." She held it out to Rachel.

"Thanks, Betts." Rachel tucked it carefully into her backpack and zipped it closed.

"Drive carefully. It's a nasty night."

She ran back to her car, her umbrella keeping her dry at least from the waist up. She pulled open the door and climbed in, trying without success to close the umbrella without getting wet. She dropped it in the passenger foot well. She slid in the key, turned it, and the motor caught. So much easier than getting Rusty all hooked up and making the poor animal trot down the road in the rain.

She headed for the exit and frowned. Something was wrong. The car wasn't responding as it should. The wheel pulled and the steering felt strange.

She threw the gear into park and climbed out, once again holding her umbrella over her head. What should she do? If there was something wrong with the motor, she was helpless. Or was it a flat tire? That wasn't as mysterious as a motor issue, but she would be just as helpless. Max had never taught her that part of having a car, and she'd never thought about it. For a smart person, she'd been very dumb.

She walked slowly around the car and found the problem. The front passenger side tire was flat.

She stared at it, then at the cars in the lot, and finally she scanned the diner. Patsy, Betts, and two other servers, both women, were in there as well as some hearty patrons who had braved the weather. Did any of them know how to change a tire? She made a face. She couldn't ask them, not in this weather. She wouldn't have the nerve even if the sun was shining and the birds singing. It was too presumptive.

She went to the trunk. That's where tire changing stuff was kept, right? She hated the feeling of helplessness. She hated the feeling of inadequacy.

She hit the icon on the key fob that showed a picture of a car with the trunk lid up. There was a click as the lock disengaged and the lid started to rise. When it stopped, she lifted it the rest of the way. She leaned forward to protect the interior from the rain and examined the contents. There was a tire. Good. The only difficulty was she had no idea how to get the bad one off and the good one on.

Rob would know. She should call him and he could tell her step-by-step.

She lowered the lid until she heard it click shut, then hurried to the driver's seat. She climbed in and grabbed her backpack. She was pulling her phone free when a car drove into the lot.

The headlights blinded her as the car drove directly to her. Suddenly she felt very vulnerable. She was the only person in the empty lot in the rain in the dark. It was what she got for not being the good Amish woman she should be. If she was obeying the Ordnung, she'd be home, not here. She'd be dry, not wet. She'd be safe, not feeling exposed and in danger.

She hit the lock buttons. Could she drive away on a bad tire even if it was difficult? Would that ruin the car? Or maybe she could just blow the horn and the people in the diner would hear and call for help.

The car shuddered to a stop beside her and the driver's window came down. Rob peered at her through the rain.

Relief made her weak. She fumbled with her own window.

"I had to come back to make sure you were okay. I had a hunch, an instinct you might need help."

"You're right. I do. I have a flat tire."

"Ah." He nodded, his hunch confirmed. "Which one?"

"Front passenger."

"Okay, let's fix it."

Just like that her problem went away.

He positioned his car so his headlights shone on the collapsed tire. He climbed into the weather, pulling on a plastic rain poncho. It billowed around him, falling to his hips. He pulled the hood of the poncho up, but it refused to stay on his head. At the slightest movement, it slid off. He gave up trying to make it stay. "At least my shirt will stay dry."

"I've got an umbrella." She reached for it.

"That's okay; don't bother. I need both hands free. Pop the trunk, will you?" He walked to the back of the car.

She climbed out, her umbrella blooming above her, and hit the fob. There was no way she could sit in the car and wait while he got wet on her behalf.

"Get back in the car." He made shooing motions. "No use both of us getting drenched."

What he said made sense. "I can't. What can I do to help?"

He looked at her. "Ever change a tire?"

She shook her head.

"Then I'll teach you how, but you should join triple A."

"Okay." She made a mental note: google triple A.

He pulled out the tire and it bounced on the asphalt. "Want to grab the jack from the clip there?"

She grabbed everything that was secured in the trunk by a clip and lugged the heavy stuff to the front of the car. Rob went down on his knees and got to work. Rachel could almost feel the chill moisture seeping into his denim-covered legs.

"Whoa." Rob sounded surprised. "Whoever put these lugs on last really tightened them. Even if you'd known what you were doing, Rachel, you probably couldn't have budged them." He grinned at her. "You don't have to feel guilty or inept anymore."

"What makes you think I feel guilty and inept?" She sounded defensive.

"It's written all over your face. Plus you don't like not knowing how to do something, right?"

How did he know her so well? "Okay. I'll no longer feel stupid and inept. I'll feel weak and puny because I couldn't have moved the lugs." Ten minutes ago she hadn't known that lugs existed.

He laughed and used all his considerable strength. Finally the lug nuts loosened. He took considerable care that the jack was positioned correctly and began ratcheting the car off the ground.

"Here." Rob handed her a lug nut. "Hold tight." He handed her another and another and another. "Don't lose them. We don't want to search for them under the car because that's where they always roll. Belly crawling in weather like this is nasty."

Rachel held the lug nuts carefully while the old wheel came off and the new slid on.

"One at a time now." He held out his hand.

In no time he was lowering the car and packing up the jack. She walked to the trunk beside him, umbrella covering neither of them effectively. Water dripped from his hair, running down his face and neck. He had to be wet under his rain poncho. It would be her fault if he got a cold. Her own hair was so thick it protected her though her face felt covered with moisture. A facial given by nature. She smiled at the thought.

"I'd still be sitting here trying to figure out what to do if it wasn't for you, Rob. Thank you so much!"

He held up a hand and smiled his charming half smile. "I'm glad I could help, pretty lady."

Pretty lady! She felt her cheeks grow hot and gave a tentative smile back.

He reached out suddenly and caught a handful of her hair, letting it wind itself around his finger. "I love the way your hair curls in the rain." He lifted his eyes from her hair and stared directly at her.

She couldn't breathe as she stared back. The moment was intimate, just the two of them caught close in a private rain world. It might just be pheromones or endorphins or some other hormones like the websites said, but the emotional tug was real. Very real.

"Thank you," she managed to whisper when she finally drew a breath. She longed to push his dripping hair off his forehead but didn't have the nerve.

His eyes lowered to her lips. She licked them in response.

A woman's laughter sounded as the diner's door opened.

Rachel blinked. What was she thinking? She spun to open her door and jerked, caught short by his grip on her hair.

"Sorry." He released her and stepped back, now completely exposed to the rain.

She climbed in and slammed her door. She threw the umbrella onto the floor and stared at the steering wheel without seeing it. After a minute she forced herself to look up at him, still standing in the rain. She gave a small smile, a little nod, and, heart thundering, drove away to safety.

Chapter 22

Monday evening Johnny pulled open the Star Diner's door and held it as Bennett and Merle shoved their way through. The evening was young, only 8:30. The Star didn't serve beer, but it had great food. They could go somewhere else to drink after they ate.

"Great fried chicken!" Merle said when he suggested they come here. "And fresh made real mashed potatoes!"

"You miss your mama's cooking," Johnny teased.

"I do miss her cooking," Merle agreed. "That's why I go home every Sunday for her big dinner. Of course she wants me to go to church first, but she can't make me. I try never to be too hung over. Makes her too sad."

"Aw, the boy loves his mama." Bennett was vocal about not liking his grumpy, critical mother, not that Johnny blamed him.

"I do," Merle said. "Love my mama and her cooking."

Johnny studied his new friend. Merle was from a family as religious as his, but Englisch. He hadn't realized Englischers could be as fanatical as the Amish. "My mom's a good cook too."

"Ah, good Amish cooking." Merle looked at him. "Do you go home for meals? You're not shunned or nothing, are you?"

Johnny shook his head. "Never baptized, so not shunned."

"So do you go home?"

"I go home as in stopping by for a visit. I was there last Sunday." And it hadn't been too bad. Of course almost an hour was a long way from living there.

Living at the farm had seemed the logical thing to do when Mick was banging on his door last week, but the passing of time made the threat seem less real. They weren't going to kill him. He couldn't pay them back if he was dead. They just wanted to scare him—which they did.

Then too, the more he thought about it, the work and the love at the farm were more than he wanted to deal with, especially the love. Hiding from Mick was less work than holding off Ma's grasping for his soul. He'd visit more often just in case things got worse with Mr. Sherman, but he didn't think they would, especially if he stayed out of sight. After all, out of sight, out of mind.

The Star was busy, but they didn't have to wait. The hostess smiled as she handed them menus.

"Don't need one," Johnny said as he eyed the buffet.

"Good choice," she said and hurried off to seat others.

"Did you see her lookin' at you, Johnny? It's your tattoos," Merle said. "They scared a sweet thing like her. That's why she ran off."

"Ha." Johnny felt offended. There was not one single scary thing about him. His tats were small and half hidden by his shirt sleeve. He was clean shaven and rosy-cheeked. Adorable. Didn't the girls at Corner Bob's always say that?

Now Merle, with his long hair, leather jacket, and biker-dude attitude? Or Bennett and his shaved head, handlebar mustache, and perpetual frown? Scary.

The three of them hit the buffet, picking it over as thoroughly as a cloud of locusts might. With heaped plates they slid back in their booth.

An Amish girl approached them hesitantly, pitcher of sweetened tea in hand. "More?"

Johnny was surprised to see her this far from what he thought of as Amish country. He wasn't aware of any Amish community this close to Lyndale. Someone must have driven her here. She held out her pitcher of tea.

"Mft," Johnny managed around a mouthful of pork and sauerkraut.

Merle and Bennett nodded, their mouths too full for even a mumbled noise.

"Excuse me," said the man at the table across the aisle. They all looked at him, but he was looking at the Amish girl. *Tourist*, Johnny thought with disdain. As if the camera in his hand wasn't sign enough, he was holding it out to the Amish girl.

"Would you mind taking our picture?" He indicated his family.

The girl looked at the camera as if it were a snake poised to bite her. She seemed momentarily paralyzed by the request.

Johnny swallowed the pork and sauerkraut and held out his hand. "I'll take it for you."

The Amish girl looked at him as if he'd saved her life. She fled, pitcher of tea held high for protection like an old Anabaptist might have held a Bible on his way to the flames.

The tourist looked after her, confused, but as Johnny took his camera, the girl was momentarily forgotten. The man and his family of wife and three kids smiled for Johnny and the camera, and Johnny took two pictures which the man checked and approved.

"Thanks," he said and looked across the room where the Amish girl was pouring more tea. "I did something wrong?"

Johnny smiled at the guy's ignorance. "Graven images." He pointed to the camera.

The man's eyebrows shot up. "Oh."

His kids laughed, and his wife said, "I told you not to bother her."

Johnny slid back into his booth and grabbed a drumstick. He took a bite as he stared across the room where the Amish girl was just finishing topping off beverages. He squinted. He blinked several times. He tilted his head. The view never changed.

Was that his sister Rachel having dinner just like him? It was! And just like him she was wearing Englisch clothes and eating with Englischers. Rachel. His sister! Englisch clothes. Englisch company. And her hair was down. Unbound. No kapp. And she was with some guy and another couple. A double date?

The chicken caught in his throat as Johnny watched her laugh at something the guy seated beside her said. He leaned in as he talked, his shoulder resting against Rachel's, and Rachel didn't move away. What was that action?

He'd always thought Rachel was pretty, even when he was a kid and knew thinking about outward appearances instead of the inner heart was vain and unworthy. But she *was* pretty. Put her next to Sally and Ruthie, and Rachel drew the eye. It was the reddish tint to her thick hair and the way it insisted on curling on her forehead no matter how severely Ma combed it back and rolled the sides.

Hanging long, all that curl broke loose, and her hair was breathtaking. *She* was breathtaking. The guy she was with slid his arm along the back of the booth and dropped it casually onto Rachel's shoulders. Again she didn't seem to mind.

Merle followed his intense gaze. "Whoa! Who's that? She's gorgeous."

Bennett looked and his eyes went wide. He spun to Johnny, his mouth open to tell Merle just who that was.

Johnny shook his head. *No*, he mouthed, desperate for a reason he couldn't articulate. *No!*

Bennett looked uncertain but shut his mouth. He swiveled to look at Rachel again as if he had to make certain he was seeing who he thought he was seeing.

Merle's eyes narrowed. "I know those two guys." He whistled and smirked. "So he's back in town. What do you know?"

"What?" Johnny looked at the guy sitting too close to his sister, completely absorbed by whatever she was saying. "What do you know about them?"

"Went to high school with them. I was a year or two behind the older one and a couple of years ahead of the younger one." He nodded his head to the men across the restaurant. "What a mess when the story broke in the paper. Talk about how the mighty are fallen!"

Johnny's stomach pitched so wildly he could barely get the mouthful of baked limas down. "What do you mean, fallen? What'd he do? They do?" And did Rachel know?

"Not them. Their father. As far as I know, he's still in jail."

"Jail?"

"He was a money guy who stole from his clients. Stole lots of money. Big deal on TV and in the papers. I think Rob over there went into the Army to get away from it all. Win, the one sitting beside the little blonde, stayed at home because he hadn't finished school yet."

Rachel's guy was or had been in the Army. The Army! Not that he thought anything bad about Army guys, but Rachel and her innocence! Just last Sunday she'd sat on the porch at Mom and Datt's in her regulation clothing. She'd attended Gmay, sat for three hours singing songs that lasted fifteen minutes each and listening to sermons that lasted an hour. And now she was hanging out with a guy who had been in the Army?

He glanced at the Amish girl with the tea. Rachel undoubtedly felt safe so far from home, but who knew when other Amish might pop up. And someone was bound to recognize her sooner or later.

As he and the guys left the restaurant, Bennett crowded close, letting Merle walk ahead. "Aren't you going to talk to her?"

Johnny shook his head. "Not now."

"But—but don't you want to know what she's doing here? I do."

"None of your business, Bennett," Johnny hissed. "I mean it."

Bennett looked back at the restaurant as if he could see Rachel through the walls. "Who'd have ever thought Rachel—"

Johnny grabbed Bennett's shirt front. "You didn't see her, Ben."

Bennett frowned. "Of course I saw her."

"You. Did. Not. See. Her."

"You mean I shouldn't tell I saw her."

How to make Bennett understand? "It's Rachel, Ben. Rachel. She's never done anything wrong in her whole life."

"Yeah, so why's she here? Dressed like that? With two Englisch guys and girl?"

Johnny shook his head. If there was one thing he never thought he'd ever see it was Rachel doing something wrong.

Not that what she was doing was wrong wrong. It was Amish

wrong. And Rachel was a good Amish girl. She was the one who always did what was expected and seemed to enjoy it. She was the one who was kind and humble and helpful and peaceable and all the other good-girl words.

"We going to Bob's for the night?" Merle asked, car key dangling from his finger as he waited impatiently for Johnny and Bennett to catch up. "There's a darts tournament I want to get in on. I'm winning tonight, so put your money on me."

"You say that every night." Bennett pulled open the passenger door. "And I keep being stupid enough to believe you. But not tonight. I'm keeping my cash in my pocket."

Johnny stood by his car only half listening. Rachel was back there with some unknown guy who was obviously leading her astray. As her brother, he had to protect her, save her.

"You guys go on," he said. "I'll catch up. I got something I got to do first. It won't take long."

Bennett got this I-got-it look that made Johnny's insides shudder. The guy might be a loyal friend, but he was stupid about keeping his mouth shut.

"Come on, Merle." Bennett contorted his face in Johnny's direction in what Johnny thought was supposed to be a wink. "Let's go. He'll catch up."

After Merle and Bennett drove off, Johnny sat in his car and stared at the restaurant door and waited. Sure enough, it wasn't long before Rachel and the guy—Rob, Merle had called him—came out. She was smiling, and he was walking close beside her, his hand on the small of her back. The other couple came out too, laughing about something, but Johnny didn't care about them.

Rachel wore a short grey jacket that looked appropriately Amish, but the pink scarf she had looped around her neck wasn't Amish any more than the slacks she wore.

Johnny had felt bad for Rachel when Aaron died. He was a nice guy, not very exciting, but he seemed to love Rachel. Johnny never quite understood what Rachel saw in him, but he was a decent guy. Amish to his toenails.

He had expected her to get remarried a year or two ago to some other good Amish guy, but no. Why hadn't some man grabbed her up? She was pretty and kind and smart and she could cook at least passably. He sat up straight as a new thought struck.

Too smart? Surely there was an Amish man out there who wasn't put off by her brains.

He knew she used to sneak down to Max's and use her computer. Even Ma and Datt knew it. But she stopped when she was baptized, didn't she? She didn't go when she was married, did she?

Another thought had him blinking in shock. What if she met Rob on some computer dating site? He wanted to laugh aloud at the absurdity of the idea, but was it that ridiculous? He knew several guys who met girls that way. He'd thought about it himself on lonely nights except his heart belonged to Becky even if she didn't want it.

But the guy was local. Merle had said. Not a dating site. So where did she meet him?

Rachel and Rob walked to a black Camry. He held the door for her as she got in the driver's seat. Then he made a lock-the-doors motion before he got into the SUV parked beside her. How sweet.

Wait a minute! The driver's seat? Rachel knew how to drive a car? Johnny almost swallowed his tongue.

The Camry began to move and the SUV followed to the exit. There Rachel turned one way and Rob turned another.

Johnny was torn. Who should he follow? The guy. He knew where Rachel would end up. He could tackle her any day. Rob was another story.

They drove to an apartment complex not too far from Wexford College. Rob climbed out, pulling a backpack out behind him. He walked to a unit and unlocked the door. Immediately a large brown dog of indeterminate parentage raced out and squatted. Rob laughed and disappeared inside, leaving the door open. The dog finished his business and ran inside. Both man and dog reappeared, and Rob cleaned up the dog's mess. He walked to the complex's trash area and disposed of the little baggie. The dog pranced happily at his side.

The pair circled the complex twice, the dog running ahead, then circling back, running ahead, circling back. By the time they went inside, Johnny figured the dog had run a mini-marathon.

He drove slowly toward the Irish Shamrock. It wasn't Corner Bob's, but Mr. Sherman didn't sit at the back table with Mick on a chain beside him. He thought as he drove. He knew where this Rob guy lived. Knew he had a dog. Knew his sister dressed Englisch to be with him.

What he didn't know was what it all meant.

Chapter 23

Rachel lay in bed long after midnight, staring at the ceiling. Something had changed between her and Rob tonight. Hints of the developing tension had shown themselves Friday at his rescue in the rain. They had become more than hints tonight. Neither she nor Rob had said anything, but the air had become thick with possibilities.

And that was the problem. There were no possibilities. There couldn't be possibilities. She was Amish. He was Englisch. She had taken her vows. He hadn't. Woudn't. Couldn't. He was an Army veteran and she believed in non-violence. They were totally incompatible.

And yet…

When he had leaned in and let his shoulder settle against hers as they ate, she'd made believe nothing of note had happened, but she hadn't moved away. Instead she'd gotten a funny yet wonderful feeling in her stomach. It had been so long since a man had touched her. She'd forgotten how unsettling and how exciting it was. When his arm settled around her shoulders, she'd felt the affection in it. When his hand found hers under the table, she'd turned hers palm up so he could hold it. Even when he walked her to her car with his hand on the small of her back, she'd tingled. Tingled!

Then he suggested they go to a movie, just the two of them. She hadn't known what to do. On one hand she wanted to yell, "Yes!" On the other, how could she possibly do such a thing? It was one thing to go to class. There was purpose there. A goal.

But a movie? Talk about letting the world invade your life! She knew Sally and Ruthie had gone during their running around. In fact Ruthie still went though she was talking about taking her vows, and that would put an end to such activities. But she'd never gone until Amy coaxed her into that first transgression just a couple of weeks ago.

She'd seen movies on television at Max and Buddy's when she was younger. When she and Ashley were friends, they sat together watching the Disney movies on rainy summer afternoons. Cartoons or real life, she loved them.

So, really, a movie was just a big TV.

But this movie would be quite something more. This would be an official date with Rob. What scared her most was how much she wanted to say yes. She had to say no.

Then Rob had said, "My last few years have been hard and lonely. Only the Lord has gotten me through. Say yes, Rachel. I need a relaxing night with someone who has no agenda, someone I can enjoy." He gave her that wonderful smile of his. "Someone sweet like you."

And as he tucked her into her car, she found herself giving him Max's address. His pleasure at her acceptance had brightened her heart and twisted her conscience.

Now staring into the night, she desperately tried to recall Aaron. His face refused to come into focus, and she was forced to face a truth she had always denied. She hadn't loved Aaron, not really loved him as he deserved. She'd liked him, respected him, enjoyed him, but she already had stronger feelings for Rob than she ever did for her husband.

The thought filled her with shame.

She threw back the bedding and stood, groping for her flashlight. By its beam she made her way downstairs. In the kitchen she filled the kettle and put it on the propane stove to heat. She got a mug and a bag of chamomile tea. The clock on the wall read 12:35. She was going to be so tired tomorrow at school!

She considered her twenty-four students, all from families she'd known her whole life. They were obedient children, trained at home and at church where they sat through the three-hour service from the time they were babies, yet they were full of mischief and adventure. Teaching them was such a privilege.

But was it enough?

She thought of Dr. Dyson, who clearly loved teaching too. What was it like to teach more than rhymes and arithmetic and geography? What was it like to read papers that had new ideas and even ideas you thought were wrong?

She stilled. Maybe it wasn't the simple subject matter she taught that was bothering her. Maybe it was the homogeneity of the thinking. Certainly the Amish way of thought had great value, but what about the way the rest of the world thought? Was everyone wrong but her People?

The churning in her stomach intensified, and she knew it would take more than a cup of tea to still it.

The kettle whistled, and she rose to fill her mug. Her bare feet were cold, so she carried her tea up to the bedroom and climbed in bed, resting her back against the headboard. As she drank her tea and warmed her feet beneath her colorful quilt, her mind whirled.

She was caught between two worlds, and it was her own fault. Her pride and arrogance led her to reach beyond.

She held out her hand and studied it in the flashlight's beam. Surely there should be something different about it. After all, as part of that reaching beyond, Rob had held it.

It looked just as it always did.

So why did she feel so different?

She remembered when Aaron singled her out. She was twenty and it seemed all her friends were getting engaged and married. She worried about being unmarried maybe for life, but she didn't know how to make the boys like her. She was quiet around them, unable to think of clever things to say. When one did begin a conversation, he soon drifted away because she asked thought questions: What did he think about the safety of buggies on high-speed roads? Should there be an option for more education if a student wanted it? Had he ever thought about learning Spanish since more and more Hispanic people were moving to the area? Did he ever worry about the damage rumspringa did to some like Johnny?

Aaron started talking to her at sings and volleyball socials. When the youth had a huge gathering at the park, he'd asked if he could pick her up and take her. She hadn't even realized it was a date until Miriam told her.

"I thought he was just taking me so you and Jonah could be together," Rachel said.

"It does have that effect, but he's coming for *you*," Miriam answered.

When she asked her thought questions of Aaron, he turned them to her. "What do *you* think, Rachel? You're a very smart girl. Should rumspringa be outlawed?"

When she told him her opinions, he just nodded and asked her to next week's social.

Maybe she married him because he accepted her, prickly mind and all. When he told her he loved her, she believed him. When he asked her to marry him, she agreed. He wasn't threatened by her, and she was threatened by a life alone.

Poor Aaron. He gave everything he had, and she only gave some, though she hadn't realized it until Rob. From the first night when he walked into class grumpy and damp, she had been drawn to him. It was ridiculous. It was scary. It was impossible.

How did you know if you loved someone? It was easy to know how to love one another in the community sense. Treat them well. Help them when needed. Pray for them. But affection between a man and a woman had always baffled her. How did you know? She thought she knew with Aaron.

Her brother Jonah loved his Miriam and she loved him back. You could see it in the way they looked at each other. There were also surreptitious touches as if they needed that physical contact for all to be well.

Mom and Datt didn't touch in public, even at home, but they were older, married for almost thirty years. Showing overt affection wasn't the Amish thing to do. Aaron had followed the same custom, touching her only in private. She had been happy with that. He had kissed her, made love to her, and she had been compliant. But she hadn't yearned.

She'd thought that was fine, maybe even good. No temptation.

But now there was Rob and there was yearning. There was temptation. There was strong emotion that grew stronger every time she saw him and even when she only thought of him. How strange that Amy could see right away that he liked her. Now she knew too, and she was more confused than ever.

She set her mug on the bedside table and got up again. In the bathroom she opened the medicine cabinet. A bottle of aspirin sat beside a tube of ointment for sore muscles. She poured out two aspirin and swallowed them with a glass of water. She went back to bed and finished her tea.

Finally about 1:30 she fell asleep, her heart as conflicted as ever.

⊙⅏⊙

Rob stood at his bedroom window and stared out at the dark commons area between the buildings. Hope nibbled at his heart, and it scared him badly. Too many things had gone wrong in his life and made him afraid to hope. The disappointment when dreams didn't come true was too painful.

But she hadn't squirmed away when he leaned into her. She hadn't pulled away when he put his arm around her. She'd held his hand, spearing her fingers between his. Hope kept rising in spite of his fear.

She was exactly what he'd been looking for. Not only was she beautiful; she was kind and warm and smart, whip smart. He'd about given up thoughts of finding such a perfect woman, at least perfect for him.

Lord, protect me if I'm not reading things right here.

There was a wonderful freshness to Rachel, an innocence that was such a contrast to her keen mind. She fascinated him. No artifice. Openness. Honesty. And she loved God.

What more could he ask?

Chapter 24

*W*ednesday night Rachel stood in line with Rob as he bought tickets for the movie. She felt a twinge of guilt about being there but more a thrill of anticipation. All the people, all the color, all the excitement made it hard for her to keep still. She felt like Abner in church, struggling to keep his little boy's inclination to activity in check.

She couldn't resist a little bounce on her toes. "I think I could become a movie buff without any trouble."

He laughed at her enthusiasm as he took her hand and led her inside. "You'd think this was your first movie."

"You would," she agreed. "You would." How about her second?

It was a totally different kind of movie than the one Amy took her to. There were scenes where she could hardly breathe with the tension of the adventure and scenes where she laughed along with everyone else. But there were scenes where people got shot and she seemed to be the only one who flinched. Blood poured and bodies jerked, and she thought she'd be sick.

The world, she thought. *The world, the flesh, and the devil.* What was she doing here?

Then Rob put the empty tub of popcorn on the floor, took her hand, and threaded their fingers, and she knew.

"Did you enjoy it?" he asked as they walked back to his car.

"Did you?"

"Fun. Great action flick."

"Didn't all the violence bother you?" Maybe it didn't. He had been a soldier after all.

He looked thoughtful, then shook his head. "It was so cartoonish it didn't."

"It seemed real to me." She'd never seen anything so graphic in her life. In truth she'd never seen a handgun in her life, just hunting guns and she couldn't even name them.

"Maybe it's because I've seen real violence, real blood, but the movie was so over the top it didn't resemble real." He looked at her, his face shadowed in the dim parking lot. "There are movies I couldn't go to anymore. They would be too accurate, too real life for me to tolerate after what I've seen." He looked away, lost for a moment.

What terrible things had he witnessed? Her heart broke for him, and she gave his hand a squeeze.

He blinked and returned to the moment. "Next time I'll take you to a rom com."

"A what?"

He laughed as he drove from the lot. "A romantic comedy."

"I think I'd like that better." And she liked that there would be a next time.

They went to the Star for something to eat though how he thought they could eat anything after that huge tub of popcorn was a mystery. But they managed to down a pair of hamburgers. Rob even had a piece of pie for dessert.

Conversation swirled from topic to topic, landing on his experiences in the Army. Rachel listened, watching his face as he talked. If there was anything about this man that made her uncomfortable— aside from the fact he was Englisch—it was his military service. Sometimes he'd start to tell a story about some Army buddy and he'd stop, his eyes moving to some middle distance where he saw things he clearly found painful.

"You were a soldier, but you don't like war," she said, surprised by that realization.

"Of course not. No soldier likes war."

"Then why?" She wanted to understand how a fine Christian man like Rob could participate in something she believed was against Jesus's admonition to turn the other cheek when struck. Instead of shooting the enemy, shouldn't he be offering him a cloak?

"When I first joined, the only reason was to get away from the mess my father had made." His smile was rueful. "A theology or philosophy of war came much later."

"You have a theology of war?" Why was she surprised? She had one against war.

He leaned toward her, his arms resting on the table. "I believe there are things worth defending, worth fighting for, Rachel. Things no one should be able to take from you without your permission. Country, honor, freedom. Faith."

She would say it differently. "Certainly there are things worth dying for."

"Exactly." He settled back in his seat, looking pleased she agreed.

She'd thought her different viewpoint had been clearly stated, but it was obvious she shouldn't join the debate team any time soon. She tried again. "What about 'Love your enemies'?"

"I'm perfectly willing to love any of those against whom I fought if they would be willing not to fight against me. If they would be willing to let me and my countrymen alone." Rob signaled for another cup of coffee.

"The Bible doesn't say love them only if they love you back. We're talking enemies here." Rachel shook her head at the waitress. "No more for me, thanks."

"I'm willing to love someone who doesn't love me." He added cream to his coffee. "I'm willing to help someone who doesn't love me—if he'll let me. But if he comes at me wearing a vest of explosives? I'm not willing to die so that he with his destructive goal might win. That isn't turning the other cheek. That's letting evil triumph."

There had to be flaws in his thinking; she just wasn't finding them. "I need to think about this some more."

"I'm dating a budding pacifist?" He laughed. "If my Army buddies could see me now."

She couldn't help but smile back. It was obvious he was proud of having served. Rob and the chaplain who introduced him to Jesus— two godly men involved in something her People considered ungodly. Her mind whirled with all the conflicting thoughts and ideas.

Rob's eyes followed someone behind Rachel, and she turned to see what he was looking at. It was an Amish girl serving tea to people a couple of tables over. Sitting here in her skirt and knit top, Rachel tried to see the girl as the world did. Was she merely a curiosity to people, or did they see someone who had hopes and dreams like any Englisch person, who yearned for her own home and people to love and to love her in return?

Rob frowned as at a puzzle. "Do you ever wonder what they think?" He looked as if he couldn't comprehend the girl and her culture. Rachel's culture.

Rachel blinked. "What do you mean, what *they* think?" She hated that he'd said "they" as if he were speaking of alien beings.

"The Amish. They live so differently. They must think differently, mustn't they? Buggies, no electricity, restricted dress."

She forced a smile. They did think differently about many things, but they were just people. "They probably think about crops and horses more than the typical Englisch person—unless the Englisch person is a farmer."

"And weather. Farmers have to think about weather. Do they watch the Weather Channel for information or have a weather app on their cells? No, wait. They can't watch TV because there's no electricity. What about cell phones? Do they use cells?"

"Most of the farmers have weather radios in their barns to track the weather, so they do know what's going on. And some use cells for business though as a rule they aren't allowed in private life."

He studied her with interest. "What about all the ones who aren't farmers? Why aren't they farmers?"

"There's not enough land to go around." Rachel thought of Jonah, who seemed happy with his nursery business. And Aaron hadn't wanted to farm. "And some don't like farming. It's hard work."

"Think of all the money tied up in their farms. All that land." Rob shook his head. "My father always wanted to get his hands on Amish money, but they were wise enough to avoid his wheeling and dealing."

Rachel frowned. "I don't understand someone like your father. It takes a lot of nerve or arrogance to think you can manage someone else's money."

"Qualities my father has in abundance." Rob smiled sadly. "He's proud he was able to pull it off for so long."

"Doesn't he feel any remorse about all the people who lost their savings because of him? If I cost someone everything, I'd be eaten alive with guilt."

"He's completely unrepentant." Rob's voice was hard. "Of all the things I find hard to forgive, that's the hardest."

It was her turn to smile sadly. Would he be able to forgive her for her deceit?

"I want to do the same thing, you know." He watched her closely.

"What same thing?"

"Be a money manager. A certified financial planner."

She studied him. "But you aren't arrogant at all."

He smiled, relieved. "I hope not. Not a very Christlike attribute."

They smiled at each other, and he reached across the table for her hand. Tingles again.

"Tell me about your father," he said.

She studied their clasped fingers resting on the table beside the ketchup. "He's a farmer."

"An Amish farmer?" he asked with that charming smile.

Tell him, Rachel. Now. Explain. But explain what? That she was Amish but was living Englisch? That she loved Amish life but wanted

Englisch perks? That she was confused? Or that she was a liar and a cheater?

No, she wasn't going to risk their relationship, still so new and fragile, by telling him what a mess she was.

Rob spoke and to her confused relief the moment of opportunity passed. "I hear they're good at saving money, probably because they don't spend it on stuff like we do."

Rachel tipped her head in agreement. "I think one of the differences between them and us—" Her voice tripped and she had to clear her throat before she could continue. Was she already one of *us*, one of the Englisch? Had she crossed some invisible line when she wasn't looking? "—is they spend it with purpose."

"So do the rest of us."

"To satisfy our wants, not needs."

Rob fiddled with her fingers, and she felt the touch in a flow of warmth running up her arm.

"You must know some Amish," he said. "You know so much about them."

Did she ever. She cleared her throat. "Some."

"No wonder you understand them."

No wonder.

"Hey, Rachel. How are you?"

She froze at that voice.

Pulling her hand free of Rob's, she forced herself to look at her brother standing beside her booth, a goofy smile lighting his face. She forced herself to smile and act pleased when what she really felt was exposed. Outed. Her castle in the clouds was about to collapse with a mighty crash.

"Johnny. What are you doing here?"

His grin broadened. "I was eating dinner. Like you." He looked at Rob, clearly wanting an introduction.

Rachel felt dread wash through her where a minute ago it had been the tingling warmth of Rob's touch. Johnny could—what could

Johnny do? This brother who was her delight and her despair could ruin her life.

"Johnny, this is my friend Rob Lanier. Rob, my brother Johnny."

Rob stood and the men shook hands. "Join us," Rob said.

Johnny slid in next to Rachel. She looked at him, but he concentrated on Rob. "So how do you guys know each other?"

"From class," Rob said. "At Wexford."

"Class?" Whatever Johnny expected, it wasn't that. He looked at Rachel with a raised eyebrow. "At college?"

Rachel took a deep breath to steady herself. She deserved any embarrassment Johnny could cause.

Rob sent her a smile that made her cheeks heat. "She sat in front of me that first night, and I was a goner. It was a rainy night and her hair, all curly and wild in spite of her barrette, kept distracting me from the lecture."

Johnny sat back and looked at Rachel. "Curly hair, huh? And wild."

She smiled weakly, aware of her hair falling free down her back.

"A comp class." Rob rolled on, unaware of Rachel's distress. "She's a great writer. I know because the professor reads her stuff to us all the time."

"I can't say I'm surprised the professor likes her, but—" Johnny reached out and pulled gently on a curl. "It *is* pretty."

Rob looked at her and smiled. "Beautiful."

In spite of her rapid pulse and churning stomach, she had to smile back.

Johnny studied her. "She usually wears it pulled back and all tucked away."

"Really? I've never seen it that way, and I'm glad."

Johnny grinned, eyes alight with something she couldn't quite decipher. She knew it was either mischief or evil intent. She held her breath.

"Well," he drew the word out to increase her anxiety. He grinned at her and she closed her eyes in expectation of the worst. "Rach has always been both smart and pretty, though hardly anyone tells her so."

She blinked. What?

He smiled at her with an understanding she never expected from him. "And she does look good in pretty clothes."

Rachel flushed while Rob nodded agreement.

Johnny stood. "I've got to go. I just wanted to say hello and meet Rach's friend."

Rob stood and the men shook hands again. "Nice to meet you, Johnny." He smiled at Rachel. "You've got a fantastic sister here."

Rachel colored while Johnny studied her. "Yeah, I do." He leaned down and whispered,

"We need to talk, sister mine." Then he smiled and flicked a wave. "See you."

As he loped off, Rachel watched him go. Her delicately balanced life was in his slightly shaky hands. She slid from the booth. "I guess we should go too. My day starts very early."

They paused to pay the bill. When they walked into the parking lot, only a few cars remained. Rob took her hand again and turned to say something. Before he could speak, they heard the unmistakable sounds of a fight: the scuff of shoes, the *thump* of the punch to the body, the grunt of pain.

In the far dark corner of the parking lot two men were attacking a third. A man with curly hair was holding the victim while the other, a big man with broad shoulders, punched him. A baseball bat leaned against the bumper of a nearby car.

Rachel froze. The deliberate violence horrified her.

"Call 911," Rob ordered and ran toward the fight.

"Rob, no!"

"Enough," Rob roared just as the puncher picked up his baseball bat and cocked it, preparing for a swing. Rob grabbed the bat on the backwards swing, and using the weapon's momentum, kept the arc going and pulled it from the puncher's hands.

"What the—"

Taken completely by surprise, the man spun. The man holding the victim was equally stunned and loosened his grip long enough for the man to pull himself free. He staggered and went down to one knee.

Rob stood with the bat cocked on his shoulder. He seemed completely at ease. "Two to one? And a baseball bat? Bit of overkill, don't you think?"

The big man Rob had stripped the bat from strode forward with a snarl. Rob swung the bat between them.

"That's far enough." He swung the bat again. "You don't want to cross into no man's land."

The man paused and pointed his finger at Rob's face. "Stay out of something that's none of your business." He grabbed the bat with both hands and wrenched it from Rob's grip. He let it fall to the ground and took a threatening step forward. "Thomas, we got ourselves a new one."

The one who had been holding the victim took a step toward Rob.

So quickly Rachel saw more the results than Rob's move, Rob grabbed the puncher's arm, turned him and twisted it behind his back. He pushed the man against the hood of a parked car.

"A bit of wisdom a guy like you should know." Rob held the man in place. "Never get close enough that they can grab you. Never." With a last push he released the man's arm and stepped out of reach.

The man straightened and glared at Rob. He rubbed his arm, flexing his hand. "You shouldn't have done that."

Rob nodded. "Probably not. Now get lost before the cops come."

"I called the cops!" shouted a man standing near the door of the Star.

"Me too," called another man standing by his car. "They're coming!"

Rachel felt relief since she'd been too upset to move, let alone call.

Thomas, the holder, took a step back, hands held with palms facing front. "I don't want nothing to do with the cops. No way." He disappeared into the darkness.

The big man, stance full of threat, stared at Rob. Then he held up a finger gun and went "Bang." He grabbed the bat from the ground and disappeared into the field behind the diner like the first man.

Rob knelt by the victim. "You okay, Johnny?"

Johnny! Rachel went cold all over.

Chapter 25

Rachel looked at Johnny slumped on the bed in her guest room. She couldn't help it; she had to ask again. "Are you sure you're okay?"

"Rachel, enough." His voice was tired and irritated. "I'm okay."

He didn't look it to her. He had a split lip and a fearsome black eye forming beside the red weal on his right cheek, but it was internal injuries she was worried about.

He had insisted he was fine to the EMTs who appeared at the Star with the ambulance and police as part of the first responders. Even a fire truck came. "I'm not going to the hospital. I don't need to go to the hospital. I'm fine."

The annoyed EMT eyed him. "If there's blood in your urine, get to the hospital. And sign this release."

"Sure," Johnny said as he signed.

"Any idea who those men were?" the police asked.

"None," Johnny said, staring at the ground.

"I've never seen them before," Rob said.

"Me neither," said both the men who called 911.

"The guy who did the punching and had the bat called the other one Thomas," Rob said. "He had curly hair if that's any help."

"You know a Thomas with curly hair?" the cop asked Johnny.

Johnny started to shake his head, then brought his hand to his forehead like he was trying to stop the pain from the movement. "No. No Thomas."

"You're sure? Very few people get jumped without provocation."

"Never saw them before," Johnny assured the officer.

"He knows who they were," Rob whispered in Rachel's ear as they stood off to the side waiting for Johnny to be able to leave.

She stared at him, not wanting to think he was right. "How do you know?"

"I just know. So do the cops."

Rachel studied the men talking to Johnny, big men wearing guns and carrying their authority like shields. She saw their looks of skepticism at Johnny's denials and realized Rob spoke the truth.

That Johnny knew men who went around beating up people frightened her. That they had attacked her brother chilled her to the bone. That he protected them confused her.

Where had he met them? What had he done to become their target? Was he following the Amish custom of not getting involved in police matters? Or was he for some unknown reason shielding evil men?

Finally the police released Johnny, who limped to his car with his arms about his middle.

He saw her look of concern.

"Don't worry, Rach. I'm fine. Just holding the organs in."

She barely understood him, garbled as he sounded because of the split lip.

Rob opened the passenger side. "Over here. You can't drive."

"Sure I can." He ruined the assertion by staggering. Rachel caught his arm.

"Rob's right. You can hardly stand upright." Rachel glared at him for even thinking he could handle a car. "I'll drive."

Complaining and groaning in equal measures, Johnny let Rob tuck him in the passenger seat. Rachel took the wheel.

Rob shut the door and went to his own car to follow. Rachel buckled in, ordered Johnny to do the same, and then pulled onto the road.

"How do you like driving, Rachel?" Johnny asked as she stopped for a light. "Beats a horse and buggy, doesn't it?"

She didn't answer; she didn't want to talk about her Englisch behavior with him, not tonight. Johnny slumped back in his seat and shut his eyes. At her house, Rob helped him up the front steps, across the living room, and up the steps to the second floor.

Rachel hurried ahead and had a kerosene lamp lit in the bedroom with a blue log cabin quilt on the double bed. As Rob lowered Johnny, her brother clutched his middle and groaned.

Rachel winced at his pain. "Johnny, please go—"

"Rach, stop. I'm fine. Just a bit sore."

"A bit?" Her fear for him made her sound angry. "You're—" He glared at her and she bit her lip.

Rob put a hand on her shoulder. She looked up at him, and he kissed her cheek, a comforting touch rather than romantic. "It's okay," he whispered.

She shook her head. "It's not."

He smiled, understanding. "No, it's not." He gave her shoulder a gentle squeeze and released her.

"You need help to the bathroom, Johnny?" Rob stepped to the bed. "I'll take you before I go."

While Johnny stumbled to the bathroom beside Rob, Rachel pulled back the quilt and put fresh sheets on the bed. By the time they got back, the room was ready and Johnny sat carefully on the edge of the bed.

"No blood," he announced as if he'd achieved a great victory. "See? I'm fine."

"He took a fistful of your pain meds," Rob said.

"Over-the-counter stuff. He could have gotten stronger medicine if he'd just—"

"I'm here. I hear you. I'm not going."

He tried to toe off his shoes and grimaced. Rachel dropped down, untied them, and pulled them off. He nodded his thanks and fell sideways, letting his head settle on the pillow. Slowly, painfully he pulled his legs onto the bed and turned on his back, shooing her when she tried to help. He took the package of frozen peas she extended and held it to his eye.

"Stubborn," she said, but softly and with affection. "Call me if you need me. I'll be just down the hall."

"You're wise to stay with him tonight," Rob said as she walked him to the front door. "Just in case."

Stay with him? Oh. Her breath caught. He thought this was Johnny's house and she was being nice to spend the night.

He pulled her into a hug that made her feel safe in the midst of her chaotic world. "Want me to stay too?"

She wrapped her arms around him and rested her head on his shoulder. They stood quietly for a few minutes, Rachel reveling in the comfort after the storm. In the storm.

She stepped back. "You've got that business trip tomorrow, and he'll probably sleep the night through with the pills he took. Go home and get a good night's rest before your big day."

Rob nodded. "Call if you need me. Promise?"

"Promise."

Rob walked onto the porch. "Nice house Johnny's got, by the way." He leaned forward and kissed her cheek. "Did he get it cheap from an Amish guy because there's no electricity?"

She hadn't given the kerosene lamps a thought in her concern for Johnny. She just smiled and didn't correct him as he went down the steps. She watched him drive away and thought about the web of deceit she'd woven for herself.

Was she supposed to give up class and her dream of getting a degree? Of exercising her mind? Of learning? Was she supposed to give up Amy? Give up Rob? Rob who had thrown himself into the fight. Rob who had swung a bat at a man though she knew it was only in threat. Rob who had twisted that man's arm behind his back and pushed him against a car.

Rob who had kept Johnny from being badly hurt.

But maybe it was God's will that Johnny be beaten. God is sovereign. Was this beating His way of teaching him to return to Amish life? Or find a better Englisch life? Had Rob interfered with God's plan?

Was there ever a time when violence was necessary or at least understandable? Forgiveable?

Jesus taught that if a man smote you, you should offer the other cheek. You should bless those who curse you. Love one another. Return good for evil. Stories from *Martyrs Mirror* flashed through her mind. Early Anabaptists went to death for their faith rather than resort to swords and violence to protect themselves and their families. Nonresistance was woven into Amish thinking from its earliest roots.

Always she agreed that pacifism was right, mere common sense as well as dogma. If people wouldn't fight, there would be no wars.

But it was her brother being beaten. And it was Rob who had saved him. Gentle, kind Rob who loved Jesus and told her the story of Chaplain Roussey and his salvation.

Was there a difference between protecting yourself and seeking vengeance? The Lord said vengeance was His. No argument there. But what about when you were attacked like Johnny? There was nothing of faith involved as there'd been for those written of in *Martyrs Mirror*. Did that make a difference? But then living out your faith was supposed to be part of everyday life, as needed as the air she breathed and as real as the ground she stood on.

She slipped her hands into her unbound hair and grabbed fistfuls. It was more than even her clever brain could parse.

"Rachel," Johnny called.

She hurried to his room. "What's wrong?"

"Nothing. I just wanted to say good night."

She nodded. "You sleep in tomorrow and get better."

He nodded. "I hope my phone holds its charge overnight so I can call work tomorrow morning."

"I can call if you want me to."

He studied her for a moment, and she shifted uncomfortably. She felt she had a red H for hypocrite embroidered on her shirt.

"Why'd you marry Aaron?" he asked.

She blinked. "What?"

"Aaron. Why?"

"Why not? He was a wonderful man."

"But not for you."

She stared at him, startled. Insight and Johnny were usually strangers. "He was my choice, Johnny. We were happy."

"You didn't know any better."

Rachel sighed. "Keep those frozen peas on your eye, and I'll see you in the morning."

She walked down the hall toward her room.

"I like him," Johnny called after her. "He fits."

She took a deep breath but didn't respond as she tried to figure out just where he fit.

Chapter 26

Rachel and her mom put out an early supper of ham, noodles with burnt butter, green beans, fresh sliced tomatoes, Rachel's applesauce, and Mom's blueberry pie. Five o'clock in the evening. Early for a farm dinner with there still being several hours of daylight.

Rachel told herself to take leftovers home for Johnny. One day after his beating he was very sore—and grumpy. He'd slept while she was at school, and now he was bored.

Every time she went to check on him, he held up a hand. "Don't ask, I'm fine."

She looked across the kitchen at her mother. If she knew what had happened to her son...

"So how is school going?" Mom asked as she made room on the table for the platter of ham.

"I love the little ones" Rachel put Johnny from her mind. "They sit there round-eyed, trying to figure out what's going on with everyone speaking English instead of German."

"It's the first time some of them even hear it." Mom put the ham in front of Datt's chair. "I always thought it was good to teach a few English words before school starts. Bathroom. Sit. Help. Lunch. Just some to help with the transition. That's why we made all you *kinder* learn the Lord's Prayer in English before you went off your first day."

"It doesn't take them long to catch up."

Levi walked in, shedding sawdust in spite of his best efforts to brush off outside.

Rachel smiled at him. "Making more outhouses?"

"Levi, go outside and brush off better," Mom ordered.

"Come on." Rachel walked to the door. "I'll brush off your back."

He stood patiently as she flicked away the remaining sawdust and then followed her back inside. He held his hand out thigh high. "This bunch is so tall. They can put them in their gardens or use them as lawn ornaments or something."

"Who would want a little outhouse in their front yard?" Mom looked perplexed.

"I don't know, but they do," Levi said with a grin.

Rachel started pouring water into the glasses. "It was clever to think of them, Levi."

Levi went to the kitchen sink to wash his hands. "Davy's starting to make bird houses. He says he's saving his money for a sulky cart."

Rachel laughed. "Just because Datt will buy a retired racer for the buggy doesn't mean he'll approve a retired cart."

"Why not?"

"You think the bishop will approve you racing up and down the street?" Rachel said.

Mom clapped her hands. "Everyone to the table."

"It's better than a car," Levi said.

Datt took his seat at the head of the table. "No car."

"A sulky cart?" Davy asked hopefully.

"I will think on it as I think on the saddle for Levi to become a cowboy."

And the discussion died.

They all took seats, Mom and Datt, Rachel, Sally, Eban, Ruthie, Levi, David, and little Abner. All bowed their heads for a silent blessing. The food was passed in silence and everyone ate quickly and efficiently. In no time the plates were empty. When Datt swallowed his last bite, he bowed his head for a second silent prayer, and everyone followed suit. Rachel prayed the Lord's Prayer and then added a spontaneous prayer like Rob prayed. *Thanks for this food, Lord. The ham was delicious. And thanks for all my family.*

She glanced around the table, thankful no one saw into her mind and knew of her Englisch prayer. Just so none of them noticed her hot face, flushed at her own audacity.

Footsteps sounded on the porch and Jonah and his family entered.

Datt stood. "All right, Jonah. This is your project. Tell us what we are to do."

Jonah pointed to the yard. "That flatbed is full of small trees. We have to plant them on the steep hill behind the new business complex over on 322. They're to help prevent erosion."

"So we're your free labor," Levi said to a laugh from everyone.

"You are. And if Miller's Nursery keeps growing, you can work for me for pay some day."

"Probably not. I'm going to work on the farm with Datt."

"*Gut.*" Datt took his hat from the peg by the door. "I need a strong young back."

Rachel slipped a black sweater on over her oldest dress. She reached behind her head and retied the scarf covering her hair and followed everyone out to the buggies and wagons. Mom stood on the porch with Jonah's children and an unhappy Abner and waved them on their way.

Rachel climbed in Jonah's buggy with Sally, Ruthie, and Miriam, with Eban driving. Jonah drove the flatbed with the trees while Datt, Levi, and Davy crowded into the seat of an open cart. With a flick of the reins the procession moved down the farm lane and onto the road toward their destination. Jonah led them a little over a mile to a mulch-covered walking path that wound its way along the top of the hill behind the businesses.

"I would not want to mow that," Levi announced as he climbed from the cart and surveyed the incline.

Rachel pictured herself trying to keep her push mower from sliding downhill. "Remember, Levi, when you and Davy were little and mowed the grass together?"

Levi grinned. "I had to pull the rope tied to the mower."

"And I had to push the mower," Davy said. "We were a good team."

From his place standing on the flatbed, Jonah began giving

instructions. "Rachel and Davy, unload the trees along the path. There are sixty trees to set in the ground this evening, and all have to be staked and protected. I'll dig the holes, and the rest of you plant the little saplings."

Jonah jumped to the ground and handed the reins of the flatbed to Rachel. With a flick of his wrist, he turned on his gas-powered auger and started digging holes in the hard earth.

Rachel climbed up on the flatbed, flicked the reins over the rumps of the big work horses, and drove slowly along the path. Davy walked beside her, lifting out flowering pears and weeping cherries, redbuds and magnolias, maples and oaks, all about a foot high, depositing them along the edge of the path.

As soon as Jonah dug a hole, one of the others set a sapling carefully in it and tamped the dirt around it. Next came a white plastic cylinder over the small tree to protect it and a stake to hold everything in place on the hill. The last step was a piece of mesh placed over the cylinder to keep out critters, bugs, anything that might hurt the fragile plant.

When Davy set out the last of the saplings, Rachel tied the horses to a tree and began helping with the planting. She looked along the hillside at the sweating Millers, bending, planting, staking.

Gott, I love these people so much!

Before the sun was on the horizon, the trees were planted and the caravan was on its way back to the farm. This time Rachel sat with Jonah on the flatbed as they rolled slowly past the dairy cows spending the mild night in the fields.

They drove past a pasture of goats of all colors and sizes, and Rachel laughed at the goat standing on top of the little storage shed. They passed the Wickersham's farm with its pristine white fences and show horses. When the Wickershams bought their farm and actually named it and hung a fancy sign that read Day's End Farm, Datt had shaken his head.

"Those Englisch. They don't even know that with farming there is no end. But they will learn, *ja?*"

They drove by Jonah's place where the closed wagon that carried the benches for church was parked in his yard. By Sunday the main floor of Jonah's house would be emptied of all furniture and filled with the benches for service. Next week the wagon, loaded again with the benches, would be driven to the home of the next to host the Gmay.

They were almost to the farm lane when a car pulled up beside them and slowed instead of passing as most cars did. An extremely handsome man behind the wheel studied them in a rude manner, his gaze moving from Jonah to Rachel and back.

He rolled down his window. "You know the Millers?"

"Who's asking?" Jonah called, pulling the horses to a stop.

"I am."

"And you are?"

The man flapped his hand, waving away the question. Muscles rippled on his forearm as he gestured. "I'm looking for Johnny Miller."

There was something about the way he said Johnny's name that made Rachel's stomach twist. *Oh, Johnny, last night wasn't enough?*

"I haven't seen Johnny Miller in a long time," Jonah answered truthfully and with a determined pleasantness. "He doesn't live here anymore."

"But I bet you know where we can get hold of him."

"I'm sorry." Jonah shook his head.

"Phone number."

"I don't have a phone."

"Address.

"I can honestly tell you I don't know it." Jonah flicked the reins gently on the horses' rumps and the flatbed began moving again.

Rachel watched the man with both fear and fascination even as she prayed he wouldn't ask her. She couldn't lie, but she didn't want to admit Johnny was sleeping mere yards from where they were.

The man's gaze settled on her. "How about you? You know where he is?"

"Me?" Her voice squeaked.

"Leave her alone," Jonah said. "How would she know if I don't?"

How indeed.

The man looked skeptical, but a car behind him honked. With a frustrated look that said he wasn't happy, he had no choice but to drive on.

Rachel watched the rear lights of the car disappear around the curve. Was he one of the men from the parking lot? If he was, he hadn't recognized her any more than she recognized him. If he wasn't the same man, just how many people were chasing Johnny?

"What's Johnny mixed up in?" Jonah looked at her and for a moment she thought he expected an answer. When she realized he didn't, her heart settled a bit.

"Whatever it is, it's bad." She knew that much for a certainty.

Jonah shook his head. "I worry about him. He has such bad friends."

Rachel couldn't disagree. "Or enemies. That man didn't strike me as friendly."

Jonah rubbed his beard. "When I ran around, I went to barn dances and drank beer. You went to Max's and used the computer and watched TV."

"I don't watch TV." The one thing she wasn't guilty of, and he refused to believe her.

"Not now maybe, but Johnny—I worry he's involved in illegal things. I don't want to see my brother in jail."

"I know. I worry about him too." The thought of jail made her shudder.

"If we worry, you can imagine how Mom and Datt worry. I want him to be the prodigal son who comes home."

They turned into the farm lane in silence.

Rachel looked at the farm, steady and stable as the people who worked it. "Do you think he'll ever come back?"

"I don't know, but at least he never took his vows. He can come visit if he wants to."

And if she went, she couldn't.

Chapter 27

As soon as Rachel walked in the house after the tree planting, she heard her cell phone ringing. Her phone never rang. No one in her world knew she had a phone nor did most of them have phones, so no one called her.

Phones represented the Englisch world, not her world. Phones were for Monday and Friday evenings, not Thursday.

She pulled her scarf off and used it to wipe her hot face as she grabbed her purse from the counter. Her dirty fingernails stared up at her as she pulled her phone out, surprised it had any power.

"Hello?"

"Where have you been? I've been trying to get you for like hours!"

"Amy?" She almost didn't recognize her friend's voice. "What's wrong?"

"Yeah, it's me." A loud sniff echoed in Rachel's ear.

"Are you crying?"

"Oh, Rachel! I don't know what to do."

Rachel's heart tripped. "What's wrong? Has something happened to your family?"

"It's Bagel!"

Visions of a car hitting the animal drew themselves in vivid color. She saw Amy on her knees hugging her injured or dead pet. She braced herself for the worst. "What happened?"

There was a long, shaky breath as Amy tried to get control. "He b-barks!"

On cue, barks sounded down the line. Rachel felt tension drain from her shoulders. The animal was alive and well enough to bark. That was good.

"Shush, baby, shush," Amy said.

Bagel quieted.

"Bagel barks." Rachel repeated, not seeing the problem. Barking was what dogs did.

"All the time! The old lady who lives on the ground floor complained to the landlord about him. She says he barks all day." Amy sounded offended on Bagel's behalf.

"Does he?"

"Not when I'm home. He's as good as gold when I'm there. I don't know about when I'm at work or class."

"He probably misses you," Rachel guessed.

"I know. And he's in a strange new place. And now I have to get rid of him or we have to m-move." Again the wail.

"Oh, Amy, I'm sorry." Though she could see the point of view of the lady downstairs. A dog barking all day would be nerve-racking to say the least.

"I can't get rid of him. I *won't.*"

Rachel pictured the happy reunion at Amy's parents' home when they'd rescued the dog from certain death. "Of course you can't get rid of him."

"I love him. He's what kept me sane back home. Him and Jesus."

Rachel wondered how Jesus felt about being paired with a beagle, but decided He was understanding of Amy's issues and hurt.

"And I don't want to move," Amy continued. "I can't afford to move. The security deposit and the first month's rent and the animal fees for another place? I don't have it. I don't. What am I going to do?"

Rachel heard the despair in her friend's voice. "Oh, Amy, I wish there was something I could do to help."

Amy jumped, ready with the answer. "I thought maybe you could keep him. You liked him on moving day."

Rachel thought a more accurate way to look at it was that she didn't dislike him on moving day. Indoor pets still seemed strange to her.

"I mean," Amy went on, "no one would hear him bark at your house, right? Except the lady you live with, but she seems nice enough. Maybe she won't mind."

The lady she lived with? "I don't—" Understanding struck. Max. Amy thought she lived at Max's because that's where she had dropped her after class and picked her up for the movies.

But how did she meet Max? She had to have met her to know she was nice, but she had never come inside. "Amy, where are you?"

"I'm parked down the street from your house waiting for you to come home. I need to t-talk—" And she started to cry again.

"Amy, I am home." She walked to the front window and looked out. She could see a car parked on the road just past Max's.

"No, you're not. I went to your house and the lady there said she didn't know where you were."

Oh, boy. Poor Max. "That's because I really live across the street and two houses down. The house with the gardens."

"But—"

"I'll explain. Come on over."

They hung up and Rachel stood with her eyes closed.

Her worlds were about to collide.

Rachel looked down at herself. Not only was she wearing Amish clothing but old and very dirty Amish clothing. She had dirt under her nails and her hair was pulled back. She grabbed her scarf and tied it on. She was about to test Amy's BFF claim.

She walked onto the porch and watched Amy pull into her drive. Amy climbed from the car and walked to the house, Bagel at her side. She stood at the foot of the stairs and looked up. Bagel had no hesitance. He surged up the steps, his toenails clicking on the treads.

"This is your house? Not there?" Amy pointed down the street at Max's brightly lit home.

"Come on in. I'll try to explain."

Rachel led the way inside. The warm glow of the lantern on the end table beside her favorite chair in front of the fireplace lit the room. It wasn't a bright light like electricity gave but a soothing light. And the soft hiss of the lantern was reassuring somehow. It was the sound of home, of family, of a safe and gentle childhood. A Plain life.

Amy stood in the doorway and looked around. Then she studied Rachel.

"Is your electricity out?" She pointed to the lantern.

Rachel shook her head. "I don't have electricity."

Amy nodded. "And that's an Amish dress."

Rachel looked down at the dirty apron and the faded dress. "A pretty ratty one. I was just helping my family plant trees for my brother Jonah's new client."

"You planted trees? I thought you were a teacher."

"I am. I teach at the Amish school."

Amy looked like she suddenly got it. "And you've got to wear their clothes."

Rachel smiled. "No. These are my everyday clothes. At least clean ones are."

Amy's mouth dropped open. "You're Amish?"

"I'm Amish."

"And you planted trees in a dress?"

Rachel smiled. "I do everything in a dress."

"Where's your hat or whatever you call it?" She waved her hand around her head.

"My kapp, you mean."

"Whatever."

"I use this scarf as a covering when I work. I wear my kapp when I'm not going to get it dirty."

"Do you wear it when you teach?"

"I do."

"I always wondered how you could teach if you're just starting college. That school board line was good."

"It's true. The school board asked me to teach at the school."

"Uh-huh. How'd you get into college with a—what is it—an eighth grade education?"

"I have my GED."

"Huh." Amy finally took a seat and Rachel thought their friendship just might survive her deceit.

"Will they kick you out if they find out?"

Rachel took a deep breath: "Probably."

Amy looked pleased. "Then you'll be like me, free as a bird."

"But I don't want—"

"Was your husband Amish?"

Rachel nodded. "Aaron was."

"Was he harsh? Did he make you obey? I bet he told you that you shouldn't go to college."

"Aaron was gentle and kind, and he didn't know I wanted to go to college." Saying it made her realize again how little of her real self Aaron had known. How very sad that was.

"No wonder I like you so much." Amy seemed to have forgotten her problems with her landlord and Bagel, who was making himself at home, exploring and sniffing. "You had the same kind of awful life I did."

"No, I didn't."

Amy didn't seem to hear. "Rules, rules, and more rules. Didn't you hate it? Didn't you hate them for making you keep them?"

Rachel checked her clock, the one shaped like a teapot. Eight-forty-five.

"Come with me." She walked to the door, Bagel padding beside her.

"What about him?" Amy pointed at the dog.

"He can come."

"Where are we going?"

Rachel pulled the door shut behind them. "I need to show you something."

They walked down the road to the farm lane, then up to Mom and Datt's. Bagel ran back and forth across the lane as if afraid he might miss a fascinating scent if he stayed on one side. Pepper slipped to Rachel's side to say hello, then slid away before Bagel had time to notice her.

The soft glow of lanterns shined from the first floor windows.

Amy hesitated when Rachel started up the steps. "Who?"

"My parents. Just don't let it slip that I'm going to college, drive a car, and wear Englisch clothes."

Amy's eyes sparkled with what had suddenly become an adventure. "Secrets, secrets."

"We can't tell them where we met."

"Right. College. Forbidden topic."

Rachel knocked on the door and let herself and Amy in. Bagel was so busy exploring he didn't mind being left outside.

Mom looked up from the kitchen and Datt from his easy chair where he held a picture book and a sleepy Abner. A small dish with the residue of ice cream sat on the end table, and Abner wore a chocolate mustache and beard.

"Rachel!" Mom smiled her greeting from the kitchen, Ruthie beside her. "I didn't expect to see you again tonight."

Rachel pulled Amy forward. Her jeans, short hair, and makeup set her apart from the other women in the room. "This is my friend Amy. She stopped to see me, and I wanted her to meet you all."

"Well, we're about to have root beer floats," Mom said. "Levi and Davy, where's that root beer?"

"Coming, Mom." Levi clattered up the cellar steps, Davy on his heels. They both held bottles of homemade root beer in their hands.

"I hope it's fizzy," Datt said as he stood with the sleepy Abner.

"It should be," Levi said. "It's had long enough to carbonate."

"I'll take Abner, Datt." Ruthie hugged her sleepy little brother and started upstairs to put him to bed. "And Levi, don't take all the ice cream!"

"There's a little bit of peach and lots of vanilla," Mom said. "Don't worry. You'll get plenty."

"Save me some of the peach, please."

"I had chocolate." Abner's little voice floated down as they disappeared upstairs. "I ate it all."

"Have a seat, Amy." Mom indicated a place at the kitchen table. "How did you and Rachel meet?"

Amy looked wide-eyed at Rachel as she slid into a chair.

"Mom, do we have any pretzels?" Rachel asked. If she could avoid this one question…

"We do," Mom said. "In the can in the closet."

"Got them."

Mom looked at Amy. "Ruthie's friend Annie is working at the pretzel factory and got us a can at a good price."

"They're great pretzels." Levi opened the root beer while Mom scooped ice cream into waiting glasses. "They're the big fat ones."

Ruthie came back downstairs, and they all sat around the table enjoying their floats.

"Because you all worked so hard for Jonah," Mom explained.

Twenty minutes later Rachel, Amy, and Bagel walked back to Rachel's.

"Are they always that nice?" Amy asked.

"They are. I know they're rule-bound, but they're Plain. It goes with the territory. They follow the Ordnung and the Bible, but Datt isn't like your father."

"He was reading to your little brother." There was wonder in Amy's voice.

"If Aaron had lived, he would have been a father like Datt."

"Do you miss him a lot?" Rachel heard the concern in Amy's question.

"Yes and no. It's complicated. My friend Max who you met?"

"Where I thought you lived."

"Her husband died about a year ago and she's still full of pain. She misses Buddy with all her heart. I miss Aaron in that he was too young to die. He was a good man and his death was very sad. But it was three years ago. I've done many things on my own since."

"Like become a rebel." Amy laughed.

Rachel forced a smile. She couldn't tell Amy that the main reason she didn't feel a hole in her heart like Max did was Rob. In fact she knew losing him when he learned who she really was would cause much greater pain than anything she felt when Aaron died. That realization, yet one more sign of the growing gap between her two lives, filled her with guilt.

They walked a few minutes in silence. Then Amy gave Rachel a gentle nudge with her shoulder. "Okay, you win. Your family is nicer than mine."

Rachel gave her a nudge back. "You can see why I don't want to leave."

"Yeah, but that doesn't help me with the Bagel problem. We need a place to live and fast!"

"When do you have to be out?"

"Saturday."

"That soon? How can they break the lease like that?"

"I'm an unsatisfactory tenant. Or my baby is."

Rachel led them inside and they took seats before the stone fireplace. Bagel jumped onto Amy's lap and licked her face. He settled quietly.

"See what a good boy he is?" Amy stroked his head and Rachel swore he smiled complacently.

A scuffle and grunt sounded, and Johnny came stiff-legged down the stairs.

"Where'd you go?" he mumbled around his split lip.

Bagel began to bark like a wild thing at the unexpected apparition, and Johnny stared, surprised, at the pair in the chair.

Rachel jumped to her feet and hurried to the stairs. "What are you doing? You shouldn't be out of bed."

"Yeah, yeah. I got hungry."

"Well, sit down and I'll get you something." She headed for the kitchen. "I could have brought you whatever you want."

"A sandwich?" He sank into the chair Rachel had vacated. "I was bored up there alone."

"Poor baby."

Johnny shifted and flinched at the jab of pain "You know it."

"Amy, this is my brother Johnny who's staying here for a few days. Johnny, my friend Amy."

Amy gave a little wave and said, "Hi," more lip read than heard over Bagel's barks.

"Yeah. I saw you at the Star with Rach and Rob and some guy."

"Really? That was Win Lanier, Rob's brother."

"He your boyfriend?"

"Johnny!" Rachel turned from the counter where she was making a sandwich.

"What? It's a legitimate question."

"It's an impolite question."

Johnny shrugged and flinched again at the discomfort. "Is he?"

Amy shook her head as she tried to quiet Bagel.

Moving carefully, Johnny held out his hand. "Hey, doggie."

Bagel jumped down and came over to investigate, curiosity winning over protection detail.

Amy studied him. "Are you okay?"

"A bit stiff," he said. "Accident."

"Ah." She sat back as Rachel brought Johnny a glass of milk and a ham and cheese sandwich made with ham from Mom's dinner.

Rachel sat on the hearth. "I've been thinking, Amy. You can stay here until you find a place."

Amy's face lit up. "Really? You'd do that for me?"

"Really?" Johnny asked around a mouthful of ham and cheese.

"BFFs and all that. I've got several bedrooms upstairs and Johnny's only filling one."

"You sure this is a good idea, Rach?" Johnny asked. "Nothing against Amy."

She wasn't the least bit sure, but waved his comment away. Amy needed help, and she was her friend.

Johnny gave another very careful shrug. "If you're not worried, I'm certainly not." He smiled at Amy. "I won't be here long, so I won't be in your way. I'm thinking of going to California."

"California?" Rachel frowned. "Do Mom and Datt know?"

"No, and you won't tell them. It's not a done deal."

Rachel studied this brother she loved and felt such concern over. "There was a man asking for you tonight."

Johnny tensed. "What did you say, you who can't tell lies."

No, she just lived them. "He asked Jonah, and he doesn't know, has never known where you've been living, let alone where you are now. I didn't have to answer."

Johnny looked at Amy like they shared some secret. "She's so Amish!"

Amy smiled. "I'm not Amish but I love Jesus and I don't lie either."

Johnny's eyes went wide, then narrowed. "Huh."

Rachel wanted to laugh at his comically suspicious expression. She was certain not many people he knew made statements like Amy's.

He took his last swallow and stood. "I'm off to sleep, ladies."

The two women watched in silence as Johnny slowly made his way upstairs, Bagel following as if shepherding him to bed.

Amy stood. "I've got to get going. It's almost ten. Breakfast comes early at the restaurant."

Rachel rose and followed her to the door.

Amy paused with a hand on the doorknob. "Did you mean it? I can stay here?"

Rachel nodded. If she could keep from answering Mom's question about where she and Amy met, there should be no big issue. It would only be for a short time.

"You won't get in trouble for having someone…um…who's not Amish in your house?"

"It'll be fine." She hoped.

"Does Rob know?" Amy waved an arm, indicating the whole Amish thing.

She swallowed. "No."

"You've got to tell him, you know. You've got to."

Chapter 28

As Rachel set Johnny's dirty dish and glass on the counter, she began to rethink having Amy here. Not that she would rescind her invitation. She'd never do that to her friend, because she had a real need. Still her presence would bring her two worlds dangerously close.

Be sure your sin will find you out.

The Bible verse, a favorite of Bishop Dan Esch, flared in her head and refused to leave. She rotated her shoulders, trying to ease the tension drawing them up, making her whole body feel as tight as Jonah's bow string when he prepared to shoot deer.

A knock sounded at the door, making Rachel jump. Had Amy forgotten something? She searched the room as she walked to the door. She opened it and felt her heart fall.

Rob.

He was wearing dress slacks and a dress shirt, his tie loose at the neck. She imagined a suit jacket draped over the car seat. She'd never seen him in anything but the casual clothes he wore to class. He looked a man of the world, a business man, a professional. He was Rob, familiar yet strange.

An Amish man might wear his best clothes, but they didn't change him that much. Same trousers but newer, same shirt, same hat, jacket added. Aaron always looked like Aaron.

But Rob, dressed up…

He swept her into a hug and, closing her eyes, she hugged him back. This handsome man, this Englisch man stirred feelings of such depth it terrified her. She blinked at the tears stinging her eyes.

He leaned back and studied her face. "Are you all right after last evening's chaos?"

Her heart turned over at his concern. "I'm fine."

He looked relieved. "And your brother?"

"Hurting, but he was well enough to come downstairs for something to eat. He's moving slowly, but he's moving."

They stood in the living room, arms still around each other. She reached out and pushed the door shut.

He gave her that half smile she loved so much, like he was glad just to be with her. She knew it was vain and foolish, very un-Amish, but she felt embarrassed that he would see her in her real clothes for the first time when she was wearing her oldest and grubbiest.

"I left my business meeting as soon as I could and drove right here," he said. "I wanted to make sure you and Johnny were all right."

Oh, my! "Johnny's upstairs. He's still awake if you want to say hi."

He gave her a quick kiss and released her. He studied her as if trying to figure out why she looked different.

She ran a hand over her scarf and secured hair and forced a smile. "I was planting trees this evening."

"Planting trees?" He laughed.

"Little trees." She held her hands a foot apart. "Sixty of them. My brother Jonah got a rush order at his nursery, and the family helped him fill it."

"Sounds more interesting than my evening."

She raised her eyebrows in question.

"Business dinner with a couple of guys who spent the whole time trying to out-brag each other. We were about to descend to my-dad's-bigger-than-your-dad when the bill finally came. Trees would be a great improvement. You'll have to tell me all about it when I come down."

He took the stairs two at a time, and she soon heard him and Johnny talking, though she couldn't make out what they were saying.

She sat in her favorite chair and stared at the empty fireplace, waiting. She felt like she was kneeling with her neck exposed and the guillotine ready to fall.

Twice in one night.

Amy had been so easy. She understood conflicting lives. She accepted that friendship could cross chasms, even the canyon of an unintended deceit, if both people were willing.

But Rob? He thought the Amish were strange, alien. *"Do you ever wonder what they think?"* And what a friendship might survive, a romance might not.

She heard footsteps in the upstairs hall. She took a deep breath and willed her stomach to stop churning. It did not obey.

"Be nice to her!" It was Johnny.

Rob came downstairs laughing. "Okay," he called back. "I'll do my best."

Johnny knew what was coming.

Rachel stood, and Rob looked at her, really looked at all of her. His eyes slid first to her hair.

"I like it loose."

She knew that. And she liked it when he fingered a curl or brushed it back over her shoulder.

He studied the scarf and frowned slightly. A scarf in the house? That would be his Englisch thought.

Then he took in her dress, its pins, its style. And her apron.

His hand waved up and down, indicating her outfit.

"Old," she said, trying to force a smile. Her lips were trembling as were her legs. "Dirty. Planting trees is hard work."

"Mmm." He looked around the room, then back at her. He studied her a minute longer. His face filled with pure disbelief. "This isn't Johnny's house, is it?"

She shook her head as a vise tightened around her heart, squeezing, squeezing.

"It's yours."

"It's mine," she admitted in a whisper.

"And you're Amish."

She wanted to sound proud of her heritage, proud in a proper, non-sinful way. There were centuries of tradition and history behind her and her People. They had stood their ground and lived their lives for God and community against great odds.

Her voice shook instead. "I'm Amish."

He studied her for a moment in silence, his disbelief slowly changing to anger. She could see it in his face. He'd been tricked, or so he must think. She forced herself to stand still under his scrutiny. She was the offender, and she deserved any embarrassment or pain she suffered.

"What are you doing at Wexford?" His voice was edged with his mounting irritation. "I don't know a lot about Amish life, but isn't eighth grade all you're allowed?"

"I never meant to deceive anyone."

He just looked at her.

"I didn't. I just wanted to learn." She took a deep breath and spoke her heart. "I didn't plan on you."

He didn't respond by as much as a flicker of an eye. He just looked away and studied the lantern on the end table. "Do your people know you take classes and run around in…civilian clothes?"

She shook her head. "No."

"Couldn't you get, like, shunned if you get caught?"

"I could."

He looked upstairs. "Is Johnny shunned?"

"Johnny never joined the Gmay."

"The Gmay?"

"Short for *gemiende* or community."

"But you did."

She nodded again.

"So you could get shunned." He dropped into one of her chairs but didn't settle back. He finally looked at her. "What does that mean exactly?"

She sat in the other, on its edge like him. "It means I lose my family and my community. I'm excommunicated."

"Can you never see them again?"

"I can see them and talk with them if they want, but I can never be part of them again. I'd never belong." Her voice caught, and she felt overwhelmed with sorrow at what might be.

Neither said anything for a few minutes, and Rachel wished it was winter and there was a fire in the fireplace. Then there'd be someplace to look, the flex of flames and the crackle of wood to absorb some of the tension.

Rob broke the silence. "Was your husband Amish?"

"Yes."

He nodded and ran a hand through his hair. "Your honesty and openness were two of the things I liked most about you, Rachel."

Talk about a knife to the heart. She actually flinched from the pain. "I'm sorry." How weak it sounded.

"I'd really hoped…" He looked at her with his heart in his eyes.

"Me too," she managed to whisper. The air vibrated with emotion and longing.

He sighed and stood. "I'd better go."

She nodded numbly and stood too.

He reached out and pulled off the head scarf. "That's a little better."

She let her head fall forward until it rested against his chest. Her tears wet his dress shirt. Being with him was so easy, so natural. Loving him was so hard, so impossible.

For a brief moment his arms came around her and she thought she felt a kiss on the top of her head. She felt hope for the first time in their conversation. Perhaps they'd survive her deceit after all.

Then he stiffened and backed away. With a small nod and a sad smile, he was gone.

She stood with her back against the door, listening to him drive away. Her shoulders shook and tears bathed her face.

All she wanted was to learn things.

Chapter 29

Friday morning when Johnny tested his various body parts, he still hurt like crazy, but he knew he wasn't going to die. He pulled himself out of bed and shuffled down the hall to the bathroom like an old man. Still no blood in his urine, thank God. He took three aspirin and grabbed the muscle soothing lotion.

When Mr. Sherman's goons had grabbed him Wednesday night and Mick had stepped up swinging that bat, Johnny had gone faint with fear. Would it be a broken skull or shattered kneecaps?

When Mick set the bat down and started with his fists, Johnny had actually felt relieved. Maybe he wouldn't get clubbed after all, unless Mick was saving the best for last.

He hadn't realized how much a fist to the solar plexus gutted you. Not only did pain swamp you, but your ability to breathe was paralyzed. No matter how he tried, he couldn't draw air. Just when he thought he was going to die, he'd managed to gasp, and precious oxygen filled his lungs. That was when Mick let him have it again.

He hadn't exactly seen stars, but flashes of red danced before him as he sagged in Thomas's arms. He started to look forward to a clean strike to the head from the bat. At least it would knock him out. Instead he got a few more punches to the ribs and one especially nasty one to his kidney.

Then Mick picked up the bat, and Johnny prepared for the end. Mick was in such a rage, he'd probably not stop with one swift bash. Before he could swing, Rachel's boyfriend rushed in, a one man rescue squad. Bing, bang, and Thomas was gone. Boom and Mick followed. Too bad he was so weak he wasn't able to appreciate Rob's moves in all their beauty. He'd get lessons when he was better.

Thursday had passed in a blur of pain. He slept most of the day. He ventured downstairs for some food in midafternoon, but hurt so much he was more than glad to return to bed. In the evening he went down again and met Rachel's cute little blonde friend Amy. What a sweetie! And Rob stopped by to see how he was.

Poor Rachel. Unmasked twice in one evening.

Now it was the second morning after the beating and he held onto the sink while he recovered from the exertion of swallowing the aspirin. After a few minutes of trying to breathe without it hurting, he started the trek back to the bedroom. When he finally made it, he painted himself with the muscle stuff. Then he lay back down as he waited for the various medicines to take effect. While he waited, he pondered his situation with Mr. Sherman.

He'd underestimated the man. He'd thought it would be all threats, like Corner Bob. Scary, scary, sure, but they could be weathered. He'd forgotten that Bob had only threats because Bob had done what Mr. Sherman asked. There was no need for stronger action in his case.

Johnny hadn't cooperated. Of course he hadn't. He couldn't. He didn't have several thousand dollars to repay that idiotic loan. He still couldn't believe how stupid he'd been.

He looked at the unadorned walls of Rachel's guest room and thought his life was as barren. The rest of her house was Plain too, but her life was full. She had her job, the family, college, Rob.

He saw a blob of color out of the corner of his eye and looked over to see a clutch of bright yellow flowers in a Mason jar on the bedside table. He was sure they hadn't been there last night. Rachel must have put them there before she left for school this morning.

Rachel loved beauty. Her gardens were spectacular. The quilt on her bed was more than functional with its soft pastels and pretty floral pattern. She was beautiful. She was smart. She was kind.

She was caught between two worlds.

He'd always wondered why she married Aaron. He was a nice enough guy, but she was made for more. Of all the Miller kids, she was far and away the standout. Not that she knew it or even thought it, but it was true.

He'd seen her and Rob look at each other when they thought no one was watching. She'd never looked at Aaron that way, poor guy. Poor Rachel.

And poor him. He went back to contemplating Mr. Sherman. No matter which way he looked at things, he realized there was only one thing to do. He was going to have to become one of the goons, at least until the loan was paid off. Then he would get as far from Mr. Sherman as he could. California was looking better by the second. He'd go today if he wasn't afraid of the man's threats toward his sisters.

Just before Rachel came home from school, he let himself out of the house and drove to his trailer. He knew he couldn't stay here. If Mick wanted to find him, this was the first place he'd look. But they wouldn't expect him to be here now. He hoped.

He stripped out of the clothes he'd worn for the last two days and lay down on his much less comfortable bed until eight o'clock. He pulled out the bottle of Rachel's aspirin that he'd borrowed and dosed himself. He showered and then rubbed on more of her muscle relaxant. He dressed, amazed that it could hurt so much to push your arms into sleeves. He drove to Corner Bob's.

"Whoa!" Bob studied his face. "Walk into an open door?"

"Yeah. One with fists."

Bob drew him a beer.

Johnny studied the empty stool at the end of the bar where unhappy Harry always sat. "Where's our friend?"

"You didn't hear? In the hospital. He's in a coma."

Johnny felt a chill slide down his body. "What happened?"

"Got attacked the other night. Beaten with a baseball bat."

Johnny pictured Mick picking up his bat. He swiped at the sweat on his lip. His chest felt as if one of Datt's plow horses sat on it.

"Robbery?" Please let it be a robbery.

Bob wiped at a spot on the bar. "Harry never had money. He's in so deep to Mr. Sherman it's all he can do to buy beer."

No wonder the man always looked so miserable. "Any suspects?"

"The cops were in here earlier. Someone told them Harry hung out here."

"Bet Mr. Sherman liked that."

"He wasn't here yet. But he's not a happy man. Take my word for it."

Johnny forced a smile. "Maybe this'll make him take his business elsewhere."

"I should be so lucky."

Johnny nursed his beer, imagining himself in that hospital bed, brain made mush by Mick's bat. When his glass was empty, he held it out. "Another."

"Better not." Bob tipped his head toward the back of the place. "Here comes Mick."

Johnny stood, forcing himself to stand straight instead of curving in on himself protectively. Standing straight hurt like the devil.

Johnny followed Mick to Mr. Sherman's table and stood in excruciating pain waiting for the great man's attention. Thomas ignored him, surveying the room as usual.

Finally Mr. Sherman deigned to look up. "Johnny." Like he hadn't known he was there all along. "Have a seat."

Trying not to sigh in relief, Johnny gingerly sat.

"Dear me," Mr. Sherman forced his pudgy face into a look of faux sympathy. "What happened to you?"

"Walked into a door in the dark."

"Ah. Of course." Faux smile. "I must say I'm surprised to see you up and about. Mick and Thomas told me about your accident."

Johnny glanced briefly at Mick who smirked at him, then at Thomas who didn't even glance his way. What had their version of the fight been like? He'd bet anything they hadn't mentioned Rob.

He dropped his gaze and tried to remember the words he had practiced all day as he lay in bed. "As you know, sir, I owe you a considerable sum of money."

Mr. Sherman tipped his head in acknowledgment.

"I wanted to ask if there is any service I can perform for you to work off the amount."

There. He'd said it. He'd offered himself a living sacrifice, not to God like they told you to in Gmay but to a bloated petty crime lord.

Mr. Sherman laced his fingers and set his hands on his table. "Why should I let you work off your debt?"

Johnny stared at the chubby fingers and tried to come up with an answer. He settled on the truth. "Because I'll never have the money."

"Never?"

"Never."

"Can't ask your Amish farmer daddy?"

Johnny didn't answer.

"Or that pretty sister of yours? What's her name? Rachel?"

All that aspirin with a beer chaser on an empty stomach was eating a hole through his abdominal lining. "Rachel's a widow, Mr. Sherman, an Amish school teacher. She has nothing to do with any of this, and she has no money."

"She doesn't have to have anything to do with this." Mr. Sherman's cold eyes peered out from below beefy lids.

Johnny's stomach pitched. He understood the threat.

"Breathe, Johnny," Mr. Sherman said with a smile. "Breathe. I'm not planning to harm her or any of the others."

Of course not. He'd send Mick and Thomas.

Feeling his strength fading fast, Johnny rushed to the point. "Whatever I can do, Mr. Sherman. Just tell me."

The man smiled, looking like the fat spider that wrapped Frodo in the cocoon. And he was Frodo, unable to escape, with no Sam to rescue him.

"I need someone to run to Philadelphia for me next Saturday," Mr. Sherman said. "There's a package that needs to be picked up. It's a trip worth a thousand dollars off your debt."

Whatever it was he was to transport, Johnny knew it was illegal. He also knew he'd do it.

What choice did he have?

"Go get a good night's sleep, Johnny." Mr. Sherman smiled as if he really cared. "We want you to feel well enough to drive into the city tomorrow."

"Let me help you to your car." Mick took a step toward him.

Johnny's stomach dropped, leaving him lightheaded and dizzy. Still he managed to hold out a hand. "No. I'll manage fine by myself."

"I'll help you, Johnny." Mick's voice was steel. "Wouldn't want you to fall on your face, would we? It's already all rainbow shades."

As Mick stepped toward him, hand out to grab, Thomas looked at him for the first time since the parking lot. Then Mick had his arm in a vice, and he was led ignominiously from Corner Bob's.

When they reached his car, Johnny felt Mick's grip slide from his arm to the muscle at the top of his shoulder. Johnny flinched as Mick squeezed.

"There will be a second package to pick up next week," Mick hissed in his ear. He squeezed harder, and Johnny was sure he'd vomit at the pain. "And you will tell no one. Got that? No one."

Johnny managed a nod. Mick released him, and Johnny grabbed the car to stay upright. Over Mick's shoulder he saw Thomas disappear back into Corner Bob's. Did Thomas think Mick couldn't handle him? Like it was a contest. After all, he was an Amish nobody and Mick could be in WWE.

Somehow he managed to drive to Rachel's and drag himself back to bed. He felt so bad he was sure he'd die. If he didn't manage it today, he'd probably manage it next week.

Chapter 30

The day after learning the truth about Rachel, Rob arrived at class before either she or Amy. He slid into his usual seat and pulled his new tablet from its pouch. He was surfing the app store when he felt her. He looked up, and sure enough, Rachel stood in the doorway looking pale, beautiful, and uncertain.

He knew how she felt. He was so confused it was a wonder he'd found the on button for the tablet. He knew he should be understanding of her dilemma, but he felt deceived, played, and thoroughly snookered. The longer he thought about the way she'd played him, the angrier he became.

He knew what she'd done was nothing like his father's crimes, but the feeling of being taken was so familiar. It made him look the fool, and it stung badly. He hadn't felt this conflicted since he watched the cops lead his father away in handcuffs, the man he had admired above all others reduced to a common con man.

He should just ignore her. He should make believe he wasn't aware of her. He should let his simmering anger surface and scorch the air with his contempt. Then she'd know.

Yet as their eyes met, he gave a little smile and patted the seat next to him. She visibly relaxed, a sure sign she'd been worried about his welcome. Well, she should be. He turned back to his tablet.

"Hi," she whispered as she sank into the chair.

He gave her a nod but didn't look up.

"Is that new?" It was Amy, all perky and uninhibited. He hadn't even noticed her come in. "Let me see."

Talk about the device managed to cover the awkwardness between him and Rachel until Dr. Dyson cleared her throat and began class.

Rachel pulled out her AlphaSmart, and all Rob's anxiety and anger focused on the innocent machine. How stupid to think a battery operated word processor was all right to use because of its battery when his new tablet wasn't because of its plug. She had to use electricity too. She had to send her material to an electric printer to get it off her "legal" machine. And what made a buggy so magical or a pinned-together dress so holy? He just didn't get it. She hadn't only deceived him. She was deceiving herself. Amish? Ha!

He tried to make himself listen to Dr. Dyson, but he only succeeded part of the time. *She* kept distracting him. She typed. She squirmed. She breathed!

What was it with people he cared for being dishonest? First his father turned all their lives into chaos. Then his mother wheedled and manipulated to get what she wanted. Win was a leech who took advantage of everyone he came in contact with. And now Rachel.

Not that he felt about her as he felt about his family. Oh, no. The pull toward her was a hundred times stronger, a thousand times stronger.

And the hurt and confusion too.

"So it's the character traits that a writer gives his people that make them interesting, and in the best scenarios, fascinating," Dr. Dyson said. "What character traits are important to you? What draws you to someone? Makes you admire them?"

Honesty! Rob wanted to shout it.

"What repels you?" she continued. "Makes you distrust or dislike someone? I want you to select two character traits, one positive, one negative, and write about why they're important to you. I want examples of times you saw them played out in real life, your life. Remember, people, personal."

"I'm writing about balance and extremism," Amy announced as they walked from class. "I lived for so long with people who had no balance and too much fanaticism. I admire people who have balance and I distrust those who don't."

It always tickled Rob that this little woman who looked like Tinker Bell was so feisty and spirited. She looked like she needed a strong man to care for her while in reality she was a scrapper who stood tall and walked proud.

"I'm trying to sort through the damage done me by extremism," she continued. "It's taken me a while to realize I can be committed to something, say Jesus, and still be balanced."

They started down the stairs to the ground floor.

"What about you, Rach?" she asked. "What are you going to write on?"

Rachel frowned. "I don't know. I have to think about it."

"You, Rob?" Amy stared up at him.

The answer was so obvious that he was surprised she asked. "Honesty and deceit. After my father and the fallout from his deceit, honesty is primary for me."

He felt Rachel, walking beside him, stiffen. He glanced at her. Her face, already paler than usual, had turned ashen. He was torn between satisfaction that his barb had hit home and guilt that he'd hurt her.

They walked out of the building. He stopped at the curb and began fiddling with his car keys. "By the way, I'm not going to the Star tonight."

"Oh, come on," Amy said. "We always go.

He shook his head. "I've got stuff I need to do." Like go home and try not to think of Rachel and their doomed relationship.

"But Win'll be at the Star."

"And that's supposed to sell me?"

Amy laughed. "Come on, Rob. We always go. Tell him, Rachel."

They both looked at Rachel who wouldn't look back. "I don't think I want to go either, Amy. Let's just go home."

Amy looked back and forth between Rob and Rachel. "Come on, you guys!"

"Let it go, Amy," Rob said.

"Why? What's wrong?"

Rachel shrugged. "Nothing. I just don't want to go."

Rachel's *nothing* was so patently untrue Amy gave Rob her pixie's version of the evil eye. She stepped close. "What did you do?" she asked softly.

"Wasn't me."

He felt like taking a step back in the face of her vehemence but forced himself to stand firm. He wasn't the one who'd done anything wrong.

"Did you know Bagel and I are living with Rachel? We moved in this afternoon." She stepped away from Rob and to Rachel. She patted her hand. "We'll talk at home, girlfriend."

"You're living with Rachel?" For some reason that irritated him. "She's living with you?" He looked at Rachel who shrugged.

"Bagel and I got kicked out because he barks when I'm not there. Rachel kept me from the streets."

He scowled at Rachel who scowled back. On one hand she lied to him. On the other she took in Amy and her dog. How could she be such a complicated mix of bad and good qualities? It was driving him crazy.

He turned to Amy. "So you knew she was Amish?" Did everyone know but him?

"Found out yesterday."

"Huh." Same day he found out. Somehow it made him feel better that Amy had been kept in the dark too.

"She took a big risk taking me in," Amy continued. "But her family's so nice. And Bagel and I won't be there too long. Just 'til I find another place."

Whereas he would have been there as long as they both should live if things had gone as he had begun to hope. So much for happily ever after.

Time to go home to Charlie and a silence broken only by canine snores and sighs. At least Charlie's love was true.

He was trying to find something on TV to occupy his mind when there was a loud knocking on his door. He looked through the peephole and saw Win's distorted face staring at him. He threw the door open.

"What are you doing here?"

Win stepped inside, forcing Rob to step back. "What did you do?"

"What did I do?"

Win all but snarled at him. "Amy called and said no Star, and I could hear Rachel crying in the background."

His chest tightened. She was crying? "It's none of your business."

"Probably not, but I thought you and she had something special going."

He wanted to be mad at Win, to resent his interference, but the genuine concern in both his expression and voice broke Rob. His shoulders slumped. "So did I."

"It's the Amish thing, isn't it?"

"Well, yeah."

"Okay. I'm trying to understand. Wouldn't that make her nice and kind and sweet and all kinds of other good things? I mean, the Amish are, you know, *good*."

"She wears pinned-together dresses and lives without electricity, Win! She drives a horse and buggy!"

"She drives a black Honda."

"You know what I mean. Talk about different worlds."

Win thought about it for a minute. "But she's so nice."

"Sometimes. But she's also a liar."

"What did she lie about?"

"About being Amish! She never said a word."

Win brushed away his statement as if it meant nothing. "It's not like she killed someone here."

"Maybe not, but it's like she lives at the North Pole and I live at the South. The distance between us is too great."

Win shrugged. "So move."

Rob stared at his brother. "I'm not going to become Amish."

"Why not?"

"I never heard of Amish certified financial planners. And that's not the point."

"What is the point?"

"She lied to me."

"Did she lie or just not tell?"

"There's a difference?"

Win wiggled his hand back and forth in a maybe, maybe not gesture. "Why did she come to class and wear normal clothes? Why did she learn to drive?"

"She's really smart and wanted an education."

"So she took a big risk just to learn stuff."

"Right."

"So maybe she'll take another risk for you."

"But the cost! Her family, her community, her vows."

"She told you she wouldn't pay the price?"

"Well, no, but how could I ever ask that of her?"

"If you feel about her like you seem to, you have to at least talk about it with her. She needs to have the choice."

Everything in Rob stilled.

Win looked at him with something like pity. "For a smart guy, you're awful dumb."

Rob didn't have much option but to agree.

"Okay." Win rubbed his hands together. "Enough of your troubles. I've got some doozies of my own. Be right back."

Rob watched as he jogged to his car and pulled two duffels out of the trunk. He ran back to the apartment, bags in hand.

Rob crossed his arms. "No way, Win. We've been through this before. You can't stay here."

"She stole from me." Win dropped the duffels on the hall floor as if they were too heavy to hold. Charlie took the opportunity to examine them thoroughly. "Four hundred and fifty dollars. Took it out of my top dresser drawer because she needed a tablet like yours but with a pink cover because your black one isn't feminine enough."

"She stole from you?" Though the real question might be how Win had four hundred and fifty dollars to be stolen.

"A new low, even for her. I can't stay there anymore. I can't trust her."

Rob studied his brother. Could he trust him? He'd thought he could trust Rachel and look how that turned out.

Rob's cell played and he answered as he tried to stare Win down.

"Rob!" His mother's shrill voice hit his eardrum and he put the phone on speaker. "He left! What am I going to do? I can't be alone! I don't like to be alone. I'm scared to be alone. Make him come back. Tell him I'm sorry. Tell him he can use the stinking tablet whenever he wants. I mean, it was only $400. It's not like it was a bundle."

"So where's the other fifty?" Win muttered in a low voice.

"Are you worried about him?" Rob asked. "Are you concerned he might be in trouble?"

There was a moment of utter silence.

"Why would I worry about him?" She sounded completely at a loss. "He's a grown man. It's me I'm worried about. It's me who's alone. It's me who's suffering here."

Rob looked at Win who shrugged.

"I've got to go, Mom." Rob got ready hit the off button.

"Don't leave me! What will I do? Where will I go?"

"Mom, you won't go anywhere but to bed. You're safe in your own house."

"Alone. I'm alone. I can't be alone. I don't do alone."

"You should have thought of that before you robbed your own son."

"Robbed? Who said I robbed anyone? I only borrowed—" There was a short pause. "He's there, isn't he? He's there telling lies about me. See what I have to put up with? My own son telling lies."

"Talk to you later after you've had a good night's sleep."

"How can I sleep? I'm alone!"

Rob hit the off button and slid the phone into its holder. He eyed his brother.

"Where'd the cash come from, Win? Just a few weeks ago you were begging me for money."

"Yeah. Not one of my finer moments. I've been working."

"Really?" Rob hoped his skepticism didn't show too much. "Where?"

"At the Star. Breakfast and lunch shift."

Rob blinked. "Doing what?"

"Waiting tables. I'm their only waiter though they call me and the girls servers. Waitress and waiter are sexist these days." He seemed proud of his job.

"How did this happen?"

"When I met you guys that first night, I got to talking to Patsy. You know Patsy? Her family owns the place?"

"I know Patsy well. We went to school together, remember?"

Win made a mumbly noise that sounded like "Oh, right." Then he continued. "Anyway she told me they needed another server and I asked for the job. I figured why not? I had to start somewhere. Isn't that what you told me? I saved that $450 as the start to getting my own place."

Rob studied his brother for a moment and then held out his hand. "Congratulations, Win. I'm proud of you."

Win flushed with pleasure as he shook it. "Thanks. I thought maybe you'd make fun of me. I mean, it's only a serving job."

"It's an honest job and a start. And the empty room is down the hall on the right. You'll have to use a sleeping bag on the floor because I haven't gotten furniture yet."

"Really?" Hope lit his face. "I can stay?"

"Really. I'd be glad to have you stay."

Win grinned. "I think maybe I'll use the sofa. It's softer."

Chapter 31

Max opened the door Saturday mid-morning to find Rachel standing there in her Amish clothes. She looked sad and the skin beneath her eyes looked bruised. Her usual spark and zip were missing. Something was clearly wrong.

Beside her was the English girl who had come here the other night looking for Rachel. Accompanying them was the cutest beagle she'd seen in a long time.

"Come in." Max stepped aside for them. "This is a nice surprise."

As the girls took chairs, Max settled back onto Buddy's recliner. She felt comfortable there. It wasn't as good as a Buddy hug, but it made her feel closer to him somehow.

She smiled at Rachel's friend. What was her name? "So you found Rachel, I see."

"This is my friend Amy who's going to be living with me for a while." Rachel pointed to the dog. "And this is Bagel, the reason she's living with me."

"He barks," Amy said.

Max looked at the dog sitting beside Amy's chair like a perfect gentleman. She listened as Amy told the story of the cranky lady who lived beneath her and caused her eviction.

"So Rachel took me in." She beamed at Rachel who smiled back with so little joy it broke Max's heart.

"How do you girls know each other?" Max found the Amish and English aspects of this friendship fascinating—and potentially troublesome for Rachel. Maybe Amy was the reason for the air of sorrow hanging over Rachel.

"We're in class together," Rachel said. "We met the first night."

"Rachel's the first person I met. I moved down here to go to Wexford and didn't know anyone. She sat next to me the first night."

Max nodded. "And you're the one she went out to eat with."

"Right! And you're the one who didn't need to come pick her up."

Max and Amy grinned at each other.

"I wanted you to meet Amy because she's going to need to come over here to use your electricity if it's okay with you."

"Sure. Anytime. I love having the company."

"I can't stay long this morning," Amy said. "I have to go to work at eleven today. I'm a waitress."

"Do you have time for a cup of coffee and a piece of coffee cake? I made Buddy's favorite this morning, and I've been sitting here wondering why." *And feeling stupid for making it with no one to eat it.*

"Buddy isn't home?"

Max shook her head. "No, he isn't."

Her expression must have become distressed because Amy looked stricken. "Buddy was your husband."

Max nodded, forcing a smile.

"I'm sorry. I knew you were a widow, but I didn't know your husband's name."

"It's okay. Don't let it worry you." She rose. "Let's go sit in the kitchen."

Everyone told Max her life would be just fine once she adjusted to her new normal, whatever that was. The problem was she wanted her old normal back. She wanted Buddy in that old chair. She wanted Buddy sniffing the air as he walked into the kitchen saying, "I smell me some good stuff!"

She sighed. She wanted her husband.

Once she was up and moving, feeding people, Max felt better, almost normal. Having people sit around her kitchen table was common for her whether it was the women in her weekly Bible study or just a drop-in friend. Entertaining was her joy.

She pulled out three mugs, the cheery ones with bouquets of daisies tied with graceful ribbons on a vivid blue background. She grabbed the cloth napkins with daisies sprinkled over them and the sugar and creamer that matched the mugs. She put slices of coffee cake on the daisy plate Buddy had given her "just because it'll make you smile."

She ran her fingers gently over the daisies in its center and realized it still did.

As they ate, Amy chattered away about how lucky she was to have Rachel as a friend, how fun it was to live with her, and how interesting learning to live Amish was. Amy was a pixie of a girl with her cropped blonde hair and her big eyes, a sprite whose hands flew as she talked. She would be a good person for Rachel to have around. Max loved Rachel's questing mind and her courage, but she needed someone to make her laugh.

Amy ate the apple coffee cake and umm-ummed with delight. Rachel broke off a small piece and played with it. Max glanced at her and looked away. Something was seriously wrong and it pained Max to see her friend this way.

After she'd eaten her second piece of coffee cake and finished her second mug of coffee, Amy glanced at the daisy clock on the wall and gave a little bleat. "Gotta go. I'm going to be late! Can't be late. They don't like that." She jumped to her feet. "Come on, Bagel. Let's go."

He jumped to his feet from his nap beneath the table.

"I'll leave him at the house, Rachel. I don't want him barking for Max. Thanks so much, Max! See you later, Rachel! Come on, Bagel!" And she was gone.

Max and Rachel sat in silence as though waiting for the air molecules to settle back into place after Amy's little whirlwind.

"I like her," Max finally said. "Perky little thing."

Rachel gave a wan smile. "Very true."

Max reached across the table and held out her hand. "What's wrong, Rachel?"

Rachel stared at the hand for a moment, her eyes filling with tears. Then she looked up, and one tear slid down her cheek. "Oh, Max!"

A mixture of compassion and yikes-what-do-I-say flashed through Max. *God, please give me wisdom! And Buddy, maybe you were right. I shouldn't have interfered.*

Max thought of a young Ashley sitting in that chair, tears in her eyes over some social disappointment or boyfriend problem. Then it had been hard enough to say the right word, the helpful word without sounding condescending or critical, but at least she and her daughter had a common world—if you didn't count teen culture with its constant turns and twists. But Rachel! The English/Amish differences went so deep.

"Are your parents upset about an English girl living with you, even if it's only for a short while?" It seemed a reasonable enough guess. One thing for sure, Rachel's distress would not come from anything academic.

"Amy?" Rachel looked surprised at the thought. "No. Well, maybe a bit, but not enough to make an issue of it." She managed a tight smile. "If I can keep from having to say where we met, I think it'll be fine."

"So they've met her?"

"The other night. I took her over. Mom was definitely fishing, but I was able to change the subject when the question came up. Datt seemed happy to leave the questioning to Mom, but Levi watched with eagle eyes. Nothing gets past him." She paused for breath. "Amy loves that my family loves each other. So far everything's good."

"So if it's not Amy bothering you, then what?"

Rachel took a deep breath. "His name's Rob."

Rob. Max sighed and waited. A single woman having sleepless nights so often meant a man. She'd learned with Ashley that the words finally erupted like a volcano whose pressure had built beyond the point of containment—if you waited.

"He found out I'm Amish. He saved Johnny and…" The whole story poured out somewhat disjointedly, a sure sign of Rachel's distress. "And he was so distant last night at class and wouldn't go out to eat and hasn't contacted me since!"

"Oh, honey." The fact that it was only a couple of days meant nothing when the heart was involved.

"And not only is he Englisch, Max. He's an Army veteran who served in Iraq and Afghanistan. His brother's a charming wastrel and his father's in jail for fraud."

Max felt a flash of foreknowledge. "What's Rob's last name?"

"Lanier."

"Eugene Lanier must be his father." Max wondered how much like father, like son applied here. "Several of our friends lost their life's savings because of him. I wanted us to put our money in his care because he had such great rates of return. Buddy said no one could honestly make that much money and refused to consider him." Max outlined the daisies on her mug with a finger. "I don't know where I'd be today if Buddy had listened to me and all our friends."

"Rob thinks I'm a liar." Rachel rested her elbow on the table and her forehead in her palm. "I *am* a liar."

She looked so desolate Max's heart broke for her. "Honey, if he's worth his stuff, he should understand that you didn't intend to trick him."

"But honesty is big to him, Max, because of his father. And I deceived him."

"You must care for him a great deal."

"I think I may…love him."

"Love is an awfully strong word, Rachel."

"I know I feel more attraction to him and affection for him than I ever did for Aaron, and that makes me feel terrible too." Another tear fell.

"Aaron was kind, considerate, and convenient," Max said.

"Yes, and isn't that so sad?"

"Was he unhappy in your marriage?"

Rachel thought a minute and then shook her head. "I've thought a lot about that, and I don't think he was. He loved me and I loved him, but not with the intensity or depth I feel for Rob."

"So don't waste guilt there. You did everything you knew to do at that time."

Rachel sat up a little straighter. "I did. I really did. If he'd lived, I would have continued as his wife, committed and faithful."

"So your problem is that you haven't heard from Rob, and it makes you sad?"

"That's half of it. It breaks my heart, but if I do hear from him, then what do I do?"

Buddy, you were right. All I did was help her reach a point of hurt and choice. Still she couldn't feel she'd done wrong. "So you'd be forced into making a decision."

"My family. My vows. Oh, Max!" She put her face in her hands and wept.

Max rounded the table and knelt before her, pulling her close. She made foolish soothing noises and rubbed her back, letting her cry herself out. There were times when no words sufficed.

"I should never have gone to class, Max. None of this would have happened if I hadn't gone out into the world. The preachers are right. The world will capture you and pull you away from *Gott*."

Max pulled a chair close to Rachel and leaned close. "Listen to me, kiddo, because I want to make a very strong point, both theological and sociological."

At that pronouncement, Rachel looked up with waterlogged eyes.

"The world can lead you astray. Your leaders are right. The world can tempt you to activities that are wrong. The world can be the devil's playground. But the world can also be full of wonderful opportunities and options and people. It's like there are two worlds out there. You get to choose which one you live in."

Max paused a moment as a new thought hit her. "Well, for you there are three worlds. There's your Amish world, circumscribed by tradition and rules, and full of safety and security because everyone knows exactly what's expected of them. You've lived there your whole life. It's what you know."

Rachel hummed agreement, encouraging Max to keep talking.

"Then there's the evil world where people break the Ten Commandments and do all kinds of wrong, evil, and cruel things. Your church is right to warn you about that world. The Bible warns us about that world, and so does my pastor. Drinking, drugs, immorality—things like that and many much worse."

Max squeezed Rachel's hands. "But between the two there exists a world where you can live a godly life and still enjoy the freedom of choice and the independence to be who God made you to be. It's not as stable a world as your Amish one because we have to figure out who we are ourselves, and that's a challenge."

Smiling wryly, Max rose. "That's where I am, Rachel. Trying to figure out who I am now that I'm no longer a wife. Trying to find my new purpose. It's hard, but I, not my community or my church, get to do the figuring and make the choices."

Rachel rose, her eyes wide and confused. "I need to go home. I need to think."

Max nodded. "Sure. Want to take some coffee cake with you?" She slipped some cake in a plastic bag and zipped it shut. She held it out to Rachel, who took it automatically.

"One last thought, my dear. Rob needs time to think and figure all this out too. He got blindsided, and he needs time. He may not be a lost cause."

But a week of no Star, no calls, no tugs on her hair made her think otherwise.

Chapter 32

*J*ohnny hated driving in Philadelphia. Everybody knew where they were going but him. The roads turned into one-way streets without warning. The cars parked at the curb made the streets too narrow. Road signs were invisible or wrong. At least they didn't agree with his GPS. And the delivery trucks parked wherever they wanted, blocking traffic while cabs blew their horns.

Give him the twisty back roads of western Chester County where buggies were your biggest obstacle and an occasional milk tanker blocked the road while it maneuvered into a farm lane in reverse.

When Mr. Sherman sent him on this errand, Johnny had assumed he would be going to a seedy part of town where gangs populated the street corners and death lurked behind every dumpster. He expected to see druggies and winos lying against abandoned buildings and hookers on every corner. He'd been telling himself he wasn't scared ever since he got the assignment.

He ended up outside a nice restaurant on Sansom Street on Saturday, a little more than a week after Mr. Sherman accepted his offer to work for him.

After he checked the address for the third time, he walked in. Tables were filled with people having late lunches. He walked to the bar that gleamed with polish along one wall. In comparison Corner Bob's looked like a dive.

A large African-American man smiled at him. "Help you?"

Johnny saw coffee on the counter behind the bar. "Coffee. Decaf." His nerves were too jumpy for caffeine. "To go."

The big man handed him his drink, a lid in place.

Johnny slipped off the lid, blew on the beverage and added some real cream from a little pitcher the bartender pushed toward him. He took a scalding sip and then drew a quick breath to cool his mouth. "Uh…I'm looking for Marco," he managed.

The big man looked him over with a dislike that hadn't been there mere seconds ago. "Why?"

All Johnny could think to say was, "Mr. Sherman sent me."

"Huh. Let me get him. I don't want no part of that man."

Which man, Mr. Sherman or Marco? Or both?

A minute later a little Hispanic man swallowed up by his white Oxford cloth shirt was at his elbow.

"I'm Marco. You from Mr. Sherman?"

Johnny nodded.

"How do I know? Maybe you're a cop."

"How do I know you're Marco? Maybe you're a cop."

"Eeny, meeny, miney, moe," Marco said it with a straight face. "Catch a tiger by the toe."

Ridiculous, Johnny thought, but easy to remember and nothing a normal man would say to another man. "One potato, two potato, three potato, four."

Marco reached behind the bar and brought out a manila envelope. It was slightly bigger than an eight and a half by eleven sheet of paper and bulged gently with—he didn't want to know with what.

He took the envelope made chubby by its contents and gave a curt nod, hoping he looked confident in spite of his heart threatening to jump from his chest.

"You got something else for me?" he asked.

"Like what?"

How was he supposed to know? "Mick sent me."

Marco grunted and reached under the counter again. This envelope was smaller and its contents harder and fatter. It made a bump in the envelope at its base. A bottle? A super-secret high-tech battery? A roll of gold coins?

Johnny took the envelope but Marco didn't let go. Johnny looked up in surprise.

"Either of these envelopes got their seals broken, you're a dea—" He stopped before he said the final D as the bartender returned to his position, a scowl aimed at Johnny and Marco. Marco smiled a most unpleasant smile. "Let's just say you don't want to get curious."

"Not curious," Johnny managed around his dry throat. "Not curious at all."

Marco released the envelope. "Good."

Johnny held the envelopes in one hand and his coffee in the other as he forced himself to walk out like he hadn't a care in the world. He climbed in his car, anxious to be out of the city, anxious to reach home, anxious to get rid of whatever he had. He put the envelopes on the passenger seat and stared at them as if they were a pair of coiled rattlers ready to sink fangs into him. The very sight of them made him shudder. He slipped his coffee in the cup holder, and started the engine. He checked behind and pulled into traffic.

And stopped. He was trapped on the narrow street behind a produce truck delivering to the restaurant he'd just left. A man wheeled his fruit and vegetables down an alley, totally oblivious to Johnny and another car now behind him. The one concession to the rest of the vehicular world was the truck's blinkers flashing.

A second truck pulled up behind the car behind him. He couldn't go back and he couldn't go forward. He was trapped! Every movie scene where trucks penned someone in flashed through his mind. Someone always died in those scenes.

He waited, fantasizing the doors on the vehicles behind him being thrown open and men with Uzis thundering toward him.

He looked in his rearview mirror, but all he saw were drivers resigned to waiting. To prove his lack of fear to anyone watching him, he casually picked up his coffee and sipped. It was still too hot, and he made a face. He managed another swallow. He'd left the lid on the bar, so he'd better drink as much as he could before he started driving.

He looked at the envelopes lying so innocently on the seat beside him, flap side up. If this was the olden days, there would be a red wax seal so Mr. Sherman would know no one had opened them. All this envelope had was the sticky stuff on the flap. All he could say was it better hold.

What was in them? Not that he'd ever look, but still…Was this how Eve felt when she studied that forbidden apple?

A horn sounded behind him, the loud blast making him jump so badly he spilled coffee all over himself—and the manila envelopes. He watched in horror as dark brown liquid seeped into the paper of the envelopes. They began to crinkle like wet paper did.

He held his breath. The seals, which took the brunt of the coffee, still looked to be holding, and he finally breathed. But what if he'd just ruined something inside? Was some important paper now wet with running ink? Was Mr. Sherman going to let Mick loose again?

The pull to look inside and see if something had been ruined was so strong his hand started to shake as it hovered over the envelope. He felt like a fish on a line being pulled closer and closer without the power to escape.

Several angry honks from behind broke his trance, and he saw the produce truck turning the corner ahead. He hit the gas and followed. Now he had to find his way back to the Schuylkill Expressway, I-76. Between his GPS and the too small signs, he finally found his way and cruised in the heavy traffic toward King of Prussia.

He glanced over at the envelopes every few seconds. In fascinated horror he watched the edges of the flaps curl as the coffee worked on the glue. Then just as he passed Conshohocken, the flap on the large envelope came loose. It didn't flip up or anything, but it was obvious it was no longer sealed.

Johnny felt the sweat pop out all over his body. Mr. Sherman was going to think he did this on purpose. All his protestations, honest and heartfelt, were going to sound lame at best and like lies at worst.

Then Mick's flap came undone too, and he added the D to Marco's *You're a dea*—.

As he turned off the Schuylkill onto 202 South, he thought longingly of California. He should just keep on driving and not stop until he reached the Pacific. Find some small town out there or maybe a big city like LA or San Francisco. Which one could he disappear into best?

But he didn't have the nerve, not so much because he feared for himself, though he did, big time. He kept remembering Corner Bob and those pictures of his little girl. He saw Rachel's concern when he was hurt, and he couldn't put her or Sally or Ruthie in danger. He wasn't that big a coward.

So he turned off 202 onto Route 30 to 322 and Honey Brook. He turned toward the farm. He wanted to go there and hide in his old room. He'd make believe none of the past few months had happened. He'd put on a pair of broadfall trousers, a white shirt, and straw hat and stand on the big green harvester as a team of work horses pulled it through the cornfields.

If only it could be so.

He was so lost in his dream of home and safety that the stop sign snuck up on him. So did the car crossing the intersection in front of him. He saw it at the last moment and stomped on the brakes. The tires screeched, the coffee went flying, and the envelopes on the passenger seat were airborne. He reached for them, but it was too late. They fell from the seat onto the floor.

And disgorged their contents at his feet.

Chapter 33

*J*ohnny stared at the papers on the floor of his car. With trembling hands he picked them up and studied them. Might as well. The damage was done. The genie couldn't go back in the bottle.

There were several birth certificates with the seal of the Commonwealth of Pennsylvania raised on each. And the little blue booklets reading United States of America that fell out with the papers were passports.

False papers. False passports. For who?

Illegals for sure. Terrorists? Or was it human trafficking? Johnny shuddered. Or maybe it was just illegal seasonal workers. What used to be the mushroom capital of the world was about twenty miles south.

But why would papers for those people find their way to Honey Brook instead of directly to Kennett Square or Oxford or one of the towns in mushroom country?

Johnny forced himself to face the truth. Mr. Sherman, sitting calmly in Corner Bob's like a fat slug, was part of some criminal network dealing in illegal papers to illegal people, and now he was too. Johnny thought he'd throw up.

There was one thing still lying on the floor, and Johnny reached for it. It was a vial of liquid, and it was what had made Mick's envelope fat. The label on the bottle had lots of print on it, most too small to read, but the word Testosterone stood out in large letters across the front of the bottle.

Anabolic steroids. Mick took illegal muscle builders.

Johnny shook his head at his own denseness. He should have known. Look at the guy's bulk, his strength. Sure, the man was a gym rat who lifted weights with the devotion and intensity other men gave their favorite football teams, and he'd assumed that was the reason for the bulging biceps.

But there was his terrible temper too. Steroid rage? With all the stories that had been in the news about the baseball players caught in the steroid scandal, he knew more than he wanted to about what the stuff did to people.

He glanced around. No one was paying him any attention in the Turkey Hill mini-mart lot where he'd pulled in after everything spilled on the floor. He looked at his watch. He had only fifteen minutes before he was supposed to meet Mick to give him the steroids. The papers were to be delivered to Mr. Sherman at Corner Bob's this evening.

Johnny thought of Mick's frenzy at the trailer, the beating at the diner, poor comatose Harry, even the pleasure Mick got from squeezing the muscle at the top of his shoulder just to inflict pain, and he shuddered. The man was crazy.

Johnny pulled his shirttail out and rubbed the bottle clean of his prints. Like Mick'd know what Johnny's prints looked like. It wasn't like he was in any database anywhere. And it wasn't as if Mick had access to any database even if he was in one.

But that temper!

He slid the bottle back in its envelope, licked the flap, and tried to make it stick. No go.

All he could do was deliver the stuff and hope Mick didn't care that he knew what was in the pouch.

It was telling, now that he thought about it, that Mick had a separate delivery spot for his package. It was a safe bet that Mr. Sherman didn't know about Mick's habit and Mick didn't want him to know.

Did the fact that he knew put Johnny in more or less danger?

Was it a bargaining chip—"Leave me alone or I'll tell"—or was it, as Marco said, a death warrant?

Without knowing the answer to that question, he pulled into the designated meeting place—a parking area adjacent to a little farm stand that had seen better days. The derelict structure was boarded up and so old it leaned to one side. Willpower alone seemed to keep it upright, and it would be only a matter of time before a strong wind flattened it. Johnny couldn't remember ever seeing it open.

Woods crowded in on one side of the parking area, and weeds grew high along the edge of the gravel. Runoff from storms had cut deep gouges in the dirt. A farm lane, rutted and stony, curled up the far side of the parking area.

He looked up the farm lane to a shabby house that had also seen better days. An old Amish lady, white haired and bent, was trying to push a hand mower over her lawn.

Johnny frowned. Where were the people from her district? They should be doing the mowing for her. When he was growing up, Mom went frequently across the street to old Mamie Weaver's to mow her lawn after Red Tim Weaver died. This lady's Gmay should be taking care of her if her children weren't.

He looked at his watch. Five minutes early. He sat in his car and waited. After ten minutes, Johnny could stand it no longer. He climbed from the car and began pacing back and forth from the woods to the farm lane. He glanced at the old farm house. The little old lady had abandoned her lawn mower and was nowhere to be seen.

Just when he was sure he'd jump out of his skin from the tension of waiting, a black convertible roared into the parking area and skidded to a stop with a spray of dirt. Johnny stepped behind his car, not so he wouldn't be seen but so he wouldn't be run over. He made his face show no emotion as Mick climbed out.

The man's shoulders and biceps strained the seams of his brown shirt. He wore tan dress slacks and tasseled loafers, ever the GQ guy. His hair looked freshly barbered. His frown chilled Johnny to his toes.

He reached into his car and picked up the envelope. His legs felt as supportive as a piece of Datt's baling twine.

"Give it," Mick ordered, holding out his hand.

Johnny handed him the envelope, flap down. The coffee stain hadn't bled through to the front and it looked almost as it should.

Mick flipped the envelope and the stain was the least of it.

Face red, eyes narrowed, Mick glared. "What happened?"

"Coffee. That's all. Coffee spilled." Johnny held his hands out in front of him. His stomach was curdling and his heart racing. Did Mick notice?

Mick upended the envelope and the bottle fell into his hand. He gave Johnny a final glare, then studied the vial.

"It's just like the guy gave me," Johnny said. "I didn't do anything to it. I swear."

Mick stepped right up to him, their toes almost touching. "So you say."

Johnny forced himself not to take a step back. "So I say." His voice was shaking only a little.

Mick grabbed him by the shirt and pulled him until they were nose to nose. "If you ever—"

Johnny never knew what threat Mick had in mind. The *pffft* was barely audible and the hole in Mick's head was small, but shot was shot, blood was blood, and dead was dead.

As Mick fell, he fell into Johnny who gasped audibly and tried to push him away. Mick's finger's still clutched his shirt, and Johnny pulled and pushed, trying to get free, trying to make believe he wasn't supporting a corpse.

After what felt like an eternity, Mick slid to the ground, his light slacks collecting dirt stains and dust settling on his polished loafers.

Where had the shot come from? Who? Johnny crouched behind his car. Would he be next?

He looked at Mick staring at nothing, his blood seeping into the ruts and cracks in the dirt. He looked up the farm lane toward the little old lady's house. He looked at the woods looming thick and menacing in the falling dusk.

Never had the haven of his parents' farm beckoned with such a golden glow of peace and safety.

He pulled open his car door and, still crouching, slipped in. Keeping as low as he could, he turned the key, threw the car into gear and hit the gas. He tore onto the road and away. After he rounded two curves, he straightened in his seat. He kept his eye on the rearview mirror and he drove and drove.

Slowly he started to think. He wasn't dead. He wasn't shot. If whoever shot Mick had wanted to shoot him, he'd already be a victim. Wouldn't he?

What if it was Mr. Sherman? Not that he'd have pulled the trigger. The fat man would never do such a dirty job. It might have been Thomas.

What would Mr. S. do if he knew Johnny had gone behind his back to get Mick his steroids? And what would he do when he saw the opened envelope? And what would he do when he knew Johnny knew what he was doing?

"Oh, God, oh, God, oh, God!"

For the first time in many years, it wasn't taking the Lord's name in vain.

Chapter 34

*L*iving with Amy proved to be easy and entertaining. Rachel was grateful for the upbeat company. They cooked dinner together the evenings Amy didn't work evening hours, Rachel teaching her how to cook good Pennsylvania Dutch dishes like ham loaf, dried corn, and shoofly pie.

"Teach me to drive a buggy," Amy asked one evening as they finished doing the dishes.

Rachel paused with a dripping pan in her hand. "You're kidding."

Amy took the pan and dried it. "If I'm going to live in an Amish house, I'd like to learn as much as I can."

Rachel emptied the dishwater and grabbed a dry towel for her hands. "Okay. No time like the present."

Bagel followed them to the barn, thrilled to go outside with his beloved Amy. Once at the barn, scents fascinated the dog and he happily explored until Rachel led Rusty from his stall. Then Bagel became an attack dog, threatened and defensive.

He barked and snarled. He ran toward Rusty, stopping just before he was in danger from the horse's large hooves and strong legs. Attack, retreat, attack, retreat, barking like a mad thing the whole time.

Rachel never anticipated a problem like this. Pepper and Corny were around the horses at her parents' all the time with never a bark. Rusty, usually very placid, grew increasingly agitated.

"Get Bagel and take him inside." Rachel held Rusty close and patted his neck. "It's okay, Rusty. You're the big guy here. It's okay."

"I'm sorry!" Amy grabbed at her pet. "I don't know what came over him."

She picked up the furious animal and carried him, snarling and squirming, to the house.

Once inside he quieted, only to start barking when Amy left him to return to the barn.

"It's a good thing I love him." Amy's expression was dark as she returned to the barn rubbing at a red welt on her arm. "Is Rusty okay?"

At first Rusty's size intimidated Amy, but in no time she was patting his neck and feeding him carrots. Rusty played his rein game with her too, and instead of getting frustrated, Amy laughed at him as she tried to push his bulk off the rein. He shook his head and lifted his foot.

"That's the secret? Laughing?" Rachel glared at Rusty who stared back unperturbed.

When Amy finally drove the buggy past the farm lane, she waved madly at Mom and Levi who were putting the little outhouses away because of a predicted storm.

"Look at me," she called. "I'm driving!"

"Both hands on the reins," Mom called. "You can't trust cars and need to be always ready."

Rachel and Amy spent each evening talking about life and men and possibilities. As a result Rachel only cried about Rob and lost opportunities in the privacy of her bedroom. Without Amy's presence she suspected she'd have moped about all week, tears leaking frequently.

Johnny moved back to his trailer early in the week.

"I feel fine," he insisted. "I appreciate all you've done for me, Rach, but I need to be alone."

Rachel suspected he needed to go back to being worldly, drinking and hanging around with undesirable people. "You take care," she said as he walked out her door.

"Don't you worry. I fixed it with those guys. Everything's fine."

Those words didn't comfort her.

Around her, life continued as always. In school, her little ones became more and more comfortable with English, and the older ones concentrated on learning new things. Mom and Datt had her and Amy for dinner twice, and she and Amy did a quick two-step to keep from saying where they met. Everyone seemed happy but Rachel.

On Saturday morning Amy slept in and finally made herself breakfast about ten o'clock. Rachel had already been working in her garden for almost two hours as she prepared it for winter. Amy wandered outside, coffee in one hand and a croissant in the other. She stood at the edge of the garden and talked the whole time she ate and drank. Rachel listened with half an ear for a while until the perky burbling suddenly became too much.

"I'm going for a walk," she announced in the middle of Amy's story. She got to her feet and dropped the spade she'd been using to the ground.

"Oh. Okay. Sure. Let me get on better shoes. And Bagel." Amy glanced at her watch. "I have a half hour before I need to leave for work."

"No." Rachel held up a hand. "I want to walk alone."

Amy studied her. "Too much cheer, huh?"

Rachel retied her scarf, a plain white rectangle folded into a triangle. "I'm sorry."

"No, don't be. I know it's been a tough week. I tried to make it not so sad, but I probably went overboard." She shrugged. "I usually do. Just one of many things that drove my father nuts. Go and walk. I'll probably be gone to work when you get back."

So Rachel walked and walked. And thought.

This gift of high intelligence was such a burden. Why couldn't she have been born ordinary? *God, why not? It would have been a kindness.*

If she were ordinary, she wouldn't be filled with this need to know everything. She'd be happy being some man's wife, some family's mother. She'd be satisfied with her allotted place in the community like her mother and Miriam and her sisters.

But she wanted more. She needed more. Something inside her compelled her to more.

Buggies rattled by and cars zoomed past as she walked. She ignored both. She barely noticed her parents' farm lane and Jonah and Miriam's house. At Eschs' place four teenage girls sat on the lawn, their kapps making little hearts above their heads, their giggles coloring the air.

Even when she was younger and sat like that with girls, giggling and talking about boys and dreams, she'd felt different, somehow apart. She loved her friends, but she knew she wasn't like them. The other girls' dreams were good and proper and fine. Husband, home, family. It was she who was wrong, she who desired the worldly, she who kept silent about her real heart because it would upset people if they knew.

Mim Stoltzfus looked up from weeding her garden as Rachel passed and waved. Peter Schwartz nodded as he drove by in his wagon laden with corn stalks to be ground for silage.

These were her People. Why couldn't she be satisfied with living among them and living like them?

"All I want is to learn things," she whispered. "That's all. Is that so terrible?"

But life was never that simple, that linear, that cooperative. At least her life wasn't. She felt like Elizabeth Hostetter who lost a lot of weight during a bad illness. Her skin never sprang back to fit her new body, only for Rachel it was her mind that couldn't spring back to the narrow world of her People. She had stretched it beyond repair.

And she wanted to stretch it more.

Therein lay a large part of her problem. She wanted to take more classes, learn more things, become her version of Dr. Dyson— whatever that would look like. And that would require leaving her community or remaining a liar. No, it would require leaving. Even she wasn't clever enough to pull off a deceit of that magnitude, even if God would allow her to without punishing her.

Do you promise before God and His church that you will support these teachings and regulations with the Lord's help, faithfully attending the services of the church and help to counsel and work in it, whether it leads you to life or to death?

She had answered *ja* to that question. She'd promised not only before the Gmay but before God. What jeopardy was her soul in if she broke that vow? She felt the fires of hell licking at her heels.

"Hi, Rachel."

Rachel looked up and found herself in front of Sauders' farm. Standing at the edge of the lawn and smiling at her were the three Sauder girls she taught: Elsie, Katie, and Kayla. As always, she wondered how an Amish daughter had as Englisch a name as Kayla, but the girl was Amish through and through with her hair pulled back in a little knot, her dress a miniature of her mother's, and her feet bare.

After talking with the girls a few minutes, Rachel walked on. What would be the effect on her students of her leaving? Confusion, disappointment, condemnation? The thought chilled her. If only she could make her choices in a vacuum, how much easier life would be.

A car slowed beside her, and she heard a window lower. A large man with curly hair leaned toward her. She leaned away instinctively. He made her nervous. The last time she'd seen a man with curly hair had been in the parking lot the night Johnny was beaten.

"Rachel Miller, right?"

When she didn't answer his question, he grinned. "Well, I know that's who you are."

In a small and probably useless attempt to protect herself and Johnny, she said, "My name is Rachel Beiler, not Rachel Miller." Not anymore.

"Yeah, that's right." He brought up a finger and pointed it at her. "You got married and got widowed. You teach at the Amish school, right?"

She felt her skin crawl that he knew so much about her.

"Want to go for a ride?" He patted the passenger seat.

She knew he was trying to upset her, and he was succeeding. Her mouth was dry and her palms wet. She was determined not to show her fear.

He was a big man, a strong man. She doubted she could run fast enough to escape if he chose to come after her. She could never defend herself against him if he got physical, nor would she try. She would have to turn the other cheek.

"You're not afraid of me, are you?" he said through a sly smile.

She looked around but found no one to help if needed, just fields of dead and dying corn edged by woods.

"Don't look so scared, Rachel honey. I'm not going to hurt you." He paused. "At least not today. Tomorrow is up to your brother. Don't forget to tell him Thomas said hi." With a flick of his hand, he was gone.

Rachel watched him disappear over a rise in the road, shaking and feeling as if she had to shower away his slime.

Oh, Johnny!

Her chest was tight and her shoulders tense as she added renewed worry about him to her already heavy burden. She resumed walking, heading back toward home.

After she mentally shook off the worst of her encounter with Thomas, Rachel found her swirling thoughts once again running circles. They made her weary as they hopped first this way, then that, like a rabbit working his way through a field of clover.

If she were a godly woman, wouldn't she just yield to the Gmay—uffgevva and all that—and live as she'd been taught? Wouldn't she become her version of her mother and all the other women in the Gmay?

But God was the one who gifted her with this questing mind, wasn't He? He was the one who planted in her a hunger for knowledge. Not just wisdom and common sense like Jonah and Datt had as well as many others she knew, but facts, ideas, theories, thoughts, and the many expressions of them?

She was a would-be academic in a culture that didn't understand and feared formal education because they thought it made you proud and separated you from God.

But did it have to? Dr. Dyson didn't seem proud. She seemed caring and kind. And she loved God. It was obvious from her lectures and assignments that she wanted her students to love Him even as they learned to think. Surely if Dr. Dyson could be both a Christian and an academic, so could she.

As she rounded the last curve and began the final leg toward home, she faced the other factor that fed her confusion: Rob.

She felt a sweet thrill and her heart beat faster at the thought of him and his smile. He was a handsome man, a strong man, and she was attracted to him for those reasons, but not for them alone. He was so much more, and it was the more that drew her. He was such a fine man, a man who loved God as she did. He would understand at least some of her vows:

Do you confess that Jesus Christ is the Son of God? Do you renounce the world, the devil with all his subtle ways, as well as your own flesh and blood, and desire to serve Jesus Christ alone, who died on the cross for you?

But could he understand the rest of that confessional question? *Do you recognize this to be a Christian order, church, and fellowship under which you now submit yourself?*

He'd understand it meant she was Amish and he wasn't.

She understood that she had committed to her church, the *gemiende*, the Gmay. She'd told God she was committed. She'd told God she was Amish. *Promised* God.

But was she Amish? Didn't her rebel heart alone put her outside the Gmay? And didn't her deceitful practices remove her from the sanctity of the community? Those practices would certainly put her in jeopardy of being denied fellowship if they were known and not repented of. And to her shame and disorientation she didn't feel regret or want to repent.

She'd always been the good girl, the one who tried to keep the rules and model the Christian walk. She did her best to avoid controversy and division. She appreciated submission and community. She loved her family and didn't want to cause them pain.

Yet here she was, willfully breaking the rules. She was a liar instead of a good Christian. She was becoming more certain by the minute she was going to cause controversy and division. She was going to rebel instead of submit, and most regretful of all, she was going to hurt her family. She was going to turn her back on things she'd believed her whole life.

The heaviness in her chest was surely her soul about to implode from the pressure.

As she walked past Max's, she could already hear Bagel complaining about being left alone. With each step his unhappiness increased in volume. She felt a flash of sympathy for the grumpy lady who lived below Amy. Then she forgot Bagel as her own problems continued to consume her.

What if she left the Gmay and things didn't work out with Rob? She knew he was unhappy with her, disappointed in her. He felt betrayed. What if he couldn't get past her deceit? Maybe his affection for her wasn't strong enough to make him tackle the monumental task of trying to understand why she'd done what she'd done. Given the pain his father's lies had caused him and his family, she understood the revulsion he must be feeling for her and her actions.

Be sure your sin will find you out.

What if she left and she spent the rest of her life as a single woman? For a person raised in a large family and an enveloping community, she would be truly alone.

But she was alone even with the People. For years she'd kept her true self hidden from everyone including those she loved most. Even Aaron hadn't known the yearnings of her heart.

Her head buzzed and her heart thundered. She was so lost in thought that it wasn't until she was climbing the front steps that she realized someone was sitting on the porch.

He stood and her heart tripped. She thought for a moment that the threatening Thomas had come for her after all.

He took a step toward her, arms stretched wide. "Rachel."

"Rob!" Without a second thought she threw herself into his embrace and felt her confusing world steady. The bubble of anxiety squeezing her chest burst like a ruptured dam, and she began to cry as all the tension rushed out.

"Shhh, baby." Rob stroked her back. "We'll work it out."

"We will?" Her tear-soaked voice wobbled.

"We will." He leaned back and looked down at her. She knew she was probably blotchy from crying, but he didn't seem to care. He brushed away her tears with his thumb. "At least I now have the answer to one question."

"What's that?"

"Would you want to see me."

She hugged him, blinking against new tears, happy tears because he was here. "I want to see you. I need to see you."

He kissed her and she kissed him back, her arms wrapped tightly around him. Her heart sang and her blood fizzed with excitement and joy. Rob had come to her! With him at her side and God at her back, she knew she'd find the courage to do what she needed to do.

As the kiss broke, she heard a buggy rattle by, and some of her joy dissolved into anxiety. As she rested her head against Rob's chest, she saw her sister-in-law Miriam drive past, eyes wide in shock.

Chapter 35

ob felt Rachel stiffen in his arms. At the same time he became
aware of a buggy driving by. He turned his head and saw a
startled young woman watching them.

"Trouble?" he asked but made no move to release her. To his relief
she made no move to pull away.

She nodded against his chest "My sister-in-law." Her voice was
small and sad.

"I'm sorry. I should have been more discreet." He kissed her forehead, and he felt her relax.

She shrugged. "It just hastens the inevitable." She took his hand.
"Let's go inside."

She opened the door and Bagel exploded onto the porch. His
frenzied barking turned to excited whines as he greeted first Rachel,
then Rob.

"Hey, little guy." Rob bent and rubbed the dog's head. Bagel made
happy sounds, and then turned and raced down the stairs. As soon
as he attended to nature, he raced back to them and followed them
into the house.

Rachel went to the kitchen table and sat. Rob took the chair next
to hers, angling so he faced her. Bagel came over and sat on the floor
between them, looking up at first one, then the other.

Rob gave him another head rub. "I was waiting for about an hour.
He barked the whole time."

"Really, Bagel?" Rachel shook her head at the dog. "No wonder you had to move."

Bagel grinned and collapsed at their feet. All that barking had worn him out.

Rob gripped Rachel's hands and she gripped back. He'd missed her this past week with an intensity that surprised him. Her sweet smile, her gentle manner, her sharp mind—when he couldn't enjoy them, he felt a hole inside.

"I'm not a liar, Rob." Her face was flushed with intensity, making her even lovelier than usual. "I'm not. I never intended to deceive. I just wanted to learn."

"I know. It just hit me hard the other night, you not being what I thought." He'd felt like he'd been punched in the gut when he understood the significance of that dress and the scarf and the lamps and the plain walls. "I needed time to think, to analyze, not just you but me."

"Your father."

Rob held up a hand to stop her. "My father has nothing to do with this. With us."

"How can he not? He deceived you. I deceived you. But I didn't mean to. I am what you thought. Really I am." Her face twisted. "And that sounds ridiculous, doesn't it, knowing what you know of me?"

"No." He rubbed his thumb across the back of her hand. "You may have been changing clothes and lives, but you were being you."

She started to cry, slow tears that ran down her cheeks. "Tears of relief," she said as she reached for a napkin sitting in a holder on the table to blot her face.

"I didn't realize you were such a crier," he said. "I'm learning something new about you."

She gave a little laugh. "I'm usually not. It's just this week…"

He nodded. "I know. Mine too."

"You felt unhappy and confused?" The thought seemed to make her happy.

"Morose and discombobulated."

"It was never meant to be a big secret, you know," she said. "It was meant to be an adventure. The beginning of realizing a dream. Then you showed up, and I didn't know how to say, 'Oh, by the way, I'm Amish.' The longer I didn't say it, the more impossible it became without ruining everything."

He studied her with her big brown eyes and earnest expression and those kissable lips. "So now I know the truth and the question is: Is everything ruined? Do we have a chance?"

She took a deep breath and let it out slowly. He knew the answer would cost her dearly whichever answer she gave.

She gripped his hand. "We have a chance. More than a chance, I hope."

He felt the tension leave his shoulders. He'd thought all week about the idea of giving her the opportunity to make her choice. What if she chose for her People and against him? It was simpler to make the choice himself. That way he could feel he'd been in control. Say no before she said no and be spared the humiliation and hurt of being rejected.

When Win had articulated what he in his anger and hurt hadn't realized, he'd been forced to take the time to ponder. He'd come to the conclusion Win was right. It wasn't about him and his pride. It wasn't about her hidden life. It was about the fact that he loved her. It was about their future. And it was about offering forgiveness for hurts given. It was about acknowledging that the hurts were unintentional and that she hurt as much or more than he did.

We have a chance. More than a chance.

He reached out and pulled off her white scarf. She made a surprised noise and reached for her head. When her hand touched her uncovered hair, she closed her eyes for a moment. Then she looked at him and smiled a somewhat sad and thoughtful smile. She took the scarf and began folding it into a small square.

"It's all for faith and family, you know. All the rules. Keep the family close by controlling what they do and where they go. Keep the family close by prescribing how you can live and believe."

"I get that. Just don't forget I believe in faith and family too, even when family is hard." And his was hard.

"Mine is wonderful. That's part of what makes this so difficult." Her face crinkled as if she was about to cry again, but all she did was blink hard.

"They're all Amish?"

"All but Johnny."

"All my family are nuts."

"Rob!" She looked shocked, but then she'd never met them. "Win's a nice guy. I know that even if I don't know the others."

"Okay, so Win's a good guy. He's improving. He's got a job." Rob heard the pride in his voice.

Rachel smiled. "Good for him. He's going to be all right, especially with you to help him."

She was giving him more credit than he deserved, but he was glad he could say, "I'm letting him live with me."

Rachel scooted her chair closer, and their knees bumped. "Good for you."

He swallowed. "Mom's having a fit. She doesn't want to be alone."

"Some people don't like being alone."

"You'll have to deal with her." He knew that was a presumptive statement, but he thought he was safe making it. "She'll drive you crazy."

"Maybe. I'd like to meet her. And your dad."

"Are you sure?" He tried to picture her going through the process of getting into Allenwood. She'd probably breeze through.

She nodded. "Will you meet my family?"

"Really?" He'd expected her relatives would remain this nebulous presence behind the scenes, shadow people he'd never know because of their lifestyle. "Will they meet me? Will they like me?"

"Of course they'll like you, but they won't like us."

He pulled her into his lap. "So there will be an *us*? Because you need to know that I love you and want there to be an us."

She rested her forehead against his. "I love you too, Rob. And I want there to be an us."

"Then there will be." He kissed her. She leaned into him and he felt happy, content, holding her. "You realize this is a marriage proposal?"

"I do." She sighed. "And I accept."

"I don't have a ring for you." With his uncertainty how he would be received, a ring was the last thing on his mind.

"I've never worn a ring in my life. Even wearing a wedding band would be a big step. A diamond would feel scandalous."

While he was thinking about the great cultural chasm she had to cross for him and for her education, there was a sharp rap on the door. Bagel surged to his feet doing what he did best. He rushed across the room, nails snick, snicking as he went.

Rob gave Rachel a last squeeze as she got to her feet. She gave him a strange look before she moved to the door. It almost seemed she was afraid. He stood and followed her.

"Jonah." Rachel stepped back from the door. "Come in."

A dark-haired Amishman stepped into the room. "Miriam said—" He stopped when he saw Rob.

"Rob, this is my brother, Jonah. Jonah, Rob Lanier."

Rob held out his hand and after the barest of hesitations, Jonah shook it.

"We were just sitting at the table talking," Rachel said. "Come join us."

Jonah looked uncomfortable. "I need to talk to you, Rachel." He shot Rob a look. "Just you."

"I know." She turned to the table. "Come. Sit."

"I…I should go." Rob took a step toward the door.

Rachel grabbed his hand. "No. Stay."

He understood she had just made a declaration with that touch and those words. He smiled at her. She smiled back, her heart in her eyes. It was one of those strange moments when everything was said with a look.

She dropped his hand and walked to the table. He followed and they took the chairs they'd had before. Jonah stood by the door for a moment before he took the chair across from Rachel. It was obvious from his expression that he understood Rachel's declaration too.

"Rachel," he began and stalled.

"I know, Jonah," she said. "I know."

"I don't have a choice."

"I know." She looked at Rob. "Jonah's a deacon."

Rob knew he was supposed to know what that meant, but he wasn't certain. Did it mean her own brother would oversee her shunning?

"What about your vows, Rachel?" Jonah asked.

"I'm not turning my back on Gott. I believe as strongly as ever."

"How can you and leave the Gmay?"

"It isn't the Gmay that saves me."

"But you vowed to serve Gott through the Gmay."

Rachel closed her eyes, a pained expression on her face. "I know. And I admit that I struggle with that."

Jonah sat back, his face suddenly stern. "I knew that devil's television would corrupt you."

"I am not watching television, Jonah," Rachel's voice was firm.

He looked unconvinced, and she shook her head at him. She took a deep breath. "I'm going to college."

She'd shocked him. "Rachel!"

"That's where I met Rob." She turned to him and smiled, and he couldn't resist covering her hand with his.

Jonah's scowl intensified as he saw the contact. "And that's where you met the woman who's staying with you?"

"Amy. Yes."

"Mom said you wouldn't say how you met. Now I know why."

"Now you know why. You need to know, Jonah, that I plan to finish college and become a professor."

Jonah turned to Rob. "This is your doing."

Rob understood Jonah needed something, someone to blame, so he didn't defend himself. Rachel did.

"Jonah, I went to Wexford *before* I met Rob. But after I met him, I admit he complicated things." She glanced at him and gave an impish smile. "A lot."

"So you will leave the Gmay for him." Jonah looked sad rather than mad.

"I will leave the Gmay only because they will not let me stay and follow the plan I believe God has for me. Jonah, I can't explain the excitement I feel when I go to class. It's like I come alive. I feel I'm finally using the gifts God gave me. I'm becoming the person God made me."

"I have worried you might leave us because of your mind." Jonah stared at the scarf lying on the table. "I have been afraid your intellect would lead you astray. When you married Aaron, I thought you were safe."

"But I was hiding such a big part of who I am, even from him."

"We are to bring every thought into submission."

"Submission to what, Jonah? The Gmay or to God?"

"Be careful, Rachel. Heresy lurks just around the corner. The world is dangerous and the people in it." He looked at Rob who blinked. He'd never been called dangerous before.

"Jonah, I love you. I love Mom and Datt. I love the *gemeinde*. And I love God no less today than I did yesterday."

"But," Jonah said, standing.

"But," Rachel agreed.

He nodded, and Rob could see tears in his eyes. Suddenly he turned a fierce expression on Rob.

"You'd better be good to her." And he stalked out of the house.

Chapter 36

Rachel stared at the closed door. She'd done it. She'd spoken the words that would mean severed ties with her People. They would no longer be her People. She stood quietly for a moment, trying to analyze how she felt.

Her heart was weighted with a deep sorrow that such a choice had to be made. Even in the loss she knew no other choice was possible given her circumstances, and she felt a whisper of excitement about what was to come next. She glanced at Rob and that whisper became a gale, blowing all the possibilities of the future into her heart. She moved to his side.

His arm came out and circled her waist. "You okay? I know that was hard."

He had no idea. "Hold me?" She needed his comfort.

"With pleasure." He pulled her onto his lap and wrapped his arms around her. She rested her head on his shoulder.

"How come making huge decisions sounds so ordinary?" she asked. "You use ordinary words, but extraordinary things happen. *We have a chance.* I said that to you, and now we're going to get married. All I said to Jonah was *But* and I will no longer be part of the Gmay. Ordinary words. Extraordinary ramifications."

Rob gave a cough of laughter, and she felt the rumble in his chest. She frowned at him. "Are you making fun of me?"

"Absolutely not. I'm just surprised at your comment." He ran a finger down her cheek. "I expect I'm in for a lifetime of interesting and unexpected observations."

"Probably. I've always been strange that way."

"Not strange. Special."

"Oh. That's good." And it was. She wouldn't have to guard her every word or thought. What a relief that would be.

She stood and grabbed his hand to pull him to his feet. "We have to go see my parents. They need to hear about all this from me, not from Jonah or Miriam or through gossip."

Rob nodded. He began fiddling with her hair, trying to undo the knot. "Let it loose. Please."

She understood that having her hair down was somehow symbolic for him. She began pulling the pins free. She remembered that first evening of school when she let her hair free for the first time. *Loose hair didn't have to be a symbol of a loose life.* But it was certainly the sign of a changed life.

As her hair fell over her shoulders and down her back, Rob grabbed a fistful and pulled her close for a quick kiss. "I love your hair. I love you."

They walked down the road to the farm, fingers threaded.

"You doing okay?" Rob asked.

She gave him a sad smile. "This is going to be so hard."

"Will they be mad?"

She shook her head. "Disappointed. Hurt. They won't understand how I could possibly choose to leave the community."

"How severe will the shunning be?"

"Oh, I think they will still love me, still visit with me, but I can no longer eat with them or work with them. I will be outside the everyday rhythms of their lives and the lives of the people I've known all my life. That distance will be the hardest."

They turned up the farm lane.

"Should I ask your father for your hand in marriage?" Rob asked. "Is that something the Amish culture does?"

Her heart swelled with love. "You would do that? Knowing he won't like the idea and would have to say no?"

"Isn't that all the more reason to? I'd like him and your mother to like me at least a little bit."

She went up on tiptoe and kissed him. He held her close.

"I know this is costing you, Rachel. I promise I'll do everything I can to make the losses you suffer less painful."

His comment touched her deeply. "You're just saying that so I'll kiss you out of gratitude."

He grinned. "Is it working?"

She kissed him again.

"Ah-ha! I knew it was you." Levi stood in the lane, a little outhouse in his arms.

Rachel stepped away from Rob and eyed her brother. "You knew what was me?"

"That day in the car when the turkeys had you surrounded. That was you with your hair down and wearing Englisch clothes." He looked her up and down. "Your hair's free again."

"Well, you see—" She stalled out.

Rob came to her rescue. He stuck out his hand. "Hi. I'm Rob Lanier."

Levi offered his hand in return, sawdust falling from his shirt cuff as he did. "Levi Miller. Her brother." He bobbed his head toward Rachel. "I make outhouses."

"For very little people?" Rob smiled.

"For tourists. You her boyfriend?"

"Her fiancé."

Levi nodded. "I knew she was going to leave."

"What do you mean, you knew?" Rachel was surprised. She thought she'd kept her lives successfully separate.

"I told Mom and Datt you would. I didn't tell them about you in the car, but I told them to be prepared. I thought it would be your girlfriend who led you into the world. I didn't realize it would be a guy."

"Rob isn't why I have chosen to…become Englisch. Well, he isn't the only reason." She swallowed. "I'm going to college."

He nodded with a definite lack of surprise. "Is that where you drive in Mr. Englerth's car?"

"You know about the car?"

"I'm every bit as smart as you, Rachel. I'm good at knowing things. At seeing things. But I'm never leaving the Gmay. I want to be an Amish farmer."

"I loved being Amish too, Levi." She felt a catch in her heart at the past tense.

"But?"

"But."

Levi set his outhouse down. "Want me to go warn the parents? Tell him there's a guy with you?"

"Thanks, Levi, but no. We'll do this ourselves."

"Hey, Levi!" Davy came running out of the barn, Abner on his heels. "Datt wants to know where you got to. Oh." He skidded to a stop as he saw Rob.

Abner kept running, throwing himself at Rachel's knees. "Rachel! I got to turn the switch!"

"On the milking machine," Davy explained.

Rachel made the little boy's suspenders snap. "Aren't you the big man."

"I am." Abner puffed out his chest. "Who's that?" He pointed at Rob.

"This is my friend Rob. I hope you will like him because I like him a lot."

"Okay," Abner said and ran back to the barn.

Davy eyed Rob with suspicion.

"They're getting married," Levi told him.

Davy frowned. "But he's not Amish."

"He's not."

Davy looked at Rachel in disbelief. "Really?"

She nodded, feeling his reaction in the roiling of her stomach. And she knew it would get worse before it would get better.

"We need to get Datt," Levi told his brother.

The boys took off at a run, the outhouse abandoned in the lane.

Rob put his arm around Rachel's shoulders and drew her close. He kissed the top of her head. "Want to change your mind?"

"About what?"

"About me. About college. About everything."

She rested her head on his shoulder. "No, I can't. This is one time I can't finesse the situation the way I'd like."

"I wish it were possible to keep what you love. I hate to see you hurt like this."

She looked up at him. "I love you."

"Well, you get to keep me forever, no matter what." He smiled that wonderful smile.

Datt came out of the barn and looked down the lane to them. She couldn't read his expression from here, but she saw the slump of his shoulders. Poor Datt.

"Mr. Miller!" Rob's voice was strong. "May I speak with you?" He didn't wait for an answer but strode toward the man. "I'll see you inside," he called over his shoulder to Rachel.

She stood for a minute watching the two men she loved talking. Pepper sidled up to her and leaned in, and it felt like comfort. Rachel fondled the animal's ears, and Pepper let herself be touched longer than usual, like she sensed Rachel's need.

With a quick lick on the hand, Pepper walked away and Rachel was left to climb the porch steps alone. She saw Mom step back from the window. When she walked in, her mother was standing at the stove stirring a large pot of what would be homemade applesauce.

"Smells good, Mom."

"Of course it does. My applesauce is always *gut*."

Rachel sat at the kitchen table. A silence noisy with nuance filled the room. Finally Mom spoke.

"Who is he?"

"His name is Rob Lanier."

"Do you make it a habit to hang on Englisch men?"

"Mom!"

"You know a man well enough to hang on him and we didn't even know about him?"

"I'm going to marry him, Mom."

"No, you are not."

"I am. He's asking Datt for permission now."

"You know he will not give it."

"I know."

"And you will still marry him?"

Seeing tears in her mother's eyes made Rachel's eyes sting. "I will."

"Rachel! Is he good like Aaron was?"

"He's very good, Mom." Better for me than Aaron. "He loves God and is a fine Christian."

Mom sniffed in distrust. "He isn't Amish."

Rachel said nothing. What could she say?

"Your hair is loose. It's uncovered."

Rachel's hand went to her head.

"The Bible says women should have their heads covered. Even the Mennonites cover their heads, at least some of them."

Another comment she couldn't counter. The Bible did say that, and a discussion about the effect of culture on some passages of Scripture was not a good idea.

"I'm going to college, Mom. I want to become a college professor."

At that pronouncement, Mom pulled her applesauce from the stove and sat. "A professor? In the world? Rachel!"

"I love you, Mom. You know that, right?" Rachel reached across the table for Mom's hands. "But I have to do this. I feel like I'm finally living true to who I am. I've been keeping me, the real me, hidden for too long. I want to learn. I want to study."

"It will take you from Gott."

"Not unless I let it."

Clearly Mom didn't agree. "So you will leave us. You will leave the Gmay so you can learn?"

"I'd stay if I was allowed to learn and be Amish."

"And what about him? You would stay Amish and give him up?"

"I don't know. Just as I need to learn, I need to be with him."

"You need to be with an Amish man."

She shook her head. "I need to be with Rob. He's a gift to me from God."

Mom's disagreement screamed in the silence.

The door opened and Datt entered, Rob behind him. Datt walked around the table to Mom and stood behind her with his hands on her shoulders. Rob came to stand beside Rachel. She looked up at him and tried to smile. He reached out a hand and she slid hers into it.

"Your young man has spoken to me, Rachel." Datt looked tired and older than she'd ever seen him. Her heart broke that she'd made him look this way.

"He asked for permission to marry you." Datt looked at their joined hands. "Of course I cannot say go and Gott bless you like I did with you and Aaron. I cannot."

Rachel nodded and felt Rob tighten his grip.

"But I will say that for an Englischer, he seems a nice man."

"Oh, Datt!" She flew around the table and hugged him. "Thank you!"

He patted her awkwardly on the shoulder. "You know I'm not happy. In fact I am very sad. To lose you to the world—" He stopped to swallow. Mom pulled up her apron and wiped her eyes.

Rachel fell to her knees beside her mother. "Mom, I'm not doing this to make you sad or because of anything you did wrong. You were the best mother there is. You *are* the best mother there is. That's why I brought Amy to meet you all. I wanted her to see how wonderful you are."

Mom sighed and looked away. "It will take me a while to get used to this, Rachel. A knife in the heart always hurts."

Rachel got to her feet wondering how to pull out the knife just driven into her own heart.

She walked to Rob. "Let's go," she mouthed.

They had reached the door when Datt spoke. "We are sad and hurt, Rachel, but you are our daughter. We will always love you. Right, Ida?"

Mom looked up from studying her lap. "You are our daughter."

Outside they found Levi, Davy, and Abner on the porch.

"Can we still talk to you?" Davy asked, his face filled with uncertainty.

"Of course," Rachel said, forcing herself to sound upbeat. "And you can come see me any time you want. After all I'm just down the road."

"We could come now," Abner said, ever ready for a new adventure.

Rachel went down on one knee and hugged her little brother, knocking his hat off in the process. "Not now, buddy. Your dinner's almost ready. And is the milking finished?"

Abner picked his hat up by its brim and set it on his head. "Are we finished?" he asked Levi.

Levi held out his hand. "Come on. Let's go check."

Rachel watched her brothers walk to the barn. Just before they disappeared inside, Levi and Davy both looked back and gave a little wave. She raised her hand in salute. And they were gone.

Her whole family whom she loved was gone. Oh, they and she and Rob would come to a détente because they did love each other, but it would never be the same.

"Oh, Rob!" Her hand covered her mouth to hold back the pain.

He pulled her close. "Shush, babe. Shush."

"Will she forgive me? Will he get back the spring in his step? Will the boys ever understand?"

"I think so. In fact I was surprised at how well things went."

"Really?"

"Really. Every day in my family is more contentious than this was."

"You're kidding."

"I wish. Now let's go back to your house where you can cry it out for as long as you need to."

Chapter 37

Rachel found going to church with Rob was both exciting and frightening. Her stomach fluttered as she worried over what to expect at an Englisch service.

"You'll keep me from doing something wrong?" she asked as they climbed from his car in the parking lot.

"We discourage arguing with the pastor during his sermon," Rob said with a straight face.

"People actually do that?" She was shocked.

He grinned. "I'm teasing. Don't worry. I'll take care of you."

How quickly her life had changed! Two weeks ago she'd gone to church with her parents at Meullers' farm, sat with the women on the backless benches, helped serve the meal after service, come home and read. Today the Gmay was gathering at Jonah and Miriam's. Everyone would be there but her, and she would be a topic of conversation.

Communion was only two weeks away. Her fall from grace would be the perfect illustration of the need to keep pure and avoid the world. Poor Mom and Datt. It hurt them so to know she had walked away from her heritage, especially as they recommitted themselves to the Gmay today in preparation for Communion. And the boys and her sisters would be hurt. Even Aaron's family would be hurt, trying to understand how their much missed son and brother could have married someone so willful and misguided.

She gripped Rob's hand. She knew she'd made the only choice she could, but whenever she thought of the rift she'd created, she had to blink away tears. Maybe it would become easier with time. Right now it was very hard and Rob was her lifeline.

Her heart thundered as he escorted her into the church. She'd never before worshipped in a building that wasn't someone's home. He led her into a large room with a stage at the front. He selected a row and they took seats, permanent seats with backs. All around her men and women sat together instead of segregated, and whole families sat together in several of the pews.

The differences from what she was used to screamed at her. Instead of a room filled with people wearing black and white, patterns and colors ran riot. Some people wore jeans and some dress clothes. When people filed onto the stage, they carried musical instruments. When they began to play, everyone stood up. Instead of slow cadenced music sung in unison and High German, the beat was fast and the English words projected on a screen.

When the service was over after a little more than an hour, she was on sensory overload.

"It's going to take time," she told Rob as he drove her home.

"Of course it is," he agreed.

"I know they sang to the Lord and the pastor preached from the Bible, but it feels like another step on the road to perdition. I know—" she tapped her head—"that God is bigger than my district, but it feels—" she placed her hand over her heart—"like I'm lost."

"God won't let you go, Rachel. He's got you firmly in His hand. Hold on to what you know, not what you feel."

They had gone to an early service because Rob wanted to drive to Allenwood to see his father.

"Can I go with you?" Doing something like visiting would make Sunday seem more normal. And she wouldn't be alone.

"He's a very difficult man, sweetheart," Rob said. "You don't have to put yourself through meeting him, especially with all you're going through right now."

"I want to meet him. He's your father."

Rob squeezed her hand. "I'd like to prep him for you. Next time, okay? The drive is about two and a half hours. The visit itself won't be long. Dad's tolerance for family is very low." He gave a sad shrug. "So I'll be home by dinner easily."

"I'll have it ready."

He took her by the shoulders. "Don't feel you have to cook if doing so on the Sabbath makes you uncomfortable."

"I've got a leftover meat loaf and some late tomatoes and some applesauce Amy and I made last week."

"Sounds wonderful. I'm hungry already." And he was gone.

After he left, she went to the refrigerator to check what other things she might have already prepared.

The meat loaf was gone.

⌒⫘⫘⫘⌒

Max enjoyed going out for brunch with friends after church. There were usually five of them besides her—Bebe, Sue, Vicki, Janice, and Janice's husband, Cliff, the only man. He called the women his harem and seemed to enjoy himself without manly backup.

Laughing with these friends each week went a great way to easing her grief, at least temporarily. It also was the extra push to go to church when it would be easier to sleep in. Sitting alone each week, singing the songs, watching the couples sitting together, shoulders touching, made Buddy's absence acute.

She hadn't been home long when there was a knock at the front door. She'd been about to check the TV for an Eagles game. Instead she went to see who was calling.

"Rachel!" On Sunday. In English clothes. "You don't have to knock. Just let yourself in."

Her cheeks were flushed as if she was either embarrassed or excited. "I came to get my clothes."

"You're going to keep them at your house?" Wasn't that risky?

"And the car, though I have to move Rusty first."

"What?" She pulled Rachel into the living room. "Okay. Tell me all! I mean, last Saturday you were despondent about life. Monday and Friday evenings you were sad and preoccupied. Now you're—" Now she was quietly effervescent, little bubbles of excitement escaping like from a soda sitting in a glass. "Tell me."

Rachel just smiled.

Curiosity finally got the better of Max. "Isn't today a church Sunday? And you're obviously not there."

Some of the sparkle dimmed. "It is and I'm not. And it hurts."

Max went to her with open arms. "I bet it does." Losing her People must feel for Rachel like losing Buddy felt for her. It was that amputated limb that kept twitching and hurting. Well, maybe not quite as bad as her ache over Buddy because her family and friends were all still here and she would see them. It was the relationship that would never be the same, fractured by her leaving. Repaired somewhat over time, but like Humpty Dumpty, never put back together.

Rachel held on tight. "I didn't really have any other choice."

"I know."

"I'm going to be a college professor." There was wonder and excitement in her voice. "Next semester I'm going to school full-time."

"And for many semesters to come! I think that's wonderful, Rachel. You're a brilliant young woman. You should be using that mind of yours in the way you're wired to use it."

"I'm wired to be an academic."

"I can picture that easily. I'm sorry your People don't understand your kind of intelligence."

"A lot of them are smart and have been able to submit their intelligence to the Gmay. I feel somewhat of a failure that I haven't been able to do so."

"You certainly tried."

"I did, but my kind of mind doesn't fit that box."

"Have you ever had your IQ tested?"

"No. Maybe someday. It doesn't matter. What matters is that I made my decision and while I feel so sad about the hurt I've dealt my family and others I love, I feel like I'm free. I can be the person God made me."

"And what about Rob?" *Buddy, there's more than just college in that glow of hers. You wait and see.*

Rachel's cheeks turned scarlet and Max laughed.

"I take it that blush is a good sign."

"He came over yesterday." Rachel stopped and grinned.

"And?" Max waved her hand in circles in a come-on-spit-it-out gesture.

"And we're going to get married."

"Yikes! That was fast. Are you *sure?*" Someone had to ask the mother type question.

Rachel's grin was slightly goofy, a delight to see. "Oh, yeah, I'm sure."

This time Max's hug was congratulatory. They sat as Rachel told all the details of last evening, including the story of Rob asking for her hand.

"Of course Datt couldn't say yes. We knew that. But he did say that for an Englischer, Rob was very nice."

Max laughed. *See, Buddy? I was right encouraging her. She's happy, really happy, happier than she is sad, and that's good.*

She didn't want to gloat, but vindication was sweet.

ᏯᎿᏯᎾ

Rob sat in the visitors' lounge at Allenwood Federal Prison across the table from his father.

"I'm going to get married, Dad." He waited to see what the reaction to this announcement would be, if any.

His father raised his eyebrows, a massive response given his usually stoic expression. Whether the eyebrows indicated positive or negative feelings, Rob couldn't tell.

"She's a former Amish girl, Dad. Her name is Rachel Beiler. I met her in my class."

"She was Amish?"

"Until recently."

"Why'd she leave?" He looked Rob up and down with a sour expression. "You?"

Rob thought of the love and sorrow at the Miller house. If there was ever a time his father had loved him and felt even a slight interest in anything he did, it was long past. Now, if Rob read things correctly, he bored the man.

"Do you like anybody, Dad?" The question came unbidden, as unexpected to Rob as it was to his father, but Rob wasn't sorry he asked it.

Eugene Lanier looked at him, arrogant and critical, then away without answering.

Rob sighed. "That's what I thought. Well, like it or not, I've decided to love you."

If anything, his father looked appalled by that statement.

"Oh, not the gooey kind of love." Why did he bother to explain himself? "The I-care-about-you love. And not for your sake, you understand, but because it's the right thing to do. God asks us to love one another, even our enemies."

His father shifted uncomfortably at the mention of God.

"Yep," Rob said. "I'm a Christian now. I pay attention to what God says."

"Stop embarrassing yourself." The statement was spit out and filled with venom.

He wanted so badly to say, "As if you didn't embarrass me many times over?" But he resisted. He wasn't here to start fights even if that's what his father wanted.

All around him smiling prisoners visited with chattering friends and family. Inside sat many who'd give anything to have a son visit them. But not his father. Not this uncommunicative and bitter old man.

Rob made his voice pleasant even though he wanted to scream. "You asked if Rachel was leaving the Amish because of me. Partly. But she was in the process of leaving before we met. She's very smart and the yearning for knowledge pulled her away."

"She wear the clothes?"

"Not anymore."

"She a Christian too?" The scorn at the word *Christian* could scorch asbestos.

"Very much so. It took her a while to realize she could keep her vows to love and serve God outside the Plain church."

"And she's going to marry you?"

"I'm a lucky man."

"Huh. Hope she doesn't regret it."

Rob shook his head. "That's it? That's all you've got to say?"

"Hope *you* don't regret it."

Rob stood in agitation, and the guards came to attention. He held up his hand to show there was no problem and sat again. "How about congratulations, son? Or best wishes?"

His father shrugged. "I never found marriage to be an institution worth valuing."

Rob studied the man. Time to leave before he said something he'd regret. This time when he stood, he nodded to the guards and went through the process of being released. His father didn't bother to say goodbye.

As he walked to his car, he felt a flash of sympathy for his mother. Had Dad treated her with the same caustic disregard and he'd just been too young and self-absorbed to notice? Or had a casual disinterest in anything but his own success been the issue?

Maybe Mom hadn't always been so demanding. Maybe she'd learned to be that way to avoid being ignored completely by her own husband. Maybe all she ever got from him was the checkbook until she'd learned to equate money and its abundance with love.

He grabbed his phone and hit Rachel's number. When she answered, he relaxed at the sound of her voice.

"I'm so glad we've got each other. Don't stop loving me, okay?"

"That bad, huh?"

"I'm sorry for the family I bring to this marriage."

"Don't be. You didn't make them what they are."

True. They'd managed that all on their own. "What about the sins of the parents being visited on the kids to the third and fourth generation?"

"There's a lot of truth in that—"

"That's what I'm afraid of."

"Let me finish. There's a lot of truth in that unless the chain is broken by someone trusting in Jesus and living differently."

The knot of frustration because he had the misfortune to be a Lanier loosened. "Thank you. Just what I needed to hear. Looking forward to that meat loaf."

Chapter 38

*R*achel walked slowly to the little barn behind the house. Her Englisch clothes now hung in her closet. Her next job was to make room for her car in the barn.

Again that strange pressure filled her chest as she looked her future in the face.

She'd made her choice. The truth was she'd made her choice the first time she'd gone to Max's as an adult to use her computer. She just hadn't realized it then.

"Hey, Rusty." She walked to her horse who was moving around his stall in an agitated manner. "What's wrong?"

Rusty was an intelligent animal as proven by the rein game, but surely he couldn't catch her conflicting emotions from this distance. He nickered and shook his head.

"Easy, boy. It's okay. You'll like it at Mom and Datt's. Levi will make you a cowboy horse."

He wouldn't, of course. Rusty was trained to the traces, not to the saddle. For Levi to be the cowboy he dreamed about, he needed a horse trained to be ridden, not easy to find in Amish country.

Rachel reached to open the stall door when a man suddenly stood inside the stall, shocking her. Scaring her. She fell back a step and grabbed her heart.

"It's only me. Don't be afraid."

Johnny had straw in his hair and his clothes were dirty and wrinkled. Dark circles made arcs beneath his eyes, and the bruises on his

291

face from the beating in the parking lot had turned pale yellow and green. Even from where she stood he reeked.

"You scared me to death!" Anger replaced the startled fear.

He held out a placating hand. "I didn't mean to."

That was Johnny's trouble. He never meant to do anything. "Why are you hiding in my barn?"

In her mind's eye she saw a man with broad shoulders and an abundance of muscles, and she thought she knew.

His shoulders hunched in. "I had to hide somewhere." He peered over her shoulder to the barn door. "Are you alone?"

"Of course I'm alone."

Relief flowed from him. "Good. Now just forget you saw me."

"I'm to walk away as if I never saw you and leave you here with Rusty?"

"You have to. No one can know I'm here."

"I don't plan to tell anyone, but you still can't stay here. You can't hide in my barn."

"Come on, Rachel. I won't bother anything."

"Johnny, this is crazy."

"It's as good a place as any until I figure out how to get away."

Running from his problem. Was that a Miller family trait? She'd been running from hers, denying it, for so long. "How long have you been here?"

"Since Saturday."

She stared at him. "You've been keeping Rusty company since yesterday?"

He shrugged as if bunking with a horse was a normal thing.

She narrowed her eyes. "Are you where my missing meat loaf went?"

"And some bread and cheese and I boiled myself some eggs while you were out." He grinned, suddenly proud. "I put the pan back so you wouldn't know."

"Johnny! Why didn't you just come into the house? I mean like a real person, not a thief?"

"I didn't want to put you and Amy at risk. What if they came looking for me? They'd come to the house, and if I was out here, you could say honestly that you didn't know where I was, and they'd go away. They wouldn't look back here."

Rachel wasn't so sure. If she was looking for someone, she'd look everywhere including barns and basements.

"They're bad guys who are after me, Rachel. Bad."

She believed that. "Why'd you get mixed up with them in the first place? You know better."

"It was a sure thing." He looked like he still couldn't believe things hadn't gone as he expected. "Even he thought it was a sure thing."

"Who is he that you need to get away from and where do you plan to go?"

"It's really one man. The others just do what he says. And I'll go to California. He'll never find me there. It's big."

"*Who* won't find you? I want a name, Johnny, a name." Though what she'd do with the information, she didn't know.

"Mr. Sherman."

Rachel waited for more, but that seemed to explain it all for Johnny. "Is he a big guy with too many muscles?"

Johnny turned paler than his already pasty look. "How do you know about him?"

"He's been around several times. He gave me the creepiest feeling."

"Well, he can't bother you anymore."

"Good."

Johnny shuddered. "He's dead."

The bubble of tension that sat in her chest and had eased slightly because she'd made her personal choices expanded like a balloon being inflated. "What happened?"

Johnny looked like he wanted to cry. "We were just standing there and boom! He got shot. He—" Johnny swept his arm down and stared at the ground. He wrapped his arms around himself.

The fake shootings of the movie flashed and Rachel couldn't imagine seeing the real thing. "You're sure he was dead?"

"Oh, yeah." Johnny turned green again. "Absolutely sure."

Rachel studied her brother, still staring at the ground, at a place only he saw. "Do you know who did it? Did you see the shooter?"

He shook his head emphatically.

"Then why are you scared? Why are you hiding?"

"Because I know who and I know why."

"Even though you didn't see him?"

"Even though I didn't see him."

"Mr. Sherman?"

He reached out and put his hand over her mouth in just short of a slap. "Don't say it, Rachel! It's not safe."

She pushed his dirty hand away. "Johnny, there's no one here but you and me."

He ignored her comment. "It wasn't him literally. He sent one of his men." He looked around as if expecting someone to jump up like a jack-in-the-box. "Thomas. It was probably Thomas."

"Does Thomas have curly hair?"

Johnny stared at her. "How do you know that?"

"He was here yesterday asking about you."

"At the house?"

"He stopped me when I was walking."

Johnny began pacing, and Rusty grew agitated again.

"You can't stay here in my barn."

"I have to until it's safe."

"You think running away will make you safe?"

"Yes."

"No." She made her voice as forceful as she could. "No running. No hiding. You have to do what's right."

"And what's that?" His voice grew sarcastic. "Confess my sin before the Gmay and hope Mr. Sherman doesn't hear about it?"

Rachel ignored the sarcasm. "You've got to go to the police."

"No. I told you. I'll get in trouble."

"Why? What did you do?"

He wouldn't look at her and had the grace to look embarrassed. "I transported bad stuff."

"Bad stuff?" What did that mean? "Drugs? What?"

"Yeah, but not bad drugs like cocaine or anything. Steroids." He pulled a vial out of his pocket. "And passports and birth certificates." He reached down and grabbed a manila envelope. He held it out to her.

She opened the flap and slid the contents out far enough to see they were indeed birth certificates and little blue books that read United States of America on their covers. She righted the envelope and tried to close the flap. It wouldn't stick.

"Have you done this transporting much?" she asked.

"Only this one time."

She felt a keen relief. "Why'd you do it if you knew it was wrong?" She heard the censure in her voice and wasn't surprised when he got defensive.

"Don't push, Rachel."

Her temper flared. "You're hiding in my barn and you say don't push? I repeat: Why did you do it if you knew it was wrong?"

His mouth was set in a stubborn line.

"Why, Johnny?" She used the tone that made her students confess whatever had gotten them in trouble. To her amazed relief it worked on Johnny too.

"Because I owe him money, and I can't pay."

"I suppose you needed this money for your sure thing?" When he nodded, she continued, "Why didn't you go to a bank or to Datt or to me?"

"The bank won't give me money. My credit's shot. And I would never ask you or Datt." He sounded scandalized at the idea. "I went to Mr. Sherman because I knew I could pay him back right away." His voice trailed off.

"Oh, Johnny." He was such a nice guy, he really was, but he was so easily led by his wild ideas. He really ought to be Amish for the parameters the life would put around him, keeping him safe from himself. Of course, that wasn't a good reason to take his vows.

"You're wearing Englisch clothes," he said all of a sudden.

She looked down at her dark blue blouse and blue flowered skirt. "I am."

He looked at her with compassion. "They found out."

She nodded. "They did, but I'd already decided."

"Mom and Datt?"

Tears burned. "Breaks my heart to hurt them." *But you will always be our daughter.* She clutched that comment close.

"Is Rob the reason?"

She smiled at the mention of his name. "Part of the reason. The rest is I'm going to college. I'm going to be a college professor."

Johnny blinked. "Wow. I'm surprised but I'm not. You always were scary smart."

Rachel brushed away his comment. "But I'm not the issue at the moment. You are."

"I have an idea that might fix stuff." Johnny looked uncertain. "I just thought of it."

"Me too." She nodded. "You first."

"Rob. He knows stuff because of the army."

"He'll know what to do," Rachel agreed. "He knows about things like police. His father's in jail."

"I knew that, but do Mom and Datt?"

She shook her head. "They had enough of a shock as it is. And it doesn't change anything. They know Rob's a wonderful guy and a Christian."

"Did that Christian part help Mom and Datt take the news any better?"

"Not really. The fact that you can be non-Amish and every bit as committed to Jesus doesn't matter. It's nice, but it's not like being Amish. It's not like being right."

Rachel walked to the barn door. "Come on, Johnny. You need a shower. Let Rusty have his stall back. I'll drive to your place and get you some clean clothes. And I'll call Rob."

Johnny followed her from the barn. "Be careful, Rachel. They're looking for me because I've got the stuff."

She looked at his empty hands. "Where is it?"

"I hid it in the stall under the straw. Rusty'll keep it safe."

Chapter 39

When Rachel got back from her trip to Johnny's trailer, she found her brother in what she'd come to think of as his bedroom. He was leaning back against the headboard wearing one of her big towels around his waist. Bagel sat beside him on the bed. They both stared at his smart phone, watching a football game.

"How can you live in a pig sty like that?" she asked as she dropped his clothes beside him.

"It's not that bad."

"Dirty dishes, unmade bed, milk left out to go sour. Oh, and there was the little colony of ants marching in a nice straight line across the counter."

"I like comfortable."

"You call that comfortable?" She put her hands on her hips. "I call it a hotbed of germs and potential disease. Mom would have a heart attack if she saw the way you live. I bet the mildew in your shower has been growing for years."

"Just because you're a neat freak…"

"And don't you forget it while you're here. And clean up after yourself when you're back home. I don't want all my work to be in vain."

His frown turned into an amazed smile. "You cleaned for me?"

"Stupid me. Now get dressed. I have to get Rusty and the buggy to Mom and Datt's before they get home."

"Can I come? Can I drive?"

She looked at his excited face. "You're kidding."

"I haven't driven a buggy in so long."

"Do you think you're safe to be in the open like that?"

He made a disappointed face. "I guess I'd better not."

"After all this is over, I'm sure Mom and Datt will let you use their buggy any time you want. All you have to do is ask."

"And they'll have me in broadfall pants and a broad brimmed hat mentally if not actually."

"They love you, Johnny. They want to see you safe and settled, not hiding in my house from some disreputable people."

"They don't know I'm here, do they?"

"Not that I know of."

"Did you get hold of Rob?"

"He's on his way, but it'll be a bit. He's coming from visiting his father at Allenwood."

"Rachel." Johnny straightened his shoulders. "I'm going to make a deal with the cops. They do it all the time on TV. I tell them what I know and go free because what I tell about the bad guys helps convict them."

"But you did wrong too, Johnny."

"Only because he threatened you and Sally and Ruthie."

"What?" He hadn't said anything about threats to anyone but himself.

"He said that if I didn't pay him back, they'd hurt you. I couldn't pay him back. I don't have the money. So I offered to work it off. For you, Rach. For you."

She wanted to believe he had a motive that was better than greed, but could she trust him? He'd been out in the world a long time, and she was still naïve about how people out there thought.

She pictured the guy with the muscles and the baseball bat and shuddered. "You never thought to tell us that we might be in danger?"

"I didn't want to worry you. You were living in your little peaceful Amish bubble. You wouldn't understand threats."

"Johnny, I'm not stupid. Of course I understand threats. I think they're wrong, but I understand them."

"Okay, I maybe should have told you. Now you know. And now I'm the one in trouble."

"How much money do you owe?"

"It started with $5000. Now it's up to $7000."

"How did it escalate so quickly?"

"Mr. Sherman sets his own rules."

"Outside the law."

"Outside the law."

"If you had the money and could repay this Mr. Sherman, would you be safe?"

His eyes turned calculating, like he was assessing her words for his benefit. "I guess. If I give him the money and the envelope."

She studied him. If she gave him the money, could she trust him not to fall into a similar situation at another time, especially if he thought she'd bail him out again? But if she could save him and didn't...

"What if I could lend you the money?"

"*You?*" He almost laughed until he saw she was serious. "I thought you were going to persuade Datt. You could lend me the money?"

"I could." Both he and she were saying lend, but she knew she had to expect him not to pay her back. She loved Johnny, but she wasn't blind to his shortcomings.

"I should have asked you originally." He laughed. "If I'd known you had money to spare."

If he only knew. "I wouldn't have given it to you to lose, Johnny. I'm only lending it to you now because I'd prefer that you not get beaten up again."

"Right. Gotcha." But he didn't.

"We're going to do this like a bank would," she said. "Paperwork. Your signature. A set amount to be paid back each month."

He frowned. "Why don't you just gi—"

"I'm *not* giving it to you. I'm *lending* it to you so you can get out of your jam. You're paying me back. Take it or leave it."

"Take it!" He grabbed her by the shoulders and gave her a big kiss on the cheek. "We won't need to go to the cops after all."

And here was the part that bothered her ethically and spiritually. "But you still did wrong, Johnny. And Mr. Sherman is still doing wrong."

"He's not my problem anymore. Just write that check and I'm free!" He gave Bagel a head rub. "Hear that, dog? I'm a free man again!"

She watched him with a sinking heart. She was used to people accepting responsibility for their actions. One of the strengths of the Amish way of life was personal responsibility and repentance.

Johnny showed no signs of admitting his wrong and accepting the consequences. He showed no interest in righting the wrong being done by lawbreakers. Certainly there was no repentance.

"Go write that check, Rach, while I get dressed. I'm going to fix this situation once and for all.

"You'll have to wait until I get back from Mom and Datt's."

"Oh, right. Rusty. Hurry up, okay? He grinned. "California here I come!"

Chapter 40

Johnny leaned against the kitchen counter eating a leftover chicken breast he'd found in the refrigerator. He'd been very considerate taking just the one. There was another piece left, not quite as large but nice and meaty. Rachel would have her dinner tonight.

He frowned. That second piece did look awfully good. The more he thought about it, the more he coveted it. There was a lot of sliced Lebanon bologna in there. She could make a sandwich with it and some cheese and have a good dinner. She could add chips, some of Mom's pickles, and maybe a soda or lemonade. She'd never miss the chicken.

He looked at the fridge. Rachel still thought Amish in spite of her Englisch clothes. It was like you could take the girl out of the Amish but you couldn't take the Amish out of the girl. He smiled at the thought. It was true. She always shared. She wouldn't mind if he took that other piece.

He should have come into the house right away instead of hiding in the barn. It was cold out there, and Rusty wasn't the best tempered roommate. What did he think? That Rachel would call Mr. Sherman and say, "My brother's here; come and get him"?

It was hard to know what to do these days. He'd never been a fugitive before. He thought for a minute. Did he have to be hiding from the police to be a fugitive or was hiding from Mr. Sherman enough? But in a very real way he was hiding from the police too. If they knew what he had transported from Philadelphia, they'd be very unhappy with him.

The chicken suddenly felt like a big indigestible lump in his stomach.

Bagel sat at his feet staring up at him, hoping his sad eyes would earn him a taste of the chicken. It was amazing how well in-house dogs did begging. Outside ones knew better.

Should he give Bagel some chicken? Would Amy mind? He shrugged. She wasn't here. The way his stomach felt, he might as well give the animal some.

He tore off a small chunk and held it out a little higher than his waist. Bagel leaped and Johnny lifted his hand over his head. Bagel fell to earth, still hopeful, still all wiggly.

Johnny lowered his hand. Bagel jumped again and he raised his hand again. Hand low. Hand high. Down, up, down, up.

Johnny laughed. He hadn't realized how much fun a house dog could be.

Finally Bagel stopped jumping and just stood, staring unhappily.

Johnny shrugged. Apparently they'd reached the end of the game. "Sit."

Bagel dropped to his haunches, vibrating again in anticipation. Johnny dropped the meat and the dog pounced. It was so weird about dogs, how they never seemed to chew. They just swallowed. Cows on the other hand chewed and chewed.

Bagel looked up all sad-eyed as if he hadn't just enjoyed that chunk. Johnny made no move to give him more, just stared at him. The dog put his paws on Johnny's thigh, his nose quivering as he inhaled the scent of the chicken. Johnny pushed him gently to the floor.

He should get a beagle. Talk about a way to impress Amy. He pictured them walking with their twin beagles on matching leads. She was smiling at him, laughing at something he said or maybe something the dogs did. She was so cute. Sure, she was a little too keen on Jesus, but he could work with that. He didn't want to spend the rest of his life hanging with Merle and Bennett. They might be great guys, but the trailer needed a woman's touch. And let's face it. Becky was a lost cause.

Just thinking about life with Amy made his stomach relax. Forget Mr. Sherman. Forget the police. He and Amy would go to California together and live happily ever after. They'd get a little house by the ocean and watch the sun set each night as they sat on their front porch. Mr. Sherman and Thomas—and poor Mick—boy, he never thought he'd use the words *poor* and *Mick* in the same sentence—would never cross his mind.

Bagel gave a tiny bark to remind him of his presence.

"Want to live in California, dog?"

Bagel cocked his head as if he was thinking about it.

Rachel's buggy rumbled down the drive, and Bagel forgot all about California. He pushed off Johnny's leg and raced across the room to the bookcase by the front window. Without pausing, he jumped. He slid a bit on the smooth wood of the bookcase's top surface, his nose bumping into the window. He went into a crouch and began barking like a mad thing at the buggy.

"Shut up, dog!" He tossed the bones into the trash and opened the fridge for the second piece. "Shut up."

Bagel ignored him.

Did Rachel know how Bagel amused himself while she and Amy were gone? If she hadn't figured it out already, the scratches on the wood were bound to give him away soon.

◦⟋⟍⟍9

Rachel guided Rusty down her driveway and then stopped at the street and looked both ways. With a flick of the reins she told Rusty to pull onto the road and head toward Mom and Datt's. She'd hoped to get there much earlier, before the family got home from church, pretty much an all-day affair today between the recommitment service and Communion preparation. She wanted to avoid any awkwardness or distress when they saw her in her English clothes, but all the issues with Johnny had made her later than she planned.

They might well be home by now with Datt reading *Die Botschaft* to anyone within earshot. Mom would be trying not to hear him, and the boys had probably escaped to the barn. Maybe Sally and Eban were visiting, sitting at the kitchen table with Mom and Ruthie while Ruthie told them all about her time with her friends last night.

Then in a disorienting shift, that familiar picture of home was skewed as she imagined a couple in English clothes standing by the door, welcomed but as visitors, not integrated into family life. She took a deep breath to ease the pain.

And she was giving up Rusty along with everything else. She and Aaron bought him when they were first married to pull their new closed buggy. He was a good horse, strong and intelligent, and he had many years of service left. Under other circumstances, she'd be driving him for years.

Instead she was going to drive a black Honda. No more cold mornings buckling Rusty into his leatherwork and tethering him to the buggy. No more mucking out his stall, filling his water trough, seeing to his feed. No more rein game.

She sighed. *Change.* No matter how desired, it hurt. At least the consequences hurt.

Rusty plodded along, head alert. The fall day seemed to invigorate him.

"I'm going to miss you, Rusty."

His ears twitched as if he understood.

When Aaron died, she'd taken to talking to Rusty. She knew Max talked to the absent Buddy a lot. She'd never talked to Aaron much, but she'd talked to Rusty. It was safe to reveal herself to him since he'd never tell on her.

Now she would be sharing her heart with Rob. The thought made her smile.

"Sorry, boy, but you've been replaced."

Rusty shook his head.

Rachel took a deep breath of the crisp fall air and grinned. Rusty trotted on and the farm lane came into view. Neither one was prepared for the car that roared up beside them and, brakes screeching, pulled to an angled stop across the road, blocking their way.

Chapter 41

Rusty snorted and shied, distressed by the large loud thing in front of him.

Mom's words, "You can't trust cars," echoed in Rachel's mind as she struggled with the reins and the unhappy Rusty. It wasn't cars that were the problem. It was those who drove them without regard for the sensitivities of high-strung animals like Rusty.

As she struggled to calm Rusty, the driver jumped from the car on the far side, a thin man with a beak nose and curly hair. Her blood chilled at the sight of him. *Thomas.*

He glared at her over the roof of the car, and she blinked at the fury in his expression. What had she ever done to call forth such venom? She pushed back against the seat as if she could get away from him.

"Where is he?" It wasn't so much a question as a demand that she answer.

"Who?" What else could she say?

"Where is he?" He brought up a handgun, pointing it at her. Not a finger gun like Mick had aimed at her but the real thing. She stared at it in horror.

He threatened you and Sally and Ruthie. He said that if I didn't pay him back, they'd hurt you.

Well, Johnny was going to pay him back; Thomas just didn't know it yet. All she had to do was tell him, and she'd be safe.

"You need to know—" she began.

"Shut up!" He gave the gun a shake as if he was shaking his index finger under her nose. His finger on the trigger looked none too steady.

She shut up.

Thomas circled the car, the gun sighted on her. When he cleared the back bumper and moved toward the buggy, his quick movements made Rusty shake his head and shuffle his feet nervously.

"Easy, boy. Easy." She wanted to jump down and go to Rusty to calm him, but she was afraid of making any sudden movement. Who knew what Thomas would do if she did.

As she stared at the gun, a terrible thought occurred. Had Thomas been the one who killed Mick? Johnny claimed he knew who the murderer was even though he hadn't seen him. How many men with guns could Johnny know? Logic and Johnny's small world said not many.

Did Thomas suspect Johnny knew? Would paying back the money be enough to ensure Johnny's safety if Thomas or Mr. Sherman knew he knew? Lack of proof might not mean a thing to men who had already killed.

Situations like this were so far out of her world that she didn't know what to do. It was one thing to pay off a loan shark and get Johnny out of trouble with Mr. Sherman. Unpalatable. Ugly. Not illegal.

It was another thing to cover for a murder. There was no way she could participate in that.

"Where is he?" Thomas roared the question again and slapped the side of the buggy.

The blow against the supple buggy skin wasn't terribly loud, but combined with the yelling it made Rusty snort and prance nervously in place. Rachel's heart slammed in her chest and her hands felt curiously weak as she fought to control the animal's movements.

"Where?" Thomas yelled again.

"I-I don't know." That wasn't exactly a lie. He could be in the house or in the barn or in his bedroom or in the living room.

Thomas's eyes narrowed and his mouth hardened. "Don't give me that. You were just at his trailer. You know where he is. You got his things for him."

She stiffened. "You spied on me?" For some reason that bothered her more than the gun.

"I didn't spy on you. I don't care about you." Scorn laced his words. "Besides I know where to find you whenever I want to."

Her skin crawled at that comment.

"I want Johnny. I was waiting at the trailer for him. He has something I want."

And with Rusty here, no one was protecting what he wanted as it lay beneath the straw in her barn.

"Where is he?" He stepped closer and pointed the gun at her head.

She stared at it. It was ugly and black, but she thought that if she hadn't gone to that movie with Rob, she wouldn't have recognized its power. She was used to guns for hunting, rifles and shotguns, big guns with big power, not handguns. This one looked so small she might have misjudged its ability to harm. She couldn't help thinking about the children at the Nickel Mines School shootings. It was speculated that those children never understood their danger because they'd never seen a handgun before.

Would it hurt when he shot her? Because she couldn't tell him where Johnny was. He was her brother, and she loved him.

She closed her eyes as she prayed for courage. She might be leaving her community, but her Anabaptist heritage ran strong in her veins. She would face her trial with the same resolute bravery as her ancestors. She wasn't about to be burned at the stake for her faith, but she was facing death for love of her family.

"Look at me!" Thomas slapped the buggy again. This time the slap cracked.

Rachel jumped and her eyes flew open. Rusty looked over his shoulder, his eyes wide with distress.

The passenger door of the black car flew open right under Rusty's nose, and a fat man jumped out.

"What are you waiting for, Thomas? Grab her and make her talk! Grab her!"

Chapter 42

Rob watched the fields of dry cornstalks glide by. Soon an Amishman pulling his John Deere with a team of huge work horses would cut the stalks, leaving behind a field that looked like the stubbled chin of a very large man.

He could feel the tension draining away the farther he got from the prison and his father.

As he drove, he repeated his frequent prayer: *Lord, don't let me be like my father. Please don't let me be like my father.*

He thought of Rachel, his lovely Rachel, who wanted to meet Eugene Lanier. Poor woman. She didn't know what she was asking. She was used to love and kindness. She'd get stony silence from his father at best, acerbic unkind comments at worst.

He'd take her with him to Allenwood because she wouldn't let it go until he did. He knew that. Her kind heart required she reach out to Dad. He smiled as he imagined the two of them together. Her sweet and gentle spirit and his sour mean one. If anyone could break through Eugene Lanier's bitterness, it would be her. It'd be a miracle, but the Lord was in the miracle business, and women like Rachel were some of His best weapons.

He knew he was almost home when he passed a farm where perhaps forty Amish young people were playing volleyball and eating from picnic tables laden with food. In a nearby field several miniature horses stood watching the activity while half a dozen fleecy sheep ignored everything but the grass they nibbled.

He smiled at the maples turning their beautiful fiery red and the pumpkins lying scattered in the fields like fat orange balls. A sign for a corn maze slid past, and No Sales on Sunday signs hung by Amish farm lanes. The sun shone brightly, filling Rob with optimism about the future.

His Rachel loved him. She was going to marry him. Life didn't get any better.

ᏊᏊ

"Did you hear me, Thomas?" the man demanded. "Grab her."

"Yes, Mr. Sherman."

Mr. Sherman? That chubby man was the man Johnny feared so much? He looked like an out of shape cartoon character, not a man to fill others with dread.

Rachel held up a hand to ward off Thomas. "We've got the money! You don't need me."

Thomas reached for her, and Rachel slid across the seat as far from him as she could get. She fumbled with the latch to the closed door.

"Did you hear me?" She spoke loudly and clearly so he couldn't help understand. "We've got the money."

She would jump out and run, losing herself in the cornstalks in the field beside the road.

Thomas reached into the buggy and grabbed her arm before she got the door unlatched and started pulling her toward him.

She struggled against his unexpected strength, hitting at him with her free arm, and shouting, "Let me go!"

The buggy shook with the struggle, and Rusty shifted in agitation.

"Johnny!" Mr. Sherman yelled. "Where is Johnny?" He took a step toward the buggy, frightening the already unnerved Rusty who whinnied in distress and sidestepped, trying to find a way to escape. The car blocked his way on one side and a shallow ditch at the edge of the cornfield stopped him on the other side.

"Be careful," Rachel yelled. "You're scaring the horse!"

"Forget the horse." Mr. Sherman waved his hands as if he intended to brush Rusty out of his path.

The upset Rusty drew his lips back and showed his teeth for an instant before he bit the appendage closest. Mr. Sherman screamed and pulled his hand away.

"He bit me!" There was as much disbelief as horror in his voice. "He bit me! Get him away from me!" He backed up against the car, cradling his bitten hand to his chest.

"Let me go to Rusty," Rachel begged Thomas who was dragging her out of the buggy with no concern for the crack of her hip against the edge of the door or the fact that she had been spun around and was about to land on her back. "I need to calm him down before he hurts someone else."

Thomas ignored her and kept hauling, wrenching her arm at the shoulder. Rachel stopped herself from landing on her back by a desperate last minute grab at the edge of the door as she was jerked past. She ended up sitting on the ground, dangling from Thomas's hand. Thomas yanked her upright and waved the gun at her. "Keep still!"

"Get this beast away from me!" Mr. Sherman looked almost as wild-eyed as Rusty did.

Rachel pulled toward her horse. "It's okay, Rusty. It's okay."

Thomas gave her a hard jerk. "Stay where you are. I'll take care of him." He dropped her arm and extended a hand to grab Rusty's halter.

"Don't!" Rachel reached out to stop him. "He's too upset for a stranger to handle him."

But it was too late. Rusty reared. When his front hooves came down, one landed on Mr. Sherman's brightly polished loafer. The man's roar of pain turned the horse rigid with shock.

Chapter 43

*J*ohnny frowned as Bagel's barking increased in volume.

"The buggy's gone, dog. Stop it!"

Bagel's bark turned to a whine as he looked over his shoulder at Johnny.

"Quiet!" The dream of getting his own beagle was fast fading as the dog began to really irritate him. "Get down and shut up."

Bagel jumped from his perch, and Johnny thought for a moment the dog was obeying. Walking beagles with Amy burst into a full color vision again.

Instead the dog raced to the front door where he began scratching and whining. He looked at Johnny, then back at the door. He went up on his hind legs, distress in every line of his quivering body as his feet scored the wood.

"What's the matter, Lassie? Timmy fall into the well?" He enjoyed his little joke based on the old *Lassie* reruns he liked laughing at.

Johnny went to the window and looked out. He actually fell back a step when he saw what the dog was barking about. Thomas with a gun, Rachel in his grasp, Rusty rearing. And Mr. Sherman's angry screams turning to ones of pain as Rusty stepped on him.

Johnny paused only long enough to grab the fireplace poker. Then he threw open the front door and rushed out. Bagel flew past him, down the steps, and into the street, barking at full volume.

"Leave her alone!" Johnny yelled as he raced toward the chaos. "Leave her alone!"

CRIMO

Max Englerth heard yelling in the brief lull between commercials on the football game. She was glad for the distraction. Her team was losing pretty badly. She glanced out the window in time to see Johnny Miller race by waving a poker. What in the world? Johnny wasn't the most stable of young men, but a poker?

She leaned forward for a better view and saw the buggy and the car blocking it. Then she saw a furious man with a gun manhandling Rachel.

Max grabbed her phone and hit 911.

"Man with a gun!" she yelled before the woman who answered had time to say, "911. What is your emergency?"

Max raced to the front door and threw it open. She didn't know what she could do to help Rachel, but there must be something. "Man with a gun!"

She stopped, reversed course, and ran to her son's room. She threw open his closet door and grabbed his baseball bat. It felt heavy in her hand as she gave a little swing. A good thunk on the head would definitely hurt. She smiled in anticipation.

"I know, Buddy. I know. Dumb as dumb. But I have to do something! It's Rachel."

She could almost hear him yelling, "Max, a gun trumps a bat any day of the week. Stay inside and wait for the cops!"

But she couldn't cower inside, peering out the window like some frightened old lady. She just couldn't. She could at least give Johnny some support, offer Rachel some hope.

Rob made the last turn onto Rachel's road. He needed her quiet and gentle manner after his father's abrasive and critical one. He wanted to sit at the table with her and eat meat loaf and plan their future. He wanted—

He blinked. Johnny was racing down the middle of the street waving a poker. And a woman was running out of her house waving a baseball bat. Both were yelling like banshees. Racing ahead of them, Bagel barked and snarled.

But the sight that chilled him to the core was the man with a gun. Thomas, the one who'd held Johnny in the parking lot. Even as the man grabbed for the bobbing and weaving Rusty, he had his gun trained on Rachel.

Rob's heart stuttered. All those times in the field expecting an IED with every mile, every step, he hadn't been this terrified, not even when the Humvee in front of his exploded and sent shrapnel flying right at him or when he and his men were pinned down by snipers firing on them from nearby rooftops. He could take danger to him and his men. They had asked for it by joining up. But Rachel?

As if the scene in front of him wasn't bad enough, rounding a curve in the road beyond Rachel and Thomas was a buggy driven by a man with a long white beard, a man he knew, a man whose daughter he planned to marry.

What would happen if Mr. and Mrs. Miller and their family drove up to Thomas? The man was clearly unstable to be waving a gun around on a public street.

I'm coming, babe! Hang in there! I'm coming!

He pushed the gas pedal and sped toward the scene.

Chapter 44

*R*achel watched in horror as Johnny raced down the street toward her brandishing a poker above his head like an old knight swinging a broadsword.

"Let her alone," he screamed. "Let her alone! We've got the money. I've got the money."

Racing in front of him, charging at full speed as he barked and growled, came Bagel.

"Shoot the dog!" ordered Mr. Sherman, his voice a croak as he held onto the car door for support with his unbitten hand.

For a minute Rachel had thought Rusty was going to play the rein game with Mr. Sherman's foot, but apparently he realized he had something too bulky under his foot to keep his weight on it. He shifted a bit and Mr. Sherman was free.

"Shoot him, Thomas! No dog's going to bite me! Shoot the horse too! Now!"

Thomas turned first to the fast advancing Bagel with his gun raised.

"No!" Rachel turned cold all over. "Don't!" Amy would be devastated if anything happened to the dog. Rachel reached for Thomas's raised arm and managed to bump his elbow.

Thomas pulled the trigger.

The percussive roar was sharp and deafening. It terrified Rusty. He screamed and reared again, his hooves flailing once again above Mr. Sherman who fell back into the car to escape the potentially lethal iron shoes.

"Get away from me! Get away!" he screamed.

Bagel kept running but Rachel watched in horror as Johnny went down. It was like watching slow motion as first his mouth opened in surprise. Then he went to his knees, then his hands, his face. The poker fell uselessly to the ground. "Johnny! No!" She lunged toward him, but Thomas grabbed her around the waist. He pulled her back against him.

"Let me go!" She twisted and struggled to get free.

Bagel came at Thomas with teeth bared. Thomas tried to aim, but the dog was too close. If he pulled the trigger, he could shoot himself in the foot. Instead he kicked, but Bagel was too quick. He darted away, then raced back, growling and snapping.

Rachel drove an elbow back into Thomas's midsection, hoping that with his attention on Bagel, he'd loosen his grip on her. She needed to get to Johnny. If he had been shot like she feared, it was her fault. Her attempt to save Bagel had skewed Thomas's aim.

Her elbow did nothing to Thomas but bump into ribs. Aside from an "*umph*," Thomas kept his strong grip about her middle.

"Forget her," Mr. Sherman yelled from the car. "It's Johnny we want!"

Rachel looked over her shoulder at Thomas in the same instant he looked down at her. Their eyes locked. Then he gave her a stiff shove. She fell, hitting the ground hard. For a moment she lay stunned, her hands burning from the scrapes made sliding on the pavement, her knees throbbing from the slam into the road, her breath compromised from hitting hard on the unforgiving ground.

Bagel abandoned Thomas and rushed to her. He licked her face, then rushed back to attack Thomas. This time, with Thomas concentrating on Johnny, he connected with Thomas's leg, his teeth finding traction through the denim.

Thomas roared and whirled to try to dislodge the dog. He stumbled against the buggy, and the jarring knocked Bagel lose. The dog dodged under the buggy and growled. Thomas cursed at Bagel but turned away toward Johnny.

Rachel caught her breath and pushed herself to her knees in time to see Thomas aim once again. It seemed he was shooting too high to hit her brother, still prone in the middle of the street. Kneeling beside him, trying to help him, was Max, her bat rolling into the little ditch running beside the road.

"No!" She threw herself at Thomas's legs as another percussive crack shattered the afternoon.

Chapter 45

Rob saw first Johnny, then Rachel, go down. In that moment he understood David's imprecatory psalms as never before and he cried out an inarticulate call for God to save them.

He narrowed his eyes in a combination of anger that someone dared hurt his Rachel and determination to get to her as quickly as possible.

He drove straight toward Thomas who finally seemed to notice a car racing down the street at him. He braced himself, legs spread, gun held steady as he drew a bead on Rob.

Rob didn't falter. Let the man shoot him. If Rachel had a chance to survive this chaos, he would give it to her. As she would to him, he thought as she lunged at Thomas's legs. Rob was filled with pride at her bravery and her pluck.

Thomas staggered a bit as she hit him, and the gun fired. Rob's windshield starred, and he heard the bullet *swhoop* as it plowed through the passenger seat.

Thomas instinctively took a couple of steps backward as Rob hurtled toward him. Rob waited for a second shot as he closed the distance, hunching as low over the wheel as he could to make himself a difficult target.

Instead of the whine of a bullet he heard Rusty whinny as the horse twisted in panic. No doubt the loud noise of the shot had terrified him.

The horse, eyes wide with terror, opened his mouth and showed his fearsome teeth. He bit hard at the closest thing—Thomas's shoulder. Rob could hear Thomas's screams through his closed windows.

Any possibility of another shot was forgotten as the gun fell uselessly to the ground as Thomas tried to pull away from the panicked animal.

Grabbing onto a wheel of the buggy, Rachel pulled herself to her feet, taking care to stay away from the flailing Rusty. She kicked the gun into the ditch.

Rob grinned. *Good girl.*

Rachel, still afraid of what might come next, raced around to the far side of the buggy and jumped across the little ditch, calling to Bagel, crouching under the buggy, to come to her.

Rob screeched to a halt with his car making the third side of a neat triangle comprised of the horse and buggy, Thomas's car, and his SUV. Thomas was neatly trapped in the middle.

"He bit me! He bit me!" Thomas stared in pained disbelief at his shoulder with its torn sleeve, flowing blood, and horse saliva, then turned white and slid down the side of his car to sit on the ground.

Rob threw the gearshift into park and then flung open his car door "Rachel!"

"Here." She jumped back across the ditch and rounded the back of the buggy. She ran toward him full tilt.

Rob grabbed her and held her close, reassuring himself she was in one piece. "Seeing that gun aimed at you—" He let the sentence dangle as he shuddered. "Are you okay? Really okay?"

"I'll be fine," she told him as she patted his chest. "Just a little sore." He covered her hand with his to still it. The last thing he wanted was to feel like Bagel being soothed.

"Johnny." She looked toward her brother. Rob felt her relax as she saw her brother was now sitting in the middle of the road holding his jaw, Max kneeling beside him.

⚬∾∾∾⚬

When Rachel heard Rob calling her name, she thought she'd never heard anything sweeter. She now rested her head softly on his shoulder, his arms around her.

Johnny stood and began limping toward her, Max at his side helping support him. Rachel felt a great wash of relief. He hadn't been shot. Her actions hadn't harmed him.

A wet nose nudged her leg and she looked down at Bagel. She rubbed his head. "Hey, boy. You did good."

He preened for a moment, then went over to Rusty and began to bark.

"No, Bagel!" As usual he ignored her as he dodged Rusty's shuffling feet.

Rob grabbed Bagel by his collar and hauled him away from the poor horse. He pulled his belt from about his waist and looped it around Bagel's collar. He held out the end to Rachel.

"You've got a better chance than anyone to quiet him."

That was a debatable comment, but she took the belt and tugged the dog close. Bagel surprised her by sitting nicely at her side.

"Rachel! What is going on here?" Datt appeared from somewhere.

"Datt! You won't believe—"

"What is wrong with Johnny?"

"Hey, Datt." Johnny limped to join them beside the buggy, walking on the ball of his right foot and putting very little pressure on that foot. He had a pained expression with every other step. He had his arm about Max's shoulders and her arm was about his waist to help bear his weight.

"You're limping." Datt frowned his concern.

"Twisted my ankle. Stepped on a stone. I heard it pop." He shuddered.

Rachel looked down. Johnny had rolled his jeans up a bit, and she could see his ankle was already swelling.

"He needs ice. I'm going to get him some," Max said. "You need to sit, Johnny. Get your weight off the injury."

"Here." Rob opened the door to the backseat of his car. "In here."

Johnny hopped over and sat.

"Leg up on the seat," Max ordered. "I'll be right back."

Johnny leaned his head back and closed his eyes. Mom climbed in beside him and took his hand.

"You will be all right." She blinked back tears as she watched her prodigal son. "You will be all right. You'll see."

"Who is that man?" Datt pointed at the sitting Thomas, his head resting against his car door. His face, filmed with perspiration, was white with pain and anger. Rachel could imagine the throbbing in his shoulder keeping time with his heartbeat.

"His name is Thomas," Rachel said. "I don't know his last name."

"And that one?" He pointed at Mr. Sherman who had slid behind the steering wheel of his car. When he patted the ignition and found no key, he tried to climb out the far side of the vehicle. He took one step on his injured foot and fell, moaning in pain. Rachel knew all the bones of his foot must be in little pieces after Rusty's stomp.

"That's Mr. Sherman. He's a bad guy. They're both bad guys, Datt. Very bad guys."

He leaned in with worried eyes and said softly and for her ears only, "Johnny's friends?"

Rachel shook her head. "You should have seen him, Datt. You'd have been proud. He was going to protect me." She decided not to mention they were planning to buy his way out of trouble and her doubts that he would remain trouble-free.

Datt looked at Johnny who looked like he was asleep in the backseat beside Mom. "Really?"

Max reappeared with a plastic bag filled with ice that she took to Johnny. As she draped a kitchen towel over his ankle and topped it with the ice, he flinched but otherwise didn't move.

The sirens grew louder and the police turned into the street, lights flashing. Rusty became agitated all over again.

"Levi!" Datt called. "Take care of the horse."

An eager Levi ran to Rusty. In no time he had calmed the distraught horse.

"He's like a horse whisperer," Datt told Rob.

And just like that, Rachel thought, a reasonable facsimile of a Sabbath calm returned—if you overlooked the police cars and ambulances and men handcuffed to their gurneys.

Chapter 46

"You're sure he's going to be all right?" Rachel asked the EMT who checked out Johnny.

"He'll be fine," the EMT assured her. "Just a twist, not a break in the ankle, is my guess."

"I'm *not* fine." Johnny shook his hands to dry the disinfectant sprayed on them. "I hurt! A lot."

Rachel looked at the bruise already forming on his jaw from the collision with the ground, and she knew how her own palms and knees stung from being sprayed. He also had his twisted ankle. Poor Johnny.

"How'd you do it?" the EMT asked.

"I hit a stone, and bam! My ankle gave way and I went down. Hard! I heard it pop!"

"Yeah, yeah." The EMT was unimpressed by his story or at least by his "poor me" attitude. "Believe me, a bullet would have hurt a lot more and I understand there were some fired here today. And I'll say again you should go to the hospital to get checked out. Get an X-ray."

Johnny shook his head, stubborn to the end, but he stopped complaining and tried to look brave when he saw Amy watching him, her face full of sympathy, Bagel on his belt lead at her side. She had arrived shortly after the action was over.

Rusty stood trembling but still as Levi stroked his neck and talked softly to him.

Mr. Sherman lay on a stretcher, his foot elevated and wrapped in cold packs. The wrist of his unbitten hand was cuffed to his gurney. He whimpered quietly as he waited for his ride to the hospital and surgery for a crushed foot. His hand would be sore for some time, but apparently Rusty hadn't broken anything with that bite. What the justice system would do with the man was yet to be determined, but when he left the hospital, he wouldn't be going home.

"We'll need you to give us an official statement," the policeman told her.

Rachel nodded. "Johnny and I will come in tomorrow."

"What? Me?" Johnny tore his eyes from Amy and looked at Rachel with something like fear. "He didn't try to grab me."

Rachel just stared at her brother, disappointment at his response welling in her. There had been that one flash of courage, of being honorable when he tried to come to her rescue. Was that all there was in him?

He squirmed and looked away. "Oh. You mean that other thing."

"What other thing?" the officer asked.

"What other thing?" Rob whispered in her ear.

Rachel said nothing and waited.

"What other thing?" the officer repeated, fixing Johnny with a steely eye.

Johnny glared at Rachel and she knew he was angry she hadn't kept quiet. She glared back. They were going to tell about the envelope and its contents. If she had to force him into talking, so be it. He was afraid of what might happen to him for having the false papers. She understood that. Still, right was right.

He cleared his throat. "I-I may have some evidence against Mr. Sherman."

"May?" The officer looked both interested and skeptical.

"Why don't you show him, Johnny?" Rachel knew she was pushing, but quite honestly she was afraid Johnny and the envelope would be on their way to California before tomorrow morning if she didn't. "I'm sure the officer will drive you to my house and the barn so you can get that evidence."

With a final if-looks-could-kill scowl in her direction, Johnny limped after the officer to his car.

"What other thing?" Rob asked as they watched the car drive slowly to Rachel's house and turn into the drive.

"Johnny was a courier for Mr. Sherman."

Rob sighed. "How deep is he in?"

"He only did it once. At least that's what he said. It started because he owed him money and couldn't pay up."

"Blood from a turnip, I imagine," Rob said.

She nodded. "Remember the beating?"

"To scare him into paying. And he couldn't because he had nothing."

"Well, Mr. Sherman then threatened Ruthie, Sally, and me." She explained the whole sad story to Rob. "The passports and birth certificates are in Rusty's stall, hidden under the straw."

Rob took her hand. "You thought he wouldn't report what happened, so you forced the issue."

"I think he'd run first. I love him, but he—" She wasn't sure how to explain Johnny.

"He should be Amish," Rob said. "Or go back to being Amish."

Rachel looked at him in surprise.

"Think about it. Living under that structure would be good for him. It'd keep him from running off the rails. It'd help the good qualities lurking in him to have a chance to come out instead of his weaknesses, like being a follower and a guy who gives in to his impulses."

She looked at Levi, who wanted to be an Amish farmer, and at her father, who was such a fine man. She thought of Aaron. Those three were what she thought an Amish man should be. Then she thought of Johnny.

"You shouldn't be Amish to hide from life, Rob. That's all it would be for Johnny. Amish life is hard. It's got just as many problems as Englisch life, just different. Johnny's got to grow up before he can be anything, Amish or Englisch. In the meantime, he's just Johnny."

"And you love him." He kissed the top of her head.

Rachel flushed and looked at her parents. They were both watching her and Rob; Datt with a stern expression, Mom with a thoughtful one.

They were all distracted as one of the ambulances drove slowly away with Mr. Sherman inside. They watched it until it turned out of sight, then looked at the other ambulance.

Thomas was being slid through the rear doors, his bitten shoulder covered, a cold pack resting on it. He still looked queasy, but that might have been due to the handcuff that held his uninjured arm to the gurney and the large policeman who climbed in after him.

Max walked over to Mom, and Rachel heard her say, "It's just like live TV." Mom looked unimpressed. Datt stood silently beside them, watching everything carefully, evaluating the Englisch world and finding it wanting. In a peaceful Amish world, such terrible things would not happen.

Everyone close to her was here: Her family, appalled by the violence, but thankful she and her brother were all right. Rob, her hero who roared to the rescue. Johnny, who showed unexpected bravery even if he did trip over his own feet and revert to character in the end. Max, who called the police and made certain the bad guys got caught. Amy, wide-eyed at it all, unhappy she'd missed the excitement. Even Bagel, who probably saved Johnny's life with the timely leap and bite. He got little more than a mouthful of jeans, but it was enough for the shot to go wild.

As Rachel looked around, something Max had said one day in her kitchen struck her. *For you there are three worlds.* And all three were here.

Her family was her old world, her secure, ordered Amish world that had cared for her and nurtured her. It was a world she loved and appreciated.

Thomas and Mr. Sherman represented the evil world, the world that was a threat to all who came near it. Just ask Johnny.

These were the two worlds she'd always known existed. But Max was right when she said there was that third world, the world populated with people like Rob and Max and Amy—even Johnny with his flawed but caring heart.

All three worlds were options for her, but she had chosen the third world.

She would miss the love and acceptance she'd known in her first world. It broke her heart that she had disappointed her family by choosing as she had. She could only hope they believed her when she told them she loved them just as fiercely as always.

That second world, the evil one, had never been attractive to her. It went against everything the Bible taught and she was committed to being a Christian who followed the Bible. She had been her whole life. The second world also seemed very illogical to her. Aside from the fact that it didn't seem wise to choose against God, it seem foolish to choose a life that was an inevitable downward spiral. A choice for a small evil led to a choice for a larger evil.

Between these two extremes was the third world, now her world. She knew that everyone in this third world didn't love God, but they did make choices to limit their wrong actions.

She thought for a moment. Maybe there were four worlds. The Amish one. The evil one. The regular-people one where people didn't particularly pay attention to God. And the regular-people one where serving God and getting to know Him better were the driving forces of life. She had chosen for this world.

She'd have to run her new idea past Rob and Max to see if they agreed, but she thought she was on to something.

Believers who lived in the world but held strong against the culture and for God, not believers who lived protected in their own private world. In this everyday world she could love God, live for Him, and be free to be who she was, not who she was told to be or expected to be. Knowledge that this world was where she belonged fizzed through her. She'd made the right choice.

A police officer got behind the wheel of Mr. Sherman's car and drove it away. Levi climbed into her buggy with Davy. They drove Rusty toward the farm lane and out of her life. Datt took Mom by the arm and led her to their buggy. With a quick glance back as if reassuring herself Rachel was all right, Mom climbed in. Datt followed, and they were gone.

The policeman who had driven Johnny to the barn was back and held the envelope in his hand. He looked at Johnny long and hard. "Tomorrow, nine a.m. Don't prove me wrong in giving you the evening to nurse your ankle. You try any tricks, and I will find you."

Johnny paled and nodded. He let out a great sigh of relief when the man drove away. "He's scary, that one."

"Just so you show," Rachel said.

"I wouldn't dare not."

Rob's stomach growled.

Rachel grinned at him. "Bad news. Johnny ate the meat loaf."

Rob looked pained.

"I've got meat loaf," Max said. "Lots of it. I was going to a dinner at church this evening but—" She spread her hands and grinned. "I got distracted. Come help me eat it."

"I've got lots of leftover macaroni and cheese from the singles dinner," Amy said. "Three of us brought the same thing."

"I love mac and cheese." Johnny smiled brightly at Amy, who smiled at him with less enthusiasm.

Rachel thought quickly. "I've got homemade applesauce and a chocolate cake in the freezer if Johnny didn't eat it."

"I didn't touch it," he said self-righteously.

"You didn't find it, you mean."

They all laughed at Rachel's comment, and it felt good after the tension of the afternoon.

"Sunday dinner in fifteen," Max said. "My house. And Johnny, let me get my car for you. You mustn't walk on that ankle."

Johnny threw his arm over Amy's slight shoulders. "I'm sure Amy can help me."

"Hurry, Max," Amy said. "He's getting delirious."

Laughing, Rachel and Rob went to Rachel's house to get her

contributions. Once the door closed behind them, Rob spun Rachel to him and kissed her thoroughly.

"Scared doesn't begin to describe it," he said as he held her close.

"I know exactly what you mean. After this afternoon I'm more a believer in nonviolence than ever."

He laughed. "Only another sign of your intelligence."

She pulled the freezer open and took out the chocolate cake. She passed it to Rob and retrieved the bowl of applesauce from the fridge. She found a basket with a handle and put the food inside. Rob picked it up.

Holding hands they walked down the street and into their new life.

Epilogue

achel looked at herself in the mirror in Max's guest bedroom. Her dress was a simple white floor-length affair, dressier than she had planned. More expensive than she had planned. She should have known better than to take Amy shopping with her.

"You look beautiful," Max assured her.

"You do." Amy reached out and adjusted Rachel's veil.

Max kissed Rachel's cheek. "I can't tell you how honored I am that you're having your wedding here."

Rachel shrugged. "It all started here."

Besides a big church wedding was scary. She was used to the form of an Amish wedding. The one Englisch wedding she'd attended had overwhelmed her with all the glitz and glamour. A few friends gathering in Max's backyard was just right for her, and Rob liked the simplicity of it too.

Max kissed Rachel's cheek. "I'll see you outside." She left the two friends.

Rachel blinked against tears as she looked at her first and best Englisch friend. "I'm going to miss you. Having you and Bagel live with me has been wonderful."

Amy handed her a tissue. "I've loved it too, but you aren't going to miss us. You'll be too busy enjoying your husband."

Rachel grinned. "You're right." She couldn't wait to be Rob's wife. "You look so pretty in that rose dress."

Amy spun in a circle. "I know. Let's go wow the troops." She picked up a bouquet of gerbera daisies in shades of pink and white and handed it to Rachel. She picked up her own of pinks and reds.

Rachel's stomach swirled with excitement. She and Amy walked through Max's house to the back door where Rob waited for her. He stepped inside to join them.

Since her father wasn't here to walk her down the aisle, Rob was going to walk with her rather than her walking alone.

"Since I plan to walk by your side for the rest of our lives, I'm just starting a few steps early," he said when he'd suggested this arrangement to her.

If she hadn't loved him before, that comment would have stolen her heart.

When he saw her in her bridal gown, his eyes lit. "You look beautiful."

She turned in a circle for him, much as Amy had spun in the bedroom minutes earlier.

He smiled approval. "I'm glad you're wearing your hair long since it's what drew me to you originally." He reached out to grab a handful.

She stepped back, out of reach of this man who made her heart sing. "Not until after the ceremony. I worked too hard to get it to cooperate to have you mess it up."

He smiled a very private smile. "I can't wait."

"Oh, brother," Amy said. "Stop embarrassing me!"

The three of them watched through the kitchen windows as Win walked Rob's mother down the little aisle between the white folding chairs rented for the day.

"She looks lovely in that pale pink dress," Amy said. "It's too young for her and too red-carpet for the occasion, but somehow it's just right for her."

Rachel looked at what everyone said was the bride's side of the seating area. Johnny sat there. She sighed. Choices.

Win walked back up the aisle looking handsome in his gray pin-striped suit, his tie a rosy pink that matched Amy's gown.

"We spent hours looking for that tie." Amy gave Win a finger wave as he took up his place at the head of the aisle as if he expected multitudes of guests to escort. He grinned at her. She sighed. "He'll never wear it again."

"I'm surprised you got him to wear it today," Rob said.

Rachel wasn't. The budding romance between the two might have been a death knell for Johnny's dreams, but it seemed a good pairing to Rachel. Amy grew stronger every day in her adjustment to life and decisions made on her own, and Win was doing well in his college courses and was now daytime manager at the Star. He'd started going to church with Amy, and Rachel knew he was asking Rob lots of questions about what being a Christian looked like. Soon, if she was any judge, he'd make a choice of his own to believe.

It was time for the keyboardist to begin the music that would cue Amy's walk down the aisle. Rachel looked at her friend and grinned. Amy had moved out two weeks ago, and so far no one had complained about Bagel.

Rob squeezed Rachel's hand. "Look, sweetheart!"

She turned back to the window to see her parents walk into the yard. Her eyes filled with tears as she squeezed his hand back. They'd come!

She forgot all wedding protocol and raced out the door. "Mom! Datt!" She threw her arms around them and hugged them. With typical Amish stoicism, Datt didn't quite know how to respond, but Mom returned her hug.

"Thank you for coming! Thank you! You have no idea how much this means to me." She knew she was gushing, but she couldn't help it.

Rob stood beside her. "Thank you, sir." He stuck out his hand. Datt shook it solemnly.

"You are our daughter, Rachel," Datt said. "Nothing can ever change that. Nothing."

Ruthie appeared beside Rachel, eyeing her gown. "Mom, can I have a dress like Rachel's when I get married?"

Datt gave her his patented look and Ruthie tried to look repentant.

"Mrs. Miller," Win said. "May I escort you to your seat?" He held out his arm.

Mom looked a bit taken aback, but she slid her arm in Win's.

"Just follow me, sir," Win said.

Frowning, Datt followed Mom down the aisle.

Rachel bit back a smile as she looked at Ruthie. In a culture where men led, this was probably the first time Mom had walked into any kind of service ahead of Datt. Soon Rachel's family sat waiting for their daughter and sister to marry, even Levi and David, shirts tucked neatly into their broadfall pants, hats firmly on their heads. All but Jonah and Miriam.

"You know he can't come," Sally whispered just before she and Eban took their seats. "Miriam sends her love."

The music began for Amy to make her entrance. She looked adorable as she floated down the aisle, her eyes fixed on Win, the best man, waiting for his brother beside the pastor.

Then "Jesu, Joy of Man's Desiring" began and Max stood. Everyone followed her example and turned to watch the bridal couple.

Rob offered Rachel his arm.

Heart filled with love, she walked beside Rob into her future.

Discussion Questions

1. Rachel takes a huge risk to ease her heart's longing for an education. Have you ever had to take a risk or make a choice your family wouldn't understand? Explain.

2. What things does Rachel stand to lose? Why does she take that risk (more than for an education)?

3. Rachel and Amy share some similarities as well as some significant differences. Discuss.

4. The four members of the Lanier family handled the fallout from Eugene's jail sentence differently. What are they? Are any healthy?

5. Rob suggests Johnny should go back to being Amish. Rachel disagrees. What do you think?

6. Max helps Rachel in her journey toward being English. Is she right to do so? What things draw Rachel and Max to each other?

7. Was Rachel a good wife? Will she be one?

8. Discuss Rob's philosophy of war and Rachel's philosophy of peace. Which is right?

9. Datt and Jonah both react to Rachel's choices. Discuss.

10. Breaking vows is very serious business. What beyond loving Rob finally allows Rachel to break hers?

Gayle Roper's many fans also love her Amish Farm trilogy, now available from Harvest House Publishers in e-book format.

Englischer Kristie Matthews' move to an Amish family farm in Lancaster County, Pennsylvania, starts on a bad note as the young schoolteacher is bitten by a dog. A trip to the local ER leads to an encounter with an old man who hands her a key and swears her to silence.

But when Kristie's life is endangered, she suspects there's a connection to the mysterious key. While solving the mystery (and staying alive), Kristie must decide whether her lawyer boyfriend, Todd Reasoner, is really right for her... or if Jon Clarke Griffin, the new local man she's met, is all he seems to be.

Cara Bentley is raised by her grandfather to appreciate family. When she discovers—quite by accident—that he was adopted, her whole perspective changes. If he wasn't a Bentley, who was he? If she isn't a Bentley, who is she? She determines to find her "real" family.

Ending up in Lancaster, Pennsylvania, she takes a room at the Zook family farm. When she seeks the help of attorney Todd Reasoner, the search for the truth begins in earnest.

But as mysterious accidents begin to happen, Cara suspects her attempt to find out the truth is not welcome—and neither is she.

Rose Martin became a nurse because she wanted to help people in pain. And she has come to realize that part of being a nurse means encountering death. But death by natural causes…not by murder. So when cancer-stricken Sophie Hostetter is murdered, Rose begins asking questions. Soon she's drawn into a maze of family secrets that endanger her own life. Her growing attraction to Amish-raised Jake Zook further complicates her life. His resentment toward her is puzzling—after all, she helped save his life. Why will he not allow her to share that life now?

About Gayle Roper

Gayle Roper is the award-winning author of more than 40 books and has been a Christy finalist three times. She has won both the RITA Award and the Carol Award as well as the Inspirational Reader's Choice twice. Gayle enjoys speaking at women's events across the nation and loves sharing the powerful truths of Scripture with humor and practicality. She lives in southeastern Pennsylvania where she enjoys reading, gardening, and her family.

To learn more about books by Gayle Roper or
other excellent Harvest House fiction authors
or to read sample chapters, visit our website:
www.harvesthousepublishers.com

HARVEST HOUSE PUBLISHERS
EUGENE, OREGON